G
Horror
Stories

50 Greatest Horror Stories

Selected and Introduced by

Terry O'Brien

RUPA

Published by
Rupa Publications India Pvt. Ltd 2018
7/16, Ansari Road, Daryaganj
New Delhi 110002

Sales Centres:

Allahabad Bengaluru Chennai
Hyderabad Jaipur Kathmandu
Kolkata Mumbai

This is a work of fiction. Names, characters, places and incidents are either the product of the author's imagination or are used fictitiously and any resemblance to any actual person, living or dead, events or locales is entirely coincidental.

ISBN: 978-93-530-4363-6

Ninth impression 2023

15 14 13 12 11 10 9

Printed in India

CONTENTS

INTRODUCTION

One is generally torn between two opposing emotions: Beauty and Fear. Beauty is the 'capacity to respond'; fear is the 'capacity to retreat'.

The oldest and strongest emotion of mankind is fear, the catechism of the unknown. Horror, scary and gothic stories send a chilling sensation down the spine. But at the end of the story, there is a sense of 'catharsis,' a sense of relief, a sigh: *alas*! However, when one looks fear in the face, one can easily gain strength, courage, confidence and much more from every experience.

50 Greatest Horror Stories deals with situations, gothic structures and the impossible, but the bottom line is that they still have a 'slice of life' reality. Reality is harsh and it stings at times. Here comes a collection of classic spooky tales that is great fun to read, perhaps on a dark, stormy night. The purpose, of course, is to scare you so you end up screaming out in fright!

Words matter; but then words impress the most with the exquisite horror of their reality. Punctuation can be the most effective tool of this genre. When one thinks of 'horror', one associates it with gloom, darkness, deafening silence and aloneness: beyond the remotest echo, silence beyond silence. But soon one finds out through these stories that horror has many more nuances.

In 'The Furnished Room', a young man commits suicide in the same room where a young woman, for whom he has vainly searched, had killed herself.

'A Ghost Story' describes the narrator's experience in a dusty New York City apartment. The very first night he spends there, he sees supernatural things invading his privacy.

'The Trail for Murder' is a perfect blend of the mysterious and the scary. The crime is solved by none other than the dead.

'The Hand' is a supernatural tale of horror that doesn't end well for one of the characters.

'The Open Window' narrates the story of a window that is kept open in the month of October so that the dead can walk in.

Ask for anything and you shall get it in 'The Monkey's Paw'. But at what cost?

'The Masque of the Red Death' has blood everywhere... especially in the royal palace when the emperors are having a gala time.

And you thought dancing with a partner was all about fun and the perfect moves! Not in the case of 'The Dancing Partner'.

He hates going out in the sun. And sleeping in a coffin is where his comfort zone lies. Meet Count Dracula in 'Dracula's Guest'.

And there is much more for the take...

Excerpted from some of the best-known classics in the horror genre, *50 Greatest Horror Stories* is guaranteed to keep you awake at night.

Hold your breath and take your sojourn into the unknown!

Happy Reading!

Terry O'Brien

1

THE ADVENTURE OF MY GRANDFATHER

Washington Irving

The old mansion shook as though it had mistaken it for an earthquake...

My grandfather was a bold dragoon, for it's a profession, d'ye see, that has run in the family. All my forefathers have been dragoons and died upon the field of honour except myself, and I hope my posterity may be able to say the same; however, I don't mean to be vainglorious. Well, my grandfather, as I said, was a bold dragoon, and had served in the Low Countries. In fact, he was one of that very army, which, according to my uncle Toby, 'swore so terribly in Flanders'. He could swear a good stick himself; and, moreover, was the very man that introduced the doctrine Corporal Trim mentions, of radical heat and radical moisture; or, in other words, the mode of keeping out the damps of ditch water by burnt brandy. Be that as it may, it's nothing to the purport of my story. I only tell it to show you that my grandfather was a man not easily to be humbugged. He had seen service; or, according to his own phrase, 'he had seen the devil'—and that's saying everything.

Well, gentlemen, my grandfather was on his way to England, for which he intended to embark at Ostend—bad luck to the place—for one where I was kept by storms and head winds for three long days, and the devil of a jolly companion or pretty face to comfort me. Well, as I was saying, my grandfather was on his way to England, or rather to Ostend—no matter which, it's all the same. So one evening, towards nightfall, he rode jollily into Bruges. Very like you all know Bruges, gentlemen, a queer, old-fashioned Flemish town, once they say a great place for trade and money-making, in old times, when the Mynheers were in their glory; but almost as large and as empty as an Irishman's pocket at the present day.

Well, gentlemen, it was the time of the annual fair. All Bruges was crowded; and the canals swarmed with Dutch boats, and the streets swarmed with Dutch merchants; and there was hardly any getting along for goods, wares, and merchandises, and peasants in big breeches, and women in half a score of petticoats.

My grandfather rode jollily along in his easy, slashing way, for he was a saucy, sunshiny fellow—staring about him at the motley crowd, and the old houses with gable ends to the street and storks' nests on the chimneys; winking at the ya vrouws who showed their faces at the windows, and joking the women right and left in the street; all of whom laughed and took it in amazing good part; for though he did not know a word of their language, yet he always had a knack of making himself understood among the women.

Well, gentlemen, it being the time of the annual fair, all the town was crowded; every inn and tavern full, and my grandfather applied in vain from one to the other for admittance. At length he rode up to an old rackety inn that looked ready to fall to pieces, and which all the rats would have run away from, if they could have found room in any other house to put their heads. It was just such a queer building as you see in Dutch pictures, with a tall roof that reached up into the clouds; and as many garrets, one over the other, as the seven heavens of Mahomet. Nothing had saved it from tumbling down but a stork's nest on the chimney, which always brings good luck to a house in the Low Countries; and at the very time of my grandfather's arrival, there were two of these long-legged birds of grace, standing like ghosts on the chimney top. Faith, but they've kept the house on its legs to this very day; for you may see it any time you pass through Bruges, as it stands there yet; only it is turned into a brewery—a brewery of strong Flemish beer; at least it was so when I came that way after the battle of Waterloo.

My grandfather eyed the house curiously as he approached. It might not altogether have struck his fancy, had he not seen in large letters over the door, HEER VERKOOPT MAN GOEDEN DRANK.

My grandfather had learnt enough of the language to know that the sign promised good liquor. 'This is the house for me,' said he, stopping short before the door.

The sudden appearance of a dashing dragoon was an event in an old inn, frequented only by the peaceful sons of traffic. A rich burgher of Antwerp, a stately ample man, in a broad Flemish hat, and who was the great man and great patron of the establishment, sat smoking a clean long pipe on one side of the door; a fat little distiller of Geneva from Schiedam, sat smoking on the other, and the bottle-nosed host stood in the door, and the comely hostess, in crimped cap, beside him; and the hostess' daughter, a plump Flanders lass, with long gold pendants in her ears, was at a side window.

'Humph!' said the rich burgher of Antwerp, with a sulky glance at the stranger. 'De duyvel!' said the fat little distiller of Schiedam.

The landlord saw with the quick glance of a publican that the new guest was not at all, at all, to the taste of the old ones; and to tell the truth, he did not himself like my grandfather's saucy eye.

He shook his head—'Not a garret in the house but was full.' 'Not a garret!' echoed the landlady. 'Not a garret!' echoed the daughter.

The burgher of Antwerp and the little distiller of Schiedam continued to smoke their pipes sullenly, eyed the enemy askance from under their broad hats, but said nothing.

My grandfather was not a man to be browbeaten. He threw the reins on his horse's neck, cocked his hat on one side, stuck one arm akimbo, slapped his broad thigh with the other hand:

'Faith and troth!' said he, 'but I'll sleep in this house this very night!'

My grandfather had on a tight pair of buckskins—the slap went to the landlady's heart.

He followed up the vow by jumping off his horse, and making his way past the staring Mynheers into the public room. Maybe you've been in the barroom of an old Flemish inn—faith, but a handsome chamber it was as you'd wish to see; with a brick floor, a great fire-place, with the whole Bible history in glazed tiles; and then the mantel-piece, pitching itself head foremost out of the wall, with a whole regiment of cracked tea-pots and earthen jugs paraded on it; not to mention half a dozen great Delft platters hung about the room by way of pictures; and the little bar in one corner, and the bouncing bar-maid inside of it with a red calico cap and yellow ear-drops.

My grandfather snapped his fingers over his head, as he cast an eye round the room: 'Faith, this is the very house I've been looking after,' said he.

There was some farther show of resistance on the part of the garrison, but my grandfather was an old soldier, and an Irishman to boot, and not easily repulsed, especially after he had got into the fortress. So he blarney'd the landlord, kissed the landlord's wife, tickled the landlord's daughter, chucked the bar-maid under the chin; and it was agreed on all hands that it would be a thousand pities, and a burning shame into the bargain, to turn such a bold dragoon into the streets. So they laid their heads together, that is to say, my grandfather and the landlady, and it was at length agreed to accommodate him with an old chamber that had for some time been shut up.

'Some say it's haunted!' whispered the landlord's daughter, 'but you're a bold dragoon, and I dare say you don't fear ghosts.'

'The devil a bit!' said my grandfather, pinching her plump cheek; 'but if I should be troubled by ghosts, I've been to the Red Sea in my time, and have a pleasant way of laying them, my darling!'

And then he whispered something to the girl which made her laugh, and give him a good-humoured box on the ear. In short, there was nobody knew better how to make his way among the petticoats than my grandfather.

In a little while, as was his usual way, he took complete possession of the house: swaggering all over it—into the stable to look after his horse; into the kitchen to look after his supper. He had something to say or do with everyone; smoked with the Dutchmen; drank with the Germans; slapped the men on the shoulders, tickled the women under the ribs: Never since the days of Ally Croaker had such a rattling blade been seen. The landlord stared at him with astonishment; the landlord's daughter hung her head and giggled whenever he came near; and as he turned his back and swaggered along, his tight jacket setting off his broad shoulders and plump buckskins, and his long sword trailing by his side, the maids whispered to one another—'What a proper man!'

At supper my grandfather took command of the table d'hôte as though he had been at home; helped everybody, not forgetting himself; talked with everyone, whether he understood their language or not; and made his way into the intimacy of the rich burgher of Antwerp, who had never been known to be sociable with anyone during his life. In fact, he revolutionized the whole establishment, and gave it such a rouse, that the very house reeled with it. He outsat everyone at table excepting the little fat distiller of Schiedam, who had sat soaking for a long time before he broke forth; but when he did, he was a very devil incarnate. He took a violent affection for my grandfather; so they sat drinking, and smoking, and telling stories, and singing Dutch and Irish songs, without understanding a word each other said, until the little Hollander was fairly swampt with his own gin and water, and carried off to bed, whooping and hiccuping, and trolling the burthen of a Low Dutch love song.

Well, gentlemen, my grandfather was shown to his quarters, up a huge staircase composed of loads of hewn timber; and through long rigmarole passages, hung with blackened paintings of fruit, and fish, and game, and country frolics, and huge kitchens, and portly burgomasters, such as you see about old-fashioned Flemish inns, till at length he arrived at his room.

An old-times chamber it was, sure enough, and crowded with all kinds of trumpery. It looked like an infirmary for decayed and superannuated furniture; where everything diseased and disabled was sent to nurse, or to be forgotten. Or rather, it might have been taken for a general congress of old legitimate movables, where every kind and country had a representative. No two chairs were alike: such high backs and low backs, and leather bottoms and worsted bottoms, and straw bottoms, and no bottoms; and cracked marble tables with curiously carved legs, holding balls in their claws, as though they were going to play at ninepins.

My grandfather made a bow to the motley assemblage as he entered, and having undressed himself, placed his light in the fire-place, asking pardon of the tongs, which seemed to be making love to the shovel in the chimney corner, and whispering soft nonsense in its ear.

The rest of the guests were by this time sound asleep; for your Mynheers are huge sleepers. The house maids, one by one, crept up yawning to their attics, and not a female head in the inn was laid on a pillow that night without dreaming of the bold dragoon.

My grandfather, for his part, got into bed, and drew over him one of those great bags of down, under which they smother a man in the Low Countries; and there he lay, melting between, two feather beds, like an anchovy sandwich between two slices of toast and butter. He was a warm-complexioned man, and this smothering played the very deuce with him. So, sure enough, in a little while it seemed as if a legion of imps were twitching at him and all the blood in his veins was in fever heat.

He lay still, however, until all the house was quiet, excepting the snoring of the Mynheers from the different chambers; who answered one another in all kinds of tones and cadences, like so many bullfrogs in a swamp. The quieter the house became, the more unquiet became my grandfather. He waxed warmer and warmer, until at length the bed became too hot to hold him.

'Maybe the maid had warmed it too much?' said the curious

gentleman, inquiringly.

'I rather think the contrary,' replied the Irishman. 'But be that as it may, it grew too hot for my grandfather.'

'Faith there's no standing this any longer,' says he; so he jumped out of bed and went strolling about the house.

'What for?' said the inquisitive gentleman.

'Why, to cool himself to be sure,' replied the other, 'or perhaps to find a more comfortable bed—or perhaps—but no matter what he went for—he never mentioned; and there's no use in taking up our time in conjecturing.'

Well, my grandfather had been for some time absent from his room, and was returning, perfectly cool, when just as he reached the door he heard a strange noise within. He paused and listened. It seemed as if someone was trying to hum a tune in defiance of the asthma. He recollected the report of the room's being haunted; but he was no believer in ghosts. So he pushed the door gently ajar, and peeped in.

Egad, gentlemen, there was a gambol carrying on within enough to have astonished St. Anthony.

By the light of the fire he saw a pale weazen-faced fellow in a long flannel gown and a tall white night-cap with a tassel to it, who sat by the fire, with a bellows under his arm by way of bagpipe, from which he forced the asthmatical music that had bothered my grandfather. As he played, too, he kept twitching about with a thousand queer contortions; nodding his head and bobbing about his tasselled night-cap.

My grandfather thought this very odd, and mighty presumptuous, and was about to demand what business he had to play his wind instruments in another gentleman's quarters, when a new cause of astonishment met his eye. From the opposite side of the room a long-backed, bandy-legged chair, covered with leather, and studded all over in a cox-comical fashion with little brass nails, got suddenly into motion; thrust out first a claw foot, then a crooked arm, and at length, making a leg, slided gracefully up to an easy chair, of tarnished brocade, with a hole in its bottom, and led it gallantly out in a ghostly minuet about the floor.

The musician now played fiercer and fiercer, and bobbed his head and his night-cap about like mad. By degrees the dancing mania seemed to seize upon all the other pieces of furniture. The antique, long-bodied chairs paired off in couples and led down a country dance; a three-legged stool danced a hornpipe, though horribly puzzled by its supernumerary leg; while the amorous tongs seized the shovel round the waist, and whirled it about the room in a German waltz. In short, all the moveables got in motion, capering about; pirouetting, hands across, right and left, like so many devils, all except a great clothes-press, which kept curtseying and curtseying, like a dowager, in one corner, in exquisite time to the music—being either too corpulent to dance, or perhaps at a loss for a partner.

My grandfather concluded the latter to be the reason; so, being, like a true Irishman, devoted to the sex, and at all times ready for a frolic, he bounced into the room, calling to the musician to strike up 'Paddy O'Rafferty,' capered up to the clothes-press and seized upon two handles to lead her out—when, whizz!—the whole revel was at an end. The chairs, tables, tongs, and shovel slunk in an instant as quietly into their places as if nothing had happened; and the musician vanished up the chimney, leaving the bellows behind him in his hurry. My grandfather found himself seated in the middle of the floor, with the clothes-press sprawling before him, and the two handles jerked off and in his hands.

'Then after all, this was a mere dream!' said the inquisitive gentleman.

'The divil a bit of a dream!' replied the Irishman: 'there never was a truer fact in this world. Faith, I should have liked to see any man tell my grandfather it was a dream.'

Well, gentlemen, as the clothes-press was a mighty heavy body, and my grandfather likewise, particularly in rear, you may easily suppose two such heavy bodies coming to the ground would make a bit of a noise. Faith, the old mansion shook as though it had mistaken it for an earthquake. The whole garrison was alarmed. The landlord, who slept just below, hurried up with a candle to inquire the cause, but with all his haste his daughter had hurried to the scene of uproar before him. The landlord was followed by the landlady, who was followed by the bouncing bar-maid, who was followed by the simpering chambermaids all holding together, as well as they could, such garments as they had first lain hands on; but all in a terrible hurry to see what the devil was to pay in the chamber of the bold dragoon.

My grandfather related the marvellous scene he had witnessed, and the prostrate clothes-press, and the broken handles, bore testimony to the fact. There was no contesting such evidence; particularly with a lad of my grandfather's complexion, who seemed able to make good every word either with sword or shillelah. So the landlord scratched his head and looked silly, as he was apt to do when puzzled. The landlady scratched—no, she did not scratch her head—but she knit her brow, and did not seem half pleased with the explanation. But the landlady's daughter corroborated it by recollecting that the last person who had dwelt in that chamber was a famous juggler who had died of St. Vitus's dance, and no doubt had infected all the furniture.

This set all things to rights, particularly when the chambermaids declared that they had all witnessed strange carryings on in that room—and as they declared this 'upon their honours', there could not remain a doubt upon the subject.

'And did your grandfather go to bed again in that room?' said the inquisitive gentleman.

'That's more than I can tell. Where he passed the rest of the night was a secret he never disclosed. In fact, though he had seen much service, he was but indifferently acquainted with geography, and apt to make blunders in his travels about inns at night, that it would have puzzled him sadly to account for in the morning.'

'Was he ever apt to walk in his sleep?' said the knowing old gentleman.

'Never that I heard of.'

There was a little pause after this rigmarole Irish romance, when the old gentleman with the haunted head observed, that the stories hitherto related had a rather a burlesque tendency. 'I recollect an adventure however,' added he, 'which I heard of during a residence in Paris, for the truth of which I can undertake to vouch, and which is of a very grave and singular nature.'

2

THE ADVENTURE OF MY AUNT

Washington Irving

The house stood in a lonely, wild part of the country...with a murderer hanging in chains on a bleak height in full view.

My aunt was a lady of large frame, strong mind, and great resolution; she was what might be termed a very manly woman. My uncle was a thin, puny little man, very meek and acquiescent, and no match for my aunt. It was observed that he dwindled and dwindled gradually away, from the day of his marriage. His wife's powerful mind was too much for him; it wore him out. My aunt, however, took all possible care of him, had half the doctors in town to prescribe for him, made him take all their prescriptions, willy nilly, and dosed him with physic enough to cure a whole hospital. All was in vain. My uncle grew worse and worse the more dosing and nursing he underwent, until in the end he added another to the long list of matrimonial victims, who have been killed with kindness.

'And was it his ghost that appeared to her?' asked the inquisitive gentleman, who had questioned the former storyteller.

'You shall hear,' replied the narrator—My aunt took on mightily for the death of her poor dear husband! Perhaps she felt some compunction at having given him so much physic, and nursed him into his grave. At any rate, she did all that a widow could do to honour his memory. She spared no expense in either the quantity or quality of her mourning weeds; she wore a miniature of him about her neck, as large as a little sun dial; and she had a full-length portrait of him always hanging in her bed chamber. All the world extolled her conduct to the skies; and it was determined, that a woman who behaved so well to the memory of one husband, deserved soon to get another.

It was not long after this that she went to take up her residence in an old country seat in Derbyshire, which had long been in the care of merely a steward and housekeeper. She took most of her servants with her, intending to make it her principal abode. The house stood in a lonely, wild part of the country among the grey Derbyshire hills; with a murderer hanging in chains on a bleak height in full view.

The servants from town were half frightened out of their wits, at the idea of living in such a dismal, pagan-looking place; especially when they got together in the servants' hall in the evening, and compared notes on all the hobgoblin stories they had picked up in the course of the day. They were afraid to venture alone about the forlorn black-looking chambers. My ladies' maid, who was troubled with nerves, declared she could never sleep alone in such a 'gashly, rummaging old building'. and the footman, who was a kind-hearted young fellow, did all in his power to cheer her up.

My aunt, herself, seemed to be struck with the lonely appearance of the house. Before she went to bed, therefore, she examined well the fastenings of the doors and windows, locked up the plate with her own hands, and carried the keys, together with a little box of money and jewels, to her own room; for she was a notable woman, and always saw to all things herself. Having put the keys under her pillow, and dismissed her maid, she sat by her toilet arranging her hair; for, being, in spite of her grief for my uncle, rather a buxom widow, she was a little particular about her person. She sat for a little while looking at her face in the glass, first on one side, then on the other, as ladies are apt to do, when they would ascertain if they have been in good looks; for a roystering country squire of the neighbourhood, with whom she had flirted when a girl, had called that day to welcome her to the country.

All of a sudden she thought she heard something move behind her. She looked hastily round, but there was nothing to be seen. Nothing but the grimly painted portrait of her poor dear man, which had been hung against the wall. She gave a heavy sigh to his memory, as she was accustomed to do, whenever she spoke of him in company; and went on adjusting her nightdress. Her sigh was re-echoed; or answered by a long-drawn breath. She looked round again, but no one was to be seen. She ascribed these sounds to the wind, oozing through the rat holes of the old mansion; and proceeded leisurely to put her hair in papers, when, all at once, she thought she perceived one of the eyes of the portrait move.

'The back of her head being towards it!' said the story-teller with the ruined head, giving a knowing wink on the sound side of his visage—'good!'

'Yes, sir!' replied drily the narrator, 'her back being towards the portrait, but her eye fixed on its reflection in the glass.'

Well, as I was saying, she perceived one of the eyes of the portrait move. So strange a circumstance, as you may well suppose, gave her a sudden shock. To assure herself cautiously of the fact, she put one hand to her forehead, as if rubbing it; peeped through her fingers, and moved the candle with the other hand. The light of the taper gleamed on the eye, and was reflected from it. She was sure it moved. Nay, more, it seemed to give her a wink, as she had sometimes known her husband to do when living! It struck a momentary chill to her heart; for she was a lone woman, and felt herself fearfully situated.

The chill was but transient. My aunt, who was almost as resolute a personage as your uncle, sir, (turning to the old story-teller,) became instantly calm and collected. She went on adjusting her dress. She even hummed a favourite air, and did not make a single false note. She casually overturned a dressing box; took a candle and picked up the articles leisurely, one by one, from the floor, pursued a rolling pin-cushion that was making the best of its way under the bed; then opened the door; looked for an instant into the corridor, as if in doubt whether to go; and then walked quietly out.

She hastened downstairs, ordered the servants to arm

themselves with the first weapons that came to hand, placed herself at their head, and returned almost immediately.

Her hastily levied army presented a formidable force. The steward had a rusty blunderbuss; the coachman a loaded whip; the footman a pair of horse pistols; the cook a huge chopping knife, and the butler a bottle in each hand. My aunt led the van with a red-hot poker; and, in my opinion, she was the most formidable of the party. The waiting maid brought up the rear, dreading to stay alone in the servants' hall, smelling to a broken bottle of volatile salts, and expressing her terror of the ghosteses.

'Ghosts!' said my aunt resolutely, 'I'll singe their whiskers for them!'

They entered the chamber. All was still and undisturbed as when she left it. They approached the portrait of my uncle.

'Pull me down that picture!' cried my aunt.

A heavy groan, and a sound like the chattering of teeth, was heard from the portrait. The servants shrunk back. The maid uttered a faint shriek, and clung to the footman.

'Instantly!' added my aunt, with a stamp of the foot.

The picture was pulled down, and from a recess behind it, in which had formerly stood a clock, they hauled forth a round-shouldered, black-bearded varlet, with a knife as long as my arm, but trembling all over like an aspen leaf.

'Well, and who was he? No ghost, I suppose!' said the inquisitive gentleman.

'A knight of the post,' replied the narrator, 'who had been smitten with the worth of the wealthy widow; or rather a marauding Tarquin, who had stolen into her chamber to violate her purse and rifle her strong box when all the house should be asleep. In plain terms,' continued he, 'the vagabond was a loose idle fellow of the neighbourhood, who had once been a servant in the house, and had been employed to assist in arranging it for the reception of its mistress. He confessed that he had contrived his hiding-place for his nefarious purposes, and had borrowed an eye from the portrait by way of a reconnoitering hole.'

'And what did they do with him—did they hang him?' resumed the questioner.

'Hang him? How could they?' exclaimed a beetle-browed barrister, with a hawk's nose—'the offence was not capital—no robbery nor assault had been committed—no forcible entry or breaking into the premises—'

'My aunt,' said the narrator, 'was a woman of spirit, and apt to take the law into her own hands. She had her own notions of cleanliness also. She ordered the fellow to be drawn through the horsepond to cleanse away all offences, and then to be well rubbed down with an oaken towel.'

'And what became of him afterwards?' said the inquisitive gentleman.

'I do not exactly know—I believe he was sent on a voyage of improvement to Botany Bay.'

'And your aunt—' said the inquisitive gentleman—'I'll warrant she took care to make her maid sleep in the room with her after that.'

'No, sir, she did better—she gave her hand shortly after to the roystering squire; for she used to observe it was a dismal thing for a woman to sleep alone in the country.'

'She was right,' observed the inquisitive gentleman, nodding his head sagaciously—'but I am sorry they did not hang that fellow.'

It was agreed on all hands that the last narrator had brought his tale to the most satisfactory conclusion; though a country clergyman present regretted that the uncle and aunt, who figured in the different stories, had not been married together. They certainly would have been well matched.

'But I don't see, after all,' said the inquisitive gentleman, 'that there was any ghost in this last story.'

'Oh, if it's ghosts you want, honey,' cried the Irish captain of dragoons, 'if it's ghosts you want, you shall have a whole regiment of them. And since these gentlemen have been giving the adventures of their uncles and aunts, faith and I'll e'en give you a chapter too, out of my own family history.'

3

THE ADVENTURE OF THE GERMAN STUDENT

Washington Irving

...a literary goul, feeding in the charnel house of decayed literature...

On a stormy night, in the tempestuous times of the French revolution, a young German was returning to his lodgings, at a late hour, across the old part of Paris. The lightning gleamed, and the loud claps of thunder rattled through the lofty, narrow streets—but I should first tell you something about this young German. Gottfried Wolfgang was a young man of good family. He had studied for some time at Göttingen, but being of a visionary and enthusiastic character, he had wandered into those wild and speculative doctrines which have so often bewildered German students. His secluded life, his intense application, and the singular nature of his studies, had an effect on both mind and body. His health was impaired; his imagination diseased. He had been indulging in fanciful speculations on spiritual essences until, like Swedenborg, he had an ideal world of his own around him. He took up a notion, I do not know from what cause, that there was an evil influence hanging over him; an evil genius or spirit seeking to ensnare him and ensure his perdition. Such an idea working on his melancholy temperament produced the most gloomy effects. He became haggard and desponding. His friends discovered the mental malady preying upon him, and determined that the best cure was a change of scene; he was sent, therefore, to finish his studies amidst the splendours and gaieties of Paris. Wolfgang arrived at Paris at the breaking out of the revolution. The popular delirium at first caught his enthusiastic mind, and he was captivated by the political and philosophical theories of the day: but the scenes of blood which followed shocked his sensitive nature; disgusted him with society and the world, and made him more than ever a recluse. He shut himself up in a solitary apartment in the Pays Latin, the quarter of students. There in a gloomy street not far from the monastic walls of the Sorbonne, he pursued his favourite speculations.

Sometimes he spent hours together in the great libraries of Paris, those catacombs of departed authors, rummaging among their hoards of dusty and obsolete works in quest of food for his unhealthy appetite. He was, in a manner, a literary goul, feeding in the charnel house of decayed literature. Wolfgang, though solitary and recluse, was of an ardent temperament, but for a time it operated merely upon his imagination. He was too shy and ignorant of the world to make any advances to the fair, but he was a passionate admirer of female beauty, and in his lonely chamber would often lose himself in reveries on forms and faces which he had seen, and his fancy would deck out images of loveliness far surpassing the reality.

While his mind was in this excited and sublimated state, a dream produced an extraordinary effect upon him. It was of a female face of transcendent beauty. So strong was the impression made, that he dreamt of it again and again. It haunted his thoughts by day, his slumbers by night; in fine, he became passionately enamoured of this shadow of a dream. This lasted so long, that it became one of those fixed ideas which haunt the minds of melancholy men, and are at times mistaken for madness.

Such was Gottfried Wolfgang, and such his situation at the time I mentioned. He was returning home late one stormy night, through some of the old and gloomy streets of the Marais, the ancient part of Paris. The loud claps of thunder rattled among the high houses of the narrow streets. He came to the Place de Grève, the square where public executions are performed.

The lightning quivered about the pinnacles of the ancient Hôtel de Ville, and shed flickering gleams over the open space in front. As Wolfgang was crossing the square, he shrank back with horror at finding himself close by the guillotine. It was the height of the reign of terror, when this dreadful instrument of death stood ever ready, and its scaffold was continually running with the blood of the virtuous and the brave. It had that very day been actively employed in the work of carnage, and there it stood in grim array amidst a silent and sleeping city, waiting for fresh victims.

Wolfgang's heart sickened within him, and he was turning shuddering from the horrible engine, when he beheld a shadowy form cowering as it were at the foot of the steps which led up to the scaffold. A succession of vivid flashes of lightning revealed it more distinctly. It was a female figure, dressed in black. She was seated on one of the lower steps of the scaffold, leaning forward, her face hid in her lap, and her long disheveled tresses hanging to the ground, streaming with the rain which fell in torrents. Wolfgang paused. There was something awful in this solitary monument of woe. The female had the appearance of being above the common order. He knew the times to be full of vicissitude, and that many a fair head, which had once been pillowed on down, now wandered houseless. Perhaps this was some poor mourner whom the dreadful axe had rendered desolate, and who sat here heartbroken on the strand of existence, from which all that was dear to her had been launched into eternity.

He approached, and addressed her in the accents of sympathy. She raised her head and gazed wildly at him. What was his astonishment at beholding, by the bright glare of the lightning, the very face which had haunted him in his dreams. It was pale and disconsolate, but ravishingly beautiful. Trembling with violent and conflicting emotions, Wolfgang again accosted her. He spoke something of her being exposed at such an hour of the night, and to the fury of such a storm, and offered to conduct her to her friends. She pointed to the guillotine with a gesture of dreadful signification. 'I have no friend on earth!' said she. 'But you have a home,' said Wolfgang.

'Yes—in the grave!'

The heart of the student melted at the words. 'If a stranger dare make an offer,' said he, 'without danger of being misunderstood, I would offer my humble dwelling as a shelter; myself as a devoted friend. I am friendless myself in Paris, and a stranger in the land; but if my life could be of service, it is at your disposal, and should be sacrificed before harm or indignity should come to you.'

There was an honest earnestness in the young man's manner that had its effect. His foreign accent, too, was in his favour; it showed him not to be a hackneyed inhabitant of Paris. Indeed there is an eloquence in true enthusiasm that is not to be doubted. The homeless stranger confided herself implicitly to the protection of the student.

He supported her faltering steps across the Pont Neuf, and by the place where the statue of Henry the Fourth had been overthrown by the populace. The storm had abated, and the thunder rumbled at a distance. All Paris was quiet; that great volcano of human passion slumbered for a while, to gather fresh strength for the next day's eruption. The student conducted his charge through the ancient streets of the Pays Latin, and by the dusky walls of the Sorbonne to the great, dingy hotel which he inhabited. The old portress who admitted them stared with surprise at the unusual sight of the melancholy Wolfgang with a female companion. On entering his apartment, the student, for the first time, blushed at the scantiness and indifference of his dwelling. He had but one chamber—an old fashioned saloon—heavily carved and fantastically furnished with the remains of former magnificence, for it was one of those hotels in the quarter of the Luxembourg palace which had once belonged to nobility. It was lumbered with books and papers, and all the usual apparatus of a student, and his bed stood in a recess at one end. When lights were brought, and Wolfgang had a better opportunity of contemplating the stranger, he was more than ever intoxicated by her beauty. Her face was pale, but of a dazzling fairness, set off by a profusion of raven hair that hung clustering about it. Her eyes were large and brilliant, with a singular expression approaching almost to wildness. As far as her black dress permitted her shape to be seen, it was of perfect symmetry.

Her whole appearance was highly striking, though she was dressed in the simplest style. The only thing approaching to an ornament which she wore was a broad, black band round her neck, clasped by diamonds. The perplexity now commenced with the student how to dispose of the helpless being thus thrown upon his protection.

He thought of abandoning his chamber to her, and seeking shelter for himself elsewhere. Still he was so fascinated by her charms, there seemed to be such a spell upon his thoughts and senses, that he could not tear himself from her presence. Her manner, too, was singular and unaccountable. She spoke no more of the guillotine. Her grief had abated. The attentions of the student had first won her confidence, and then, apparently, her heart. She was evidently an enthusiast like himself, and enthusiasts soon understand each other.

In the infatuation of the moment Wolfgang avowed his passion for her. He told her the story of his mysterious dream, and how she had possessed his heart before he had even seen her. She was strangely affected by his recital, and acknowledged to have felt an impulse towards him equally unaccountable.

It was the time for wild theory and wild actions. Old prejudices and superstitions were done away; everything was under the sway of the 'Goddess of Reason'. Among other rubbish of the old times, the forms and ceremonies of marriage began to be considered superfluous bonds for honourable minds. Social compacts were the vogue. Wolfgang was too much of a theorist not to be tainted by the liberal doctrines of the day.

'Why should we separate?' said he: 'Our hearts are united; in the eye of reason and honour we are as one. What need is there of sordid forms to bind high souls together?' The stranger listened with emotion: she had evidently received illumination at the same school. 'You have no home nor family,' continued he; 'let me be every thing to you, or rather let us be every thing to one another. If form is necessary, form shall be observed—there is my hand. I pledge myself to you for ever.'

'For ever?' said the stranger, solemnly.

'For ever!' repeated Wolfgang.

The stranger clasped the hand extended to her: 'Then I am yours,' murmured she, and sank upon his bosom. The next morning the student left his bride sleeping, and sallied forth at an early hour to seek more spacious apartments, suitable to the change in his situation. When he returned, he found the stranger lying with her head hanging over the bed, and one arm thrown over it. He spoke to her, but received no reply. He advanced to awaken her from her uneasy posture.

On taking her hand, it was cold—there was no pulsation—her face was pallid and ghastly. In a word—she was a corpse. Horrified and frantic, he alarmed the house. A scene of confusion ensued. The police was summoned. As the officer of police entered the room, he started back on beholding the corpse.

'Great heaven!' cried he, 'how did this woman come here?' 'Do you know any thing about her?' said Wolfgang, eagerly. 'Do I?' exclaimed the police officer: 'she was guillotined yesterday!'

He stepped forward; undid the black collar round the neck of the corpse, and the head rolled on the floor! The student burst into a frenzy. 'The fiend! The fiend has gained possession of me!' shrieked he: 'I am lost for ever!' They tried to soothe him, but in vain. He was possessed with the frightful belief that an evil spirit had reanimated the dead body to ensnare him. He went distracted, and died in a madhouse.

Here the old gentleman with the haunted head finished his narrative. 'And is this really a fact?' said the inquisitive gentleman. 'A fact not to be doubted,' replied the other. 'I had it from the best authority. The student told it me himself. I saw him in a madhouse at Paris.'

4
THE PALE MAN

Julius Long

It is odd, too, that, with so many vacant rooms in the hotel, he should have chosen No. 212 at the extreme rear....

I have not yet met the man in No. 212. I do not even know his name. He never patronizes the hotel restaurant, and he does not use the lobby. On the three occasions when we passed each other by, we did not speak, although we nodded in a semi-cordial, noncommittal way. I should like very much to make his acquaintance. It is lonesome in this dreary place. With the exception of the aged lady down the corridor, the only permanent guests are the man in No. 212 and myself. However, I should not complain, for this utter quiet is precisely what the doctor prescribed.

I wonder if the man in No. 212, too, has come here for a rest. He is so very pale. Yet I can not believe that he is ill, for his paleness is not of a sickly cast, but rather wholesome in its ivory clarity. His carriage is that of a man enjoying the best of health. He is tall and straight. He walks erectly and with a brisk, athletic stride. His pallor is no doubt congenital, else he would quickly tan under this burning, summer sun.

He must have traveled here by auto, for he certainly was not a passenger on the train that brought me, and he checked in only a short time after my arrival. I had briefly rested in my room and was walking down the stairs when I encountered him ascending with his bag. It is odd that our venerable bell-boy did not show him to his room.

It is odd, too, that, with so many vacant rooms in the hotel, he should have chosen No. 212 at the extreme rear. The building is a long, narrow affair three stories high. The rooms are all on the east side, as the west wall is flush with a decrepit business building. The corridor is long and drab, and its stiff, bloated paper exudes a musty, unpleasant odor. The feeble electric bulbs that light it shine dimly as from a tomb. Revolted by this corridor, I insisted vigorously upon being given No. 201, which is at the front and blessed with southern exposure. The room clerk, a disagreeable fellow with a Hitler mustache, was very reluctant to let me have it, as it is ordinarily reserved for his more profitable transient trade. I fear my stubborn insistence has made him an enemy.

If only I had been as self-assertive thirty years ago! I should now be a full-fledged professor instead of a broken-down assistant. I still smart from the cavalier manner in which the president of the university summarily recommended my vacation. No doubt he acted for my best interests. The people who have dominated my poor life invariably have.

Oh, well, the summer's rest will probably do me considerable good. It is pleasant to be away from the university. There is something positively gratifying about the absence of the graduate student face.

If only it were not so lonely! I must devise a way of meeting the pale man in No. 212. Perhaps the room clerk can arrange matters.

◆

I have been here exactly a week, and if there is a friendly soul in this miserable little town, he has escaped my notice. Although the tradespeople accept my money with flattering eagerness, they studiously avoid even the most casual conversation. I am afraid I can never cultivate their society unless I can arrange to have my ancestors recognized as local residents for the last hundred and fifty years.

Despite the coolness of my reception, I have been frequently venturing abroad. In the back of my mind I have cherished hopes that I might encounter the pale man in No. 211. Incidentally, I wonder why he has moved from No. 212. There is certainly little advantage in coming only one room nearer to the front. I noticed the change yesterday when I saw him coming out of his new room.

We nodded again, and this time I thought I detected a certain malign satisfaction in his somber, black eyes. He must know that I am eager to make his acquaintance, yet his manner forbids overtures. If he wants to make me go all the way, he can go to the devil. I am not the sort to run after anybody. Indeed, the surly diffidence of the room clerk has been enough to prevent me from questioning him about his mysterious guest.

◆

I wonder where the pale man takes his meals. I have been absenting myself from the hotel restaurant and patronizing the restaurants outside. At each I have ventured inquiries about the man in No. 210. No one at any restaurant remembered his having been there. Perhaps he has entrée into the Brahmin homes of this town. And again, he may have found a boarding-house. I shall have to learn if there be one.

The pale man must be difficult to please, for he has again changed his room. I am baffled by his conduct. If he is so desirous of locating himself more conveniently in the hotel, why does he not move to No. 202, which is the nearest available room to the front?

Perhaps I can make his inability to locate himself permanently an excuse for starting a conversation. 'I see we are closer neighbours now,' I might casually say. But that is too banal. I must await a better opportunity.

◆

He has done it again! He is now occupying No. 209. I am intrigued by his little game. I waste hours trying to fathom its point. What possible motive could he have? I should think he would get on the hotel people's nerves. I wonder what our combination bellhop-chambermaid thinks of having to prepare four rooms for a single guest. If he were not stone-deaf, I would ask him. At present I feel too exhausted to attempt such an enervating conversation.

I am tremendously interested in the pale man's next move. He must either skip a room or remain where he is, for a permanent guest, a very old lady, occupies No. 208. She has not budged-from her room since I have been here, and I imagine that she does not intend to.

I wonder what the pale man will do. I await his decision with the nervous excitement of a devotee of the track on the eve of a big race. After all, I have so little diversion.

◆

Well, the mysterious guest was not forced to remain where he was, nor did he have to skip a room. The lady in No. 208 simplified matters by conveniently dying. No one knows the cause of her death, but it is generally attributed to old age. She was buried this morning. I was among the curious few who attended her funeral. When I returned home from the mortuary, I was in time to see the pale man leaving her room. Already he has moved in. He favored me with a smile whose meaning I have tried in vain to decipher. I cannot but believe that he meant it to have some significance. He acted as if there were between us some secret that I failed to appreciate. But, then, perhaps his smile was meaningless after all and only ambiguous by chance, like that of the Mona Lisa.

◆

My man of mystery now resides in No. 207, and I am not the least surprised. I would have been astonished if he had not made his scheduled move, I have almost given up trying to understand his eccentric conduct. I do not know a single thing more about him than I knew the day he arrived. I wonder whence he came. There is something indefinably foreign about his manner. I am curious to hear his voice. I like to imagine that he speaks the exotic tongue of some far-away country. If only I could somehow inveigle him into conversation! I wish that I were possessed of the glib assurance of a college boy, who can address himself to the most distinguished celebrity without batting an eye. It is no wonder that I am only an assistant professor.

◆

I am worried. This morning I awoke to find myself lying prone upon the floor. I was fully clothed. I must have fallen exhausted there after I returned to my room last night.

I wonder if my condition is more serious than I had suspected. Until now I have been inclined to discount the fears of those who have pulled a long face about me. For the first time I recall the prolonged handclasp of the president when he bade me goodbye from the university. Obviously he never expected to see me alive again.

Of course I am not that unwell. Nevertheless, I must be more careful. Thank heaven I have no dependents to worry about. I have not even a wife, for I was never willing to exchange the loneliness of a bachelor for the loneliness of a husband. I can say in all sincerity that the prospect of death does not frighten me. Speculation about life beyond the grave has always bored me. Whatever it is, or is not, I'll try to get along.

I have been so preoccupied about the sudden turn of my own affairs that I have neglected to make note of a most extraordinary incident. The pale man has done an astounding thing. He has skipped three rooms and moved all the way to No.

203. We are now very close neighbours. We shall meet oftener, and my chances for making his acquaintance are now greater.

◆

I have confined myself to my bed during the last few days and have had my food brought to me. I even called a local doctor, whom I suspect to be a quack. He looked me over with professional indifference and told me not to leave my room. For some reason he does not want me to climb stairs. For this bit of information he received a ten-dollar bill which, as I directed him, he fished out of my coat pocket. A pickpocket could not have done it better.

He had not been gone long when I was visited by the room clerk. That worthy suggested with a great show of kindly concern that I use the facilities of the local hospital. It was so modern and all that. With more firmness than I have been able to muster in a long time, I gave him to understand that I intended to remain where I am. Frowning sullenly, he stiffly retired. The doctor must have paused long enough downstairs to tell him a pretty story. It is obvious that he is afraid I shall die in his best room.

The pale man is up to his old tricks. Last night, when I tottered down the hall, the door of No. 202 was ajar. Without thinking, I looked inside. The pale man sat in a rocking-chair idly smoking a cigarette. He looked up into my eyes and smiled that peculiar, ambiguous smile that has so deeply puzzled me. I moved on down the corridor, not so much mystified as annoyed. The whole mystery of the man's conduct is beginning to irk me. It is all so inane, so utterly lacking in motive.

I feel that I shall never meet the pale man. But, at least, I am going to learn his identity. Tomorrow I shall ask for the room clerk and deliberately interrogate him.

◆

I know now. I know the identity of the pale man, and I know the meaning of his smile.

Early this afternoon I summoned the room clerk to my bedside.

'Please tell me,' I asked abruptly, 'who is the man in No. 202?'

The clerk stared wearily and uncomprehendingly.

'You must be mistaken. That room is unoccupied.'

'Oh, but it is,' I snapped in irritation. 'I myself saw the man there only two nights ago. He is a tall, handsome fellow with dark eyes and hair. He is unusually pale. He checked in the day that I arrived.'

The hotel man regarded me dubiously, as if I were trying to impose upon him.

'But I assure you there is no such person in the house. As for his checking in when you did, you were the only guest we registered that day.'

'What? Why, I've seen him twenty times! First he had No. 212 at the end of the corridor. Then he kept moving toward the front. Now he's next door in No. 202.'

The room clerk threw up his hands.

'You're crazy!' he exclaimed, and I saw that he meant what he said.

I shut up at once and dismissed him. After he had gone, I heard him rattling the knob of the pale man's door. There is no doubt that he believes the room to be empty.

Thus it is that I can now understand the events of the past few weeks. I now comprehend the significance of the death in No. 207. I even feel partly responsible for the old lady's passing. After all, I brought the pale man with me. But it was not I who fixed his path. Why he chose to approach me room after room through the length of this dreary hotel, why his path crossed the threshold of the woman in No. 207, those mysteries I can not explain.

I suppose I should have guessed his identity when he skipped the three rooms the night I fell unconscious upon the floor. In a single night of triumph he advanced until he was almost to my door.

He will be coming by and by to inhabit this room, his ultimate goal. When he comes, I shall at least be able to return his smile of grim recognition.

Meanwhile, I have only to wait beyond my bolted door.

◆

The door swings slowly open...

5

BEYOND THE WALL

Ambrose Bierce

Three or four trees, writhing and moaning in the torment of the tempest, appeared to be trying to escape from their dismal environment...

Many years ago, on my way from Hong Kong to New York, I passed a week in San Francisco. A long time had gone by since I had been in that city, during which my ventures in the Orient had prospered beyond my hope; I was rich and could afford to revisit my own country to renew my friendship with such of the companions of my youth as still lived and remembered me with the old affection. Chief of these, I hoped, was Mohun Dampier, an old schoolmate with whom I had held a desultory correspondence which had long ceased, as is the way of correspondence between men. You may have observed that the indisposition to write a merely social letter is in the ratio of the square of the distance between you and your correspondent. It is a law.

I remembered Dampier as a handsome, strong young fellow of scholarly tastes, with an aversion to work and a marked indifference to many of the things that the world cares for, including wealth, of which, however, he had inherited enough to put him beyond the reach of want. In his family, one of the oldest and most aristocratic in the country, it was, I think, a matter of pride that no member of it had ever been in trade nor politics, nor suffered any kind of distinction. Mohun was a trifle sentimental, and had in him a singular element of superstition, which led him to the study of all manner of occult subjects, although his sane mental health safeguarded him against fantastic and perilous faiths. He made daring incursions into the realm of the unreal without renouncing his residence in the partly surveyed and charted region of what we are pleased to call certitude.

The night of my visit to him was stormy. The Californian winter was on, and the incessant rain splashed in the deserted streets, or, lifted by irregular gusts of wind, was hurled against the houses with incredible fury. With no small difficulty my cabman found the right place, away out toward the ocean beach, in a sparsely populated suburb. The dwelling, a rather ugly one, apparently, stood in the centre of its grounds, which as nearly as I could make out in the gloom were destitute of either flowers or grass. Three or four trees, writhing and moaning in the torment of the tempest, appeared to be trying to escape from their dismal environment and take the chance of finding a better one out at sea. The house was a two-story brick structure with a tower, a story higher, at one corner. In a window of that was the only visible light. Something in the appearance of the place made me shudder, a performance that may have been assisted by a rill of rainwater down my back as I scuttled to cover in the doorway.

In answer to my note apprising him of my wish to call, Dampier had written, 'Don't ring—open the door and come up.' I did so. The staircase was dimly lighted by a single gas-jet at the top of the second flight. I managed to reach the landing without disaster and entered by an open door into the lighted square room of the tower. Dampier came forward in gown and slippers to receive me, giving me the greeting that I wished, and if I had held a thought that it might more fitly have been accorded me at the front door the first look at him dispelled any sense of his inhospitality.

He was not the same. Hardly past middle age, he had gone grey and had acquired a pronounced stoop. His figure was thin and angular, his face deeply lined, his complexion dead-white, without a touch of colour. His eyes, unnaturally large, glowed with a fire that was almost uncanny.

He seated me, proffered a cigar, and with grave and obvious sincerity assured me of the pleasure that it gave him to meet me. Some unimportant conversation followed, but all the while I was dominated by a melancholy sense of the great change in him. This he must have perceived, for he suddenly said with a bright enough smile, 'You are disappointed in me—*non sum qualis eram*.'

I hardly knew what to reply, but managed to say: 'Why, really, I don't know; your Latin is about the same.'

He brightened again. 'No,' he said, 'being a dead language, it grows in appropriateness. But please have the patience to wait: where I am going there is perhaps a better tongue. Will you care to have a message in it?'

The smile faded as he spoke, and as he concluded he was looking into my eyes with a gravity that distressed me. Yet I would not surrender myself to his mood, nor permit him to see how deeply his prescience of death affected me.

'I fancy that it will be long,' I said, 'before human speech will cease to serve our need; and then the need, with its possibilities of service, will have passed.'

He made no reply, and I too was silent, for the talk had taken a dispiriting turn, yet I knew not how to give it a more agreeable character. Suddenly, in a pause of the storm, when the dead silence was almost startling by contrast with the previous uproar, I heard a gentle tapping, which appeared to come from the wall behind my chair. The sound was such as might have been made by a human hand, not as upon a door by one asking admittance, but rather, I thought, as an agreed signal, an assurance of someone's presence in an adjoining room; most of us, I fancy, have had more experience of such communications than we should care to relate. I glanced at Dampier. If possibly there was something of amusement in the look he did not observe it. He appeared to have forgotten my presence, and was staring at the wall behind me with an expression in his eyes that I am unable to name, although my memory of it is as vivid today as was my sense of it then. The situation was embarrassing! I rose to take my leave. At this he seemed to recover himself. 'Please be seated,' he said; 'it is nothing—no one is there.' But the tapping was repeated, and with the same gentle, slow insistence as before. 'Pardon me,' I said, 'it is late. May I call tomorrow?' He smiled—a little mechanically, I thought. 'It is very delicate of you,' said he, 'but quite needless. Really, this is the only room in the tower, and no one is there. At least—' He left the sentence incomplete, rose, and threw up a window, the only opening in the wall from which the sound seemed to come. 'See.'

Not clearly knowing what else to do I followed him to the window and looked out. A street-lamp some little distance away gave enough light through the murk of the rain that was again falling in torrents to make it entirely plain that 'no one was there'. In truth there was nothing but the sheer blank wall of the tower. Dampier closed the window and signing me to my seat resumed his own.

The incident was not in itself particularly mysterious; anyone of a dozen explanations was possible (though none has occurred to me), yet it impressed me strangely, the more, perhaps, from my friend's effort to reassure me, which seemed to dignify it with a certain significance and importance. He had proved that no one was there, but in that fact lay all the interest; and he proffered no explanation. His silence was irritating and made me resentful.

'My good friend,' I said, somewhat ironically, I fear, 'I am not disposed to question your right to harbour as many spooks as you find agreeable to your taste and consistent with your notions of companionship; that is no business of mine. But being just a plain man of affairs, mostly of this world, I find spooks needless to my peace and comfort. I am going to my hotel, where my fellow-guests are still in the flesh.'

It was not a very civil speech, but he manifested no feeling about it. 'Kindly remain', he said. 'I am grateful for your presence here. What you have heard tonight I believe myself to have heard twice before. Now I *know* it was no illusion. That is much to me—more than you know. Have a fresh cigar and a good stock of patience while I tell you the story.'

The rain was now falling more steadily, with a low, monotonous susurration, interrupted at long intervals by the sudden slashing of the boughs of the trees as the wind rose and failed. The night was well advanced, but both sympathy and curiosity held me a willing listener to my friend's monologue, which I did not interrupt by a single word from beginning to end.

'Ten years ago,' he said, 'I occupied a ground-floor apartment in one of a row of houses, all alike, away at the other end of the town, on what we call Rincon Hill. This had been the best quarter of San Francisco, but had fallen into neglect and decay, partly because the primitive character of its domestic architecture no longer suited the maturing tastes of our wealthy citizens, partly because certain public improvements had made a wreck of it. The row of dwellings in one of which I lived stood a little way back from the street, each having a miniature garden, separated from its neighbours by low iron fences and bisected with mathematical precision by a box-bordered gravel walk from gate to door.

'One morning as I was leaving my lodging I observed a young girl entering the adjoining garden on the left. It was a warm day in June, and she was lightly gowned in white. From her shoulders hung a broad straw hat profusely decorated with flowers and wonderfully beribboned in the fashion of the time. My attention was not long held by the exquisite simplicity of her costume, for no one could look at her face and think of anything earthly. Do not fear; I shall not profane it by description; it was beautiful exceedingly. All that I had ever seen or dreamed of loveliness was in that matchless living picture by the hand of the Divine Artist. So deeply did it move me that, without a thought of the impropriety of the act, I unconsciously bared my head, as a devout Catholic or well-bred Protestant uncovers before an image of the Blessed Virgin. The maiden showed no displeasure; she merely turned her glorious dark eyes upon me with a look that made me catch my breath, and without other recognition of my act passed into the house. For a moment I stood motionless, hat in hand, painfully conscious of my rudeness, yet so dominated by the emotion inspired by that vision of incomparable beauty that my penitence was less poignant than it should have been. Then I went my way, leaving my heart behind. In the natural course of things I should probably have remained away until nightfall, but by the middle of the afternoon I was back in the little garden, affecting an interest in the few foolish flowers that I had never before observed. My hope was vain; she did not appear.

'To a night of unrest succeeded a day of expectation and disappointment, but on the day after, as I wandered aimlessly about the neighbourhood, I met her. Of course I did not repeat my folly of uncovering, nor venture by even so much as too long a look to manifest an interest in her; yet my heart was beating audibly. I trembled and consciously coloured as she turned her big black eyes upon me with a look of obvious recognition entirely devoid of boldness or coquetry.

'I will not weary you with particulars; many times afterward I met the maiden, yet never either addressed her or sought to fix her attention. Nor did I take any action toward making her acquaintance. Perhaps my forbearance, requiring so supreme an effort of self-denial, will not be entirely clear to you. That I was heels over head in love is true, but who can overcome his habit of thought, or reconstruct his character?

'I was what some foolish persons are pleased to call, and others, more foolish, are pleased to be called—an aristocrat; and despite her beauty, her charms and graces, the girl was not of my class. I had learned her name—which it is needless to speak—and something of her family. She was an orphan, a dependent niece of the impossible elderly fat woman in whose lodging-house she lived. My income was small and I lacked the talent for marrying; it is perhaps a gift. An alliance with that family would condemn me to its manner of life, part me from my books and studies, and in a social sense reduce me to the ranks. It is easy to deprecate such considerations as these and I have not retained myself for the defence. Let judgement be entered against me, but in strict justice all my ancestors for generations should be made co-defendants and I be permitted to plead in mitigation of punishment the imperious mandate of heredity. To a mésalliance of that kind every globule of my ancestral blood spoke in opposition. In brief, my tastes, habits, instinct, with whatever of reason my love had left me—all fought against it. Moreover, I was an irreclaimable sentimentalist, and found a subtle charm in an impersonal and spiritual relation which acquaintance might vulgarise and marriage would certainly dispel. No woman, I argued, is what this lovely creature seems. Love is a delicious dream; why should I bring about my own awakening?

'The course dictated by all this sense and sentiment was obvious. Honour, pride, prudence, preservation of my ideals—all commanded me to go away, but for that I was too weak. The utmost that I could do by a mighty effort of will was to cease meeting the girl, and that I did. I even avoided the chance encounters of the garden, leaving my lodging only when I knew that she had gone to her music lessons, and returning after nightfall. Yet all the while I was as one in a trance, indulging the most fascinating fancies and ordering my entire intellectual life in accordance with my dream. Ah, my friend, as one whose actions have a traceable relation to reason, you cannot know the fool's paradise in which I lived.

'One evening the devil put it into my head to be an unspeakable idiot. By apparently careless and purposeless questioning I learned from my gossipy landlady that the young woman's bedroom adjoined my own, a partywall between. Yielding to a sudden and coarse impulse I gently rapped on the wall. There was no response, naturally, but I was in no mood to accept a rebuke. A madness was upon me and I repeated the folly, the offence, but again ineffectually, and I had the decency to desist.

'An hour later, while absorbed in some of my infernal studies, I heard, or thought I heard, my signal answered. Flinging down my books I sprang to the wall and as steadily as my beating heart would permit gave three slow taps upon it. This time the response was distinct, unmistakable: one, two, three—an exact repetition of my signal. That was all I could elicit, but it was enough—too much.

'The next evening, and for many evenings afterward, that folly went on, I always having "the last word". During the whole period I was deliriously happy, but with the perversity of my nature I persevered in my resolution not to see her. Then, as I should have expected, I got no further answers. "She is disgusted," I said to myself, "with what she thinks my timidity in making no more definite advances"; and I resolved to seek her and make her acquaintance and—what? I did not know, nor do I now know, what might have come of it. I know only that I passed days and days trying to meet her, and all in vain; she was invisible as well as inaudible. I haunted the streets where we had met, but she did not come. From my window I watched the garden in front of her house, but she passed neither in nor out. I fell into the deepest dejection, believing that she had gone away, yet took no steps to resolve my doubt by inquiry of my landlady, to whom, indeed, I had taken an unconquerable aversion from her having once spoken of the girl with less of reverence than I thought befitting.

'There came a fateful night. Worn out with emotion, irresolution and despondency, I had retired early and fallen into such sleep as was still possible to me. In the middle of the night something—some malign power bent upon the wrecking of my peace forever—caused me to open my eyes and sit up, wide awake and listening intently for I knew not what. Then I thought I heard a faint tapping on the wall—the mere ghost of the familiar signal. In a few moments it was repeated: one, two, three—no louder than before, but addressing a sense alert and strained to receive it. I was about to reply when the Adversary of Peace again intervened in my affairs with a rascally suggestion of retaliation. She had long and cruelly ignored me; now I would ignore her. Incredible fatuity—may God forgive it!

All the rest of the night I lay awake, fortifying my obstinacy with shameless justifications and—listening.

'Late the next morning, as I was leaving the house, I met my landlady, entering. "Good morning, Mr Dampier," she said. "Have you heard the news?" I replied in words that I had heard no news; in manner, that I did not care to hear any. The manner escaped her observation. "About the sick young lady next door," she babbled on. "What! You did not know? Why, she has been ill for weeks. And now—" I almost sprang upon her. "And now," I cried, "now what?' "She is dead."

'That is not the whole story. In the middle of the night, as I learned later, the patient, awakening from a long stupor after a week of delirium, had asked—it was her last utterance—that her bed be moved to the opposite side of the room. Those in attendance had thought the request a vagary of her delirium, but had complied. And there the poor passing soul had exerted its failing will to restore a broken connection—a golden thread of sentiment between its innocence and a monstrous baseness owing a blind, brutal allegiance to the Law of Self.

'What reparation could I make? Are there masses that can be said for the repose of souls that are abroad such nights as this—spirits "blown about by the viewless winds"—coming in the storm and darkness with signs and portents, hints of memory and presages of doom?

'This is the third visitation. On the first occasion I was too sceptical to do more than verify by natural methods the character of the incident; on the second, I responded to the signal after it had been several times repeated, but without result. Tonight's recurrence completes the "fatal triad" expounded by Parapelius Necromantius. There is no more to tell.'

When Dampier had finished his story I could think of nothing relevant that I cared to say, and to question him would have been a hideous impertinence. I rose and bade him good night in a way to convey to him a sense of my sympathy, which he silently acknowledged by a pressure of the hand. That night, alone with his sorrow and remorse, he passed into the Unknown.

6

THE BOARDED WINDOW

Ambrose Bierce

He lived alone in a house of logs surrounded on all sides by the great forest, of whose gloom and silence he seemed a part...

In 1830, only a few miles away from what is now the great city of Cincinnati, lay an immense and almost unbroken forest. The whole region was sparsely settled by people of the frontier—restless souls who no sooner had hewn fairly habitable homes out of the wilderness and attained to that degree of prosperity which today we should call indigence, than, impelled by some mysterious impulse of their nature, they abandoned all and pushed farther westward, to encounter new perils and privations in the effort to regain the meagre comforts which they had voluntarily renounced. Many of them had already forsaken that region for the remoter settlements, but among those remaining was one who had been of those first arriving. He lived alone in a house of logs surrounded on all sides by the great forest, of whose gloom and silence he seemed a part, for no one had ever known him to smile nor speak a needless word. His simple wants were supplied by the sale or barter of skins of wild animals in the river town, for not a thing did he grow upon the land which, if needful, he might have claimed by right of undisturbed possession. There were evidences of 'improvement'—a few acres of ground immediately about the house had once been cleared of its trees, the decayed stumps of which were half concealed by the new growth that had been suffered to repair the ravage wrought by the axe. Apparently the man's zeal for agriculture had burned with a failing flame, expiring in penitential ashes.

The little log house, with its chimney of sticks, its roof of warping clapboards weighted with traversing poles and its 'chinking' of clay, had a single door and, directly opposite, a window. The latter, however, was boarded up—nobody could remember a time when it was not. And none knew why it was so closed; certainly not because of the occupant's dislike of light and air, for on those rare occasions when a hunter had passed that lonely spot the recluse had commonly been seen sunning himself on his doorstep if heaven had provided sunshine for his need. I fancy there are few persons living today who ever knew the secret of that window, but I am one, as you shall see.

The man's name was said to be Murlock. He was apparently seventy years old, actually about fifty. Something besides years had had a hand in his ageing. His hair and long, full beard were white, his grey, lustreless eyes sunken, his face singularly seamed with wrinkles which appeared to belong to two intersecting systems. In figure he was tall and spare, with a stoop of the shoulders—a burden bearer. I never saw him; these particulars I learned from my grandfather, from whom also I got the man's story when I was a lad. He had known him when living nearby in that early day.

One day Murlock was found in his cabin, dead. It was not a time and place for coroners and newspapers, and I suppose it was agreed that he had died from natural causes or I should have been told, and should remember. I know only that with what was probably a sense of the fitness of things the body was buried near the cabin, alongside the grave of his wife, who had preceded him by so many years that local tradition had retained hardly a hint of her existence. That closes the final chapter of this true story—excepting, indeed, the circumstance that many years afterward, in company with an equally intrepid spirit, I penetrated to the place and ventured near enough to the ruined cabin to throw a stone against it, and ran away to avoid the ghost which every well-informed boy thereabout knew haunted the spot. But there is an earlier chapter—that supplied by my grandfather.

When Murlock built his cabin and began laying sturdily about with his axe to hew out a farm—the rifle, meanwhile, his means of support—he was young, strong and full of hope. In that eastern country whence he came he had married, as was the fashion, a young woman in all ways worthy of his honest devotion, who shared the dangers and privations of his lot with a willing spirit and light heart. There is no known record of her name; of her charms of mind and person tradition is silent and the doubter is at liberty to entertain his doubt; but God forbid that I should share it! Of their affection and happiness there is abundant assurance in every added day of the man's widowed life; for what but the magnetism of a blessed memory could have chained that venturesome spirit to a lot like that?

One day Murlock returned from gunning in a distant part of the forest to find his wife prostrate with fever, and delirious. There was no physician within miles, no neighbour; nor was she in a condition to be left, to summon help. So he set about the task of nursing her back to health, but at the end of the third day she fell into unconsciousness and so passed away, apparently, with never a gleam of returning reason.

From what we know of a nature like his we may venture to sketch in some of the details of the outline picture drawn by my grandfather. When convinced that she was dead, Murlock had sense enough to remember that the dead must be prepared for burial. In performance of this sacred duty he blundered now and again, did certain things incorrectly, and others which he did correctly were done over and over. His occasional failures to accomplish some simple and ordinary act filled him with astonishment, like that of a drunken man who wonders at the suspension of familiar natural laws. He was surprised, too, that he did not weep—surprised and a little ashamed; surely it is unkind not to weep for the dead. 'Tomorrow,' he said aloud, 'I shall have to make the coffin and dig the grave; and then I shall miss her, when she is no longer in sight; but now—she is dead, of course, but it is all right—it must be all right, somehow.

Things cannot be so bad as they seem.'

He stood over the body in the fading light, adjusting the hair and putting the finishing touches to the simple toilet, doing all mechanically, with soulless care. And still through his consciousness ran an undersense of conviction that all was right—that he should have her again as before, and everything explained. He had had no experience in grief; his capacity had not been enlarged by use. His heart could not contain it all, nor his imagination rightly conceive it. He did not know he was so hard struck; that knowledge would come later, and never go. Grief is an artist of powers as various as the instruments upon which he plays his dirges for the dead, evoking from some the sharpest, shrillest notes, from others the low, grave chords that throb recurrent like the slow beating of a distant drum. Some natures it startles; some it stupefies. To one it comes like the stroke of an arrow, stinging all the sensibilities to a keener life; to another as the blow of a bludgeon, which in crushing benumbs. We may conceive Murlock to have been that way affected, for (and here we are upon surer ground than that of conjecture) no sooner had he finished his pious work than, sinking into a chair by the side of the table upon which the body lay, and noting how white the profile showed in the deepening gloom, he laid his arms upon the table's edge, and dropped his face into them, tearless yet and unutterably weary. At that moment came in through the open window a long, wailing sound like the cry of a lost child in the far deeps of the darkening woods! But the man did not move. Again, and nearer than before, sounded that unearthly cry upon his failing sense. Perhaps it was a wild beast; perhaps it was a dream. For Murlock was asleep.

Some hours later, as it afterward appeared, this unfaithful watcher awoke and lifting his head from his arms intently listened—he knew not why. There in the black darkness by the side of the dead, recalling all without a shock, he strained his eyes to see—he knew not what. His senses were all alert, his breath was suspended, his blood had stilled its tides as if to assist the silence. Who—what had waked him, and where was it?

Suddenly the table shook beneath his arms, and at the same moment he heard, or fancied that he heard, a light, soft step—another—sounds as of bare feet upon the floor!

He was terrified beyond the power to cry out or move. Perforce he waited—waited there in the darkness through seeming centuries of such dread as one may know, yet live to tell. He tried vainly to speak the dead woman's name, vainly to stretch forth his hand across the table to learn if she were there. His throat was powerless, his arms and hands were like lead. Then occurred something most frightful. Some heavy body seemed hurled against the table with an impetus that pushed it against his breast so sharply as nearly to overthrow him, and at the same instant he heard and felt the fall of something upon the floor with so violent a thump that the whole house was shaken by the impact. A scuffling ensued, and a confusion of sounds impossible to describe. Murlock had risen to his feet. Fear had by excess forfeited control of his faculties. He flung his hands upon the table. Nothing was there!

There is a point at which terror may turn to madness; and madness incites to action. With no definite intent, from no motive but the wayward impulse of a madman, Murlock sprang to the wall, with a little groping seized his loaded rifle, and without aim discharged it. By the flash which lit up the room with a vivid illumination, he saw an enormous panther dragging the dead woman toward the window, its teeth fixed in her throat! Then there were darkness blacker than before, and silence; and when he returned to consciousness the sun was high and the wood vocal with songs of birds.

The body lay near the window, where the beast had left it when frightened away by the flash and report of the rifle. The clothing was deranged, the long hair in disorder, the limbs lay anyhow. From the throat, dreadfully lacerated, had issued a pool of blood not yet entirely coagulated. The ribbon with which he had bound the wrists was broken; the hands were tightly clenched. Between the teeth was a fragment of the animal's ear.

7

THE COBWEB

Saki

The yellow, wrinkled old dame who hobbled and muttered about the kitchen... like a dead autumn leaf which the winter winds still pushed hither and thither...

The farmhouse kitchen probably stood where it did as a matter of accident or haphazard choice; yet its situation might have been planned by a master-strategist in farmhouse architecture. Dairy and poultry-yard, and herb garden, and all the busy places of the farm seemed to lead by easy access into its wide flagged haven, where there was room for everything and where muddy boots left traces that were easily swept away. And yet, for all that it stood so well in the centre of human bustle, its long, latticed window, with the wide window-seat, built into an embrasure beyond the huge fireplace, looked out on a wild spreading view of hill and heather and wooded combe. The window nook made almost a little room in itself, quite the pleasantest room in the farm as far as situation and capabilities went. Young Mrs Ladbruk, whose husband had just come into the farm by way of inheritance, cast covetous eyes on this snug corner, and her fingers itched to make it bright and cosy with chintz curtains and bowls of flowers, and a shelf or two of old china. The musty farm parlour, looking out on to a prim, cheerless garden imprisoned within high, blank walls, was not a room that lent itself readily either to comfort or decoration.

'When we are more settled I shall work wonders in the way of making the kitchen habitable,' said the young woman to her occasional visitors. There was an unspoken wish in those words, a wish which was unconfessed as well as unspoken. Emma Ladbruk was the mistress of the farm; jointly with her husband she might have her say, and to a certain extent her way, in ordering its affairs. But she was not mistress of the kitchen.

On one of the shelves of an old dresser, in company with chipped sauce-boats, pewter jugs, cheese-graters, and paid bills, rested a worn and ragged Bible, on whose front page was the record, in faded ink, of a baptism dated ninety-four years ago. 'Martha Crale' was the name written on that yellow page. The yellow, wrinkled old dame who hobbled and muttered about the kitchen, looking like a dead autumn leaf which the winter winds still pushed hither and thither, had once been Martha Crale; for seventy odd years she had been Martha Mountjoy. For longer than anyone could remember she had pattered to and fro between oven and wash-house and dairy, and out to chicken-run and garden, grumbling and muttering and scolding, but working unceasingly. Emma Ladbruk, of whose coming she took as little notice as she would of a bee wandering in at a window on a summer's day, used at first to watch her with a kind of frightened curiosity. She was so old and so much a part of the place, it was difficult to think of her exactly as a living thing. Old Shep, the white-nozzled, stiff-limbed collie, waiting for his time to die, seemed almost more human than the withered, dried-up old woman. He had been a riotous, roystering puppy, mad with the joy of life, when she was already a tottering, hobbling dame; now he was just a blind, breathing carcase, nothing more, and she still worked with frail energy, still swept and baked and washed, fetched and carried. If there were something in these wise old dogs that did not perish utterly with death, Emma used to think to herself, what generations of ghost-dogs there must be out on those hills, that Martha had reared and fed and tended and spoken a last goodbye word to in that old kitchen. And what memories she must have of human generations that had passed away in her time. It was difficult for anyone, let alone a stranger like Emma, to get her to talk of the days that had been; her shrill, quavering speech was of doors that had been left unfastened, pails that had got mislaid, calves whose feeding-time was overdue, and the various little faults and lapses that chequer a farmhouse routine. Now and again, when election time came round, she would unstore her recollections of the old names round which the fight had waged in the days gone by. There had been a Palmerston, that had been a name down Tiverton way; Tiverton was not a far journey as the crow flies, but to Martha it was almost a foreign country. Later there had been Northcotes and Aclands, and many other newer names that she had forgotten; the names changed, but it was always Libruls and Toories, Yellows and Blues. And they always quarrelled and shouted as to who was right and who was wrong. The one they quarrelled about most was a fine old gentleman with an angry face—she had seen his picture on the walls. She had seen it on the floor too, with a rotten apple squashed over it, for the farm had changed its politics from time to time. Martha had never been on one side or the other; none of 'they' had ever done the farm a stroke of good. Such was her sweeping verdict, given with all a peasant's distrust of the outside world.

When the half-frightened curiosity had somewhat faded away, Emma Ladbruk was uncomfortably conscious of another feeling towards the old woman. She was a quaint old tradition, lingering about the place, she was part and parcel of the farm itself, she was something at once pathetic and picturesque—but she was dreadfully in the way. Emma had come to the farm full of plans for little reforms and improvements, in part the result of training in the newest ways and methods, in part the outcome of her own ideas and fancies. Reforms in the kitchen region, if those deaf old ears could have been induced to give them even a hearing, would have met with short shrift and scornful rejection, and the kitchen region spread over the zone of dairy and market business and half the work of the household. Emma, with the latest science of dead-poultry dressing at her finger-tips, sat by, an unheeded watcher, while old Martha trussed the chickens for the market-stall as she had trussed them for nearly four-score years—all leg and no breast. And the hundred hints about effective cleaning and labour-lightening and the things that make for wholesomeness which the young woman was ready to impart or to put into action dropped away into nothingness before that wan, muttering, unheeding presence. Above all, the coveted window corner, that was to be a dainty, cheerful oasis in the gaunt old kitchen, stood now choked and lumbered with a litter of odds and ends that Emma, for all her nominal authority, would not have dared or cared to displace; over them seemed to be spun the protection of something that was like a human cobweb. Decidedly Martha was in the way. It would have been an unworthy meanness to have wished to see the span of that brave old life shortened by a few paltry months, but as the days sped by Emma was conscious that the wish was there, disowned though it might be, lurking at the back of her mind.

She felt the meanness of the wish come over her with a qualm of self-reproach one day when she came into the kitchen and found an unaccustomed state of things in that usually busy quarter. Old Martha was not working. A basket of corn was on the floor by her side, and out in the yard the poultry were beginning to clamour a protest of overdue feeding-time. But Martha sat huddled in a shrunken bunch on the window seat, looking out with her dim old eyes as though she saw something stranger than the autumn landscape. 'Is anything the matter, Martha?' asked the young woman. ''Tis death, 'tis death a-coming,' answered the quavering voice; 'I knew 'twere coming. I knew it. 'Tweren't for nothing that old Shep's been howling all morning. An' last night I heard the screech-owl give the death-cry, and there were something white as run across the yard yesterday; 'tweren't a cat nor a stoat, 'twere something. The fowls knew 'twere something; they all drew off to one side. Ay, there's been warnings. I knew it were a-coming.'

The young woman's eyes clouded with pity. The old thing sitting there so white and shrunken had once been a merry, noisy child, playing about in lanes and hay-lofts and farmhouse garrets; that had been eighty odd years ago, and now she was just a frail old body cowering under the approaching chill of the death that was coming at last to take her. It was not probable that much could be done for her, but Emma hastened away to get assistance and counsel. Her husband, she knew, was down at a tree-felling some little distance off, but she might find some other intelligent soul who knew the old woman better than she did. The farm, she soon found out, had that faculty common to farmyards of swallowing up and losing its human population. The poultry followed her in interested fashion, and swine grunted interrogations at her from behind the bars of their styes, but barnyard and rickyard, orchard and stables and dairy, gave no reward to her search. Then, as she retraced her steps towards the kitchen, she came suddenly on her cousin, young Mr Jim, as everyone called him, who divided his time between amateur horse-dealing, rabbit-shooting, and flirting with the farm maids.

'I'm afraid old Martha is dying,' said Emma. Jim was not the sort of person to whom one had to break news gently. 'Nonsense,' he said; 'Martha means to live to a hundred. She told me so, and she'll do it.' 'She may be actually dying at this moment, or it may just be the beginning of the break-up,' persisted Emma, with a feeling of contempt for the slowness and dullness of the young man.

A grin spread over his good-natured features. 'It don't look like it,' he said, nodding towards the yard. Emma turned to catch the meaning of his remark. Old Martha stood in the middle of a mob of poultry, scattering handfuls of grain around her. The turkey-cock, with the bronzed sheen of his feathers and the purple-red of his wattles, the gamecock, with the glowing metallic lustre of his Eastern plumage, the hens, with their ochres and buffs and umbers and their scarlet combs, and the drakes, with their bottle-green heads, made a medley of rich colour, in the centre of which the old woman looked like a withered stalk standing amid a riotous growth of gaily-hued flowers. But she threw the grain deftly amid the wilderness of beaks, and her quavering voice carried as far as the two people who were watching her. She was still harping on the theme of death coming to the farm. 'I knew 'twere a-coming. There's been signs an' warnings.' 'Who's dead, then, old Mother?' called out the young man. "Tis young Mister Ladbruk,' she shrilled back; 'they've just a-carried his body in. Run out of the way of a tree that was coming down an' ran hisself on to an iron post. Dead when they picked un up. Aye, I knew 'twere coming.' And she turned to fling a handful of barley at a belated group of guinea-fowl that came racing toward her.

The farm was a family property, and passed to the rabbit-shooting cousin as the next-of-kin. Emma Ladbruk drifted out of its history as a bee that had wandered in at an open window might flit its way out again. On a cold grey morning she stood waiting, with her boxes already stowed in the farm cart, till the last of the market produce should be ready, for the train she was to catch was of less importance than the chickens and butter and eggs that were to be offered for sale. From where she stood she could see an angle of the long latticed window that was to have been cosy with curtains and gay with bowls of flowers. Into her mind came the thought that for months, perhaps for years, long after she had been utterly forgotten, a white, unheeding face would be seen peering out through those latticed panes, and a weak muttering voice would be heard quavering up and down those flagged passages. She made her way to a narrow barred casement that opened into the farm larder. Old Martha was standing at a table trussing a pair of chickens for the market stall as she had trussed them for nearly fourscore years.

8

A CURIOUS DREAM

Mark Twain

...a broken and worm-eaten coffin on its shoulder and a bundle of something in its hand...

Night before last I had a singular dream. I seemed to be sitting on a doorstep (in no particular city perhaps) ruminating, and the time of night appeared to be about twelve or one o'clock. The weather was balmy and delicious. There was no human sound in the air, not even a footstep. There was no sound of any kind to emphasize the dead stillness, except the occasional hollow barking of a dog in the distance and the fainter answer of a further dog. Presently up the street I heard a bony clack-clacking, and guessed it was the castanets of a serenading party. In a minute more a tall skeleton, hooded, and half clad in a tattered and moldy shroud, whose shreds were flapping about the ribby latticework of its person, swung by me with a stately stride and disappeared in the gray gloom of the starlight. It had a broken and worm-eaten coffin on its shoulder and a bundle of something in its hand. I knew what the clack-clacking was then; it was this party's joints working together, and his elbows knocking against his sides as he walked. I may say I was surprised. Before I could collect my thoughts and enter upon any speculations as to what this apparition might portend, I heard another one coming for I recognized his clack-clack. He had two-thirds of a coffin on his shoulder, and some foot and head boards under his arm. I mightily wanted to peer under his hood and speak to him, but when he turned and smiled upon me with his cavernous sockets and his projecting grin as he went by, I thought I would not detain him. He was hardly gone when I heard the clacking again, and another one issued from the shadowy half-light. This one was bending under a heavy gravestone, and dragging a shabby coffin after him by a string. When he got to me he gave me a steady look for a moment or two, and then rounded to and backed up to me, saying:

'Ease this down for a fellow, will you?'

I eased the gravestone down till it rested on the ground, and in doing so noticed that it bore the name of 'John Baxter Copmanhurst,' with 'May, 1839,' as the date of his death. Deceased sat wearily down by me, and wiped his os frontis with his major maxillary—chiefly from former habit I judged, for I could not see that he brought away any perspiration.

'It is too bad, too bad,' said he, drawing the remnant of the shroud about him and leaning his jaw pensively on his hand. Then he put his left foot up on his knee and fell to scratching his anklebone absently with a rusty nail which he got out of his coffin.

'What is too bad, friend?'

'Oh, everything, everything. I almost wish I never had died.'

'You surprise me. Why do you say this? Has anything gone wrong? What is the matter?'

'Matter! Look at this shroud-rags. Look at this gravestone, all battered up. Look at that disgraceful old coffin. All a man's property going to ruin and destruction before his eyes, and ask him if anything is wrong? Fire and brimstone!'

'Calm yourself, calm yourself,' I said. 'It is too bad—it is certainly too bad, but then I had not supposed that you would much mind such matters situated as you are.'

'Well, my dear sir, I do mind them. My pride is hurt, and my comfort is impaired—destroyed, I might say. I will state my case—I will put it to you in such a way that you can comprehend it, if you will let me,' said the poor skeleton, tilting the hood of his shroud back, as if he were clearing for action, and thus unconsciously giving himself a jaunty and festive air very much at variance with the grave character of his position in life—so to speak—and in prominent contrast with his distressful mood.

'Proceed,' said I.

'I reside in the shameful old graveyard a block or two above you here, in this street—there, now, I just expected that cartilage would let go!—third rib from the bottom, friend, hitch the end of it to my spine with a string, if you have got such a thing about you, though a bit of silver wire is a deal pleasanter, and more durable and becoming, if one keeps it polished—to think of shredding out and going to pieces in this way, just on account of the indifference and neglect of one's posterity!'—and the poor ghost grated his teeth in a way that gave me a wrench and a shiver—for the effect is mightily increased by the absence of muffling flesh and cuticle. 'I reside in that old graveyard, and have for these thirty years; and I tell you things are changed since I first laid this old tired frame there, and turned over, and stretched out for a long sleep, with a delicious sense upon me of being done with bother, and grief, and anxiety, and doubt, and fear, forever and ever, and listening with comfortable and increasing satisfaction to the sexton's work, from the startling clatter of his first spadeful on my coffin till it dulled away to the faint patting that shaped the roof of my new home—delicious! My! I wish you could try it tonight!' and out of my reverie deceased fetched me a rattling slap with a bony hand.

'Yes, sir, thirty years ago I laid me down there, and was happy. For it was out in the country then—out in the breezy, flowery, grand old woods, and the lazy winds gossiped with the leaves, and the squirrels capered over us and around us, and the creeping things visited us, and the birds filled the tranquil solitude with music. Ah, it was worth ten years of a man's life to be dead then! Everything was pleasant. I was in a good neighbourhood, for all the dead people that lived near me belonged to the best families in the city. Our posterity appeared to think the world of us. They kept our graves in the very best condition; the fences were always in faultless repair, head-boards were kept painted or whitewashed, and were replaced with new ones as soon as they began to look rusty or decayed; monuments were kept upright, railings intact and bright, the rose-bushes and shrubbery trimmed, trained, and free from blemish, the walks clean and smooth and graveled. But that day is gone by. Our descendants have forgotten us. My grandson lives in a stately house built with money made by these old hands of mine, and I sleep in a neglected grave with invading vermin that gnaw my shroud to build them nests withal! I and friends that lie with me founded and secured the prosperity of this fine city, and the stately bantling of our loves leaves us to rot in a dilapidated cemetery which neighbours curse and strangers scoff at. See the difference between the old time and this—for instance: Our graves are all caved in now; our head-boards have rotted away and tumbled down; our railings reel this way and that, with one foot in the air, after a fashion of unseemly levity; our monuments lean wearily, and our gravestones bow their heads discouraged; there be no adornments any more—no roses, nor shrubs, nor graveled walks, nor anything that is a comfort to the eye; and even the paintless old board fence that did make a show of holding us sacred from companionship with beasts and the defilement of heedless feet, has tottered till it overhangs the street, and only advertises the presence of our dismal resting-place and invites yet more derision to it. And now we cannot hide our poverty and tatters in the friendly woods, for the city has stretched its withering arms abroad and taken us in, and all that remains of the cheer of our old home is the cluster of lugubrious forest trees that stand, bored and weary of a city life, with their feet in our coffins, looking into the hazy distance and wishing they were there. I tell you it is disgraceful!

'You begin to comprehend—you begin to see how it is. While our descendants are living sumptuously on our money, right around us in the city, we have to fight hard to keep skull and bones together. Bless you, there isn't a grave in our cemetery that doesn't leak, not one. Every time it rains in the night we have to climb out and roost in the trees and sometimes we are wakened suddenly by the chilly water trickling down the back of our necks. Then I tell you there is a general heaving up of old graves and kicking over of old monuments, and scampering of old skeletons for the trees! Bless me, if you had gone along there some such nights after twelve you might have seen as many as fifteen of us roosting on one limb, with our joints rattling drearily and the wind wheezing through our ribs! Many a time we have perched there for three or four dreary hours, and then come down, stiff and chilled through and drowsy, and borrowed each other's skulls to bail out our graves with—if you will glance up in my mouth now as I tilt my head back, you can see that my head-piece is half full of old dry sediment—how top-heavy and stupid it makes me sometimes! Yes, sir, many a time if you had happened to come along just before the dawn you'd have caught us bailing out the graves and hanging our shrouds on the fence to dry. Why, I had an elegant shroud stolen from there one morning—think a party by the name of Smith took it, that resides in a plebeian graveyard over yonder—I think so because the first time I ever saw him he hadn't anything on but a check shirt, and the last time I saw him, which was at a social gathering in the new cemetery, he was the best-dressed corpse in the company—and it is a significant fact that he left when he saw me; and presently an old woman from here missed her coffin—she generally took it with her when she went anywhere, because she was liable to take cold and bring on the spasmodic rheumatism that originally killed her if she exposed herself to the night air much. She was named Hotchkiss—Anna Matilda Hotchkiss—you might know her? She has two upper front teeth, is tall, but a good deal inclined to stoop, one rib on the left side gone, has one shred of rusty hair hanging from the left side of her head, and one little tuft just above and a little forward of her right ear, has her under jaw wired on one side where it had worked loose, small bone of left forearm gone—lost in a fight—has a kind of swagger in her gait and a 'gallus' way of going with her arms akimbo and her nostrils in the air—has been pretty free and easy, and is all damaged and battered up till she looks like a queensware crate in ruins—maybe you have met her?'

'God forbid!' I involuntarily ejaculated, for somehow I was not looking for that form of question, and it caught me a little off my guard. But I hastened to make amends for my rudeness, and say, 'I simply meant I had not had the honour—for I would not deliberately speak discourteously of a friend of yours. You were saying that you were robbed—and it was a shame, too—but it appears by what is left of the shroud you have on that it was a costly one in its day. How did—'

A most ghastly expression began to develop among the decayed features and shriveled integuments of my guest's face, and I was beginning to grow uneasy and distressed, when he told me he was only working up a deep, sly smile, with a wink in it, to suggest that about the time he acquired his present garment a ghost in a neighbouring cemetery missed one. This reassured me, but I begged him to confine himself to speech thenceforth, because his facial expression was uncertain. Even with the most elaborate care it was liable to miss fire. Smiling should especially be avoided. What he might honestly consider a shining success was likely to strike me in a very different light. I said I liked to see a skeleton cheerful, even decorously playful, but I did not think smiling was a skeleton's best hold.

'Yes, friend,' said the poor skeleton, 'the facts are just as I have given them to you. Two of these old graveyards—the one that I resided in and one further along—have been deliberately neglected by our descendants of today until there is no occupying them any longer. Aside from the osteological discomfort of it—and that is no light matter this rainy weather—the present state of things is ruinous to property. We have got to move or be content to see our effects wasted away and utterly destroyed.

'Now, you will hardly believe it, but it is true, nevertheless, that there isn't a single coffin in good repair among all my acquaintance—now that is an absolute fact. I do not refer to low people who come in a pine box mounted on an express-wagon, but I am talking about your high-toned, silver-mounted burial-case, your monumental sort, that travel under black plumes at the head of a procession and have choice of cemetery lots—I mean folks like the Jarvises, and the Bledsoes and Burlings, and such. They are all about ruined. The most substantial people in our set, they were. And now look at them—utterly used up and poverty-stricken. One of the Bledsoes actually traded his monument to a late barkeeper for some fresh shavings to put under his head. I tell you it speaks volumes, for there is nothing a corpse takes so much pride in as his monument. He loves to read the inscription. He comes after a while to believe what it says himself, and then you may see him sitting on the fence night after night enjoying it. Epitaphs are cheap, and they do a poor chap a world of good after he is dead, especially if he had hard luck while he was alive. I wish they were used more. Now I don't complain, but confidentially I do think it was a little shabby in my descendants to give me nothing but this old slab of a gravestone—and all the more that there isn't a compliment on it. It used to have: "GONE TO HIS JUST REWARD" on it, and I was proud when I first saw it, but by and by I noticed that whenever an old friend of mine came along he would hook his chin on the railing and pull a long face and read along down till he came to that, and then he would chuckle to himself and walk off, looking satisfied and comfortable. So I scratched it off to get rid of those fools. But a dead man always takes a deal of pride in his monument. Yonder goes half a dozen of the Jarvises now, with the family monument along. And Smithers and some hired specters went by with his awhile ago. Hello, Higgins, good-by, old friend! That's Meredith Higgins—died in '44—belongs to our set in the cemetery—fine old family—great-grand mother was an Injun—I am on the most familiar terms with him—he didn't hear me was the reason he didn't answer me. And I am sorry, too, because I would have liked to introduce you. You would admire him. He is the most disjointed, sway-backed, and generally distorted old skeleton you ever saw, but he is full of fun. When he laughs it sounds like rasping two stones together, and he always starts it off with a cheery screech like raking a nail across a window-pane. Hey, Jones! That is old Columbus Jones—shroud cost four hundred dollars—entire trousseau, including monument, twenty-seven hundred. This was in the spring of '26. It was enormous style for those days. Dead people came all the way from the Alleghanies to see his things—the party that occupied the grave next to mine remembers it well. Now do you see that individual going along with a piece of a head-board under his arm, one leg-bone below his knee gone, and not a thing in the world on? That is Barstow Dalhousie, and next to Columbus Jones he was the most sumptuously outfitted person that ever entered our cemetery. We are all leaving. We cannot tolerate the treatment we are receiving at the hands of our descendants. They open new cemeteries, but they leave us to our ignominy. They mend the streets, but they never mend anything that is about us or belongs to us. Look at that coffin of mine—yet I tell you in its day it was a piece of furniture that would have attracted attention in any drawing-room in this city. You may have it if you want it—I can't afford to repair it. Put a new bottom in her, and part of a new top, and a bit of fresh lining along the left side, and you'll find her about as comfortable as any receptacle of her species you ever tried. No thanks—no, don't mention it—you have been civil to me, and I would give you all the property I have got before I would seem ungrateful. Now this winding-sheet is a kind of a sweet thing in its way, if you would like to—No? Well, just as you say, but I wished to be fair and liberal—there's nothing mean about me. Good-by, friend, I must be going. I may have a good way to go tonight—don't know. I only know one thing for certain, and that is that I am on the emigrant trail now, and I'll never sleep in that crazy old cemetery again. I will travel till I find respectable quarters, if I have to hoof it to New Jersey. All the boys are going. It was decided in public conclave, last night, to emigrate, and by the time the sun rises there won't be a bone left in our old habitations. Such cemeteries may suit my surviving friends, but they do not suit the remains that have the honour to make these remarks. My opinion is the general opinion. If you doubt it, go and see how the departing ghosts upset things before they started. They were almost riotous in their demonstrations of distaste. Hello, here are some of the Bledsoes, and if you will give me a lift with this tombstone I guess I will join company and jog along with them—mighty respectable old family, the Bledsoes, and used to always come out in six-horse hearses and all that sort of thing fifty years ago when I walked these streets in daylight. Good-by, friend.'

And with his gravestone on his shoulder he joined the grisly procession, dragging his damaged coffin after him, for notwithstanding he pressed it upon me so earnestly, I utterly refused his hospitality. I suppose that for as much as two hours these sad outcasts went clacking by, laden with their dismal effects, and all that time I sat pitying them. One or two of the youngest and least dilapidated among them inquired about midnight trains on the railways, but the rest seemed unacquainted with that mode of travel, and merely asked about common public roads to various towns and cities, some of which are not on the map now, and vanished from it and from the earth as much as thirty years ago, and some few of them never had existed anywhere but on maps, and private ones in real-estate agencies at that. And they asked about the condition of the cemeteries in these towns and cities, and about the reputation the citizens bore as to reverence for the dead.

This whole matter interested me deeply, and likewise compelled my sympathy for these homeless ones. And it all seeming real, and I not knowing it was a dream, I mentioned to one shrouded wanderer an idea that had entered my head to publish an account of this curious and very sorrowful exodus, but said also that I could not describe it truthfully, and just as it occurred, without seeming to trifle with a grave subject and exhibit an irreverence for the dead that would shock and distress their surviving friends. But this bland and stately remnant of a former citizen leaned him far over my gate and whispered in my ear, and said:

'Do not let that disturb you. The community that can stand such graveyards as those we are emigrating from can stand anything a body can say about the neglected and forsaken dead that lie in them.'

At that very moment a cock crowed, and the weird procession vanished and left not a shred or a bone behind. I awoke, and found myself lying with my head out of the bed and 'sagging' downward considerably—a position favorable to dreaming dreams with morals in them, maybe, but not poetry.

NOTE: The reader is assured that if the cemeteries in his town are kept in good order, this dream is not levelled at his town at all, but is levelled particularly and venomously at the next town.

9

THE EVIL CLERGYMAN

H.P. Lovecraft

...the man got frightened and shot himself...

I was shown into the attic chamber by a grave, intelligent-looking man with quiet clothes and an iron-gray beard, who spoke to me in this fashion: 'Yes, he lived here—but I don't advise your doing anything. Your curiosity makes you irresponsible. We never come here at night, and it's only because of his will that we keep it this way. You know what he did. That abominable society took charge at last, and we don't know where he is buried. There was no way the law or anything else could reach the society.

'I hope you won't stay till after dark. And I beg of you to let that thing on the table—the thing that looks like a match-box—alone. We don't know what it is, but we suspect it has something to do with what he did. We even avoid looking at it very steadily.' After a time the man left me alone in the attic room. It was very dingy and dusty, and only primitively furnished, but it had a neatness which showed it was not a slum-denizen's quarters. There were shelves full of theological and classical books, and another bookcase containing treatises on magic—Paracelsus, Albertus Magnus, Trithemius, Hermes Trismegistus, Borellus, and others in a strange alphabet whose titles I could not decipher. The furniture was very plain. There was a door, but it led only into a closet. The only egress was the aperture in the floor up to which the crude, steep staircase led. The windows were of bull's-eye pattern, and the black oak beams bespoke unbelievable antiquity. Plainly, this house was of the Old World. I seemed to know where I was, but cannot recall what I then knew. Certainly the town was not London. My impression is of a small seaport. The small object on the table fascinated me intensely. I seemed to know what to do with it, for I drew a pocket electric light—or what looked like one—out of my pocket and nervously tested its flashes. The light was not white but violet, and seemed less like true light than like some radioactive bombardment. I recall that I did not regard it as a common flashlight—indeed, I had a common flashlight in another pocket. It was getting dark, and the ancient roofs and chimney-pots outside looked very queer through the bull's-eye window-panes. Finally I summoned up courage and propped the small object up on the table against a book—then turned the rays of the peculiar violet light upon it. The light seemed now to be more like a rain of hail or small violet particles than like a continuous beam. As the particles struck the glassy surface at the center of the strange device, they seemed to produce a crackling noise like the sputtering of a vacuum tube through which sparks are passed. The dark glassy surface displayed a pinkish glow, and a vague white shape seemed to be taking form at its center. Then I noticed that I was not alone in the room—and put the ray-projector back in my pocket.

But the newcomer did not speak—nor did I hear any sound whatever during all the immediately following moments. Everything was shadowy pantomime, as if seen at a vast distance through some intervening haze—although on the other hand the newcomer and all subsequent comers loomed large and close, as if both near and distant, according to some abnormal geometry. The newcomer was a thin, dark man of medium height attired in the clerical garb of the Anglican church. He was apparently about thirty years old, with a sallow, olive complexion and fairly good features, but an abnormally high forehead. His black hair was well cut and neatly brushed, and he was clean-shaven though blue-chinned with a heavy growth of beard. He wore rimless spectacles with steel bows. His build and lower facial features were like other clergymen I had seen, but he had a vastly higher forehead, and was darker and more intelligent-looking—also more subtly and concealedly evil-looking. At the present moment—having just lighted a faint oil lamp—he looked nervous, and before I knew it he was casting all his magical books into a fireplace on the window side of the room (where the wall slanted sharply) which I had not noticed before. The flames devoured the volumes greedily—leaping up in strange colours and emitting indescribably hideous odors as the strangely hieroglyphed leaves and wormy bindings succumbed to the devastating element. All at once I saw there were others in the room—grave-looking men in clerical costume, one of whom wore the bands and knee-breeches of a bishop. Though I could hear nothing, I could see that they were bringing a decision of vast import to the first-comer. They seemed to hate and fear him at the same time, and he seemed to return these sentiments. His face set itself into a grim expression, but I could see his right hand shaking as he tried to grip the back of a chair. The bishop pointed to the empty case and to the fireplace (where the flames had died down amidst a charred, non-committal mass), and seemed filled with a peculiar loathing. The first-comer then gave a wry smile and reached out with his left hand toward the small object on the table. Everyone then seemed frightened. The procession of clerics began filing down the steep stairs through the trapdoor in the floor, turning and making menacing gestures as they left. The bishop was last to go.

The first-comer now went to a cupboard on the inner side of the room and extracted a coil of rope. Mounting a chair, he attached one end of the rope to a hook in the great exposed central beam of black oak, and began making a noose with the other end. Realizing he was about to hang himself, I started forward to dissuade or save him. He saw me and ceased his preparations, looking at me with a kind of triumph which puzzled and disturbed me. He slowly stepped down from the chair and began gliding toward me with a positively wolfish grin on his dark, thin-lipped face.

I felt somehow in deadly peril, and drew out the peculiar

ray-projector as a weapon of defense. Why I thought it could help me, I do not know. I turned it on—full in his face, and saw the sallow features glow first with violet and then with pinkish light. His expression of wolfish exultation began to be crowded aside by a look of profound fear—which did not, however, wholly displace the exultation. He stopped in his tracks—then, flailing his arms wildly in the air, began to stagger backwards. I saw he was edging toward the open stair-well in the floor, and tried to shout a warning, but he did not hear me. In another instant he had lurched backward through the opening and was lost to view.

I found difficulty in moving toward the stair-well, but when I did get there I found no crushed body on the floor below. Instead there was a clatter of people coming up with lanterns, for the spell of phantasmal silence had broken, and I once more heard sounds and saw figures as normally tri-dimensional. Something had evidently drawn a crowd to this place. Had there been a noise I had not heard?

Presently the two people (simple villagers, apparently) farthest in the lead saw me—and stood paralyzed. One of them shrieked loudly and reverberantly: '*Ahrrh!...It be'ee, zur? Again?*'

Then they all turned and fled frantically. All, that is, but one. When the crowd was gone I saw the grave-bearded man who had brought me to this place—standing alone with a lantern. He was gazing at me gaspingly and fascinatedly, but did not seem afraid. Then he began to ascend the stairs, and joined me in the attic. He spoke:

'So you didn't let it alone! I'm sorry. I know what has happened. It happened once before, but the man got frightened and shot himself. You ought not to have made him come back. You know what he wants. But you mustn't get frightened like the other man he got. Something very strange and terrible has happened to you, but it didn't get far enough to hurt your mind and personality. If you'll keep cool, and accept the need for making certain radical readjustments in your life, you can keep right on enjoying the world, and the fruits of your scholarship.

But you can't live here—and I don't think you'll wish to go back to London. I'd advise America.

'You mustn't try anything more with that—thing. Nothing can be put back now. It would only make matters worse to do—or summon—anything. You are not as badly off as you might be—but you must get out of here at once and stay away. You'd better thank Heaven it didn't go further...

'I'm going to prepare you as bluntly as I can. There's been a certain change—in your personal appearance. He always causes that. But in a new country you can get used to it. There's a mirror up at the other end of the room, and I'm going to take you to it. You'll get a shock—though you will see nothing repulsive.'

I was now shaking with a deadly fear, and the bearded man almost had to hold me up as he walked me across the room to the mirror, the faint lamp (i.e. that formerly on the table, not the still fainter lantern he had brought) in his free hand. This is what I saw in the glass:

A thin, dark man of medium stature attired in the clerical garb of the Anglican church, apparently about thirty, and with rimless, steel-bowed glasses glistening beneath a sallow, olive forehead of abnormal height.

It was the silent first-comer who had burned his books.

For all the rest of my life, in outward form, I was to be that man!

10

THE FACTS IN THE CASE OF M. VALDEMAR

Edgar Allan Poe

...the unutterable, shuddering horror which these few words, thus uttered, were so well calculated to convey...

Of course I shall not pretend to consider it any matter for wonder, that the extraordinary case of M. Valdemar has excited discussion. It would have been a miracle had it not—especially under the circumstances. Through the desire of all parties concerned, to keep the affair from the public, at least for the present, or until we had farther opportunities for investigation—through our endeavors to effect this—a garbled or exaggerated account made its way into society, and became the source of many unpleasant misrepresentations, and, very naturally, of a great deal of disbelief. It is now rendered necessary that I give the facts—as far as I comprehend them myself. They are, succinctly, these:

My attention, for the last three years, had been repeatedly drawn to the subject of Mesmerism; and, about nine months ago it occurred to me, quite suddenly, that in the series of experiments made hitherto, there had been a very remarkable and most unaccountable omission—no person had as yet been mesmerized in articulo mortis. It remained to be seen, first, whether, in such condition, there existed in the patient any susceptibility to the magnetic influence; secondly, whether, if any existed, it was impaired or increased by the condition; thirdly, to what extent, or for how long a period, the encroachments of Death might be arrested by the process. There were other points to be ascertained, but these most excited my curiosity—

the last in especial, from the immensely important character of its consequences.

In looking around me for some subject by whose means I might test these particulars, I was brought to think of my friend, M. Ernest Valdemar, the well-known compiler of the *Bibliotheca Forensica*, and author (under the nom de plume of Issachar Marx) of the Polish versions of *Wallenstein* and *Gargantua*. M. Valdemar, who has resided principally at Harlaem, N.Y., since the year 1839, is (or was) particularly noticeable for the extreme spareness of his person—his lower limbs much resembling those of John Randolph; and, also, for the whiteness of his whiskers, in violent contrast to the blackness of his hair—the latter, in consequence, being very generally mistaken for a wig. His temperament was markedly nervous, and rendered him a good subject for mesmeric experiment. On two or three occasions I had put him to sleep with little difficulty, but was disappointed in other results which his peculiar constitution had naturally led me to anticipate. His will was at no period positively, or thoroughly, under my control, and in regard to clairvoyance, I could accomplish with him nothing to be relied upon. I always attributed my failure at these points to the disordered state of his health. For some months previous to my becoming acquainted with him, his physicians had declared him in a confirmed phthisis. It was his custom, indeed, to speak calmly of his approaching dissolution, as of a matter neither to be avoided nor regretted.

When the ideas to which I have alluded first occurred to me, it was of course very natural that I should think of M. Valdemar. I knew the steady philosophy of the man too well to apprehend any scruples from him; and he had no relatives in America who would be likely to interfere. I spoke to him frankly upon the subject; and, to my surprise, his interest seemed vividly excited. I say to my surprise, for, although he had always yielded his person freely to my experiments, he had never before given me any tokens of sympathy with what I did. His disease was of that character which would admit of exact calculation in respect to the epoch of its termination in death; and it was finally arranged between us that he would send for me about twenty-four hours before the period announced by his physicians as that of his decease.

It is now rather more than seven months since I received, from M Valdemar himself, the subjoined note:

My DEAR P—,

You may as well come now. D— and F— are agreed that I cannot hold out beyond tomorrow midnight; and I think they have hit the time very nearly.

VALDEMAR

I received this note within half an hour after it was written, and in fifteen minutes more I was in the dying man's chamber. I had not seen him for ten days, and was appalled by the fearful alteration which the brief interval had wrought in him. His face wore a leaden hue; the eyes were utterly lustreless; and the emaciation was so extreme that the skin had been broken through by the cheek-bones. His expectoration was excessive. The pulse was barely perceptible. He retained, nevertheless, in a very remarkable manner, both his mental power and a certain degree of physical strength. He spoke with distinctness—took some palliative medicines without aid—and, when I entered the room, was occupied in penciling memoranda in a pocket-book. He was propped up in the bed by pillows. Doctors D— and F— were in attendance.

After pressing Valdemar's hand, I took these gentlemen aside, and obtained from them a minute account of the patient's condition. The left lung had been for eighteen months in a semi-osseous or cartilaginous state, and was, of course, entirely useless for all purposes of vitality. The right, in its upper portion, was also partially, if not thoroughly, ossified, while the lower region was merely a mass of purulent tubercles, running one into another. Several extensive perforations existed; and, at one point, permanent adhesion to the ribs had taken place.

These appearances in the right lobe were of comparatively recent date. The ossification had proceeded with very unusual rapidity; no sign of it had been discovered a month before, and the adhesion had only been observed during the three previous days. Independently of the phthisis, the patient was suspected of aneurism of the aorta; but on this point the osseous symptoms rendered an exact diagnosis impossible. It was the opinion of both physicians that M. Valdemar would die about midnight on the morrow (Sunday). It was then seven o'clock on Saturday evening. On quitting the invalid's bedside to hold conversation with myself, Doctors D— and F— had bidden him a final farewell. It had not been their intention to return; but, at my request, they agreed to look in upon the patient about ten the next night.

When they had gone, I spoke freely with M. Valdemar on the subject of his approaching dissolution, as well as, more particularly, of the experiment proposed. He still professed himself quite willing and even anxious to have it made, and urged me to commence it at once. A male and a female nurse were in attendance; but I did not feel myself altogether at liberty to engage in a task of this character with no more reliable witnesses than these people, in case of sudden accident, might prove. I therefore postponed operations until about eight the next night, when the arrival of a medical student with whom I had some acquaintance, (Mr Theodore L—l,) relieved me from farther embarrassment. It had been my design, originally, to wait for the physicians; but I was induced to proceed, first, by the urgent entreaties of M. Valdemar, and secondly, by my conviction that I had not a moment to lose, as he was evidently sinking fast.

Mr L—l was so kind as to accede to my desire that he would take notes of all that occurred, and it is from his memoranda that what I now have to relate is, for the most part, either condensed or copied verbatim.

It wanted about five minutes of eight when, taking the patient's hand, I begged him to state, as distinctly as he could, to Mr L—l, whether he (M. Valdemar) was entirely willing that I should make the experiment of mesmerizing him in his then condition.

He replied feebly, yet quite audibly, 'Yes, I wish to be mesmerized'—adding immediately afterwards, 'I fear you have deferred it too long.'

While he spoke thus, I commenced the passes which I had already found most effectual in subduing him. He was evidently influenced with the first lateral stroke of my hand across his forehead; but although I exerted all my powers, no farther perceptible effect was induced until some minutes after ten o'clock, when Doctors D— and F— called, according to appointment. I explained to them, in a few words, what I designed, and as they opposed no objection, saying that the patient was already in the death agony, I proceeded without hesitation—exchanging, however, the lateral passes for downward ones, and directing my gaze entirely into the right eye of the sufferer.

By this time his pulse was imperceptible and his breathing was stertorous, and at intervals of half a minute.

This condition was nearly unaltered for a quarter of an hour. At the expiration of this period, however, a natural although a very deep sigh escaped the bosom of the dying man, and the stertorous breathing ceased—that is to say, its stertorousness was no longer apparent; the intervals were undiminished. The patient's extremities were of an icy coldness.

At five minutes before eleven I perceived unequivocal signs of the mesmeric influence. The glassy roll of the eye was changed for that expression of uneasy inward examination which is never seen except in cases of sleep-waking, and which it is quite impossible to mistake. With a few rapid lateral passes I made the lids quiver, as in incipient sleep, and with a few more I closed them altogether. I was not satisfied, however, with this, but continued the manipulations vigorously, and with the fullest exertion of the will, until I had completely stiffened the limbs of the slumberer, after placing them in a seemingly easy position. The legs were at full length; the arms were nearly so, and reposed on the bed at a moderate distance from the loin. The head was very slightly elevated.

When I had accomplished this, it was fully midnight, and I requested the gentlemen present to examine M Valdemar's condition. After a few experiments, they admitted him to be an unusually perfect state of mesmeric trance. The curiosity of both the physicians was greatly excited. Dr D— resolved at once to remain with the patient all night, while Dr F— took leave with a promise to return at daybreak. Mr L—l and the nurses remained.

We left M Valdemar entirely undisturbed until about three o'clock in the morning, when I approached him and found him in precisely the same condition as when Dr F— went away—that is to say, he lay in the same position; the pulse was imperceptible; the breathing was gentle (scarcely noticeable, unless through the application of a mirror to the lips); the eyes were closed naturally; and the limbs were as rigid and as cold as marble. Still, the general appearance was certainly not that of death.

As I approached M Valdemar I made a kind of half effort to influence his right arm into pursuit of my own, as I passed the latter gently to and fro above his person. In such experiments with this patient I had never perfectly succeeded before, and assuredly I had little thought of succeeding now; but to my astonishment, his arm very readily, although feebly, followed every direction I assigned it with mine. I determined to hazard a few words of conversation.

'M. Valdemar,' I said, 'are you asleep?' He made no answer, but I perceived a tremor about the lips, and was thus induced to repeat the question, again and again. At its third repetition, his whole frame was agitated by a very slight shivering; the eyelids unclosed themselves so far as to display a white line of the ball; the lips moved sluggishly, and from between them, in a barely audible whisper, issued the words:

'Yes—asleep now. Do not wake me!—let me die so!'

I here felt the limbs and found them as rigid as ever.

The right arm, as before, obeyed the direction of my hand. I questioned the sleep-waker again:

'Do you still feel pain in the breast, M. Valdemar?'

The answer now was immediate, but even less audible than before:

'No pain—I am dying.'

I did not think it advisable to disturb him farther just then, and nothing more was said or done until the arrival of Dr F—, who came a little before sunrise, and expressed unbounded astonishment at finding the patient still alive. After feeling the pulse and applying a mirror to the lips, he requested me to speak to the sleep-waker again. I did so, saying:

'M. Valdemar, do you still sleep?'

As before, some minutes elapsed ere a reply was made; and during the interval the dying man seemed to be collecting his energies to speak. At my fourth repetition of the question, he said very faintly, almost inaudibly:

'Yes; still asleep—dying.'

It was now the opinion, or rather the wish, of the physicians, that M. Valdemar should be suffered to remain undisturbed in his present apparently tranquil condition, until death should supervene—and this, it was generally agreed, must now take place within a few minutes. I concluded, however, to speak to him once more, and merely repeated my previous question.

While I spoke, there came a marked change over the countenance of the sleep-waker. The eyes rolled themselves slowly open, the pupils disappearing upwardly; the skin generally assumed a cadaverous hue, resembling not so much parchment as white paper; and the circular hectic spots which, hitherto, had been strongly defined in the centre of each cheek, went out at once. I use this expression, because the suddenness of their departure put me in mind of nothing so much as the extinguishment of a candle by a puff of the breath. The upper lip, at the same time, writhed itself away from the teeth, which it had previously covered completely; while the lower jaw fell with an audible jerk, leaving the mouth widely extended, and disclosing in full view the swollen and blackened tongue. I presume that no member of the party then present had been unaccustomed to death-bed horrors; but so hideous beyond conception was the appearance of M. Valdemar at this moment, that there was a general shrinking back from the region of the bed.

I now feel that I have reached a point of this narrative at which every reader will be startled into positive disbelief. It is my business, however, simply to proceed.

There was no longer the faintest sign of vitality in M. Valdemar; and concluding him to be dead, we were consigning him to the charge of the nurses, when a strong vibratory motion was observable in the tongue. This continued for perhaps a minute. At the expiration of this period, there issued from the distended and motionless jaws a voice—such as it would be madness in me to attempt describing. There are, indeed, two or three epithets which might be considered as applicable to it in part; I might say, for example, that the sound was harsh, and broken and hollow; but the hideous whole is indescribable, for the simple reason that no similar sounds have ever jarred upon the ear of humanity. There were two particulars, nevertheless, which I thought then, and still think, might fairly be stated as characteristic of the intonation—as well adapted to convey some idea of its unearthly peculiarity. In the first place, the voice seemed to reach our ears—at least mine—from a vast distance, or from some deep cavern within the earth. In the second place, it impressed me (I fear, indeed, that it will be impossible to make myself comprehended) as gelatinous or glutinous matters impress the sense of touch.

I have spoken both of 'sound' and of 'voice.' I mean to say that the sound was one of distinct—of even wonderfully, thrillingly distinct—syllabification. M. Valdemar spoke—obviously in reply to the question I had propounded to him a few minutes before. I had asked him, it will be remembered, if he still slept. He now said:

'Yes—no—I have been sleeping—and now—now—I am dead.'

No person present even affected to deny, or attempted to repress, the unutterable, shuddering horror which these few words, thus uttered, were so well calculated to convey. Mr L—l (the student) swooned. The nurses immediately left the chamber, and could not be induced to return. My own impressions I would not pretend to render intelligible to the reader. For nearly an hour, we busied ourselves, silently—without the utterance of a word—in endeavors to revive Mr L—l. When he came to himself, we addressed ourselves again to an investigation of M. Valdemar's condition.

It remained in all respects as I have last described it, with the exception that the mirror no longer afforded evidence of respiration. An attempt to draw blood from the arm failed. I should mention, too, that this limb was no farther subject to my will. I endeavored in vain to make it follow the direction of my hand. The only real indication, indeed, of the mesmeric influence, was now found in the vibratory movement of the tongue, whenever I addressed M. Valdemar a question. He seemed to be making an effort to reply, but had no longer sufficient volition. To queries put to him by any other person than myself he seemed utterly insensible—although I endeavored to place each member of the company in mesmeric rapport with him. I believe that I have now related all that is necessary to an understanding of the sleep-waker's state at this epoch. Other nurses were procured; and at ten o'clock I left the house in company with the two physicians and Mr L—l.

In the afternoon we all called again to see the patient. His condition remained precisely the same. We had now some discussion as to the propriety and feasibility of awakening him; but we had little difficulty in agreeing that no good purpose would be served by so doing. It was evident that, so far, death (or what is usually termed death) had been arrested by the mesmeric process. It seemed clear to us all that to awaken M. Valdemar would be merely to insure his instant, or at least his speedy dissolution.

From this period until the close of last week—an interval of nearly seven months—we continued to make daily calls at M. Valdemar's house, accompanied, now and then, by medical and other friends. All this time the sleeper-waker remained exactly as I have last described him. The nurses' attentions were continual.

It was on Friday last that we finally resolved to make the experiment of awakening or attempting to awaken him; and it is the (perhaps) unfortunate result of this latter experiment which has given rise to so much discussion in private circles—to so much of what I cannot help thinking unwarranted popular feeling.

For the purpose of relieving M. Valdemar from the mesmeric trance, I made use of the customary passes. These, for a time, were unsuccessful. The first indication of revival was afforded by a partial descent of the iris. It was observed, as especially remarkable, that this lowering of the pupil was accompanied by the profuse out-flowing of a yellowish ichor (from beneath the lids) of a pungent and highly offensive odor.

It was now suggested that I should attempt to influence the patient's arm, as heretofore. I made the attempt and failed. Dr F— then intimated a desire to have me put a question. I did so, as follows:

'M. Valdemar, can you explain to us what are your feelings or wishes now?'

There was an instant return of the hectic circles on the cheeks; the tongue quivered, or rather rolled violently in the mouth (although the jaws and lips remained rigid as before;) and at length the same hideous voice which I have already described, broke forth:

'For God's sake!—quick!—quick!—put me to sleep—or, quick!—waken me!—quick!—I say to you that I am dead!'

I was thoroughly unnerved, and for an instant remained undecided what to do. At first I made an endeavor to re-compose the patient; but, failing in this through total abeyance of the will, I retraced my steps and as earnestly struggled to awaken him. In this attempt I soon saw that I should be successful—or at least I soon fancied that my success would be complete—and I am sure that all in the room were prepared to see the patient awaken.

For what really occurred, however, it is quite impossible that any human being could have been prepared.

As I rapidly made the mesmeric passes, amid ejaculations of 'dead! dead!' absolutely bursting from the tongue and not from the lips of the sufferer, his whole frame at once—within the space of a single minute, or even less, shrunk—crumbled—absolutely rotted away beneath my hands. Upon the bed, before that whole company, there lay a nearly liquid mass of loathsome—of detestable putridity.

11

A GHOST STORY

Mark Twain

...groping among the tombs and invading the privacy of the dead...

I took a large room, far up Broadway, in a huge old building whose upper stories had been wholly unoccupied for years; until I came. The place had long been given up to dust and cobwebs, to solitude and silence. I seemed groping among the tombs and invading the privacy of the dead, that first night I climbed up to my quarters. For the first time in my life a superstitious dread came over me; and as I turned a dark angle of the stairway and an invisible cobweb swung its lazy woof in my face and clung there, I shuddered as one who had encountered a phantom.

I was glad enough when I reached my room and locked out the mould and darkness. A cheery fire was burning in the grate, and I sat down before it with a comforting sense of relief. For two hours I sat there, thinking of bygone times; recalling old scenes, and summoning half-forgotten faces out of the mists of the past; listening, in fancy, to voices that long ago grew silent for all time, and to once familiar songs that nobody sings now. And as my reverie softened down to a sadder and sadder pathos, the shrieking of the winds outside softened to a wail, the angry beating of the rain against the panes diminished to a tranquil patter, and one by one the noises in the street subsided, until the hurrying footsteps of the last belated straggler died away in the distance and left no sound behind.

The fire had burned low. A sense of loneliness crept over

me. I arose and undressed, moving on tiptoe about the room, doing stealthily what I had to do, as if I were environed by sleeping enemies whose slumbers it would be fatal to break. I covered up in bed, and lay listening to the rain and wind and the faint creaking of distant shutters, till they lulled me to sleep.

I slept profoundly, but how long I do not know. All at once I found myself awake, and filled with a shuddering expectancy. All was still. All but my own heart—I could hear it beat.

Presently the bedclothes began to slip away slowly toward the foot of the bed, as if someone were pulling them! I could not stir; I could not speak. Still the blankets slipped deliberately away, till my breast was uncovered. Then with a great effort I seized them and drew them over my head. I waited, listened, waited. Once more that steady pull began, and once more I lay torpid a century of dragging seconds till my breast was naked again. At last I roused my energies and snatched the covers back to their place and held them with a strong grip. I waited. By and by I felt a faint tug, and took a fresh grip. The rug strengthened to a steady strain—it grew stronger and stronger. My hold parted, and for the third time the blankets slid away. I groaned. An answering groan came from the foot of the bed! Beaded drops of sweat stood upon my forehead.

I was more dead than alive. Presently I heard a heavy footstep in my room—the step of an elephant it seemed to me—it was not like anything human. But it was moving from me—there was relief in that. I heard it approach the door—pass out without moving bolt or lock—and wander away among the dismal corridors, straining the floors and joists till they creaked again as it passed; and then silence reigned once more.

When my excitement had calmed, I said to myself, 'This is a dream—simply a hideous dream.' And so I lay thinking it over until I convinced myself that it was a dream, and then a comforting laugh relaxed my lips and I was happy again. I got up and struck a light; and when I found the locks and bolts were just as I had left them, another soothing laugh welled in my heart and rippled from my lips. I took my pipe and lit it, and was just sitting down before the fire, when—down went the pipe out of my nerveless fingers, the blood forsook my cheeks, and my placid breathing was cut short with a gasp! In the ashes on the hearth, side by side with my own bare footprint, was another, so vast that in comparison, mine was but an infant's! Then I had had a visitor, and the elephant tread was explained.

I put out the light and returned to bed, palsied with fear. I lay a long time, peering into the darkness, and listening. Then I heard a grating noise overhead, like the dragging of a heavy body across the floor; then the throwing down of the body, and the shaking of my windows in response to the concussion. In distant parts of the building I heard the muffled slamming of doors. I heard, at intervals, stealthy footsteps creeping in and out among the corridors, and up and down the stairs. Sometimes these noises approached my door, hesitated, and went away again. I heard the clanking of chains faintly, in remote passages, and listened while the clanking grew nearer—while it wearily climbed the stairways, marking each move by the loose surplus of chain that fell with an accented rattle upon each succeeding step as the goblin that bore it advanced. I heard muttered sentences, half-uttered screams that seemed smothered violently; and the swish of invisible garments and the rush of invisible wings. Then I became conscious that my chamber was invaded—that I was not alone. I heard sighs and breathings about my bed, and mysterious whisperings. Three little spheres of phosphorescent light appeared on the ceiling directly over my head, clung and glowed there a moment, and then dropped—two of them upon my face and one upon the pillow. They spattered, liquidly, and felt warm. Intuition told me they had turned to gouts of blood as they fell—I needed no light to satisfy myself of that. Then I saw pallid faces, dimly luminous, and white uplifted hands, floating bodiless in the air—floating a moment and then disappearing. The whispering ceased, and the voices and the sounds, and a solemn stillness followed. I waited and listened. I felt that I must have light or die. I was weak with fear. I slowly raised myself toward a sitting posture, and my face came in contact with a clammy hand! All strength went from me apparently, and I fell back like a stricken invalid. Then I heard the rustle of a garment—it seemed to pass to the door and go out.

When everything was still once more, I crept out of bed, sick and feeble, and lit the gas with a hand that trembled as if it were aged with a hundred years. The light brought some little cheer to my spirits. I sat down and fell into a dreamy contemplation of that great footprint in the ashes. By and by its outlines began to waver and grow dim. I glanced up and the broad gas flame was slowly wilting away. In the same moment I heard that elephantine tread again. I noted its approach, nearer and nearer, along the musty halls, and dimmer and dimmer the light waned. The tread reached my very door and paused—the light had dwindled to a sickly blue, and all things about me were in a spectral twilight. The door did not open, and yet I felt a faint gust of air fan my cheek, and presently was conscious of a huge, cloudy presence before me. I watched it with fascinated eyes. A pale glow stole over the Thing; gradually its cloudy folds took shape—an arm appeared, then legs, then a body, and last a great sad face looked out of the vapour. Stripped of its filmy housings, naked, muscular and comely, the majestic Cardiff Giant loomed above me!

All my misery vanished—for a child might know that no harm could come with that benignant countenance. My cheerful spirits returned at once, and in sympathy with them the gas turned up brightly again. Never a lone outcast was so glad to welcome company as I was to greet the friendly giant. I said: 'Why, is it nobody but you? Do you know, I have been scared to death for the last two or three hours? I am most honestly glad to see you. I wish I had a chair—Here, here, don't try to sit down in that thing!'

But it was too late. He was in before I could stop him, and down he went—I never saw a chair shivered so in my life.

'Stop, stop, you'll ruin ev—' Too late again. There was

another crash, and another chair was resolved into its original elements.

'Confound it, haven't you got any judgment at all? Do you want to ruin all the furniture on the place? Here, here, you petrified fool—' But it was no use. Before I could arrest him he had sat down on the bed, and it was a melancholy ruin.

'Now what sort of a way is that to do? First you come lumbering about the place bringing a legion of vagabond goblins along with you to worry me to death, and then, when I overlook an indelicacy of costume which would not be tolerated anywhere by cultivated people except in a respectable theater, and not even there if the nudity were of your sex, you repay me by wrecking all the furniture you can find to sit down on. And why will you? You damage yourself as much as you do me. You have broken off the end of your spinal column, and littered up the floor with chips of your hands till the place looks like a marble yard. You ought to be ashamed of yourself—you are big enough to know better.'

'Well, I will not break any more furniture. But what am I to do? I have not had a chance to sit down for a century.' And the tears came into his eyes. 'Poor devil,' I said, 'I should not have been so harsh with you. And you are an orphan, too, no doubt. But sit down on the floor here—nothing else can stand your weight—and, besides, we cannot be sociable with you away up there above me; I want you down where I can perch on this high counting-house stool and gossip with you face to face.'

So he sat down on the floor, and lit a pipe which I gave him, threw one of my red blankets over his shoulders, inverted my sitz-bath on his head, helmet fashion, and made himself picturesque and comfortable. Then he crossed his ankles, while I renewed the fire, and exposed the flat, honey-combed bottoms of his prodigious feet to the grateful warmth.

'What is the matter with the bottom of your feet and the back of your legs, that they are gouged up so?'

'Infernal chilblains—I caught them clear up to the back of my head, roosting out there under Newell' s farm. But I love the place; I love it as one loves his old home. There is no peace for me like the peace I feel when I am there.'

We talked along for half an hour, and then I noticed that he looked tired, and I spoke of it.

'Tired?' he said. 'Well, I should think so. And now I will tell you all about it, since you have treated me so well. I am the spirit of the Petrified Man that lies across the street there in the museum. I am the ghost of the Cardiff Giant. I can have no rest, no peace, till they have given that poor body burial again. Now what was the most natural thing for me to do, to make men satisfy this wish? Terrify them into it!—haunt the place where the body lay! So I haunted the museum night after night. I got the other spirits to help me. But it did no good, for nobody ever came to the museum at midnight. Then it occurred to me to come over the way and haunt this place a little. I felt that if I ever got a hearing I must succeed, for I had the most efficient company that tradition could furnish. Night after night we have shivered around through these mildewed halls, dragging chains, groaning, whispering, tramping up and down stairs, till, to tell you the truth, I am almost worn out. But when I saw a light in your room tonight, I roused my energies again and went at it with a deal of the old freshness. But I am tired out—entirely fagged out. Give me, I beseech you, give me some hope!'

I lit off my perch in a burst of excitement, and exclaimed: 'This transcends everything! Everything that ever did occur—why, you poor blundering old fossil, you have had all your trouble for nothing—you have been haunting a plaster cast of yourself—the real Cardiff Giant is in Albany ! Confound it, don't you know your own remains?' I never saw such an eloquent look of shame, of pitiable humiliation, overspread a countenance before. The Petrified Man rose slowly to his feet, and said: 'Honestly, is that true?' 'As true as I am sitting here.'

He took the pipe from his mouth and laid it on the mantle, then stood irresolute a moment (unconsciously, from old habit, thrusting his hands where his pantaloon pockets should have been, and meditatively dropping his chin on his breast), and finally said: 'Well—I never felt so absurd before. The Petrified Man has sold everything else and now the mean fraud has ended by selling his own ghost! My son, if there is any charity left in your heart for a poor friendless phantom like me, don't let this get out. Think how you would feel if you had made such an ass of yourself.'

I heard his stately tramp die away, step by step down the stairs and out into the deserted street, and felt sorry that he had gone, poor fellow—and sorrier still that he had carried off my red blanket and my bathtub.

12

THE HOUND

H.P. Lovecraft

...museum was a blasphemous, unthinkable place, where with the satanic taste of neurotic virtuosi we had assembled an universe of terror and decay...

In my tortured ears there sounds unceasingly a nightmare whirring and flapping, and a faint, distant baying as of some gigantic hound. It is not dream—it is not, I fear, even madness—for too much has already happened to give me these merciful doubts. St John is a mangled corpse; I alone know why, and such is my knowledge that I am about to blow out my brains for fear I shall be mangled in the same way. Down unlit and illimitable corridors of eldritch phantasy sweeps the black, shapeless Nemesis that drives me to self-annihilation.

May heaven forgive the folly and morbidity which led us both to so monstrous a fate! Wearied with the commonplaces of a prosaic world, where even the joys of romance and adventure soon grow stale, St John and I had followed enthusiastically every aesthetic and intellectual movement which promised respite from our devastating ennui. The enigmas of the Symbolists and the ecstasies of the pre-Raphaelites all were ours in their time, but each new mood was drained too soon of its diverting novelty and appeal. Only the sombre philosophy of the Decadents could hold us, and this we found potent only by increasing gradually the depth and diabolism of our penetrations. Baudelaire and Huysmans were soon exhausted of thrills, till finally there remained for us only the more direct stimuli of unnatural personal experiences and adventures. It was this frightful emotional need which led us eventually to that detestable course which even in my present fear I mention with shame and timidity—that hideous extremity of human outrage, the abhorred practice of grave-robbing.

I cannot reveal the details of our shocking expeditions, or catalogue even partly the worst of the trophies adorning the nameless museum we prepared in the great stone house where we jointly dwelt, alone and servantless. Our museum was a blasphemous, unthinkable place, where with the satanic taste of neurotic virtuosi we had assembled a universe of terror and decay to excite our jaded sensibilities. It was a secret room, far, far underground; where huge winged daemons carven of basalt and onyx vomited from wide grinning mouths weird green and orange light, and hidden pneumatic pipes ruffled into kaleidoscopic dances of death the lines of red charnel things hand in hand woven in voluminous black hangings. Through these pipes came at will the odours our moods most craved; sometimes the scent of pale funeral lilies, sometimes the narcotic incense of imagined Eastern shrines of the kingly dead, and sometimes—how I shudder to recall it!—the frightful, soul-upheaving stenches of the uncovered grave.

Around the walls of this repellent chamber were cases of antique mummies alternating with comely, life-like bodies perfectly stuffed and cured by the taxidermist's art, and with headstones snatched from the oldest churchyards of the world. Niches here and there contained skulls of all shapes, and heads preserved in various stages of dissolution. There one might find the rotting, bald pates of famous noblemen, and the fresh and radiantly golden heads of new-buried children. Statues and paintings there were, all of fiendish subjects and some executed by St John and myself. A locked portfolio, bound in tanned human skin, held certain unknown and unnamable drawings which it was rumoured Goya had perpetrated but dared not acknowledge. There were nauseous musical instruments, stringed, brass, and wood-wind, on which St John and I sometimes produced dissonances of exquisite morbidity and cacodaemoniacal ghastliness; whilst in a multitude of inlaid ebony cabinets reposed the most incredible and unimaginable variety of tomb-loot ever assembled by human madness and perversity. It is of this loot in particular that I must not speak—thank God I had the courage to destroy it long before I thought of destroying myself.

The predatory excursions on which we collected our unmentionable treasures were always artistically memorable events. We were no vulgar ghouls, but worked only under certain conditions of mood, landscape, environment, weather, season, and moonlight. These pastimes were to us the most exquisite form of aesthetic expression, and we gave their details a fastidious technical care. An inappropriate hour, a jarring lighting effect, or a clumsy manipulation of the damp sod, would almost totally destroy for us that ecstatic titillation which followed the exhumation of some ominous, grinning secret of the earth. Our quest for novel scenes and piquant conditions was feverish and insatiate—St John was always the leader, and he it was who led the way at last to that mocking, that accursed spot which brought us our hideous and inevitable doom.

By what malign fatality were we lured to that terrible Holland churchyard? I think it was the dark rumour and legendry, the tales of one buried for five centuries, who had himself been a ghoul in his time and had stolen a potent thing from a mighty sepulchre. I can recall the scene in these final moments—the pale autumnal moon over the graves, casting long horrible shadows; the grotesque trees, drooping sullenly to meet the neglected grass and the crumbling slabs; the vast legions of strangely colossal bats that flew against the moon; the antique ivied church pointing a huge spectral finger at the livid sky; the phosphorescent insects that danced like death-fires under the yews in a distant corner; the odours of mould, vegetation, and less explicable things that mingled feebly with the night-wind from over far swamps and seas; and worst of all, the faint deep-toned baying of some gigantic hound which we could neither see nor definitely place. As we heard this suggestion of baying we shuddered, remembering the tales of the peasantry; for he whom we sought had centuries before been found in this selfsame spot, torn and mangled by the claws and teeth of some unspeakable beast.

I remembered how we delved in this ghoul's grave with our spades, and how we thrilled at the picture of ourselves, the grave, the pale watching moon, the horrible shadows, the grotesque trees, the titanic bats, the antique church, the dancing death-fires, the sickening odours, the gently moaning night-wind, and the strange, half-heard, directionless baying, of whose objective existence we could scarcely be sure. Then we struck a substance harder than the damp mould, and beheld a rotting oblong box crusted with mineral deposits from the long undisturbed ground. It was incredibly tough and thick, but so old that we finally pried it open and feasted our eyes on what it held.

Much—amazingly much—was left of the object despite the lapse of five hundred years. The skeleton, though crushed in places by the jaws of the thing that had killed it, held together with surprising firmness, and we gloated over the clean white skull and its long, firm teeth and its eyeless sockets that once had glowed with a charnel fever like our own. In the coffin lay an amulet of curious and exotic design, which had apparently been worn around the sleeper's neck. It was the oddly conventionalised figure of a crouching winged hound, or sphinx with a semi-canine face, and was exquisitely carved in antique Oriental fashion from a small piece of green jade. The expression on its features was repellent in the extreme, savouring at once of death, bestiality, and malevolence. Around the base was an inscription in characters which neither St John nor I could identify; and on the bottom, like a maker's seal, was graven a grotesque and formidable skull.

Immediately upon beholding this amulet we knew that we must possess it; that this treasure alone was our logical pelf from the centuried grave. Even had its outlines been unfamiliar we would have desired it, but as we looked more closely we saw that it was not wholly unfamiliar. Alien it indeed was to all art and literature which sane and balanced readers know, but we recognised it as the thing hinted of in the forbidden *Necronomicon* of the mad Arab Abdul Alhazred; the ghastly soul-symbol of the corpse-eating cult of inaccessible Leng, in Central Asia. All too well did we trace the sinister lineaments described by the old Arab daemonologist; lineaments, he wrote, drawn from some obscure supernatural manifestation of the souls of those who vexed and gnawed at the dead.

Seizing the green jade object, we gave a last glance at the bleached and cavern-eyed face of its owner and closed up the grave as we found it. As we hastened from that abhorrent spot, the stolen amulet in St John's pocket, we thought we saw the bats descend in a body to the earth we had so lately rifled, as if seeking for some cursed and unholy nourishment. But the autumn moon shone weak and pale, and we could not be sure. So, too, as we sailed the next day away from Holland to our home, we thought we heard the faint distant baying of some gigantic hound in the background. But the autumn wind moaned sad and wan, and we could not be sure.

Less than a week after our return to England, strange things began to happen. We lived as recluses; devoid of friends, alone, and without servants in a few rooms of an ancient manor-house on a bleak and unfrequented moor; so that our doors were seldom disturbed by the knock of the visitor. Now, however, we were troubled by what seemed to be frequent fumblings in the night, not only around the doors but around the windows also, upper as well as lower. Once we fancied that a large, opaque body darkened the library window when the moon was shining against it, and another time we thought we heard a whirring or flapping sound not far off. On each occasion investigation revealed nothing, and we began to ascribe the occurrences to imagination alone—that same curiously disturbed imagination which still prolonged in our ears the faint far baying we thought we had heard in the Holland churchyard. The jade amulet now reposed in a niche in our museum, and sometimes we burned strangely scented candles before it. We read much in Alhazred's *Necronomicon* about its properties, and about the relation of ghouls' souls to the objects it symbolised; and were disturbed by what we read. Then terror came.

On the night of September 24, 19––, I heard a knock at my chamber door. Fancying it St John's, I bade the knocker enter, but was answered only by a shrill laugh. There was no one in the corridor. When I aroused St John from his sleep, he professed entire ignorance of the event, and became as worried as I. It was that night that the faint, distant baying over the moor became to us a certain and dreaded reality. Four days later, whilst we were both in the hidden museum, there came a low, cautious scratching at the single door which led to the secret library staircase. Our alarm was now divided, for besides our fear of the unknown, we had always entertained a dread that our grisly collection might be discovered. Extinguishing all lights, we proceeded to the door and threw it suddenly open; whereupon we felt an unaccountable rush of air, and heard as if receding far away a queer combination of rustling, tittering, and articulate chatter. Whether we were mad, dreaming, or in our senses, we did not try to determine. We only realised, with the blackest of apprehensions, that the apparently disembodied chatter was beyond a doubt *in the Dutch language.*

After that we lived in growing horror and fascination. Mostly we held to the theory that we were jointly going mad from our life of unnatural excitements, but sometimes it pleased us more to dramatise ourselves as the victims of some creeping and appalling doom. Bizarre manifestations were now too frequent to count. Our lonely house was seemingly alive with the presence of some malign being whose nature we could not guess, and every night that daemoniac baying rolled over the windswept moor, always louder and louder. On October 29 we found in the soft earth underneath the library window a series of footprints utterly impossible to describe. They were as baffling as the hordes of great bats which haunted the old manor-house in unprecedented and increasing numbers.

The horror reached a culmination on November 18, when St John, walking home after dark from the distant railway station, was seized by some frightful carnivorous thing and torn to ribbons. His screams had reached the house, and I had hastened to the terrible scene in time to hear a whir of wings and see a vague black cloudy thing silhouetted against the rising moon. My friend was dying when I spoke to him, and he could not answer coherently. All he could do was to whisper, 'The amulet—that damned thing—.' Then he collapsed, an inert mass of mangled flesh.

I buried him the next midnight in one of our neglected gardens, and mumbled over his body one of the devilish rituals he had loved in life. And as I pronounced the last daemoniac sentence I heard afar on the moor the faint baying of some gigantic hound. The moon was up, but I dared not look at it. And when I saw on the dim-litten moor a wide nebulous shadow sweeping from mound to mound, I shut my eyes and threw myself face down upon the ground. When I arose trembling, I know not how much later, I staggered into the house and made shocking obeisances before the enshrined amulet of green jade.

Being now afraid to live alone in the ancient house on the moor, I departed on the following day for London, taking with me the amulet after destroying by fire and burial the rest of the impious collection in the museum. But after three nights I heard the baying again, and before a week was over felt strange eyes upon me whenever it was dark. One evening as I strolled on Victoria Embankment for some needed air, I saw a black shape obscure one of the reflections of the lamps in the water. A wind stronger than the night-wind rushed by, and I knew that what had befallen St John must soon befall me.

The next day I carefully wrapped the green jade amulet and sailed for Holland. What mercy I might gain by returning the thing to its silent, sleeping owner I knew not; but I felt that I must at least try any step conceivably logical. What the hound was, and why it pursued me, were questions still vague; but I had first heard the baying in that ancient churchyard, and every subsequent event including St John's dying whisper had served to connect the curse with the stealing of the amulet. Accordingly I sank into the nethermost abysses of despair when, at an inn in Rotterdam, I discovered that thieves had despoiled me of this sole means of salvation.

The baying was loud that evening, and in the morning I read of a nameless deed in the vilest quarter of the city. The rabble were in terror, for upon an evil tenement had fallen a red death beyond the foulest previous crime of the neighbourhood. In a squalid thieves' den an entire family had been torn to shreds by an unknown thing which left no trace, and those around had heard all night above the usual clamour of drunken voices a faint, deep, insistent note as of a gigantic hound.

So at last I stood again in that unwholesome churchyard where a pale winter moon cast hideous shadows, and leafless trees drooped sullenly to meet the withered, frosty grass and cracking slabs, and the ivied church pointed a jeering finger at the unfriendly sky, and the night-wind howled maniacally from over frozen swamps and frigid seas. The baying was very faint now, and it ceased altogether as I approached the ancient grave I had once violated, and frightened away an abnormally large horde of bats which had been hovering curiously around it.

I know not why I went thither unless to pray, or gibber out insane pleas and apologies to the calm white thing that lay within; but, whatever my reason, I attacked the half-frozen sod with a desperation partly mine and partly that of a dominating will outside myself. Excavation was much easier than I expected, though at one point I encountered a queer interruption; when a lean vulture darted down out of the cold sky and pecked frantically at the grave-earth until I killed him with a blow of my spade. Finally I reached the rotting oblong box and removed the damp nitrous cover. This is the last rational act I ever performed.

For crouched within that centuried coffin, embraced by a close-packed nightmare retinue of huge, sinewy, sleeping bats, was the bony thing my friend and I had robbed; not clean and placid as we had seen it then, but covered with caked blood and shreds of alien flesh and hair, and leering sentiently at me with phosphorescent sockets and sharp ensanguined fangs yawning twistedly in mockery of my inevitable doom. And when it gave from those grinning jaws a deep, sardonic bay as of some gigantic hound, and I saw that it held in its gory, filthy claw the lost and fateful amulet of green jade, I merely screamed and ran away idiotically, my screams soon dissolving into peals of hysterical laughter.

Madness rides the star-wind... claws and teeth sharpened on centuries of corpses... dripping death astride a Bacchanale of bats from night-black ruins of buried temples of Belial... Now, as the baying of that dead, fleshless monstrosity grows louder and louder, and the stealthy whirring and flapping of those accursed web-wings circles closer and closer, I shall seek with my revolver the oblivion which is my only refuge from the unnamed and unnamable.

13
THE SPHINX WITHOUT A SECRET

Oscar Wilde

...simply a woman with a mania for mystery...

One afternoon I was sitting outside the Cafe de la Paix, watching the splendour and shabbiness of Parisian life, and wondering over my vermouth at the strange panorama of pride and poverty that was passing before me, when I heard someone call my name. I turned round, and saw Lord Murchison. We had not met since we had been at college together, nearly ten years before, so I was delighted to come across him again, and we shook hands warmly. At Oxford we had been great friends. I had liked him immensely, he was so handsome, so high-spirited, and so honourable. We used to say of him that he would be the best of fellows, if he did not always speak the truth, but I think we really admired him all the more for his frankness. I found him a good deal changed. He looked anxious and puzzled, and seemed to be in doubt about something. I felt it could not be modern scepticism, for Murchison was the stoutest of Tories, and believed in the Pentateuch as firmly as he believed in the House of Peers; so I concluded that it was a woman, and asked him if he was married yet.

'I don't understand women well enough,' he answered. 'My dear Gerald,' I said, 'women are meant to be loved, not to be understood.'

'I cannot love where I cannot trust,' he replied.

'I believe you have a mystery in your life, Gerald,' I exclaimed; 'tell me about it.'

'Let us go for a drive,' he answered, 'it is too crowded here.

No, not a yellow carriage, any other colour—there, that dark-green one will do;' and in a few moments we were trotting down the boulevard in the direction of the Madeleine. 'Where shall we go to?' I said.

'Oh, anywhere you like!' he answered—'to the restaurant in the Bois; we will dine there, and you shall tell me all about yourself.'

'I want to hear about you first,' I said. 'Tell me your mystery.'

He took from his pocket a little silver-clasped morocco case, and handed it to me. I opened it. Inside there was the photograph of a woman. She was tall and slight, and strangely picturesque with her large vague eyes and loosened hair. She looked like a clairvoyante, and was wrapped in rich furs.

'What do you think of that face?' he said; 'is it truthful?'

I examined it carefully. It seemed to me the face of someone who had a secret, but whether that secret was good or evil I could not say. Its beauty was a beauty moulded out of many mysteries—the beauty, in fact, which is psychological, not plastic—and the faint smile that just played across the lips was far too subtle to be really sweet. 'Well,' he cried impatiently, 'what do you say?'

'She is the Gioconda in sables,' I answered. 'Let me know all about her.'

'Not now,' he said; 'after dinner;' and began to talk of other things.

When the waiter brought us our coffee and cigarettes I reminded Gerald of his promise. He rose from his seat, walked two or three times up and down the room, and, sinking into an armchair, told me the following story: 'One evening,' he said, 'I was walking down Bond Street about five o'clock. There was a terrific crush of carriages, and the traffic was almost stopped. Close to the pavement was standing a little yellow brougham, which, for some reason or other, attracted my attention. As I passed by there looked out from it the face I showed you this afternoon. It fascinated me immediately. All that night I kept thinking of it, and all the next day. I wandered up and down that wretched Row, peering into every carriage, and waiting for the yellow brougham; but I could not find *ma belle inconnue*, and at last I began to think she was merely a dream. About a week afterwards I was dining with Madame de Rastail. Dinner was for eight o'clock; but at half-past eight we were still waiting in the drawing-room. Finally the servant threw open the door, and announced Lady Alroy. It was the woman I had been looking for. She came in very slowly, looking like a moon-beam in grey lace, and, to my intense delight, I was asked to take her in to dinner. After we had sat down I remarked quite innocently, "I think I caught sight of you in Bond Street some time ago, Lady Alroy." She grew very pale, and said to me in a low voice, "Pray do not talk so loud; you may be overheard." I felt miserable at having made such a bad beginning, and plunged recklessly into the subject of French plays. She spoke very little, always in the same low musical voice, and seemed as if she was afraid of someone listening. I fell passionately, stupidly in love, and the indefinable atmosphere of mystery that surrounded her excited my most ardent curiosity. When she was going away, which she did very soon after dinner, I asked her if I might call and see her. She hesitated for a moment, glanced round to see if anyone was near us, and then said, "Yes; tomorrow at a quarter to five." I begged Madame de Rastail to tell me about her; but all that I could learn was that she was a widow with a beautiful house in Park Lane, and as some scientific bore began a dissertation of widows, as exemplifying the survival of the matrimonially fittest, I left and went home.

'The next day I arrived at Park Lane punctual to the moment, but was told by the butler that Lady Alroy had just gone out. I went down to the club quite unhappy and very much puzzled, and after long consideration wrote her a letter, asking if I might be allowed to try my chance some other afternoon. I had no answer for several days, but at last I got a little note saying she would be at home on Sunday at four, and with this extraordinary postscript: "Please do not write to me here again; I will explain when I see you." On Sunday she received me, and was perfectly charming; but when I was going away she begged of me, if I ever had occasion to write to her again, to address my letter to "Mrs Knox, care of Whittaker's Library, Green Street." "There are reasons," she said, "why I cannot receive letters in my own house."

'All through the season I saw a great deal of her, and the atmosphere of mystery never left her. Sometimes I thought that she was in the power of some man, but she looked so unapproachable that I could not believe it. It was really very difficult for me to come to any conclusion, for she was like one of those strange crystals that one sees in museums, which are at one moment clear, and at another clouded. At last I determined to ask her to be my wife: I was sick and tired of the incessant secrecy that she imposed on all my visits, and on the few letters I sent her. I wrote to her at the library to ask her if she could see me the following Monday at six. She answered yes, and I was in the seventh heaven of delight. I was infatuated with her: in spite of the mystery, I thought then—in consequence of it, I see now. No; it was the woman herself I loved. The mystery troubled me, maddened me. Why did chance put me in its track?'

'You discovered it, then?' I cried.

'I fear so,' he answered. 'You can judge for yourself.

'When Monday came round I went to lunch with my uncle, and about four o'clock found myself in the Marylebone Road. My uncle, you know, lives in Regent's Park. I wanted to get to Piccadilly, and took a short cut through a lot of shabby little streets. Suddenly I saw in front of me Lady Alroy, deeply veiled and walking very fast. On coming to the last house in the street, she went up the steps, took out a latch-key, and let herself in. "Here is the mystery," I said to myself; and I hurried on and examined the house. It seemed a sort of place for letting lodgings. On the doorstep lay her handkerchief, which she had dropped. I picked it up and put it in my pocket. Then I began to consider what I should do. I came to the conclusion that I had no right to spy on her, and I drove down to the club. At six I called to see her. She was lying on a sofa, in a tea-gown of silver tissue looped up by some strange moonstones that she always wore. She was looking quite lovely. "I am so glad to see you," she said; "I have not been out all day." I stared at her in amazement, and pulling the handkerchief out of my pocket, handed it to her. "You dropped this in Cumnor Street this afternoon, Lady Alroy," I said very calmly. She looked at me in terror, but made no attempt to take the handkerchief. "What were you doing there?" I asked. "What right have you to question me?" she answered. "The right of a man who loves you," I replied; "I came here to ask you to be my wife." She hid her face in her hands, and burst into floods of tears. "You must tell me," I continued. She stood up, and, looking me straight in the face, said, "Lord Murchison, there is nothing to tell you."—"You went to meet someone," I cried; "this is your mystery." She grew dreadfully white, and said, "I went to meet no one,"—"Can't you tell the truth?" I exclaimed. "I have told it," she replied. I was mad, frantic; I don't know what I said, but I said terrible things to her. Finally I rushed out of the house. She wrote me a letter the next day; I sent it back unopened, and started for Norway with Alan Colville. After a month I came back, and the first thing I saw in the Morning Post was the death of Lady Alroy. She had caught a chill at the Opera, and had died in five days of congestion of the lungs. I shut myself up and saw no one. I had loved her so much, I had loved her so madly. Good God! how I had loved that woman!'

'You went to the street, to the house in it?' I said. 'Yes,' he answered.

'One day I went to Cumnor Street. I could not help it; I was tortured with doubt. I knocked at the door, and a respectable-looking woman opened it to me. I asked her if she had any rooms to let. "Well, sir," she replied, "the drawing-rooms are supposed to be let; but I have not seen the lady for three months, and as rent is owing on them, you can have them."—"Is this the lady?" I said, showing the photograph. "That's her, sure enough," she exclaimed; "and when is she coming back, sir?"—"The lady is dead," I replied. "Oh, sir, I hope not!" said the woman; "she was my best lodger. She paid me three guineas a week merely to sit in my drawing-rooms now and then."—"She met someone here?" I said; but the woman assured me that it was not so, that she always came alone, and saw no one. "What on earth did she do here?" I cried. "She simply sat in the drawing-room, sir, reading books, and sometimes had tea," the woman answered. I did not know what to say, so I gave her a sovereign and went away. Now, what do you think it all meant? You don't believe the woman was telling the truth?'

'I do.'

'Then why did Lady Alroy go there?'

'My dear Gerald,' I answered, 'Lady Alroy was simply a woman with a mania for mystery. She took these rooms for the pleasure of going there with her veil down, and imagining she was a heroine. She had a passion for secrecy, but she herself was merely a Sphinx without a secret.'

'Do you really think so?'

'I am sure of it,' I replied.

He took out the morocco case, opened it, and looked at the photograph. 'I wonder?' he said at last.

14
THE STRANGER

Ambrose Bierce

...somewhere in the darkness that seemed to enclose us like a black wall...

A man stepped out of the darkness into the little illuminated circle about our failing camp-fire and seated himself upon a rock.

'You are not the first to explore this region,' he said gravely. Nobody controverted his statement; he was himself proof of its truth, for he was not of our party and must have been somewhere near when we camped. Moreover, he must have companions not far away; it was not a place where one would be living or travelling alone. For more than a week we had seen, besides ourselves and our animals, only such living things as rattlesnakes and horned toads. In an Arizona desert one does not long coexist with only such creatures as these: one must have pack animals, supplies, arms—'an outfit.' And all these imply comrades. It was perhaps a doubt as to what manner of men this unceremonious stranger's comrades might be, together with something in his words interpretable as a challenge that caused every man of our half-dozen 'gentlemen adventurers' to rise to a sitting posture and lay his hand upon a weapon—an act signifying, in that time and place, a policy of expectation. The stranger gave the matter no attention and began again to speak in the same deliberate, uninflected monotone in which he had delivered his first sentence:

'Thirty years ago Ramon Gallegos, William Shaw, George W. Kent, and Berry Davis, all of Tucson, crossed the Santa Catalina mountains and travelled due west, as nearly as the configuration of the country permitted. We were prospecting and it was our intention, if we found nothing, to push through to the Gila river at some point near Big Bend, where we understood there was a settlement. We had a good outfit, but no guide—just Ramon Gallegos, William Shaw, George W. Kent, and Berry Davis.'

The man repeated the names slowly and distinctly, as if to fix them in the memories of his audience, every member of which was now attentively observing him, but with a slackened apprehension regarding his possible companions somewhere in the darkness that seemed to enclose us like a black wall; in the manner of this volunteer historian was no suggestion of an unfriendly purpose. His act was rather that of a harmless lunatic than an enemy. We were not so new to the country as not to know that the solitary life of many a plainsman had a tendency to develop eccentricities of conduct and character not always easily distinguishable from mental aberration. A man is like a tree: in a forest of his fellows he will grow as straight as his generic and individual nature permits; alone in the open, he yields to the deforming stresses and tortions that environ him. Some such thoughts were in my mind as I watched the man from the shadow of my hat, pulled low to shut out the firelight. A witless fellow, no doubt, but what could he be doing there in the heart of a desert?

Having undertaken to tell this story, I wish that I could describe the man's appearance; that would be a natural thing to do. Unfortunately, and somewhat strangely, I find myself unable to do so with any degree of confidence, for afterward no two of us agreed as to what he wore and how he looked; and when I try to set down my own impressions they elude me. Anyone can tell some kind of story; narration is one of the elemental powers of the race. But the talent for description is a gift. Nobody having broken silence the visitor went on to say:

'This country was not then what it is now. There was not a ranch between the Gila and the Gulf. There was a little game here and there in the mountains, and near the infrequent water-holes grass enough to keep our animals from starvation. If we should be so fortunate as to encounter no Indians we might get through. But within a week the purpose of the expedition had altered from discovery of wealth to preservation of life. We had gone too far to go back, for what was ahead could be no worse than what was behind; so we pushed on, riding by night to avoid Indians and the intolerable heat, and concealing ourselves by day as best we could. Sometimes, having exhausted our supply of wild meat and emptied our casks, we were days without food or drink; then a water-hole or a shallow pool in the bottom of an arroyo so restored our strength and sanity that we were able to shoot some of the wild animals that sought it also. Sometimes it was a bear, sometimes an antelope, a coyote, a cougar—that was as God pleased; all were food.

'One morning as we skirted a mountain range, seeking a practicable pass, we were attacked by a band of Apaches who had followed our trail up a gulch—it is not far from here. Knowing that they outnumbered us ten to one, they took none of their usual cowardly precautions, but dashed upon us at a gallop, firing and yelling. Fighting was out of the question: we urged our feeble animals up the gulch as far as there was footing for a hoof, then threw ourselves out of our saddles and took to the chaparral on one of the slopes, abandoning our entire outfit to the enemy. But we retained our rifles, every man—Ramon Gallegos, William Shaw, George W. Kent, and Berry Davis.'

'Same old crowd,' said the humorist of our party. He was an Eastern man, unfamiliar with the decent observances of social intercourse. A gesture of disapproval from our leader silenced him, and the stranger proceeded with his tale:

'The savages dismounted also, and some of them ran up the gulch beyond the point at which we had left it, cutting off further retreat in that direction and forcing us on up the side. Unfortunately the chaparral extended only a short distance up the slope, and as we came into the open ground above we took the fire of a dozen rifles; but Apaches shoot badly when in a hurry, and God so willed it that none of us fell. Twenty yards up the slope, beyond the edge of the brush, were vertical cliffs, in which, directly in front of us, was a narrow opening. Into that we ran, finding ourselves in a cavern about as large as an ordinary room in a house. Here for a time we were safe: a single man with a repeating rifle could defend the entrance against all the Apaches in the land. But against hunger and thirst we had no defence. Courage we still had, but hope was a memory.

'Not one of those Indians did we afterward see, but by the smoke and glare of their fires in the gulch we knew that by day and by night they watched with ready rifles in the edge of the bush—knew that if we made a sortie, not a man of us would live to take three steps into the open. For three days, watching in turn, we held out before our suffering became insupportable. Then—it was the morning of the fourth day—Ramon Gallegos said: '"Senores, I know not well of the good God and what please Him. I have live without religion, and I am not acquaint with that of you. Pardon, senores, if I shock you, but for me the time is come to beat the game of the Apache."

'He knelt upon the rock floor of the cave and pressed his pistol against his temple. "Madre de Dios," he said, "comes now the soul of Ramon Gallegos."

'And so he left us—William Shaw, George W. Kent, and Berry Davis.

'I was the leader: it was for me to speak.

'"He was a brave man," I said—"he knew when to die, and how. It is foolish to go mad from thirst and fall by Apache bullets, or be skinned alive—it is in bad taste. Let us join Ramon Gallegos."

'"That is right," said William Shaw.

'"That is right," said George W. Kent.

'I straightened the limbs of Ramon Gallegos and put a handkerchief over his face. Then William Shaw said: "I should like to look like that—a little while."

'And George W. Kent said that he felt that way, too.

'"It shall be so," I said: "the red devils will wait a week. William Shaw and George W. Kent, draw and kneel."

'They did so and I stood before them.

'"Almighty God, our Father," said I.

'"Almighty God, our Father," said William Shaw.

'"Almighty God, our Father," said George W. Kent.

'"Forgive us our sins," said I.

'"Forgive us our sins," said they.

'"And receive our souls."

'"And receive our souls."

'"Amen!"

'"Amen!"

'I laid them beside Ramon Gallegos and covered their faces.'

There was a quick commotion on the opposite side of the camp-fire: one of our party had sprung to his feet, pistol in hand.

'And you!' he shouted—'you dared to escape?—You dare to be alive? You cowardly hound, I'll send you to join them if I hang for it!'

But with the leap of a panther the captain was upon him, grasping his wrist. 'Hold it in, Sam Yountsey, hold it in!' We were now all upon our feet—except the stranger, who sat motionless and apparently inattentive. Someone seized Yountsey's other arm.

'Captain,' I said, 'there is something wrong here. This fellow is either a lunatic or merely a liar—just a plain, everyday liar whom Yountsey has no call to kill. If this man was of that party it had five members, one of whom—probably himself—he has not named.'

'Yes,' said the captain, releasing the insurgent, who sat down, 'there is something—unusual. Years ago four dead bodies of white men, scalped and shamefully mutilated, were found about the mouth of that cave. They are buried there; I have seen the graves—we shall all see them tomorrow.'

The stranger rose, standing tall in the light of the expiring fire, which in our breathless attention to his story we had neglected to keep going.

'There were four,' he said—'Ramon Gallegos, William Shaw, George W. Kent, and Berry Davis.'

With this reiterated roll-call of the dead he walked into

the darkness and we saw him no more. At that moment one of our party, who had been on guard, strode in among us, rifle in hand and somewhat excited.

'Captain,' he said, 'for the last half-hour three men have been standing out there on the mesa.' He pointed in the direction taken by the stranger. 'I could see them distinctly, for the moon is up, but as they had no guns and I had them covered with mine I thought it was their move. They have made none, but damn it! They have got on to my nerves.'

'Go back to your post, and stay till you see them again,' said the captain. 'The rest of you lie down again, or I'll kick you all into the fire.'

The sentinel obediently withdrew, swearing, and did not return. As we were arranging our blankets the fiery Yountsey said: 'I beg your pardon, Captain, but who the devil do you take them to be?'

'Ramon Gallegos, William Shaw, and George W. Kent.'

'But how about Berry Davis? I ought to have shot him.'

'Quite needless; you couldn't have made him any deader. Go to sleep.'

15

THE TERRIBLE OLD MAN

H.P. Lovecraft

It was a design... to call on the Terrible Old Man... when one is aged and feeble one's reserve is doubly strong....

It was the design of Angelo Ricci and Joe Czanek and Manuel Silva to call on the Terrible Old Man. This old man dwells all alone in a very ancient house on Water Street near the sea, and is reputed to be both exceedingly rich and exceedingly feeble; which forms a situation very attractive to men of the profession of Messrs Ricci, Czanek, and Silva, for that profession was nothing less dignified than robbery.

The inhabitants of Kingsport say and think many things about the Terrible Old Man which generally keep him safe from the attention of gentlemen like Mr Ricci and his colleagues, despite the almost certain fact that he hides a fortune of indefinite magnitude somewhere about his musty and venerable abode. He is, in truth, a very strange person, believed to have been a captain of East India clipper ships in his day; so old that no one can remember when he was young, and so taciturn that few know his real name. Among the gnarled trees in the front yard of his aged and neglected place he maintains a strange collection of large stones, oddly grouped and painted so that they resemble the idols in some obscure Eastern temple. This collection frightens away most of the small boys who love to taunt the Terrible Old Man about his long white hair and beard, or to break the small-paned windows of his dwelling with wicked missiles; but there are other things which frighten the older and more curious folk who sometimes steal up to the house to peer in through the dusty panes. These folk say that on a table in a bare room on the ground floor are many peculiar bottles, in each a small piece of lead suspended pendulum-wise from a string. And they say that the Terrible Old Man talks to these bottles, addressing them by such names as Jack, Scar-Face, Long Tom, Spanish Joe, Peters, and Mate Ellis, and that whenever he speaks to a bottle the little lead pendulum within makes certain definite vibrations as if in answer. Those who have watched the tall, lean, Terrible Old Man in these peculiar conversations, do not watch him again. But Angelo Ricci and Joe Czanek and Manuel Silva were not of Kingsport blood; they were of that new and heterogeneous alien stock which lies outside the charmed circle of New England life and traditions, and they saw in the Terrible Old Man merely a tottering, almost helpless greybeard, who could not walk without the aid of his knotted cane, and whose thin, weak hands shook pitifully. They were really quite sorry in their way for the lonely, unpopular old fellow, whom everybody shunned, and at whom all the dogs barked singularly. But business is business, and to a robber whose soul is in his profession, there is a lure and a challenge about a very old and very feeble man who has no account at the bank, and who pays for his few necessities at the village store with Spanish gold and silver minted two centuries ago.

Messrs Ricci, Czanek, and Silva selected the night of April 11th for their call. Mr Ricci and Mr Silva were to interview the poor old gentleman, whilst Mr Czanek waited for them and their presumable metallic burden with a covered motor-car in Ship Street, by the gate in the tall rear wall of their host's grounds. Desire to avoid needless explanations in case of unexpected police intrusions prompted these plans for a quiet and unostentatious departure.

As prearranged, the three adventurers started out separately in order to prevent any evil-minded suspicions afterward. Messrs Ricci and Silva met in Water Street by the old man's front gate, and although they did not like the way the moon shone down upon the painted stones through the budding branches of the gnarled trees, they had more important things to think about than mere idle superstition. They feared it might be unpleasant work making the Terrible Old Man loquacious concerning his hoarded gold and silver, for aged sea-captains are notably stubborn and perverse. Still, he was very old and very feeble, and there were two visitors. Messrs Ricci and Silva were experienced in the art of making unwilling persons voluble, and the screams of a weak and exceptionally venerable man can be easily muffled. So they moved up to the one lighted window and heard the Terrible Old Man talking childishly to his bottles with pendulums. Then they donned masks and knocked politely at the weather-stained oaken door.

Waiting seemed very long to Mr Czanek as he fidgeted restlessly in the covered motor-car by the Terrible Old Man's back gate in Ship Street. He was more than ordinarily tender-hearted, and he did not like the hideous screams he had heard in the ancient house just after the hour appointed for the deed. Had he not told his colleagues to be as gentle as possible with the pathetic old sea-captain? Very nervously he watched that narrow oaken gate in the high and ivy-clad stone wall. Frequently he consulted his watch, and wondered at the delay. Had the old man died before revealing where his treasure was hidden, and had a thorough search become necessary? Mr Czanek did not like to wait so long in the dark in such a place. Then he sensed a soft tread or tapping on the walk inside the gate, heard a gentle fumbling at the rusty latch, and saw the narrow, heavy door swing inward. And in the pallid glow of the single dim street-lamp he strained his eyes to see what his colleagues had brought out of that sinister house which loomed so close behind. But when he looked, he did not see what he had expected; for his colleagues were not there at all, but only the Terrible Old Man leaning quietly on his knotted cane and smiling hideously. Mr Czanek had never before noticed the colour of that man's eyes; now he saw that they were yellow.

Little things make considerable excitement in little towns, which is the reason that Kingsport people talked all that spring and summer about the three unidentifiable bodies, horribly slashed as with many cutlasses, and horribly mangled as by the tread of many cruel boot-heels, which the tide washed in. And some people even spoke of things as trivial as the deserted motor-car found in Ship Street, or certain especially inhuman cries, probably of a stray animal or migratory bird, heard in the night by wakeful citizens. But in this idle village gossip the Terrible Old Man took no interest at all. He was by nature reserved, and when one is aged and feeble one's reserve is doubly strong. Besides, so ancient a sea-captain must have witnessed scores of things much more stirring in the far-off days of his unremembered youth.

16

THE FURNISHED ROOM

O. Henry

They flit from furnished room to furnished room, transients forever—transients in abode, transients in heart and mind...

Restless, shifting, fugacious as time itself is a certain vast bulk of the population of the red brick district of the lower West Side. Homeless, they have a hundred homes. They flit from furnished room to furnished room, transients forever—transients in abode, transients in heart and mind. They sing 'Home, Sweet Home' in ragtime; they carry their *lares et penates* in a bandbox; their vine is entwined about a picture hat; a rubber plant is their fig tree.

Hence the houses of this district, having had a thousand dwellers, should have a thousand tales to tell, mostly dull ones, no doubt; but it would be strange if there could not be found a ghost or two in the wake of all these vagrant guests.

One evening after dark a young man prowled among these crumbling red mansions, ringing their bells. At the twelfth he rested his lean hand baggage upon the step and wiped the dust from his hatband and forehead. The bell sounded faint and far away in some remote, hollow depths.

To the door of this, the twelfth house whose bell he had rung, came a housekeeper who made him think of an unwholesome, surfeited worm that had eaten its nut to a hollow shell and now sought to fill the vacancy with edible lodgers.

He asked if there was a room to let.

'Come in,' said the housekeeper. Her voice came from her throat; her throat seemed lined with fur. 'I have the third-floor-back, vacant since a week back. Should you wish to look at it?'

The young man followed her up the stairs. A faint light from no particular source mitigated the shadows of the halls. They trod noiselessly upon a stair carpet that its own loom would have forsworn. It seemed to have become vegetable; to have degenerated in that rank, sunless air to lush lichen or spreading moss that grew in patches to the staircase and was viscid under the foot like organic matter. At each turn of the stairs were vacant niches in the wall. Perhaps plants had once been set within them. If so, they had died in that foul and tainted air. It may be that statues of the saints had stood there, but it was not difficult to conceive that imps and devils had dragged them forth in the darkness and down to the unholy depths of some furnished pit below.

'This is the room,' said the housekeeper, from her furry throat. 'It's a nice room. It ain't often vacant. I had some most elegant people in it last summer—no trouble at all, and paid in advance to the minute. The water's at the end of the hall. Sprowls and Mooney kept it three months. They done a vaudeville sketch. Miss B'retta Sprowls—you may have heard of her—oh, that was just the stage names—right there over the dresser is where the marriage certificate hung, framed. The gas is here, and you see there is plenty of closet room. It's a room everybody likes. It never stays idle long.'

'Do you have many theatrical people rooming here?' asked the young man.

'They comes and goes. A good proportion of my lodgers is connected with the theaters. Yes, sir, this is the theatrical district. Actor people never stays long anywhere. I get my share. Yes, they comes and they goes.'

He engaged the room, paying for a week in advance. He was tired, he said, and would take possession at once. He counted out the money. The room had been made ready, she said, even to towels and water. As the housekeeper moved away he put, for the thousandth time, the question that he carried at the end of his tongue.

'A young girl—Miss Vashner—Miss Eloise Vashner—do you remember such a one among your lodgers? She would be singing on the stage, most likely. A fair girl, of medium height and slender, with reddish gold hair and a dark mole near her left eyebrow.'

'No, I don't remember the name. Them stage people has names they change as often as their rooms. No, I don't call that one to mind.'

No. Always no. Five months of ceaseless interrogation and the inevitable negative. So much time spent by day in questioning managers, agents, schools and choruses; by night among the audiences of theaters from all-star casts down to music halls so low that he dreaded to find what he most hoped for. He who had loved her best had tried to find her. He was sure that since her disappearance from home this great, water-girt city held her somewhere, but it was like a monstrous quicksand, shifting its particles constantly, with no foundation, its upper granules of today buried tomorrow in ooze and slime.

The furnished room received its latest guest with a first glow of pseudo hospitality, a hectic, haggard, perfunctory welcome like the specious smile of a demirep. The sophistical comfort came in reflected gleams from the decayed furniture, the ragged brocade upholstery of a couch and two chairs, a foot-wide cheap pier glass between the two windows, from one or two gilt picture frames and a brass bedstead in a corner.

The guest reclined, inert, upon a chair, while the room, confused in speech as though it were an apartment in Babel, tried to discourse to him of its divers tenantry.

A polychromatic rug like some brilliant-fowered, rectangular, tropical islet lay surrounded by a billowy sea of soiled matting. Upon the gay-papered wall were those pictures that pursue the homeless one from house to house—The Huguenot Lovers, The First Quarrel, The Wedding Breakfast, Psyche at the Fountain. The mantel's chastely severe outline was ingloriously veiled behind some pert drapery drawn rakishly askew like the sashes of the Amazonian ballet. Upon it was some desolate flotsam cast aside by the room's marooned when a lucky sail had borne them to a fresh port—a trifling vase or two, pictures of actresses, a medicine bottle, some stray cards out of a deck. One by one, as the characters of a cryptograph became explicit, the little signs left by the furnished room's procession of guests developed a significance. The threadbare space in the rug in front of the dresser told that lovely women had marched in the throng. The tiny fingerprints on the wall spoke of little prisoners trying to feel their way to sun and air. A splattered stain, raying like the shadow of a bursting bomb, witnessed where a hurled glass or bottle had splintered with its contents against the wall. Across the pier glass had been scrawled with a diamond in staggering letters the name Marie. It seemed that the succession of dwellers in the furnished room had turned in fury—perhaps tempted beyond forbearance by its garish coldness—and wreaked upon it their passions. The furniture was chipped and bruised; the couch, distorted by bursting springs, seemed a horrible monster that had been slain during the stress of some grotesque convulsion. Some more potent upheaval had cloven a great slice from the marble mantel. Each plank in the floor owned its particular cant and shriek as from a separate and individual agony. It seemed incredible that all this malice and injury had been wrought upon the room by those who had called it for a time their home; and yet it may have been the cheated home instinct surviving blindly, the resentful rage at false household gods that had kindled their wrath. A hut that is our own we can sweep and adorn and cherish.

The young tenant in the chair allowed these thoughts to file, softshod, through his mind, while there drifted into the room furnished sounds and furnished scents. He heard in one room a tittering and incontinent, slack laughter; in others the monologue of a scold, the rattling of dice, a lullaby, and one crying dully; above him a banjo tinkled with spirit. Doors banged somewhere; the elevated trains roared intermittently; a cat yowled miserably upon a back fence. And he breathed the breath of the house—a dank savor rather than a smell—a cold, musty effluvium as from underground vaults mingled with the reeking exhalations of linoleum and mildewed and rotten woodwork.

Then suddenly, as he rested there, the room was filled with the strong, sweet odor of mignonette. It came as upon a single buffet of wind with such sureness and fragrance and emphasis that it almost seemed a living visitant. And the man cried aloud, 'What, dear?' as if he had been called, and sprang up and faced about. The rich odor clung to him and wrapped him around. He reached out his arms for it, all his senses for the time confused and commingled. How could one be peremptorily called by an odor? Surely it must have been a sound. But was it not the sound that had touched, that had caressed him?

'She has been in this room,' he cried, and he sprang to wrest from it a token, for he knew he would recognize the smallest thing that had belonged to her or that she had touched. This enveloping scent of mignonette, the odor that she had loved and made her own—whence came it?

The room had been but carelessly set in order. Scattered upon the flimsy dresser scarf were half a dozen hairpins—those discreet, indistinguishable friends of womankind, feminine of gender, infinite of mood and uncommunicative of tense. These he ignored, conscious of their triumphant lack of identity. Ransacking the drawers of the dresser he came upon a discarded, tiny, ragged handkerchief. He pressed it to his face. It was racy and insolent with heliotrope; he hurled it to the floor. In another drawer he found odd buttons, a theater program, a pawnbroker's card, two lost marshmallows, a book on the divination of dreams. In the last was a woman's black satin hair bow, which halted him, poised between ice and fire. But the black satin hair bow also is femininity's demure, impersonal common ornament and tells no tales.

And then he traversed the room like a hound on the scent, skimming the walls, considering the corners of the bulging matting on his hands and knees, rummaging mantel and tables, the curtains and hangings, the drunken cabinet in the corner, for a visible sign, unable to perceive that she was there beside, around, against, within, above him, clinging to him, wooing him, calling him so poignantly through the finer senses that even his grosser ones became cognizant of the call. Once again he answered loudly, 'Yes, dear!' and turned, wild-eyed, to gaze on vacancy, for he could not yet discern form and colour and love and outstretched arms in the odor of mignonette. Oh, God! Whence that odor, and since when have odors had a voice to call! Thus he groped.

He burrowed in crevices and corners, and found corks and cigarettes. These he passed in passive contempt. But once he found in a fold of the matting a half-smoked cigar, and this he ground beneath his heel with a green and trenchant oath. He sifted the room, from end to end. He found dreary and ignoble small records of many a peripatetic tenant; but of her whom he sought, and who may have lodged there, and whose spirit seemed to hover there, he found no trace.

And then he thought of the housekeeper.

He ran from the haunted room downstairs and to a door that showed a crack of light. She came out to his knock. He smothered his excitement as best he could.

'Will you tell me, madam,' he besought her, 'who occupied the room I have before I came?'

'Yes, sir. I can tell you again. 'Twas Sprowls and Mooney, as I said. Miss B'retta Sprowls it was in the theaters, but Missis Mooney she was. My house is well known for respectability. The marriage certificate hung, framed, on a nail over——'

'What kind of a lady was Miss Sprowls—in looks, I mean?'

'Why, black-haired, sir, short, and stout, with a comical face. They left a week ago Tuesday.'

'And before they occupied it?'

'Why, there was a single gentleman connected with the draying business. He left owing me a week. Before him was Missis Crowder and her two children, that stayed four months; and back of them was old Mr Doyle, whose sons paid for him. He kept the room six months. That goes back a year, sir, and further I do not remember.'

He thanked her and crept back to his room. The room was dead. The essence that had vivified it was gone. The perfume of mignonette had departed. In its place was the old, stale odor of moldy house furniture, of atmosphere in storage.

The ebbing of his hope drained his faith. He sat staring at the yellow, singing gaslight. Soon he walked to the bed and began to tear the sheets into strips. With the blade of his knife he drove them tightly into every crevice around windows and door. When all was snug and taut he turned out the light, turned the gas full on again and laid himself gratefully upon the bed.

◆

It was Mrs McCool's night to go with the can for beer. So she fetched it and sat with Mrs Purdy in one of those subterranean retreats where housekeepers forgather and the worm dieth seldom.

'I rented out my third-floor-back this evening,' said Mrs Purdy, across a fine circle of foam. 'A young man took it. He went up to bed two hours ago.'

'Now, did ye, Mrs Purdy, ma'am?' said Mrs McCool, with intense admiration. 'You do be a wonder for rentin' rooms of that kind. And did ye tell him, then?' she concluded in a husky whisper laden with mystery.

'Rooms,' said Mrs Purdy, in her furriest tones, 'are furnished for to rent. I did not tell him, Mrs McCool.'

''Tis right ye are, ma'am; 'tis by renting rooms we kape alive. Ye have the rale sense for business, ma'am. There be many people will rayjict the rentin' of a room if they be tould a suicide has been after dyin' in the bed of it.'

'As you say, we has our living to be making,' remarked Mrs Purdy.

'Yis, ma'am; 'tis true.' Tis just one wake ago this day I helped ye lay out the third-floor-back. A pretty slip of a colleen she was to be killin' herself wid the gas—a swate little face she had, Mrs Purdy, ma'am.'

'She'd a-been called handsome, as you say,' said Mrs Purdy, assenting but critical, 'but for that mole she had a-growin' by her left eyebrow. Do fill up your glass again, Mrs McCool.'

17

THE SIGNAL MAN

Charles Dickens

...He was a dark sallow man, with a dark beard and rather heavy eyebrows... His post was in as solitary and dismal a place...

'Halloa! Below there!' When he heard a voice thus calling to him, he was standing at the door of his box, with a flag in his hand, furled round its short pole. One would have thought, considering the nature of the ground, that he could not have doubted from what quarter the voice came; but, instead of looking up to where I stood on the top of the steep cutting nearly over his head, he turned himself about and looked down the Line. There was something remarkable in his manner of doing so, though I could not have said, for my life, what. But, I know it was remarkable enough to attract my notice, even though his figure was foreshortened and shadowed, down in the deep trench, and mine was high above him, so steeped in the glow of an angry sunset that I had shaded my eyes with my hand before I saw him at all.

'Halloa! Below!' From looking down the Line, he turned himself about again, and, raising his eyes, saw my figure high above him. 'Is there any path by which I can come down and speak to you?' He looked up at me without replying, and I looked down at him without pressing him too soon with a repetition of my idle question. Just then, there came a vague vibration in the earth and air, quickly changing into a violent pulsation, and an oncoming rush that caused me to start back, as though it had force to draw me down. When such vapour as rose to my height from this rapid train, had passed me and was skimming away over the landscape, I looked down again, and saw him re-furling the flag he had shown while the train went by. I repeated my inquiry. After a pause, during which he seemed to regard me with fixed attention, he motioned with his rolled-up flag towards a point on my level, some two or three hundred yards distant. I called down to him, 'All right!' and made for that point. There, by dint of looking closely about me, I found a rough zig-zag descending path notched out: which I followed.

The cutting was extremely deep, and unusually precipitate. It was made through a clammy stone that became oozier and wetter as I went down. For these reasons, I found the way long enough to give me time to recall a singular air of reluctance or compulsion with which he had pointed out the path.

When I came down low enough upon the zig-zag descent, to see him again, I saw that he was standing between the rails on the way by which the train had lately passed, in an attitude as if he were waiting for me to appear. He had his left hand at his chin, and that left elbow rested on his right hand crossed over his breast. His attitude was one of such expectation and watchfulness, that I stopped a moment, wondering at it.

I resumed my downward way, and, stepping out upon the level of the railroad and drawing nearer to him, saw that he was a dark sallow man, with a dark beard and rather heavy eyebrows. His post was in as solitary and dismal a place as ever I saw. On either side, a dripping-wet wall of jagged stone, excluding all view but a strip of sky; the perspective one way, only a crooked prolongation of this great dungeon; the shorter perspective in the other direction, terminating in a gloomy red light, and the gloomier entrance to a black tunnel, in whose massive architecture there was a barbarous, depressing, and forbidding air. So little sunlight ever found its way to this spot, that it had an earthy deadly smell; and so much cold wind rushed through it, that it struck chill to me, as if I had left the natural world.

Before he stirred, I was near enough to him to have touched him. Not even then removing his eyes from mine, he stepped back one step, and lifted his hand. This was a lonesome post to occupy (I said), and it had riveted my attention when I looked down from up yonder. A visitor was a rarity, I should suppose; not an unwelcome rarity, I hoped? In me, he merely saw a man who had been shut up within narrow limits all his life, and who, being at last set free, had a newly-awakened interest in these great works. To such purpose I spoke to him; but I am far from sure of the terms I used, for, besides that I am not happy in opening any conversation, there was something in the man that daunted me.

He directed a most curious look towards the red light near the tunnel's mouth, and looked all about it, as if something were missing from it, and then looked at me. That light was part of his charge? Was it not?

He answered in a low voice: 'Don't you know it is?'

The monstrous thought came into my mind as I perused the fixed eyes and the saturnine face, that this was a spirit, not a man. I have speculated since, whether there may have been infection in his mind.

In my turn, I stepped back. But in making the action, I detected in his eyes some latent fear of me. This put the monstrous thought to flight.

'You look at me,' I said, forcing a smile, 'as if you had a dread of me.'

'I was doubtful,' he returned, 'whether I had seen you before.'

'Where?' He pointed to the red light he had looked at. 'There?' I said.

Intently watchful of me, he replied (but without sound), Yes.

'My good fellow, what should I do there? However, be that as it may, I never was there, you may swear.' 'I think I may,' he rejoined. 'Yes. I am sure I may.' His manner cleared, like my own. He replied to my remarks with readiness, and in well-chosen words. Had he much to do there? Yes; that was to say, he had enough responsibility to bear; but exactness and watchfulness were what was required of him, and of actual work—manual labour he had next to none. To change that signal, to trim those lights, and to turn this iron handle now and then, was all he had to do under that head. Regarding those many long and lonely hours of which I seemed to make so much, he could only say that the routine of his life had shaped itself into that form, and he had grown used to it. He had taught himself a language down here—if only to know it by sight, and to have formed his own crude ideas of its pronunciation, could be called learning it. He had also worked at fractions and decimals, and tried a little algebra; but he was, and had been as a boy, a poor hand at figures. Was it necessary for him when on duty, always to remain in that channel of damp air, and could he never rise into the sunshine from between those high stone walls? Why, that depended upon times and circumstances. Under some conditions there would be less upon the Line than under others, and the same held good as to certain hours of the day and night. In bright weather, he did choose occasions for getting a little above these lower shadows; but, being at all times liable to be called by his electric bell, and at such times listening for it with redoubled anxiety, the relief was less than I would suppose.

He took me into his box, where there was a fire, a desk for an official book in which he had to make certain entries, a telegraphic instrument with its dial face and needles, and the little bell of which he had spoken. On my trusting that he would excuse the remark that he had been well-educated, and (I hoped I might say without offence), perhaps educated above that station, he observed that instances of slight incongruity in such-wise would rarely be found wanting among large bodies of men; that he had heard it was so in workhouses, in the police force, even in that last desperate resource, the army; and that he knew it was so, more or less, in any great railway staff. He had been, when young (if I could believe it, sitting in that hut; he scarcely could), a student of natural philosophy, and had attended lectures; but he had run wild, misused his opportunities, gone down, and never risen again. He had no complaint to offer about that. He had made his bed and he lay upon it. It was far too late to make another.

All that I have here condensed, he said in a quiet manner, with his grave dark regards divided between me and the fire. He threw in the word 'Sir' from time to time, and especially when he referred to his youth: as though to request me to understand that he claimed to be nothing but what I found him. He was several times interrupted by the little bell, and had to read off messages, and send replies. Once, he had to stand without the door, and display a flag as a train passed, and make some verbal communication to the driver. In the discharge of his duties I observed him to be remarkably exact and vigilant, breaking off his discourse at a syllable, and remaining silent until what he had to do was done. In a word, I should have set this man down as one of the safest of men to be employed in that capacity, but for the circumstance that while he was speaking to me he twice broke off with a fallen colour, turned his face towards the little bell when it did NOT ring, opened the door of the hut (which was kept shut to exclude the unhealthy damp), and looked out towards the red light near the mouth of the tunnel. On both of those occasions, he came back to the fire with the inexplicable air upon him which I had remarked, without being able to define, when we were so far asunder. Said I when I rose to leave him: 'You almost make me think that I have met with a contented man.'

(I am afraid I must acknowledge that I said it to lead him on.)

'I believe I used to be so,' he rejoined, in the low voice in which he had first spoken; 'but I am troubled, sir, I am troubled.' He would have recalled the words if he could. He had said them, however, and I took them up quickly. 'With what? What is your trouble?' 'It is very difficult to impart, sir. It is very, very difficult to speak of. If ever you make me another visit, I will try to tell you.' 'But I expressly intend to make you another visit. Say, when shall it be?' 'I go off early in the morning, and I shall be on again at ten tomorrow night, sir.' 'I will come at eleven.'

He thanked me, and went out at the door with me. 'I'll show my white light, sir,' he said, in his peculiar low voice, 'till you have found the way up. When you have found it, don't call out! And when you are at the top, don't call out!'

His manner seemed to make the place strike colder to me, but I said no more than 'Very well.' 'And when you come down tomorrow night, don't call out! Let me ask you a parting question. What made you cry "Halloa! Below there!" tonight?' 'Heaven knows,' said I. 'I cried something to that effect—' 'Not to that effect, sir. Those were the very words. I know them well.' 'Admit those were the very words. I said them, no doubt, because I saw you below.' 'For no other reason?' 'What other reason could I possibly have!' 'You had no feeling that they were conveyed to you in any supernatural way?'

'No.'

He wished me good night, and held up his light. I walked by the side of the down line of rails (with a very disagreeable sensation of a train coming behind me), until I found the path. It was easier to mount than to descend, and I got back to my inn without any adventure.

Punctual to my appointment, I placed my foot on the first notch of the zig-zag next night, as the distant clocks were striking eleven. He was waiting for me at the bottom, with his white light on. 'I have not called out,' I said, when we came close together; 'may I speak now?' 'By all means, sir.' 'Good night then, and here's my hand.' 'Good night, sir, and here's mine.' With that, we walked side by side to his box, entered it, closed the door, and sat down by the fire.

'I have made up my mind, sir,' he began, bending forward as soon as we were seated, and speaking in a tone but a little above a whisper, 'that you shall not have to ask me twice what troubles me. I took you for someone else yesterday evening. That troubles me.'

'That mistake?' 'No. That someone else.'

'Who is it?' 'I don't know.' 'Like me?' 'I don't know. I never saw the face. The left arm is across the face, and the right arm is waved. Violently waved. This way.'

I followed his action with my eyes, and it was the action of an arm gesticulating with the utmost passion and vehemence: 'For God's sake clear the way!'

'One moonlight night,' said the man, 'I was sitting here, when I heard a voice cry "Halloa! Below there!" I started up, looked from that door, and saw this someone else standing by the red light near the tunnel, waving as I just now showed you. The voice seemed hoarse with shouting, and it cried, "Look out! Look out!" And then again "Halloa! Below there! Look out!" I caught up my lamp, turned it on red, and ran towards the figure, calling, "What's wrong? What has happened? Where?" It stood just outside the blackness of the tunnel. I advanced so close upon it that I wondered at its keeping the sleeve across its eyes. I ran right up at it, and had my hand stretched out to pull the sleeve away, when it was gone.'

'Into the tunnel,' said I.

'No. I ran on into the tunnel, five hundred yards. I stopped and held my lamp above my head, and saw the figures of the measured distance, and saw the wet stains stealing down the walls and trickling through the arch. I ran out again, faster than I had run in (for I had a mortal abhorrence of the place upon me), and I looked all round the red light with my own red light, and I went up the iron ladder to the gallery atop of it, and I came down again, and ran back here. I telegraphed both ways, "An alarm has been given. Is anything wrong?" The answer came back, both ways: "All well."'

Resisting the slow touch of a frozen finger tracing out my spine, I showed him how that this figure must be a deception of his sense of sight, and how that figures, originating in disease of the delicate nerves that minister to the functions of the eye, were known to have often troubled patients, some of whom had become conscious of the nature of their affliction, and had even proved it by experiments upon themselves. 'As to an imaginary cry,' said I, 'do but listen for a moment to the wind in this unnatural valley while we speak so low, and to the wild harp it makes of the telegraph wires!' That was all very well, he returned, after we had sat listening for a while, and he ought to know something of the wind and the wires, he who so often passed long winter nights there, alone and watching. But he would beg to remark that he had not finished.

I asked his pardon, and he slowly added these words, touching my arm: 'Within six hours after the Appearance, the memorable accident on this line happened, and within ten hours the dead and wounded were brought along through the tunnel over the spot where the figure had stood.'

A disagreeable shudder crept over me, but I did my best against it. It was not to be denied, I rejoined, that this was a remarkable coincidence, calculated deeply to impress his mind. But it was unquestionable that remarkable coincidences did continually occur, and they must be taken into account in dealing with such a subject. Though to be sure I must admit, I added (for I thought I saw that he was going to bring the objection to bear upon me), men of common sense did not allow much for coincidences in making the ordinary calculations of life. He again begged to remark that he had not finished. I again begged his pardon for being betrayed into interruptions. 'This,' he said, again laying his hand upon my arm, and glancing over his shoulder with hollow eyes, 'was just a year ago. Six or seven months passed, and I had recovered from the surprise and shock, when one morning, as the day was breaking, I, standing at that door, looked towards the red light, and saw the spectre again.' He stopped, with a fixed look at me.

'Did it cry out?' 'No. It was silent.' 'Did it wave its arm?' 'No. It leaned against the shaft of the light, with both hands before the face. Like this.'

Once more, I followed his action with my eyes. It was an action of mourning. I have seen such an attitude in stone figures on tombs.

'Did you go up to it?'

'I came in and sat down, partly to collect my thoughts, partly because it had turned me faint. When I went to the door again, daylight was above me, and the ghost was gone.'

'But nothing followed? Nothing came of this?'

He touched me on the arm with his forefinger twice or thrice, giving a ghastly nod each time: 'That very day, as a train came out of the tunnel, I noticed, at a carriage window on my side, what looked like a confusion of hands and heads, and something waved. I saw it, just in time to signal the driver, Stop! He shut off, and put his brake on, but the train drifted past here a hundred and fifty yards or more. I ran after it, and, as I went along, heard terrible screams and cries. A beautiful young lady had died instantaneously in one of the compartments, and was brought in here, and laid down on this floor between us.'

Involuntarily, I pushed my chair back, as I looked from the boards at which he pointed, to himself. 'True, sir. True. Precisely as it happened, so I tell it you.' I could think of nothing to say, to any purpose, and my mouth was very dry. The wind and the wires took up the story with a long lamenting wail.

He resumed. 'Now, sir, mark this, and judge how my mind is troubled. The spectre came back, a week ago. Ever since, it has been there, now and again, by fits and starts.'

'At the light?'

'At the Danger-light.'

'What does it seem to do?'

He repeated, if possible with increased passion and vehemence, that former gesticulation of 'For God's sake clear the way!'

Then, he went on. 'I have no peace or rest for it. It calls to me, for many minutes together, in an agonised manner, "Below there! Look out! Look out!" It stands waving to me. It rings my little bell—'

I caught at that. 'Did it ring your bell yesterday evening when I was here, and you went to the door?'

'Twice.'

'Why, see,' said I, 'how your imagination misleads you. My

eyes were on the bell, and my ears were open to the bell, and if I am a living man, it did NOT ring at those times. No, nor at any other time, except when it was rung in the natural course of physical things by the station communicating with you.'

He shook his head. 'I have never made a mistake as to that, yet, sir. I have never confused the spectre's ring with the man's. The ghost's ring is a strange vibration in the bell that it derives from nothing else, and I have not asserted that the bell stirs to the eye. I don't wonder that you failed to hear it. But I heard it.'

'And did the spectre seem to be there, when you looked out?'

'It WAS there.'

'Both times?'

He repeated firmly: 'Both times.'

'Will you come to the door with me, and look for it now?'

He bit his under-lip as though he were somewhat unwilling, but arose. I opened the door, and stood on the step, while he stood in the doorway. There, was the Danger-light. There, was the dismal mouth of the tunnel. There, were the high wet stone walls of the cutting. There, were the stars above them.

'Do you see it?' I asked him, taking particular note of his face. His eyes were prominent and strained; but not very much more so, perhaps, than my own had been when I had directed them earnestly towards the same spot.

'No,' he answered. 'It is not there.'

'Agreed,' said I.

We went in again, shut the door, and resumed our seats. I was thinking how best to improve this advantage, if it might be called one, when he took up the conversation in such a matter of course way, so assuming that there could be no serious question of fact between us, that I felt myself placed in the weakest of positions.

'By this time you will fully understand, sir,' he said, 'that what troubles me so dreadfully, is the question, What does the spectre mean?'

I was not sure, I told him, that I did fully understand.

'What is its warning against?' he said, ruminating, with his eyes on the fire, and only by times turning them on me. 'What is the danger? Where is the danger? There is danger overhanging, somewhere on the line. Some dreadful calamity will happen. It is not to be doubted this third time, after what has gone before. But surely this is a cruel haunting of me. What can I do?'

He pulled out his handkerchief, and wiped the drops from his heated forehead.

'If I telegraph Danger, on either side of me, or on both, I can give no reason for it,' he went on, wiping the palms of his hands. 'I should get into trouble, and do no good. They would think I was mad. This is the way it would work—Message: "Danger! Take care!" Answer: "What danger? Where?" Message: "Don't know. But for God's sake take care!" They would displace me. What else could they do?'

His pain of mind was most pitiable to see. It was the mental torture of a conscientious man, oppressed beyond endurance by an unintelligible responsibility involving life.

'When it first stood under the Danger-light,' he went on, putting his dark hair back from his head, and drawing his hands outward across and across his temples in an extremity of feverish distress, 'Why not tell me where that accident was to happen—if it must happen? Why not tell me how it could be averted—if it could have been averted? When on its second coming it hid its face, why not tell me instead: "She is going to die. Let them keep her at home"? If it came, on those two occasions, only to show me that its warnings were true, and so to prepare me for the third, why not warn me plainly now? And I, Lord help me! A mere poor signalman on this solitary station! Why not go to somebody with credit to be believed, and power to act!'

When I saw him in this state, I saw that for the poor man's sake, as well as for the public safety, what I had to do for the time was, to compose his mind. Therefore, setting aside all question of reality or unreality between us, I represented to him that whoever thoroughly discharged his duty, must do well, and that at least it was his comfort that he understood his duty, though he did not understand these confounding Appearances. In this effort I succeeded far better than in the attempt to reason him out of his conviction. He became calm; the occupations incidental to his post as the night advanced, began to make larger demands on his attention; and I left him at two in the morning. I had offered to stay through the night, but he would not hear of it.

That I more than once looked back at the red light as I ascended the pathway, that I did not like the red light, and that I should have slept but poorly if my bed had been under it, I see no reason to conceal. Nor did I like the two sequences of the accident and the dead girl. I see no reason to conceal that, either.

But, what ran most in my thoughts was the consideration how ought I to act, having become the recipient of this disclosure? I had proved the man to be intelligent, vigilant, painstaking, and exact; but how long might he remain so, in his state of mind? Though in a subordinate position, still he held a most important trust, and would I (for instance) like to stake my own life on the chances of his continuing to execute it with precision?

Unable to overcome a feeling that there would be something treacherous in my communicating what he had told me, to his superiors in the Company, without first being plain with himself and proposing a middle course to him, I ultimately resolved to offer to accompany him (otherwise keeping his secret for the present) to the wisest medical practitioner we could hear of in those parts, and to take his opinion. A change in his time of duty would come round next night, he had apprised me, and he would be off an hour or two after sunrise, and on again soon after sunset. I had appointed to return accordingly.

Next evening was a lovely evening, and I walked out early to enjoy it. The sun was not yet quite down when I traversed the field-path near the top of the deep cutting. I would extend my walk for an hour, I said to myself, half an hour on and half an hour back, and it would then be time to go to my signalman's box.

Before pursuing my stroll, I stepped to the brink, and mechanically looked down, from the point from which I had first seen him. I cannot describe the thrill that seized upon me, when, close at the mouth of the tunnel, I saw the appearance of a man, with his left sleeve across his eyes, passionately waving his right arm.

The nameless horror that oppressed me, passed in a moment, for in a moment I saw that this appearance of a man was a man indeed, and that there was a little group of other men standing at a short distance, to whom he seemed to be rehearsing the gesture he made. The Danger-light was not yet lighted. Against its shaft, a little low hut, entirely new to me, had been made of some wooden supports and tarpaulin. It looked no bigger than a bed.

With an irresistible sense that something was wrong—with a flashing self-reproachful fear that fatal mischief had come of my leaving the man there, and causing no one to be sent to overlook or correct what he did—I descended the notched path with all the speed I could make.

'What is the matter?' I asked the men.

'Signalman killed this morning, sir.'

'Not the man belonging to that box?'

'Yes, sir.'

'Not the man I know?'

'You will recognise him, sir, if you knew him,' said the man who spoke for the others, solemnly uncovering his own head and raising an end of the tarpaulin, 'for his face is quite composed.'

'O! how did this happen, how did this happen?' I asked, turning from one to another as the hut closed in again.

'He was cut down by an engine, sir. No man in England knew his work better. But somehow he was not clear of the outer rail. It was just at broad day. He had struck the light, and had the lamp in his hand. As the engine came out of the tunnel, his back was towards her, and she cut him down. That man drove her, and was showing how it happened. Show the gentleman, Tom.'

The man, who wore a rough dark dress, stepped back to his former place at the mouth of the tunnel!

'Coming round the curve in the tunnel, sir,' he said, 'I saw him at the end, like as if I saw him down a perspective-glass. There was no time to check speed, and I knew him to be very careful. As he didn't seem to take heed of the whistle, I shut it off when we were running down upon him, and called to him as loud as I could call.'

'What did you say?'

'I said, Below there! Look out! Look out! For God's sake clear the way!'

I started.

'Ah! it was a dreadful time, sir. I never left off calling to him. I put this arm before my eyes, not to see, and I waved this arm to the last; but it was no use.'

Without prolonging the narrative to dwell on anyone of its curious circumstances more than on any other, I may, in closing it, point out the coincidence that the warning of the Engine-Driver included, not only the words which the unfortunate Signalman had repeated to me as haunting him, but also the words which I myself—not he—had attached, and that only in my own mind, to the gesticulation he had imitated.

18

THE DEVIL AND TOM WALKER

Washington Irving

...dark and stagnant pools, the abodes of the tadpole, the bullfrog, and the water-snake, where the trunks of pines and hemlocks lay half-drowned, half-rotting, looking like alligators sleeping in the mire...

A few miles from Boston, in Massachusetts, there is a deep inlet winding several miles into the interior of the country from Charles Bay, and terminating in a thickly wooded swamp, or morass. On one side of this inlet is a beautiful dark grove; on the opposite side the land rises abruptly from the water's edge, into a high ridge on which grow a few scattered oaks of great age and immense size. Under one of these gigantic trees, according to old stories, there was a great amount of treasure buried by Kidd the pirate. The inlet allowed a facility to bring the money in a boat secretly and at night to the very foot of the hill. The elevation of the place permitted a good look out to be kept that no one was at hand, while the remarkable trees formed good landmarks by which the place might easily be found again. The old stories add, moreover, that the devil presided at the hiding of the money, and took it under his guardianship; but this, it is well known, he always does with buried treasure, particularly when it has been ill gotten. Be that as it may, Kidd never returned to recover his wealth; being shortly after seized at Boston, sent out to England, and there hanged for a pirate.

About the year 1727, just at the time when earthquakes were prevalent in New England, and shook many tall sinners down upon their knees, there lived near this place a meagre miserly fellow of the name of Tom Walker. He had a wife as miserly as himself; they were so miserly that they even conspired to cheat each other. Whatever the woman could lay hands on she hid away: a hen could not cackle but she was on the alert to secure the new-laid egg. Her husband was continually prying about to detect her secret hoards, and many and fierce were the conflicts that took place about what ought to have been common property. They lived in a forlorn looking house that stood alone and had an air of starvation. A few straggling savin trees, emblems of sterility, grew near it; no smoke ever curled from its chimney; no traveler stopped at its door. A miserable horse, whose ribs were as articulate as the bars of a gridiron, stalked about a field where a thin carpet of moss, scarcely covering the ragged beds of pudding stone, tantalized and balked his hunger; and sometimes he would lean his head over the fence, look piteously at the passer by, and seem to petition deliverance from this land of famine. The house and its inmates had altogether a bad name. Tom's wife was a tall termagant, fierce of temper, loud of tongue, and strong of arm. Her voice was often heard in wordy warfare with her husband; and his face sometimes showed signs that their conflicts were not confined to words. No one ventured, however, to interfere between them; the lonely wayfarer shrunk within himself at the horrid clamor and clapper clawing; eyed the den of discord askance, and hurried on his way, rejoicing, if a bachelor, in his celibacy.

One day that Tom Walker had been to a distant part of the neighbourhood, he took what he considered a short cut homewards through the swamp. Like most short cuts, it was an ill chosen route. The swamp was thickly grown with great gloomy pines and hemlocks, some of them ninety feet high; which made it dark at noonday, and a retreat for all the owls of the neighbourhood. It was full of pits and quagmires, partly covered with weeds and mosses; where the green surface often betrayed the traveler into a gulf of black smothering mud; there were also dark and stagnant pools, the abodes of the tadpole, the bullfrog, and the water snake, and where trunks of pines and hemlocks lay half drowned, half rotting, looking like alligators, sleeping in the mire.

Tom had long been picking his way cautiously through this treacherous forest; stepping from tuft to tuft of rushes and roots which afforded precarious footholds among deep sloughs; or pacing carefully, like a cat, along the prostrate trunks of trees; startled now and then by the sudden screaming of the bittern, or the quacking of a wild duck, rising on the wing from some solitary pool. At length he arrived at a piece of firm ground, which ran out like a peninsula into the deep bosom of the swamp. It had been one of the strongholds of the Indians during their wars with the first colonists. Here they had thrown up a kind of fort, which they had looked upon as almost impregnable, and had used as a place of refuge for their squaws and children. Nothing remained of the Indian fort but a few embankments gradually sinking to the level of the surrounding earth, and already overgrown in part by oaks and other forest trees, the foliage of which formed a contrast to the dark pines and hemlocks of the swamp.

It was late in the dusk of evening that Tom Walker reached the old fort, and he paused there for a while to rest himself. Anyone but he would have felt unwilling to linger in this lonely melancholy place, for the common people had a bad opinion of it from the stories handed down from the time of the Indian wars; when it was asserted that the savages held incantations here and made sacrifices to the evil spirit. Tom Walker, however, was not a man to be troubled with any fears of the kind.

He reposed himself for some time on the trunk of a fallen hemlock, listening to the boding cry of the tree toad, and delving with his walking staff into a mound of black mould at his feet. As he turned up the soil unconsciously, his staff struck against something hard. He raked it out of the vegetable mould, and lo! A cloven skull with an Indian tomahawk buried deep in it, lay before him. The rust on the weapon showed the time that had elapsed since this death blow had been given. It was a dreary memento of the fierce struggle that had taken place in this last foothold of the Indian warriors.

'Humph!' said Tom Walker, as he gave the skull a kick to shake the dirt from it.

'Let that skull alone!' said a gruff voice.

Tom lifted up his eyes and beheld a great black man, seated directly opposite him on the stump of a tree. He was exceedingly surprised, having neither seen nor heard anyone approach, and he was still more perplexed on observing, as well as the gathering gloom would permit, that the stranger was neither negro nor Indian. It is true, he was dressed in a rude, half Indian garb, and had a red belt or sash swathed round his body, but his face was neither black nor copper colour, but swarthy and dingy and begrimed with soot, as if he had been accustomed to toil among fires and forges. He had a shock of coarse black hair, that stood out from his head in all directions; and bore an axe on his shoulder.

He scowled for a moment at Tom with a pair of great red eyes.

'What are you doing in my grounds?' said the black man, with a hoarse growling voice.

'Your grounds?' said Tom, with a sneer; 'no more your grounds than mine: they belong to Deacon Peabody.'

'Deacon Peabody be d——d,' said the stranger, 'as I flatter myself he will be, if he does not look more to his own sins and less to his neighbour's. Look yonder, and see how Deacon Peabody is faring.'

Tom looked in the direction that the stranger pointed, and beheld one of the great trees, fair and flourishing without, but rotten at the core, and saw that it had been nearly hewn through, so that the first high wind was likely to below it down. On the bark of the tree was scored the name of Deacon Peabody. He now looked round and found most of the tall trees marked with the name of some great men of the colony, and all more or less scored by the axe. The one on which he had been seated, and which had evidently just been hewn down, bore the name of Crowninshield; and he recollected a mighty rich man of that name, who made a vulgar display of wealth, which it was whispered he had acquired by buccaneering.

'He's just ready for burning!' said the black man, with a growl of triumph. 'You see I am likely to have a good stock of firewood for winter.'

'But what right have you,' said Tom, 'to cut down Deacon Peabody's timber?'

'The right of prior claim,' said the other. 'This woodland belonged to me long before one of your white faced race put foot upon the soil.'

'And pray, who are you, if I may be so bold?' said Tom.

'Oh, I go by various names. I am the Wild Huntsman in some countries; the Black Miner in others. In this neighbourhood I am known by the name of the Black Woodsman. I am he to whom the red men devoted this spot, and now and then roasted a white man by way of sweet smelling sacrifice. Since the red men have been exterminated by you white savages, I amuse myself by presiding at the persecutions of Quakers and Anabaptists; I am the great patron and prompter of slave dealers, and the grand master of the Salem witches.'

'The upshot of all which is, that, if I mistake not,' said Tom, sturdily, 'you are he commonly called Old Scratch.'

'The same at your service!' replied the black man, with a half civil nod.

Such was the opening of this interview, according to the old story, though it has almost too familiar an air to be credited. One would think that to meet with such a singular personage in this wild lonely place, would have shaken any man's nerves: but Tom was a hard-minded fellow, not easily daunted, and he had lived so long with a termagant wife, that he did not even fear the devil.

It is said that after this commencement, they had a long and earnest conversation together, as Tom returned homewards. The black man told him of great sums of money which had been buried by Kidd the pirate, under the oak trees on the high ridge not far from the morass. All these were under his command and protected by his power, so that none could find them but such as propitiated his favor. These he offered to place within Tom Walker's reach, having conceived an especial kindness for him: but they were to be had only on certain conditions. What these conditions were, may easily be surmised, though Tom never disclosed them publicly. They must have been very hard, for he required time to think of them, and he was not a man to stick at trifles where money was in view. When they had reached the edge of the swamp the stranger paused.

'What proof have I that all you have been telling me is true?' said Tom.

'There is my signature,' said the black man, pressing his finger on Tom's forehead. So saying, he turned off among the thickets of the swamp, and seemed, as Tom said, to go down, down, down, into the earth, until nothing but his head and shoulders could be seen, and so on until he totally disappeared.

When Tom reached home he found the black print of a finger burnt, as it were, into his forehead, which nothing could obliterate.

The first news his wife had to tell him was the sudden death of Absalom Crowninshield the rich buccaneer. It was announced in the papers with the usual flourish, that 'a great man had fallen in Israel'.

Tom recollected the tree which his black friend had just hewn down, and which was ready for burning. 'Let the freebooter roast,' said Tom, 'who cares!' He now felt convinced that all he had heard and seen was no illusion.

He was not prone to let his wife into his confidence; but as this was an uneasy secret, he willingly shared it with her. All her avarice was awakened at the mention of hidden gold, and she urged her husband to comply with the black man's terms and secure what would make them wealthy for life. However Tom might have felt disposed to sell himself to the devil, he was determined not to do so to oblige his wife; so he flatly refused out of the mere spirit of contradiction. Many and bitter were the quarrels they had on the subject, but the more she talked the more resolute was Tom not to be damned to please her. At length she determined to drive the bargain on her own account, and if she succeeded, to keep all the gain to herself.

Being of the same fearless temper as her husband, she set off for the old Indian fort towards the close of a summer's day. She was many hours absent. When she came back she was reserved and sullen in her replies. She spoke something of a black man whom she had met about twilight, hewing at the root of a tall tree. He was sulky, however, and would not come to terms; she was to go again with a propitiatory offering, but what it was she forbore to say.

The next evening she set off again for the swamp, with her apron heavily laden. Tom waited and waited for her, but in vain: midnight came, but she did not make her appearance; morning, noon, night returned, but still she did not come. Tom now grew uneasy for her safety; especially as he found she had carried off in her apron the silver teapot and spoons and every portable article of value. Another night elapsed, another morning came; but no wife. In a word, she was never heard of more.

What was her real fate nobody knows, in consequence of so many pretending to know. It is one of those facts that have become confounded by a variety of historians. Some asserted that she lost her way among the tangled mazes of the swamp and sunk into some pit or slough; others, more uncharitable, hinted that she had eloped with the household booty, and made off to some other province; while others assert that the tempter had decoyed her into a dismal quagmire on top of which her hat was found lying. In confirmation of this, it was said a great black man with an axe on his shoulder was seen late that very evening coming out of the swamp, carrying a bundle tied in a check apron, with an air of surly triumph.

The most current and probable story, however, observes that Tom Walker grew so anxious about the fate of his wife and his property that he sat out at length to seek them both at the Indian fort. During a long summer's afternoon he searched about the gloomy place, but no wife was to be seen. He called her name repeatedly, but she was no where to be heard. The bittern alone responded to his voice, as he flew screaming by; or the bullfrog croaked dolefully from a neighbouring pool. At length, it is said, just in the brown hour of twilight, when the owls began to hoot and the bats to flit about, his attention was attracted by the clamor of carrion crows that were hovering about a cypress tree. He looked and beheld a bundle tied in a check apron and hanging in the branches of the tree; with a great vulture perched hard by, as if keeping watch upon it. He leaped with joy, for he recognized his wife's apron, and supposed it to contain the household valuables.

'Let us get hold of the property,' said he, consolingly to himself, 'and we will endeavor to do without the woman.'

As he scrambled up the tree the vulture spread its wide wings, and sailed off screaming into the deep shadows of the forest. Tom seized the check apron, but, woeful sight! Found nothing but a heart and liver tied up in it.

Such, according to the most authentic old story, was all that was to be found of Tom's wife. She had probably attempted to deal with the black man as she had been accustomed to deal with her husband; but though a female scold is generally considered a match for the devil, yet in this instance she appears to have had the worst of it. She must have died game however; for it is said Tom noticed many prints of cloven feet deeply stamped about the tree, and several handfuls of hair, that looked as if they had been plucked from the coarse black shock of the woodsman. Tom knew his wife's prowess by experience. He shrugged his shoulders as he looked at the signs of a fierce clapper clawing. 'Egad,' said he to himself, 'Old Scratch must have had a tough time of it!'

Tom consoled himself for the loss of his property with the loss of his wife; for he was a man of fortitude. He even felt something like gratitude towards the black woodsman, who he considered had done him a kindness. He sought, therefore, to cultivate a farther acquaintance with him, but for some time without success; the old black legs played shy, for whatever people may think, he is not always to be had for calling for; he knows how to play his cards when pretty sure of his game.

At length, it is said, when delay had whetted Tom's eagerness to the quick, and prepared him to agree to any thing rather than not gain the promised treasure, he met the black man one evening in his usual woodman dress, with his axe on his shoulder, sauntering along the edge of the swamp, and humming a tune. He affected to receive Tom's advance with great indifference, made brief replies, and went on humming his tune.

By degrees, however, Tom brought him to business, and they began to haggle about the terms on which the former was to have the pirate's treasure. There was one condition, which need not be mentioned, being generally understood in all cases where the devil grants favors; but there were others about which, though of less importance, he was inflexibly obstinate. He insisted that the money found through his means should be employed in his service. He proposed, therefore, that Tom should employ it in the black traffic; that is to say, that he should fit out a slave ship. This, however, Tom resolutely refused; he was bad enough in all conscience; but the devil himself could not tempt him to turn slave dealer.

Finding Tom so squeamish on this point, he did not insist upon it, but proposed instead that he should turn usurer; the devil being extremely anxious for the increase of usurers, looking upon them as his peculiar people.

To this no objections were made, for it was just to Tom's taste.

'You shall open a broker's shop in Boston next month,' said the black man.

'I'll do it tomorrow, if you wish,' said Tom Walker.

'You shall lend money at 2 per cent a month.'

'Egad, I'll charge four!' replied Tom Walker.

'You shall extort bonds, foreclose mortgages, drive the merchant to bankruptcy—'

'I'll drive him to the d——l,' cried Tom Walker, eagerly.

'You are the usurer for my money!' said the black legs, with delight. 'When will you want the rhino?'

'This very night.'

'Done!' said the devil.

'Done!' said Tom Walker. So they shook hands, and struck a bargain.

A few days' time saw Tom Walker seated behind his desk in a counting house in Boston. His reputation for a ready moneyed man, who would lend money out for a good consideration, soon spread abroad. Every body remembers the days of Governor Belcher, when money was particularly scarce. It was a time of paper credit. The country had been deluged with government bills; the famous Land Bank had been established; there had been a rage for speculating; the people had run mad with schemes for new settlements; for building cities in the wilderness; land jobbers went about with maps of grants, and townships, and Eldorados, lying nobody knew where, but which every body was ready to purchase. In a word, the great speculating fever which breaks out every now and then in the country, had raged to an alarming degree, and every body was dreaming of making sudden fortunes from nothing. As usual the fever had subsided; the dream had gone off, and the imaginary fortunes with it; the patients were left in doleful plight, and the whole country resounded with the consequent cry of 'hard times.'

At this propitious time of public distress did Tom Walker set up as a usurer in Boston. His door was soon thronged by customers. The needy and the adventurous; the gambling speculator; the dreaming land jobber; the thriftless tradesman; the merchant with cracked credit; in short, everyone driven to raise money by desperate means and desperate sacrifices, hurried to Tom Walker.

Thus Tom was the universal friend of the needy, and he acted like a 'friend in need'; that is to say, he always exacted good pay and good security. In proportion to the distress of the applicant was the hardness of his terms. He accumulated bonds and mortgages; gradually squeezed his customers closer and closer; and sent them at length, dry as a sponge from his door.

In this way he made money hand over hand; became a rich and mighty man, and exalted his cocked hat upon change. He built himself, as usual, a vast house, out of ostentation; but left the greater part of it unfinished and unfurnished out of parsimony. He even set up a carriage in the fullness of his vain glory, though he nearly starved the horses which drew it; and as the ungreased wheels groaned and screeched on the axle trees, you would have thought you heard the souls of the poor debtors he was squeezing.

As Tom waxed old, however, he grew thoughtful. Having secured the good things of this world, he began to feel anxious about those of the next. He thought with regret on the bargain he had made with his black friend, and set his wits to work to cheat him out of the conditions. He became, therefore, all of a sudden, a violent churchgoer. He prayed loudly and strenuously as if heaven were to be taken by force of lungs. Indeed, one might always tell when he had sinned most during the week, by the clamor of his Sunday devotion. The quiet Christians who had been modestly and steadfastly traveling Zion ward, were struck with self reproach at seeing themselves so suddenly outstripped in their career by this new-made convert. Tom was as rigid in religious, as in money matters; he was a stern supervisor and censurer of his neighbours, and seemed to think every sin entered up to their account became a credit on his own side of the page. He even talked of the expediency of reviving the persecution of Quakers and Anabaptists. In a word, Tom's zeal became as notorious as his riches.

Still, in spite of all this strenuous attention to forms, Tom had a lurking dread that the devil, after all, would have his due. That he might not be taken unawares, therefore, it is said he always carried a small Bible in his coat pocket. He had also a great folio Bible on his counting house desk, and would frequently be found reading it when people called on business; on such occasions he would lay his green spectacles on the book, to mark the place, while he turned round to drive some usurious bargain.

Some say that Tom grew a little crack brained in his old days, and that fancying his end approaching, he had his horse new shod, saddled and bridled, and buried with his feet uppermost; because he supposed that at the last day the world would be turned upside down; in which case he should find his horse standing ready for mounting, and he was determined at the worst to give his old friend a run for it. This, however, is probably a mere old wives' fable. If he really did take such a precaution it was totally superfluous; at least so says the authentic old legend, which closes his story in the following manner.

On one hot afternoon in the dog days, just as a terrible black thunder gust was coming up, Tom sat in his counting house in his white linen cap and India silk morning gown. He was on the point of foreclosing a mortgage, by which he would complete the ruin of an unlucky land speculator for whom he had professed the greatest friendship. The poor land jobber begged him to grant a few months indulgence. Tom had grown testy and irritated and refused another day.

'My family will be ruined and brought upon the parish,' said the land jobber. 'Charity begins at home,' replied Tom, 'I must take care of myself in these hard times.'

'You have made so much money out of me,' said the speculator.

Tom lost his patience and his piety—'The devil take me,' said he, 'if I have made a farthing!'

Just then there were three loud knocks at the street door. He stepped out to see who was there. A black man was holding a black horse, which neighed and stamped with impatience.

'Tom, you're come for!' said the black fellow, gruffly. Tom shrunk back, but too late. He had left his little Bible at the bottom of his coat pocket, and his big Bible on the desk buried under the mortgage he was about to foreclose: never was a sinner taken more unawares. The black man whisked him like a child astride the horse and away he galloped in the midst of a thunderstorm. The clerks stuck their pens behind their ears and stared after him from the windows. Away went Tom Walker, dashing down the streets; his white cap bobbing up and down; his morning gown fluttering in the wind, and his steed striking fire out of the pavement at every bound. When the clerks turned to look for the black man he had disappeared.

Tom Walker never returned to foreclose the mortgage. A countryman who lived on the borders of the swamp, reported that in the height of the thunder gust he had heard a great clattering of hoofs and a howling along the road, and that when he ran to the window he just caught sight of a figure, such as I have described, on a horse that galloped like mad across the fields, over the hills and down into the black hemlock swamp towards the old Indian fort; and that shortly after a thunderbolt fell in that direction which seemed to set the whole forest in a blaze.

The good people of Boston shook their heads and shrugged their shoulders, but had been so much accustomed to witches and goblins and tricks of the devil in all kinds of shapes from the first settlement of the colony, that they were not so much horror struck as might have been expected. Trustees were appointed to take charge of Tom's effects. There was nothing, however, to administer upon. On searching his coffers all his bonds and mortgages were found reduced to cinders. In place of gold and silver his iron chest was filled with chips and shavings; two skeletons lay in his stable instead of his half starved horses, and the very next day his great house took fire and was burnt to the ground.

Such was the end of Tom Walker and his ill gotten wealth. Let all griping money brokers lay this story to heart. The truth of it is not to be doubted. The very hole under the oak trees, from whence he dug Kidd's money is to be seen to this day; and the neighbouring swamp and old Indian fort is often haunted in stormy nights by a figure on horseback, in a morning gown and white cap, which is doubtless the troubled spirit of the usurer. In fact, the story has resolved itself into a proverb, and is the origin of that popular saying, prevalent throughout New England, of 'The Devil and Tom Walker.'

19

DRACULA'S GUEST

Bram Stoker

...something so strange in all this,
something so weird and impossible to imagine...

When we started for our drive the sun was shining brightly on Munich, and the air was full of the joyousness of early summer. Just as we were about to depart, Herr Delbrück (the maître d'hôtel of the Quatre Saisons, where I was staying) came down, bareheaded, to the carriage and, after wishing me a pleasant drive, said to the coachman, still holding his hand on the handle of the carriage door:

'Remember you are back by nightfall. The sky looks bright but there is a shiver in the north wind that says there may be a sudden storm. But I am sure you will not be late.' Here he smiled, and added, 'for you know what night it is.'

Johann answered with an emphatic, 'Ja, mein Herr,' and, touching his hat, drove off quickly. When we had cleared the town, I said, after signalling to him to stop: 'Tell me, Johann, what is tonight?' He crossed himself, as he answered laconically: 'Walpurgis nacht.' Then he took out his watch, a great, old-fashioned German silver thing as big as a turnip, and looked at it, with his eyebrows gathered together and a little impatient shrug of his shoulders. I realised that this was his way of respectfully protesting against the unnecessary delay, and sank back in the carriage, merely motioning him to proceed. He started off rapidly, as if to make up for lost time. Every now and then the horses seemed to throw up their heads and sniffed the air suspiciously. On such occasions I often looked round in alarm. The road was pretty bleak, for we were traversing a sort of high, wind-swept plateau. As we drove, I saw a road that looked but little used, and which seemed to dip through a little, winding valley. It looked so inviting that, even at the risk of offending him, I called Johann to stop—and when he had pulled up, I told him I would like to drive down that road. He made all sorts of excuses, and frequently crossed himself as he spoke. This somewhat piqued my curiosity, so I asked him various questions. He answered fencingly, and repeatedly looked at his watch in protest. Finally I said: 'Well, Johann, I want to go down this road. I shall not ask you to come unless you like; but tell me why you do not like to go, that is all I ask.' For answer he seemed to throw himself off the box, so quickly did he reach the ground. Then he stretched out his hands appealingly to me, and implored me not to go. There was just enough of English mixed with the German for me to understand the drift of his talk. He seemed always just about to tell me something—the very idea of which evidently frightened him; but each time he pulled himself up, saying, as he crossed himself: 'Walpurgis nacht!'

I tried to argue with him, but it was difficult to argue with a man when I did not know his language. The advantage certainly rested with him, for although he began to speak in English, of a very crude and broken kind, he always got excited and broke into his native tongue—and every time he did so, he looked at his watch. Then the horses became restless and sniffed the air. At this he grew very pale, and, looking around in a frightened way, he suddenly jumped forward, took them by the bridles and led them on some twenty feet. I followed, and asked why he had done this. For answer he crossed himself, pointed to the spot we had left and drew his carriage in the direction of the other road, indicating a cross, and said, first in German, then in English: 'Buried him—him what killed themselves.'

I remembered the old custom of burying suicides at cross-roads: 'Ah! I see, a suicide. How interesting!' But for the life of me I could not make out why the horses were frightened.

Whilst we were talking, we heard a sort of sound between a yelp and a bark. It was far away; but the horses got very restless, and it took Johann all his time to quiet them. He was pale, and said, 'It sounds like a wolf—but yet there are no wolves here now.'

'No?' I said, questioning him; 'isn't it long since the wolves were so near the city?'

'Long, long,' he answered, 'in the spring and summer; but with the snow the wolves have been here not so long.'

Whilst he was petting the horses and trying to quiet them, dark clouds drifted rapidly across the sky. The sunshine passed away, and a breath of cold wind seemed to drift past us. It was only a breath, however, and more in the nature of a warning than a fact, for the sun came out brightly again. Johann looked under his lifted hand at the horizon and said:

'The storm of snow, he comes before long time.' Then he looked at his watch again, and, straightway holding his reins firmly—for the horses were still pawing the ground restlessly and shaking their heads—he climbed to his box as though the time had come for proceeding on our journey.

I felt a little obstinate and did not at once get into the carriage.

'Tell me,' I said, 'about this place where the road leads,' and I pointed down.

Again he crossed himself and mumbled a prayer, before he answered, 'It is unholy.'

'What is unholy?' I enquired.

'The village.'

'Then there is a village?'

'No, no. No one lives there hundreds of years.' My curiosity was piqued, 'But you said there was a village.'

'There was.'

'Where is it now?'

Whereupon he burst out into a long story in German and English, so mixed up that I could not quite understand exactly what he said, but roughly I gathered that long ago, hundreds of years, men had died there and been buried in their graves; and sounds were heard under the clay, and when the graves were opened, men and women were found rosy with life, and their mouths red with blood. And so, in haste to save their lives (aye, and their souls!—and here he crossed himself) those who were left fled away to other places, where the living lived, and the dead were dead and not—not something. He was evidently afraid to speak the last words. As he proceeded with his narration, he grew more and more excited. It seemed as if his imagination had got hold of him, and he ended in a perfect paroxysm of fear—white-faced, perspiring, trembling and looking round him, as if expecting that some dreadful presence would manifest itself there in the bright sunshine on the open plain. Finally, in an agony of desperation, he cried:

'Walpurgis nacht!' and pointed to the carriage for me to get in. All my English blood rose at this, and, standing back, I said:

'You are afraid, Johann—you are afraid. Go home; I shall return alone; the walk will do me good.' The carriage door was open. I took from the seat my oak walking-stick—which I always carry on my holiday excursions—and closed the door, pointing back to Munich, and said, 'Go home, Johann—Walpurgis nacht doesn't concern Englishmen.'

The horses were now more restive than ever, and Johann was trying to hold them in, while excitedly imploring me not to do anything so foolish. I pitied the poor fellow, he was deeply in earnest; but all the same I could not help laughing. His English was quite gone now. In his anxiety he had forgotten that his only means of making me understand was to talk my language, so he jabbered away in his native German. It began to be a little tedious. After giving the direction, 'Home!' I turned to go down the cross-road into the valley.

With a despairing gesture, Johann turned his horses towards Munich. I leaned on my stick and looked after him. He went slowly along the road for a while: then there came over the crest of the hill a man tall and thin. I could see so much in the distance. When he drew near the horses, they began to jump and kick about, then to scream with terror. Johann could not hold them in; they bolted down the road, running away madly. I watched them out of sight, then looked for the stranger, but I found that he, too, was gone.

With a light heart I turned down the side road through the deepening valley to which Johann had objected. There was not the slightest reason, that I could see, for his objection; and I daresay I tramped for a couple of hours without thinking of time or distance, and certainly without seeing a person or a house. So far as the place was concerned, it was desolation itself. But I did not notice this particularly till, on turning a bend in the road, I came upon a scattered fringe of wood; then I recognised that I had been impressed unconsciously by the desolation of the region through which I had passed.

I sat down to rest myself, and began to look around. It struck me that it was considerably colder than it had been at the commencement of my walk—a sort of sighing sound seemed to be around me, with, now and then, high overhead, a sort of muffled roar. Looking upwards I noticed that great thick clouds were drifting rapidly across the sky from North to South at a great height. There were signs of coming storm in some lofty stratum of the air. I was a little chilly, and, thinking that it was the sitting still after the exercise of walking, I resumed my journey.

The ground I passed over was now much more picturesque. There were no striking objects that the eye might single out; but in all there was a charm of beauty. I took little heed of time and it was only when the deepening twilight forced itself upon me that I began to think of how I should find my way home. The brightness of the day had gone. The air was cold, and the drifting of clouds high overhead was more marked. They were accompanied by a sort of far-away rushing sound, through which seemed to come at intervals that mysterious cry which the driver had said came from a wolf. For a while I hesitated. I had said I would see the deserted village, so on I went, and presently came on a wide stretch of open country, shut in by hills all around. Their sides were covered with trees which spread down to the plain, dotting, in clumps, the gentler slopes and hollows which showed here and there. I followed with my eye the winding of the road, and saw that it curved close to one of the densest of these clumps and was lost behind it.

As I looked there came a cold shiver in the air, and the snow began to fall. I thought of the miles and miles of bleak country I had passed, and then hurried on to seek the shelter of the wood in front. Darker and darker grew the sky, and faster and heavier fell the snow, till the earth before and around me was a glistening white carpet the further edge of which was lost in misty vagueness. The road was here but crude, and when on the level its boundaries were not so marked, as when it passed through the cuttings; and in a little while I found that I must have strayed from it, for I missed underfoot the hard surface, and my feet sank deeper in the grass and moss. Then the wind grew stronger and blew with ever increasing force, till I was fain to run before it. The air became icy-cold, and in spite of my exercise I began to suffer. The snow was now falling so thickly and whirling around me in such rapid eddies that I could hardly keep my eyes open. Every now and then the heavens were torn asunder by vivid lightning, and in the flashes I could see ahead of me a great mass of trees, chiefly yew and cypress all heavily coated with snow.

I was soon amongst the shelter of the trees, and there, in comparative silence, I could hear the rush of the wind high overhead. Presently the blackness of the storm had become merged in the darkness of the night. By-and-by the storm seemed to be passing away: it now only came in fierce puffs or blasts. At such moments the weird sound of the wolf appeared to be echoed by many similar sounds around me.

Now and again, through the black mass of drifting cloud, came a straggling ray of moonlight, which lit up the expanse, and showed me that I was at the edge of a dense mass of cypress and yew trees. As the snow had ceased to fall, I walked out from the shelter and began to investigate more closely. It appeared to me that, amongst so many old foundations as I had passed, there might be still standing a house in which, though in ruins, I could find some sort of shelter for a while. As I skirted the edge of the copse, I found that a low wall encircled it, and following this I presently found an opening. Here the cypresses formed an alley leading up to a square mass of some kind of building. Just as I caught sight of this, however, the drifting clouds obscured the moon, and I passed up the path in darkness. The wind must have grown colder, for I felt myself shiver as I walked; but there was hope of shelter, and I groped my way blindly on.

I stopped, for there was a sudden stillness. The storm had passed; and, perhaps in sympathy with nature's silence, my heart seemed to cease to beat. But this was only momentarily; for suddenly the moonlight broke through the clouds, showing me that I was in a graveyard, and that the square object before me was a great massive tomb of marble, as white as the snow that lay on and all around it. With the moonlight there came a fierce sigh of the storm, which appeared to resume its course with a long, low howl, as of many dogs or wolves. I was awed and shocked, and felt the cold perceptibly grow upon me till it seemed to grip me by the heart. Then while the flood of moonlight still fell on the marble tomb, the storm gave further evidence of renewing, as though it was returning on its track. Impelled by some sort of fascination, I approached the sepulchre to see what it was, and why such a thing stood alone in such a place. I walked around it, and read, over the Doric door, in German:

COUNTESS DOLINGEN OF GRATZ IN STYRIA
SOUGHT AND FOUND DEATH
1801

On the top of the tomb, seemingly driven through the solid marble—for the structure was composed of a few vast blocks of stone—was a great iron spike or stake. On going to the back I saw, graven in great Russian letters:

'The dead travel fast.'

There was something so weird and uncanny about the whole thing that it gave me a turn and made me feel quite faint. I began to wish, for the first time, that I had taken Johann's advice. Here a thought struck me, which came under almost mysterious circumstances and with a terrible shock. This was Walpurgis Night!

Walpurgis Night, when, according to the belief of millions of people, the devil was abroad—when the graves were opened and the dead came forth and walked. When all evil things of earth and air and water held revel. This very place the driver had specially shunned. This was the depopulated village of centuries ago. This was where the suicide lay; and this was the place where I was alone—unmanned, shivering with cold in a shroud of snow with a wild storm gathering again upon me! It took all my philosophy, all the religion I had been taught, all my courage, not to collapse in a paroxysm of fright.

And now a perfect tornado burst upon me. The ground shook as though thousands of horses thundered across it; and this time the storm bore on its icy wings, not snow, but great hailstones which drove with such violence that they might have come from the thongs of Balearic slingers—hailstones that beat down leaf and branch and made the shelter of the cypresses of no more avail than though their stems were standing-corn. At the first I had rushed to the nearest tree; but I was soon fain to leave it and seek the only spot that seemed to afford refuge, the deep Doric doorway of the marble tomb. There, crouching against the massive bronze door, I gained a certain amount of protection from the beating of the hailstones, for now they only drove against me as they ricocheted from the ground and the side of the marble.

As I leaned against the door, it moved slightly and opened inwards. The shelter of even a tomb was welcome in that pitiless tempest, and I was about to enter it when there came a flash of forked-lightning that lit up the whole expanse of the heavens. In the instant, as I am a living man, I saw, as my eyes were turned into the darkness of the tomb, a beautiful woman, with rounded cheeks and red lips, seemingly sleeping on a bier. As the thunder broke overhead, I was grasped as by the hand of a giant and hurled out into the storm. The whole thing was so sudden that, before I could realise the shock, moral as well as physical, I found the hailstones beating me down. At the same time I had a strange, dominating feeling that I was not alone. I looked towards the tomb. Just then there came another blinding flash, which seemed to strike the iron stake that surmounted the tomb and to pour through to the earth, blasting and crumbling the marble, as in a burst of flame. The dead woman rose for a moment of agony, while she was lapped in the flame, and her bitter scream of pain was drowned in the thundercrash. The last thing I heard was this mingling of dreadful sound, as again I was seized in the giant-grasp and dragged away, while the hailstones beat on me, and the air around seemed reverberant with the howling of wolves. The last sight that I remembered was a vague, white, moving mass, as if all the graves around me had sent out the phantoms of their sheeted-dead, and that they were closing in on me through the white cloudiness of the driving hail.

Gradually there came a sort of vague beginning of consciousness; then a sense of weariness that was dreadful. For a time I remembered nothing; but slowly my senses returned. My feet seemed positively racked with pain, yet I could not move them. They seemed to be numbed. There was an icy feeling at the back of my neck and all down my spine, and my ears, like my feet, were dead, yet in torment; but there was in my breast a sense of warmth which was, by comparison, delicious. It was as a nightmare—a physical nightmare, if one may use such an expression; for some heavy weight on my chest made it difficult for me to breathe.

This period of semi-lethargy seemed to remain a long time, and as it faded away I must have slept or swooned. Then came a sort of loathing, like the first stage of sea-sickness, and a wild desire to be free from something—I knew not what. A vast stillness enveloped me, as though all the world were asleep or dead—only broken by the low panting as of some animal close to me. I felt a warm rasping at my throat, then came a consciousness of the awful truth, which chilled me to the heart and sent the blood surging up through my brain. Some great animal was lying on me and now licking my throat. I feared to stir, for some instinct of prudence bade me lie still; but the brute seemed to realise that there was now some change in me, for it raised its head. Through my eyelashes I saw above me the two great flaming eyes of a gigantic wolf. Its sharp white teeth gleamed in the gaping red mouth, and I could feel its hot breath fierce and acrid upon me.

For another spell of time I remembered no more. Then I became conscious of a low growl, followed by a yelp, renewed again and again. Then, seemingly very far away, I heard a 'Holloa! holloa!' as of many voices calling in unison. Cautiously I raised my head and looked in the direction whence the sound came; but the cemetery blocked my view. The wolf still continued to yelp in a strange way, and a red glare began to move round the grove of cypresses, as though following the sound. As the voices drew closer, the wolf yelped faster and louder. I feared to make either sound or motion. Nearer came the red glow, over the white pall which stretched into the darkness around me. Then all at once from beyond the trees there came at a trot a troop of horsemen bearing torches. The wolf rose from my breast and made for the cemetery. I saw one of the horsemen (soldiers by their caps and their long military cloaks) raise his carbine and take aim. A companion knocked up his arm, and I heard the ball whizz over my head. He had evidently taken my body for that of the wolf. Another sighted the animal as it slunk away, and a shot followed. Then, at a gallop, the troop rode forward—some towards me, others following the wolf as it disappeared amongst the snow-clad cypresses.

As they drew nearer I tried to move, but was powerless, although I could see and hear all that went on around me. Two or three of the soldiers jumped from their horses and knelt beside me. One of them raised my head, and placed his hand over my heart.

'Good news, comrades!' he cried. 'His heart still beats!'

Then some brandy was poured down my throat; it put vigour into me, and I was able to open my eyes fully and look around. Lights and shadows were moving among the trees, and I heard men call to one another. They drew together, uttering frightened exclamations; and the lights flashed as the others came pouring out of the cemetery pell-mell, like men possessed. When the further ones came close to us, those who were around me asked them eagerly:

'Well, have you found him?'

The reply rang out hurriedly:

'No! no! Come away quick—quick! This is no place to stay, and on this of all nights!'

'What was it?' was the question, asked in all manner of keys. The answer came variously and all indefinitely as though the men were moved by some common impulse to speak, yet were restrained by some common fear from giving their thoughts.

'It—it—indeed!' gibbered one, whose wits had plainly given out for the moment.

'A wolf—and yet not a wolf!' another put in shudderingly.

'No use trying for him without the sacred bullet,' a third remarked in a more ordinary manner.

'Serve us right for coming out on this night! Truly we have earned our thousand marks!' were the ejaculations of a fourth.

'There was blood on the broken marble,' another said after a pause—'the lightning never brought that there. And for him—is he safe? Look at his throat! See, comrades, the wolf has been lying on him and keeping his blood warm.'

The officer looked at my throat and replied:

'He is all right; the skin is not pierced. What does it all mean? We should never have found him but for the yelping of the wolf.'

'What became of it?' asked the man who was holding up my head, and who seemed the least panic-stricken of the party, for his hands were steady and without tremor. On his sleeve was the chevron of a petty officer.

'It went to its home,' answered the man, whose long face was pallid, and who actually shook with terror as he glanced around him fearfully. 'There are graves enough there in which it may lie. Come, comrades—come quickly! Let us leave this cursed spot.'

The officer raised me to a sitting posture, as he uttered a word of command; then several men placed me upon a horse. He sprang to the saddle behind me, took me in his arms, gave the word to advance; and, turning our faces away from the cypresses, we rode away in swift, military order.

As yet my tongue refused its office, and I was perforce silent. I must have fallen asleep; for the next thing I remembered was finding myself standing up, supported by a soldier on each side of me. It was almost broad daylight, and to the north a red streak of sunlight was reflected, like a path of blood, over the waste of snow. The officer was telling the men to say nothing of what they had seen, except that they found an English stranger, guarded by a large dog.

'Dog! That was no dog,' cut in the man who had exhibited such fear. 'I think I know a wolf when I see one.'

The young officer answered calmly: 'I said a dog.'

'Dog!' reiterated the other ironically. It was evident that his courage was rising with the sun; and, pointing to me, he said, 'Look at his throat. Is that the work of a dog, master?'

Instinctively I raised my hand to my throat, and as I touched it I cried out in pain. The men crowded round to look, some stooping down from their saddles; and again there came the calm voice of the young officer:

'A dog, as I said. If aught else were said we should only be laughed at.'

I was then mounted behind a trooper, and we rode on into the suburbs of Munich. Here we came across a stray carriage, into which I was lifted, and it was driven off to the Quatre Saisons—the young officer accompanying me, whilst a trooper followed with his horse, and the others rode off to their barracks.

When we arrived, Herr Delbrück rushed so quickly down the steps to meet me, that it was apparent he had been watching within. Taking me by both hands he solicitously led me in. The officer saluted me and was turning to withdraw, when I recognised his purpose, and insisted that he should come to my rooms. Over a glass of wine I warmly thanked him and his brave comrades for saving me. He replied simply that he was more than glad, and that Herr Delbrück had at the first taken steps to make all the searching party pleased; at which ambiguous utterance the maître d'hôtel smiled, while the officer pleaded duty and withdrew.

'But Herr Delbrück,' I enquired, 'how and why was it that the soldiers searched for me?'

He shrugged his shoulders, as if in depreciation of his own deed, as he replied:

'I was so fortunate as to obtain leave from the commander of the regiment in which I served, to ask for volunteers.'

'But how did you know I was lost?' I asked.

'The driver came hither with the remains of his carriage, which had been upset when the horses ran away.'

'But surely you would not send a search-party of soldiers merely on this account?'

'Oh, no!' he answered; 'but even before the coachman arrived, I had this telegram from the Boyar whose guest you are,' and he took from his pocket a telegram which he handed to me, and I read:

> *Bistritz*. Be careful of my guest—his safety is most precious to me. Should aught happen to him, or if he be missed, spare nothing to find him and ensure his safety. He is English and therefore adventurous. There are often dangers from snow and wolves and night. Lose not a moment if you suspect harm to him. I answer your zeal with my fortune.—*Dracula*.

As I held the telegram in my hand, the room seemed to whirl

around me; and, if the attentive maître d'hôtel had not caught me, I think I should have fallen. There was something so strange in all this, something so weird and impossible to imagine, that there grew on me a sense of my being in some way the sport of opposite forces—the mere vague idea of which seemed in a way to paralyse me. I was certainly under some form of mysterious protection. From a distant country had come, in the very nick of time, a message that took me out of the danger of the snow-sleep and the jaws of the wolf.

20

THE APPARITION

Guy de Maupassant

'I also know of something strange, so strange that it has haunted me all my life.'

The subject of sequestration of the person came up in speaking of a recent lawsuit, and each of us had a story to tell—a true story, he said. We had been spending the evening together at an old family mansion in the Rue de Grenelle, just a party of intimate friends. The old Marquis de la Tour-Samuel, who was eighty-two, rose, and, leaning his elbow on the mantelpiece, said in his somewhat shaky voice:

'I also know of something strange, so strange that it has haunted me all my life. It is now fifty-six years since the incident occurred, and yet not a month passes that I do not see it again in a dream, so great is the impression of fear it has left on my mind. For ten minutes I experienced such horrible fright that ever since then a sort of constant terror has remained with me. Sudden noises startle me violently, and objects imperfectly distinguished at night inspire me with a mad desire to flee from them. In short, I am afraid of the dark!

'But I would not have acknowledged that before I reached my present age. Now I can say anything. I have never receded before real danger, ladies. It is, therefore, permissible, at eighty-two years of age, not to be brave in presence of imaginary danger.

'That affair so completely upset me, caused me such deep and mysterious and terrible distress, that I never spoke of it to anyone. I will now tell it to you exactly as it happened, without any attempt at explanation.

'In July, 1827, I was stationed at Rouen. One day as I was walking along the quay I met a man whom I thought I recognized without being able to recall exactly who he was. Instinctively I made a movement to stop. The stranger perceived it and at once extended his hand.

'He was a friend to whom I had been deeply attached as a youth. For five years I had not seen him; he seemed to have aged half a century. His hair was quite white and he walked bent over as though completely exhausted. He apparently understood my surprise, and he told me of the misfortune which had shattered his life.

'Having fallen madly in love with a young girl, he had married her, but after a year of more than earthly happiness she died suddenly of an affection of the heart. He left his country home on the very day of her burial and came to his town house in Rouen, where he lived, alone and unhappy, so sad and wretched that he thought constantly of suicide.

'"Since I have found you again in this manner," he said, "I will ask you to render me an important service. It is to go and get me out of the desk in my bedroom—our bedroom—some papers of which I have urgent need. I cannot send a servant or a business clerk, as discretion and absolute silence are necessary. As for myself, nothing on earth would induce me to reenter that house. I will give you the key of the room, which I myself locked on leaving, and the key of my desk, also a few words for my gardener, telling him to open the chateau for you. But come and breakfast with me tomorrow and we will arrange all that."

'I promised to do him the slight favor he asked. It was, for that matter, only a ride which I could make in an hour on horseback, his property being but a few miles distant from Rouen.

'At ten o'clock the following day I breakfasted, tete-a-tete, with my friend, but he scarcely spoke.

'He begged me to pardon him; the thought of the visit I was about to make to that room, the scene of his dead happiness, overcame him, he said. He, indeed, seemed singularly agitated and preoccupied, as though undergoing some mysterious mental struggle.

'At length he explained to me exactly what I had to do. It was very simple. I must take two packages of letters and a roll of papers from the first right-hand drawer of the desk, of which I had the key. He added:

'"I need not beg you to refrain from glancing at them."

'I was wounded at that remark and told him so somewhat sharply. He stammered:

'"Forgive me, I suffer so," and tears came to his eyes.

'At about one o'clock I took leave of him to accomplish my mission.

'The weather was glorious, and I trotted across the fields, listening to the song of the larks and the rhythmical clang of my sword against my boot. Then I entered the forest and walked my horse. Branches of trees caressed my face as I passed, and now and then I caught a leaf with my teeth and chewed it, from sheer gladness of heart at being alive and vigorous on such a radiant day.

'As I approached the chateau I took from my pocket the letter I had for the gardener, and was astonished at finding it sealed. I was so irritated that I was about to turn back without having fulfilled my promise, but reflected that I should thereby display undue susceptibility. My friend in his troubled condition might easily have fastened the envelope without noticing that he did so.

'The manor looked as if it had been abandoned for twenty years. The open gate was falling from its hinges, the walks were overgrown with grass and the flower beds were no longer distinguishable.

'The noise I made by kicking at a shutter brought out an old man from a side door. He seemed stunned with astonishment at seeing me. On receiving my letter, he read it, reread it, turned it over and over, looked me up and down, put the paper in his pocket and finally said:

'"Well, what is it you wish?"

'I replied shortly:

'"You ought to know, since you have just read your master's orders. I wish to enter the chateau."

'He seemed overcome.

'"Then you are going in—into her room?"

'I began to lose patience.

'"Damn it! Are you presuming to question me?"

'He stammered in confusion:

'"No—sir—but—but it has not been opened since—since the death. If you will be kind enough to wait five minutes I will go and—and see if—"

'I interrupted him angrily:

'"See here, what do you mean by your tricks?

'"You know very well you cannot enter the room, since here is the key!"

'He no longer objected.

'"Then, sir, I will show you the way."

'"Show me the staircase and leave me. I'll find my way without you."

'"But—sir—indeed—"

'This time I lost patience, and pushing him aside, went into the house.

'I first went through the kitchen, then two rooms occupied by this man and his wife. I then crossed a large hall, mounted a staircase and recognized the door described by my friend.

'I easily opened it, and entered the apartment. It was so dark that at first I could distinguish nothing. I stopped short, disagreeably affected by that disagreeable, musty odor of closed, unoccupied rooms. As my eyes slowly became accustomed to the darkness I saw plainly enough a large and disordered bedroom, the bed without sheets but still retaining its mattresses and pillows, on one of which was a deep impression, as though an elbow or a head had recently rested there.

'The chairs all seemed out of place. I noticed that a door, doubtless that of a closet, had remained half open.

'I first went to the window, which I opened to let in the

light, but the fastenings of the shutters had grown so rusty that I could not move them. I even tried to break them with my sword, but without success. As I was growing irritated over my useless efforts and could now see fairly well in the semi-darkness, I gave up the hope of getting more light, and went over to the writing desk.

'I seated myself in an armchair and, letting down the lid of the desk, I opened the drawer designated. It was full to the top. I needed but three packages, which I knew how to recognize, and began searching for them.

'I was straining my eyes in the effort to read the superscriptions when I seemed to hear, or, rather, feel, something rustle back of me. I paid no attention, believing that a draught from the window was moving some drapery. But in a minute or so another movement, almost imperceptible, sent a strangely disagreeable little shiver over my skin. It was so stupid to be affected, even slightly, that self-respect prevented my turning around. I had just found the second package I needed and was about to lay my hand on the third when a long and painful sigh, uttered just at my shoulder, made me bound like a madman from my seat and land several feet off. As I jumped I had turned round my hand on the hilt of my sword, and, truly, if I had not felt it at my side I should have taken to my heels like a coward.

'A tall woman dressed in white, stood gazing at me from the back of the chair where I had been sitting an instant before.

'Such a shudder ran through all my limbs that I nearly fell backward. No one who has not experienced it can understand that frightful, unreasoning terror! The mind becomes vague, the heart ceases to beat, the entire body grows as limp as a sponge.

'I do not believe in ghosts, nevertheless I collapsed from a hideous dread of the dead, and I suffered, oh! I suffered in a few moments more than in all the rest of my life from the irresistible terror of the supernatural. If she had not spoken I should have died perhaps. But she spoke, she spoke in a sweet, sad voice that set my nerves vibrating. I dare not say that I became master of myself and recovered my reason. No! I was terrified and scarcely knew what I was doing. But a certain innate pride, a remnant of soldierly instinct, made me, almost in spite of myself, maintain a bold front. She said:

'"Oh, sir, you can render me a great service."

'I wanted to reply, but it was impossible for me to pronounce a word. Only a vague sound came from my throat. She continued:

'"Will you? You can save me, cure me. I suffer frightfully. I suffer, oh! how I suffer!" and she slowly seated herself in my armchair, still looking at me.

'"Will you?" she said.

'I nodded in assent, my voice still being paralyzed.

'Then she held out to me a tortoise-shell comb and murmured:

'"Comb my hair, oh! comb my hair; that will cure me; it must be combed. Look at my head—how I suffer; and my hair pulls so!"

'Her hair, unbound, very long and very black, it seemed to me, hung over the back of the armchair and touched the floor.

'Why did I promise? Why did I take that comb with a shudder, and why did I hold in my hands her long black hair that gave my skin a frightful cold sensation, as though I were handling snakes? I cannot tell.

'That sensation has remained in my fingers, and I still tremble in recalling it.

'I combed her hair. I handled, I know not how, those icy locks. I twisted, knotted, and unknotted, and braided them. She sighed, bowed her head, seemed happy. Suddenly she said, "Thank you!" snatched the comb from my hands and fled by the door that I had noticed ajar.

'Left alone, I experienced for several seconds the horrible agitation of one who awakens from a nightmare. At length I regained my senses. I ran to the window and with a mighty effort burst open the shutters, letting a flood of light into the room. Immediately I sprang to the door by which that being had departed. I found it closed and immovable!

'Then the mad desire to flee overcame me like a panic—the

panic which soldiers know in battle. I seized the three packets of letters on the open desk, ran from the room, dashed down the stairs four steps at a time, found myself outside, I know not how, and, perceiving my horse a few steps off, leaped into the saddle and galloped away.

'I stopped only when I reached Rouen and alighted at my lodgings. Throwing the reins to my orderly, I fled to my room and shut myself in to reflect. For an hour I anxiously asked myself if I were not the victim of a hallucination. Undoubtedly I had had one of those incomprehensible nervous attacks, those exaltations of mind that give rise to visions and are the stronghold of the supernatural. And I was about to believe I had seen a vision, had a hallucination, when, as I approached the window, my eyes fell, by chance, upon my breast. My military cape was covered with long black hairs! One by one, with trembling fingers, I plucked them off and threw them away.

'I then called my orderly. I was too disturbed, too upset to go and see my friend that day, and I also wished to reflect more fully upon what I ought to tell him. I sent him his letters, for which he gave the soldier a receipt. He asked after me most particularly, and, on being told I was ill—had had a sunstroke—appeared exceedingly anxious. Next morning I went to him, determined to tell him the truth. He had gone out the evening before and had not yet returned. I called again during the day; my friend was still absent. After waiting a week longer without news of him, I notified the authorities and a judicial search was instituted. Not the slightest trace of his whereabouts or manner of disappearance was discovered.

'A minute inspection of the abandoned chateau revealed nothing of a suspicious character. There was no indication that a woman had been concealed there.

'After fruitless researches all further efforts were abandoned, and for fifty-six years I have heard nothing; I know no more than before.'

21

THE MINISTER'S BLACK VEIL

Nathaniel Hawthorne

...such were the terrors of the black veil,
even when Death had bared his visage...

The sexton stood in the porch of Milford meeting-house, pulling busily at the bell-rope. The old people of the village came stooping along the street. Children, with bright faces, tripped merrily beside their parents, or mimicked a graver gait, in the conscious dignity of their Sunday clothes. Spruce bachelors looked sidelong at the pretty maidens, and fancied that the Sabbath sunshine made them prettier than on week days. When the throng had mostly streamed into the porch, the sexton began to toll the bell, keeping his eye on the Reverend Mr Hooper's door. The first glimpse of the clergyman's figure was the signal for the bell to cease its summons.

'But what has good Parson Hooper got upon his face?' cried the sexton in astonishment.

All within hearing immediately turned about, and beheld the semblance of Mr Hooper, pacing slowly his meditative way towards the meeting-house. With one accord they started, expressing more wonder than if some strange minister were coming to dust the cushions of Mr Hooper's pulpit.

'Are you sure it is our parson?' inquired Goodman Gray of the sexton.

'Of a certainty it is good Mr Hooper,' replied the sexton. 'He was to have exchanged pulpits with Parson Shute, of Westbury; but Parson Shute sent to excuse himself yesterday, being to preach a funeral sermon.'

The cause of so much amazement may appear sufficiently slight. Mr Hooper, a gentlemanly person, of about thirty, though still a bachelor, was dressed with due clerical neatness, as if a careful wife had starched his band, and brushed the weekly dust from his Sunday's garb. There was but one thing remarkable in his appearance. Swathed about his forehead, and hanging down over his face, so low as to be shaken by his breath, Mr Hooper had on a black veil. On a nearer view it seemed to consist of two folds of crape, which entirely concealed his features, except the mouth and chin, but probably did not intercept his sight, further than to give a darkened aspect to all living and inanimate things. With this gloomy shade before him, good Mr Hooper walked onward, at a slow and quiet pace, stooping somewhat, and looking on the ground, as is customary with abstracted men, yet nodding kindly to those of his parishioners who still waited on the meeting-house steps. But so wonder-struck were they that his greeting hardly met with a return.

'I can't really feel as if good Mr Hooper's face was behind that piece of crape,' said the sexton.

'I don't like it,' muttered an old woman, as she hobbled into the meeting-house. 'He has changed himself into something awful, only by hiding his face.'

'Our parson has gone mad!' cried Goodman Gray, following him across the threshold.

A rumour of some unaccountable phenomenon had preceded Mr Hooper into the meeting-house, and set all the congregation astir. Few could refrain from twisting their heads towards the door; many stood upright, and turned directly about; while several little boys clambered upon the seats, and came down again with a terrible racket. There was a general bustle, a rustling of the women's gowns and shuffling of the men's feet, greatly at variance with that hushed repose which should attend the entrance of the minister. But Mr Hooper appeared not to notice the perturbation of his people. He entered with an almost noiseless step, bent his head mildly to the pews on each side, and bowed as he passed his oldest parishioner, a white-haired great grandsire, who occupied an arm-chair in the centre of the aisle. It was strange to observe how slowly this venerable man became conscious of something singular in the appearance of his pastor. He seemed not fully to partake of the prevailing wonder, till Mr Hooper had ascended the stairs, and showed himself in the pulpit, face to face with his congregation, except for the black veil. That mysterious emblem was never once withdrawn. It shook with his measured breath, as he gave out the psalm; it threw its obscurity between him and the holy page, as he read the Scriptures; and while he prayed, the veil lay heavily on his uplifted countenance. Did he seek to hide it from the dread Being whom he was addressing?

Such was the effect of this simple piece of crape, that more than one woman of delicate nerves was forced to leave the meeting-house. Yet perhaps the pale-faced congregation was almost as fearful a sight to the minister, as his black veil to them.

Mr Hooper had the reputation of a good preacher, but not an energetic one: he strove to win his people heavenward by mild, persuasive influences, rather than to drive them thither by the thunders of the Word. The sermon which he now delivered was marked by the same characteristics of style and manner as the general series of his pulpit oratory. But there was something, either in the sentiment of the discourse itself, or in the imagination of the auditors, which made it greatly the most powerful effort that they had ever heard from their pastor's lips. It was tinged, rather more darkly than usual, with the gentle gloom of Mr Hooper's temperament. The subject had reference to secret sin, and those sad mysteries which we hide from our nearest and dearest, and would fain conceal from our own consciousness, even forgetting that the Omniscient can detect them. A subtle power was breathed into his words. Each member of the congregation, the most innocent girl, and the man of hardened breast, felt as if the preacher had crept upon them, behind his awful veil, and discovered their hoarded iniquity of deed or thought. Many spread their clasped hands on their bosoms. There was nothing terrible in what Mr Hooper said, at least, no violence; and yet, with every tremor of his melancholy voice, the hearers quaked. An unsought pathos came hand in hand with awe. So sensible were the audience of some unwonted attribute in their minister, that they longed for a breath of wind to blow aside the veil, almost believing that a stranger's visage would be discovered, though the form, gesture, and voice were those of Mr Hooper.

At the close of the services, the people hurried out with indecorous confusion, eager to communicate their pent-up amazement, and conscious of lighter spirits the moment they lost sight of the black veil. Some gathered in little circles, huddled closely together, with their mouths all whispering in the centre; some went homeward alone, wrapt in silent meditation; some talked loudly, and profaned the Sabbath day with ostentatious laughter. A few shook their sagacious heads, intimating that they could penetrate the mystery; while one or two affirmed that there was no mystery at all, but only that Mr Hooper's eyes were so weakened by the midnight lamp, as to require a shade. After a brief interval, forth came good Mr Hooper also, in the rear of his flock. Turning his veiled face from one group to another, he paid due reverence to the hoary heads, saluted the middle aged with kind dignity as their friend and spiritual guide, greeted the young with mingled authority and love, and laid his hands on the little children's heads to bless them. Such was always his custom on the Sabbath day. Strange and bewildered looks repaid him for his courtesy. None; as on former occasions, aspired to the honour of walking by their pastor's side. Old Squire Saunders, doubtless by an accidental lapse of memory, neglected to invite Mr Hooper to his table, where the good clergyman had been wont to bless the food, almost every Sunday since his settlement. He returned, therefore, to the parsonage, and, at the moment of closing the door, was observed to look back upon the people, all of whom had their eyes fixed upon the minister. A sad smile gleamed faintly from beneath the black veil, and flickered about his mouth, glimmering as he disappeared.

'How strange,' said a lady, 'that a simple black veil, such as any woman might wear on her bonnet, should become such a terrible thing on Mr Hooper's face!'

'Something must surely be amiss with Mr Hooper's intellects,' observed her husband, the physician of the village. 'But the strangest part of the affair is the effect of this vagary, even on a sober-minded man like myself. The black veil, though it covers only our pastor's face, throws its influence over his whole person, and makes him ghostlike from head to foot. Do you not feel it so?'

'Truly do I,' replied the lady; 'and I would not be alone with him for the world. I wonder he is not afraid to be alone with himself!'

'Men sometimes are so,' said her husband.

The afternoon service was attended with similar circumstances. At its conclusion, the bell tolled for the funeral of a young lady. The relatives and friends were assembled in the house, and the more distant acquaintances stood about the door, speaking of the good qualities of the deceased, when their talk was interrupted by the appearance of Mr Hooper, still covered with his black veil. It was now an appropriate emblem. The clergyman stepped into the room where the corpse was laid, and bent over the coffin, to take a last farewell of his deceased parishioner. As he stooped, the veil hung straight down from his forehead, so that, if her eye-lids had not been closed forever, the dead maiden might have seen his face. Could Mr Hooper be fearful of her glance, that he so hastily caught back the black veil? A person who watched the interview between the dead and living, scrupled not to affirm, that, at the instant when the clergyman's features were disclosed, the corpse had slightly shuddered, rustling the shroud and muslin cap, though the countenance retained the composure of death. A superstitious old woman was the only witness of this prodigy. From the coffin Mr Hooper passed into the chamber of the mourners, and thence to the head of the staircase, to make the funeral prayer. It was a tender and heart-dissolving prayer, full of sorrow, yet so imbued with celestial hopes, that the music of a heavenly harp, swept by the fingers of the dead, seemed faintly to be heard among the saddest accents of the minister. The people trembled, though they but darkly understood him when he prayed that they, and himself, and all of mortal race, might be ready, as he trusted this young maiden had been, for the dreadful hour that should snatch the veil from their faces. The bearers went heavily forth, and the mourners followed, saddening all the street, with the dead before them, and Mr Hooper in his black veil behind.

'Why do you look back?' said one in the procession to his partner.

'I had a fancy,' replied she, 'that the minister and the maiden's spirit were walking hand in hand.'

'And so had I, at the same moment,' said the other.

That night, the handsomest couple in Milford village were to be joined in wedlock. Though reckoned a melancholy man, Mr Hooper had a placid cheerfulness for such occasions, which often excited a sympathetic smile where livelier merriment would have been thrown away. There was no quality of his disposition which made him more beloved than this. The company at the wedding awaited his arrival with impatience, trusting that the strange awe, which had gathered over him throughout the day, would now be dispelled. But such was not the result. When Mr Hooper came, the first thing that their eyes rested on was the same horrible black veil, which had added deeper gloom to the funeral, and could portend nothing but evil to the wedding. Such was its immediate effect on the guests that a cloud seemed to have rolled duskily from beneath the black crape, and dimmed the light of the candles. The bridal pair stood up before the minister. But the bride's cold fingers quivered in the tremulous hand of the bridegroom, and her deathlike paleness caused a whisper that the maiden who had been buried a few hours before was come from her grave to be married. If ever another wedding were so dismal, it was that famous one where they tolled the wedding knell. After performing the ceremony, Mr Hooper raised a glass of wine to his lips, wishing happiness to the new-married couple in a strain of mild pleasantry that ought to have brightened the features of the guests, like a cheerful gleam from the hearth. At that instant, catching a glimpse of his figure in the looking-glass, the black veil involved his own spirit in the horror with which it overwhelmed all others. His frame shuddered, his lips grew white, he spilt the untasted wine upon the carpet, and rushed forth into the darkness. For the Earth, too, had on her Black Veil.

The next day, the whole village of Milford talked of little else than Parson Hooper's black veil. That, and the mystery concealed behind it, supplied a topic for discussion between acquaintances meeting in the street, and good women gossiping at their open windows. It was the first item of news that the tavern-keeper told to his guests. The children babbled of it on their way to school. One imitative little imp covered his face with an old black handkerchief, thereby so affrighting his playmates that the panic seized himself, and he well-nigh lost his wits by his own waggery.

It was remarkable that of all the busybodies and impertinent people in the parish, not one ventured to put the plain question to Mr Hooper, wherefore he did this thing. Hitherto, whenever there appeared the slightest call for such interference, he had never lacked advisers, nor shown himself averse to be guided by their judgment. If he erred at all, it was by so painful a degree of self-distrust, that even the mildest censure would lead him to consider an indifferent action as a crime. Yet, though so well acquainted with this amiable weakness, no individual among his parishioners chose to make the black veil a subject of friendly remonstrance. There was a feeling of dread, neither plainly confessed nor carefully concealed, which caused each to shift the responsibility upon another, till at length it was found expedient to send a deputation of the church, in order to deal with Mr Hooper about the mystery, before it should grow into a scandal. Never did an embassy so ill discharge its duties. The minister received then with friendly courtesy, but became silent, after they were seated, leaving to his visitors the whole burden of introducing their important business. The topic, it might be supposed, was obvious enough. There was the black veil swathed round Mr Hooper's forehead, and concealing every feature above his placid mouth, on which, at times, they could perceive the glimmering of a melancholy smile. But that piece of crape, to their imagination, seemed to hang down before his heart, the symbol of a fearful secret between him and them. Were the veil but cast aside, they might speak freely of it, but not till then. Thus they sat a considerable time, speechless, confused, and shrinking uneasily from Mr Hooper's eye, which they felt to be fixed upon them with an invisible glance. Finally, the deputies returned abashed to their constituents, pronouncing the matter too weighty to be handled, except by a council of the churches, if, indeed, it might not require a general synod.

But there was one person in the village unappalled by the awe with which the black veil had impressed all beside herself. When the deputies returned without an explanation, or even venturing to demand one, she, with the calm energy of her character, determined to chase away the strange cloud that appeared to be settling round Mr Hooper, every moment more darkly than before. As his plighted wife, it should be her privilege to know what the black veil concealed. At the minister's first visit, therefore, she entered upon the subject with a direct simplicity, which made the task easier both for him and her. After he had seated himself, she fixed her eyes steadfastly upon the veil, but could discern nothing of the dreadful gloom that had so overawed the multitude: it was but a double fold of crape, hanging down from his forehead to his mouth, and slightly stirring with his breath.

'No,' said she aloud, and smiling, 'there is nothing terrible in this piece of crape, except that it hides a face which I am always glad to look upon. Come, good sir, let the sun shine from behind the cloud. First lay-aside your black veil: then tell me why you put it on.'

Mr Hooper's smile glimmered faintly.

'There is an hour to come,' said he, 'when all of us shall cast aside our veils. Take it not amiss, beloved friend, if I wear this piece of crape till then.'

'Your words are a mystery, too,' returned the young lady. 'Take away the veil from them, at least.'

'Elizabeth, I will,' said he, 'so far as my vow may suffer me. Know, then, this veil is a type and a symbol, and I am bound to wear it ever, both in light and darkness, in solitude and before the gaze of multitudes, and as with strangers, so with my familiar friends. No mortal eye will see it withdrawn. This dismal shade must separate me from the world: even you, Elizabeth, can never come behind it!'

'What grievous affliction hath befallen you,' she earnestly inquired, 'that you should thus darken your eyes forever?'

'If it be a sign of mourning,' replied Mr Hooper, 'I, perhaps, like most other mortals, have sorrows dark enough to be typified by a black veil.'

'But what if the world will not believe that it is the type of an innocent sorrow?' urged Elizabeth. 'Beloved and respected as you are, there may be whispers that you hide your face under the consciousness of secret sin. For the sake of your holy office, do away this scandal!'

The colour rose into her cheeks as she intimated the nature of the rumors that were already abroad in the village. But Mr Hooper's mildness did not forsake him. He even smiled again—that same sad smile, which always appeared like a faint glimmering of light, proceeding from the obscurity beneath the veil.

'If I hide my face for sorrow, there is cause enough,' he merely replied; 'and if I cover it for secret sin, what mortal might not do the same?'

And with this gentle, but unconquerable obstinacy did he resist all her entreaties. At length Elizabeth sat silent. For a few moments she appeared lost in thought, considering, probably, what new methods might be tried to withdraw her lover from so dark a fantasy, which, if it had no other meaning, was perhaps a symptom of mental disease. Though of a firmer character than his own, the tears rolled down her cheeks. But, in an instant, as it were, a new feeling took the place of sorrow: her eyes were fixed insensibly on the black veil, when, like a sudden twilight in the air, its terrors fell around her. She arose, and stood trembling before him.

'And do you feel it then, at last?' said he mournfully.

She made no reply, but covered her eyes with her hand, and turned to leave the room. He rushed forward and caught her arm.

'Have patience with me, Elizabeth!' cried he, passionately. 'Do not desert me, though this veil must be between us here on earth. Be mine, and hereafter there shall be no veil over my face, no darkness between our souls! It is but a mortal veil—it is not for eternity! O! you know not how lonely I am, and how frightened, to be alone behind my black veil. Do not leave me in this miserable obscurity forever!'

'Lift the veil but once, and look me in the face,' said she.

'Never! It cannot be!' replied Mr Hooper.

'Then farewell!' said Elizabeth.

She withdrew her arm from his grasp, and slowly departed, pausing at the door, to give one long shuddering gaze, that seemed almost to penetrate the mystery of the black veil. But, even amid his grief, Mr Hooper smiled to think that only a material emblem had separated him from happiness, though the horrors, which it shadowed forth, must be drawn darkly between the fondest of lovers.

From that time no attempts were made to remove Mr Hooper's black veil, or, by a direct appeal, to discover the secret which it was supposed to hide. By persons who claimed a superiority to popular prejudice, it was reckoned merely an eccentric whim, such as often mingles with the sober actions of men otherwise rational, and tinges them all with its own semblance of insanity. But with the multitude, good Mr Hooper was irreparbly a bugbear. He could not walk the street with any peace of mind, so conscious was he that the gentle and timid would turn aside to avoid him, and that others would make it a point of hardihood to throw themselves in his way. The impertinence of the latter class compelled him to give up his customary walk at sunset to the burial ground; for when he leaned pensively over the gate, there would always be faces behind the gravestones, peeping at his black veil. A fable went the rounds that the stare of the dead people drove him thence. It grieved him, to the very depth of his kind heart, to observe how the children fled from his approach, breaking up their merriest sports, while his melancholy figure was yet afar off. Their instinctive dread caused him to feel more strongly than aught else, that a preternatural horror was interwoven with the threads of the black crape. In truth, his own antipathy to the veil was known to be so great, that he never willingly passed before a mirror, nor stooped to drink at a still fountain, lest, in its peaceful bosom, he should be affrighted by himself. This was what gave plausibility to the whispers, that Mr Hooper's conscience tortured him for some great crime too horrible to be entirely concealed, or otherwise than so obscurely intimated. Thus, from beneath the black veil, there rolled a cloud into the sunshine, an ambiguity of sin or sorrow, which enveloped the poor minister, so that love or sympathy could never reach him. It was said that ghost and fiend consorted with him there. With self-shudderings and outward terrors, he walked continually in its shadow, groping darkly within his own soul, or gazing through a medium that saddened the whole world. Even the lawless wind, it was believed, respected his dreadful secret, and never blew aside the veil. But still good Mr Hooper sadly smiled at the pale visages of the worldly throng as he passed by.

Among all its bad influences, the black veil had the one desirable effect, of making its wearer a very efficient clergyman. By the aid of his mysterious emblem—for there was no other apparent cause—he became a man of awful power over souls that were in agony for sin. His converts always regarded him with a dread peculiar to themselves, affirming, though but figuratively, that, before he brought them to celestial light, they had been with him behind the black veil. Its gloom, indeed, enabled him to sympathize with all dark affections. Dying sinners cried aloud for Mr Hooper, and would not yield their breath till he appeared; though ever, as he stooped to whisper consolation, they shuddered at the veiled face so near their own. Such were the terrors of the black veil, even when Death had bared his visage! Strangers came long distances to attend service at his church, with the mere idle purpose of gazing at his figure, because it was forbidden them to behold his face. But many were made to quake ere they departed! Once, during Governor Belcher's administration, Mr Hooper was appointed to preach the election sermon. Covered with his black veil, he stood before the chief magistrate, the council, and the representatives, and wrought so deep an impression, that the legislative measures of that year were characterized by all the gloom and piety of our earliest ancestral sway.

In this manner Mr Hooper spent a long life, irreproachable in outward act, yet shrouded in dismal suspicions; kind and loving, though unloved, and dimly feared; a man apart from men, shunned in their health and joy, but ever summoned to their aid in mortal anguish. As years wore on, shedding their snows above his sable veil, he acquired a name throughout the New England churches, and they called him Father Hooper. Nearly all his parishioners, who were of mature age when he was settled, had been borne away by many a funeral: he had one congregation in the church, and a more crowded one in the churchyard; and having wrought so late into the evening, and done his work so well, it was now good Father Hooper's turn to rest.

Several persons were visible by the shaded candlelight, in the death chamber of the old clergyman. Natural connections he had none. But there was the decorously grave, though unmoved physician, seeking only to mitigate the last pangs of the patient whom he could not save. There were the deacons, and other eminently pious members of his church. There, also, was the Reverend Mr Clark, of Westbury, a young and zealous divine, who had ridden in haste to pray by the bedside of the expiring minister. There was the nurse, no hired handmaiden of death, but one whose calm affection had endured thus long in secrecy, in solitude, amid the chill of age, and would not perish, even at the dying hour. Who, but Elizabeth! And there lay the hoary head of good Father Hooper upon the death pillow, with the black veil still swathed about his brow, and reaching down over his face, so that each more difficult gasp of his faint breath caused it to stir. All through life that piece of crape had hung between him and the world: it had separated him from cheerful brotherhood and woman's love, and kept him in that saddest of all prisons, his own heart; and still it lay upon his face, as if to deepen the gloom of his darksome chamber, and shade him from the sunshine of eternity.

For some time previous, his mind had been confused, wavering doubtfully between the past and the present, and hovering forward, as it were, at intervals, into the indistinctness of the world to come. There had been feverish turns, which tossed him from side to side, and wore away what little strength he had. But in his most convulsive struggles, and in the wildest vagaries of his intellect, when no other thought retained its sober influence, he still showed an awful solicitude lest the black veil should slip aside. Even if his bewildered soul could have forgotten, there was a faithful woman at this pillow, who, with averted eyes, would have covered that aged face, which she had last beheld in the comeliness of manhood. At length the death-stricken old man lay quietly in the torpor of mental and bodily exhaustion, with an imperceptible pulse, and breath that grew fainter and fainter, except when a long, deep, and irregular inspiration seemed to prelude the flight of his spirit.

The minister of Westbury approached the bedside.

'Venerable Father Hooper,' said he, 'the moment of your release is at hand. Are you ready for the lifting of the veil that shuts in time from eternity?'

Father Hooper at first replied merely by a feeble motion of

his head; then, apprehensive, perhaps, that his meaning might be doubted, he exerted himself to speak.

'Yea,' said he, in faint accents, 'my soul hath a patient weariness until that veil be lifted.'

'And is it fitting,' resumed the Reverend Mr Clark, 'that a man so given to prayer, of such a blameless example, holy in deed and thought, so far as mortal judgment may pronounce; is it fitting that a father in the church should leave a shadow on his memory, that may seem to blacken a life so pure? I pray you, my venerable brother, let not this thing be! Suffer us to be gladdened by your triumphant aspect as you go to your reward. Before the veil of eternity be lifted, let me cast aside this black veil from your face!'

And thus speaking, the Reverend Mr Clark bent forward to reveal the mystery of so many years. But, exerting a sudden energy, that made all the beholders stand aghast, Father Hooper snatched both his hands from beneath the bedclothes, and pressed them strongly on the black veil, resolute to struggle, if the minister of Westbury would contend with a dying man.

'Never!' cried the veiled clergyman. 'On earth, never!'

'Dark old man!' exclaimed the affrighted minister, 'with what horrible crime upon your soul are you now passing to the judgment?'

Father Hooper's breath heaved; it rattled in his throat; but, with a mighty effort, grasping forward with his hands, he caught hold of life, and held it back till he should speak. He even raised himself in bed; and there he sat, shivering with the arms of death around him, while the black veil hung down, awful, at that last moment, in the gathered terrors of a life-time. And yet the faint, sad smile, so often there, now seemed to glimmer from its obscurity, and linger on Father Hooper's lips.

'Why do you tremble at me alone?' cried he, turning his veiled face round the circle of pale spectators. 'Tremble also at each other! Have men avoided me, and women shown no pity, and children screamed and fled, only for my black veil? What, but the mystery which it obscurely typifies, has made this piece of crape so awful? When the friend shows his inmost heart to his friend; the lover to his best beloved; when man does not vainly shrink from the eye of his Creator, loathsomely treasuring up the secret of his sin; then deem me a monster, for the symbol beneath which I have lived, and die! I look around me, and, lo! On every visage a Black Veil!'

While his auditors shrank from one another, in mutual affright, Father Hooper fell back upon his pillow, a veiled corpse, with a faint smile lingering on the lips. Still veiled, they laid him in his coffin, and a veiled corpse they bore him to the grave. The grass of many years has sprung up and withered on that grave, the burial stone is moss-grown, and good Mr Hooper's face is dust; but awful is still the thought that it mouldered beneath the Black Veil!

22
THE TRIAL FOR MURDER

Charles Dickens

I would bury the memory of this particular brute, if I could, as his body was buried, in Newgate Jail...

I have always noticed a prevalent want of courage, even among persons of superior intelligence and culture, as to imparting their own psychological experiences when those have been of a strange sort. Almost all men are afraid that what they could relate in such wise would find no parallel or response in a listener's internal life, and might be suspected or laughed at. A truthful traveller, who should have seen some extraordinary creature in the likeness of a sea-serpent, would have no fear of mentioning it; but the same traveller, having had some singular presentiment, impulse, vagary of thought, vision (so-called), dream, or other remarkable mental impression, would hesitate considerably before he would own to it. To this reticence I attribute much of the obscurity in which such subjects are involved. We do not habitually communicate our experiences of these subjective things as we do our experiences of objective creation. The consequence is, that the general stock of experience in this regard appears exceptional, and really is so, in respect of being miserably imperfect.

In what I am going to relate, I have no intention of setting up, opposing, or supporting, any theory whatever. I know the history of the Bookseller of Berlin, I have studied the case of the wife of a late Astronomer Royal as related by Sir David Brewster, and I have followed the minutest details of a much more remarkable case of Spectral Illusion occurring within my private circle of friends. It may be necessary to state as to this last, that the sufferer (a lady) was in no degree, however distant, related to me. A mistaken assumption on that head might suggest an explanation of a part of my own case—but only a part—which would be wholly without foundation. It cannot be referred to my inheritance of any developed peculiarity, nor had I ever before any at all similar experience, nor have I ever had any at all similar experience since.

It does not signify how many years ago, or how few, a certain murder was committed in England, which attracted great attention. We hear more than enough of murderers as they rise in succession to their atrocious eminence, and I would bury the memory of this particular brute, if I could, as his body was buried, in Newgate Jail. I purposely abstain from giving any direct clue to the criminal's individuality.

When the murder was first discovered, no suspicion fell—or I ought rather to say, for I cannot be too precise in my facts, it was nowhere publicly hinted that any suspicion fell—on the man who was afterwards brought to trial. As no reference was at that time made to him in the newspapers, it is obviously impossible that any description of him can at that time have been given in the newspapers. It is essential that this fact be remembered.

Unfolding at breakfast my morning paper, containing the account of that first discovery, I found it to be deeply interesting, and I read it with close attention. I read it twice, if not three times. The discovery had been made in a bedroom, and, when I laid down the paper, I was aware of a flash—rush—flow—I do not know what to call it—no word I can find is satisfactorily descriptive—in which I seemed to see that bedroom passing through my room, like a picture impossibly painted on a running river. Though almost instantaneous in its passing, it was perfectly clear; so clear that I distinctly, and with a sense of relief, observed the absence of the dead body from the bed.

It was in no romantic place that I had this curious sensation, but in chambers in Piccadilly, very near to the corner of St

James's Street. It was entirely new to me. I was in my easy-chair at the moment, and the sensation was accompanied with a peculiar shiver which started the chair from its position. (But it is to be noted that the chair ran easily on castors.) I went to one of the windows (there are two in the room, and the room is on the second floor) to refresh my eyes with the moving objects down in Piccadilly. It was a bright autumn morning, and the street was sparkling and cheerful. The wind was high. As I looked out, it brought down from the Park a quantity of fallen leaves, which a gust took, and whirled into a spiral pillar. As the pillar fell and the leaves dispersed, I saw two men on the opposite side of the way, going from West to East. They were one behind the other. The foremost man often looked back over his shoulder. The second man followed him, at a distance of some thirty paces, with his right hand menacingly raised. First, the singularity and steadiness of this threatening gesture in so public a thoroughfare attracted my attention; and next, the more remarkable circumstance that nobody heeded it. Both men threaded their way among the other passengers with a smoothness hardly consistent even with the action of walking on a pavement; and no single creature, that I could see, gave them place, touched them, or looked after them. In passing before my windows, they both stared up at me. I saw their two faces very distinctly, and I knew that I could recognise them anywhere. Not that I had consciously noticed anything very remarkable in either face, except that the man who went first had an unusually lowering appearance, and that the face of the man who followed him was of the colour of impure wax.

I am a bachelor, and my valet and his wife constitute my whole establishment. My occupation is in a certain Branch Bank, and I wish that my duties as head of a Department were as light as they are popularly supposed to be. They kept me in town that autumn, when I stood in need of change. I was not ill, but I was not well. My reader is to make the most that can be reasonably made of my feeling jaded, having a depressing sense upon me of a monotonous life, and being 'slightly dyspeptic.' I am assured by my renowned doctor that my real state of health at that time justifies no stronger description, and I quote his own from his written answer to my request for it.

As the circumstances of the murder, gradually unravelling, took stronger and stronger possession of the public mind, I kept them away from mine by knowing as little about them as was possible in the midst of the universal excitement. But I knew that a verdict of Wilful Murder had been found against the suspected murderer, and that he had been committed to Newgate for trial. I also knew that his trial had been postponed over one Sessions of the Central Criminal Court, on the ground of general prejudice and want of time for the preparation of the defence. I may further have known, but I believe I did not, when, or about when, the Sessions to which his trial stood postponed would come on.

My sitting-room, bedroom, and dressing-room, are all on one floor. With the last there is no communication but through the bedroom. True, there is a door in it, once communicating with the staircase; but a part of the fitting of my bath has been—and had then been for some years—fixed across it. At the same period, and as a part of the same arrangement,—the door had been nailed up and canvased over.

I was standing in my bedroom late one night, giving some directions to my servant before he went to bed. My face was towards the only available door of communication with the dressing-room, and it was closed. My servant's back was towards that door. While I was speaking to him, I saw it open, and a man look in, who very earnestly and mysteriously beckoned to me. That man was the man who had gone second of the two along Piccadilly, and whose face was of the colour of impure wax.

The figure, having beckoned, drew back, and closed the door. With no longer pause than was made by my crossing the bedroom, I opened the dressing-room door, and looked in. I had a lighted candle already in my hand. I felt no inward expectation of seeing the figure in the dressing-room, and I did not see it there.

Conscious that my servant stood amazed, I turned round to him, and said: 'Derrick, could you believe that in my cool senses I fancied I saw a—' As I there laid my hand upon his breast, with a sudden start he trembled violently, and said, 'O Lord, yes, sir! A dead man beckoning!'

Now I do not believe that this John Derrick, my trusty and attached servant for more than twenty years, had any impression whatever of having seen any such figure, until I touched him. The change in him was so startling, when I touched him, that I fully believe he derived his impression in some occult manner from me at that instant.

I bade John Derrick bring some brandy, and I gave him a dram, and was glad to take one myself. Of what had preceded that night's phenomenon, I told him not a single word. Reflecting on it, I was absolutely certain that I had never seen that face before, except on the one occasion in Piccadilly. Comparing its expression when beckoning at the door with its expression when it had stared up at me as I stood at my window, I came to the conclusion that on the first occasion it had sought to fasten itself upon my memory, and that on the second occasion it had made sure of being immediately remembered.

I was not very comfortable that night, though I felt a certainty, difficult to explain, that the figure would not return. At daylight I fell into a heavy sleep, from which I was awakened by John Derrick's coming to my bedside with a paper in his hand.

This paper, it appeared, had been the subject of an altercation at the door between its bearer and my servant. It was a summons to me to serve upon a Jury at the forthcoming Sessions of the Central Criminal Court at the Old Bailey. I had never before been summoned on such a Jury, as John Derrick well knew. He believed—I am not certain at this hour whether with reason or otherwise—that that class of Jurors were customarily chosen on a lower qualification than mine, and he had at first refused to accept the summons. The man who served it had taken the matter very coolly. He had said that my attendance or non-attendance was nothing to him; there the summons was; and

I should deal with it at my own peril, and not at his.

For a day or two I was undecided whether to respond to this call, or take no notice of it. I was not conscious of the slightest mysterious bias, influence, or attraction, one way or other. Of that I am as strictly sure as of every other statement that I make here. Ultimately I decided, as a break in the monotony of my life, that I would go.

The appointed morning was a raw morning in the month of November. There was a dense brown fog in Piccadilly, and it became positively black and in the last degree oppressive east of Temple Bar. I found the passages and staircases of the Court-House flaringly lighted with gas, and the Court itself similarly illuminated. I *think* that, until I was conducted by officers into the Old Court and saw its crowded state, I did not know that the Murderer was to be tried that day. I *think* that, until I was so helped into the Old Court with considerable difficulty, I did not know into which of the two Courts sitting my summons would take me. But this must not be received as a positive assertion, for I am not completely satisfied in my mind on either point.

I took my seat in the place appropriated to Jurors in waiting, and I looked about the Court as well as I could through the cloud of fog and breath that was heavy in it. I noticed the black vapour hanging like a murky curtain outside the great windows, and I noticed the stifled sound of wheels on the straw or tan that was littered in the street; also, the hum of the people gathered there, which a shrill whistle, or a louder song or hail than the rest, occasionally pierced. Soon afterwards the Judges, two in number, entered, and took their seats. The buzz in the Court was awfully hushed. The direction was given to put the Murderer to the bar. He appeared there. And in that same instant I recognised in him the first of the two men who had gone down Piccadilly.

If my name had been called then, I doubt if I could have answered to it audibly. But it was called about sixth or eighth in the panel, and I was by that time able to say, 'Here!' Now, observe. As I stepped into the box, the prisoner, who had been looking on attentively, but with no sign of concern, became violently agitated, and beckoned to his attorney. The prisoner's wish to challenge me was so manifest, that it occasioned a pause, during which the attorney, with his hand upon the dock, whispered with his client, and shook his head. I afterwards had it from that gentleman, that the prisoner's first affrighted words to him were, '*At all hazards, challenge that man*!' But that, as he would give no reason for it, and admitted that he had not even known my name until he heard it called and I appeared, it was not done.

Both on the ground already explained, that I wish to avoid reviving the unwholesome memory of that Murderer, and also because a detailed account of his long trial is by no means indispensable to my narrative, I shall confine myself closely to such incidents in the ten days and nights during which we, the Jury, were kept together, as directly bear on my own curious personal experience. It is in that, and not in the Murderer, that I seek to interest my reader. It is to that, and not to a page of the Newgate Calendar, that I beg attention.

I was chosen Foreman of the Jury. On the second morning of the trial, after evidence had been taken for two hours (I heard the church clocks strike), happening to cast my eyes over my brother jurymen, I found an inexplicable difficulty in counting them. I counted them several times, yet always with the same difficulty. In short, I made them one too many.

I touched the brother jurymen whose place was next me, and I whispered to him, 'Oblige me by counting us.' He looked surprised by the request, but turned his head and counted. 'Why,' says he, suddenly, 'we are thirt-; but no, it's not possible. No. We are twelve.'

According to my counting that day, we were always right in detail, but in the gross we were always one too many. There was no appearance—no figure—to account for it; but I had now an inward foreshadowing of the figure that was surely coming.

The Jury were housed at the London Tavern. We all slept

in one large room on separate tables, and we were constantly in the charge and under the eye of the officer sworn to hold us in safe-keeping. I see no reason for suppressing the real name of that officer. He was intelligent, highly polite, and obliging, and (I was glad to hear) much respected in the City. He had an agreeable presence, good eyes, enviable black whiskers, and a fine sonorous voice. His name was Mr Harker.

When we turned into our twelve beds at night, Mr Harker's bed was drawn across the door. On the night of the second day, not being disposed to lie down, and seeing Mr Harker sitting on his bed, I went and sat beside him, and offered him a pinch of snuff. As Mr Harker's hand touched mine in taking it from my box, a peculiar shiver crossed him, and he said, 'Who is this?'

Following Mr Harker's eyes, and looking along the room, I saw again the figure I expected—the second of the two men who had gone down Piccadilly. I rose, and advanced a few steps; then stopped, and looked round at Mr Harker. He was quite unconcerned, laughed, and said in a pleasant way, 'I thought for a moment we had a thirteenth juryman, without a bed. But I see it is the moonlight.'

Making no revelation to Mr Harker, but inviting him to take a walk with me to the end of the room, I watched what the figure did. It stood for a few moments by the bedside of each of my eleven brother jurymen, close to the pillow. It always went to the right-hand side of the bed, and always passed out crossing the foot of the next bed. It seemed, from the action of the head, merely to look down pensively at each recumbent figure. It took no notice of me, or of my bed, which was that nearest to Mr Harker's. It seemed to go out where the moonlight came in, through a high window, as by an aerial flight of stairs.

Next morning at breakfast, it appeared that everybody present had dreamed of the murdered man last night, except myself and Mr Harker.

I now felt as convinced that the second man who had gone down Piccadilly was the murdered man (so to speak), as if it had been borne into my comprehension by his immediate testimony. But even this took place, and in a manner for which I was not at all prepared.

On the fifth day of the trial, when the case for the prosecution was drawing to a close, a miniature of the murdered man, missing from his bedroom upon the discovery of the deed, and afterwards found in a hiding-place where the Murderer had been seen digging, was put in evidence. Having been identified by the witness under examination, it was handed up to the Bench, and thence handed down to be inspected by the Jury. As an officer in a black gown was making his way with it across to me, the figure of the second man who had gone down Piccadilly impetuously started from the crowd, caught the miniature from the officer, and gave it to me with his own hands, at the same time saying, in a low and hollow tone—before I saw the miniature, which was in a locket—'*I was younger then, and my face was not then drained of blood.*' It also came between me and the brother juryman to whom I would have given the miniature, and between him and the brother juryman to whom he would have given it, and so passed it on through the whole of our number, and back into my possession. Not one of them, however, detected this.

At table, and generally when we were shut up together in Mr Harker's custody, we had from the first naturally discussed the day's proceedings a good deal. On that fifth day, the case for the prosecution being closed, and we having that side of the question in a completed shape before us, our discussion was more animated and serious. Among our number was a vestryman—the densest idiot I have ever seen at large—who met the plainest evidence with the most preposterous objections, and who was sided with by two flabby parochial parasites; all the three impanelled from a district so delivered over to Fever that they ought to have been upon their own trial for five hundred Murders. When these mischievous blockheads were at their loudest, which was towards midnight, while some of us were already preparing for bed, I again saw the murdered man. He stood grimly behind them, beckoning to me. On my going towards them, and striking into the conversation, he immediately retired. This was the beginning of a separate series of appearances, confined to that long room in which we were confined. Whenever a knot of my brother jurymen laid their heads together, I saw the head of the murdered man among theirs. Whenever their comparison of notes was going against him, he would solemnly and irresistibly beckon to me.

It will be borne in mind that down to the production of the miniature, on the fifth day of the trial, I had never seen the Appearance in Court. Three changes occurred now that we entered on the case for the defence. Two of them I will mention together, first. The figure was now in Court continually, and it never there addressed itself to me, but always to the person who was speaking at the time. For instance: the throat of the murdered man had been cut straight across. In the opening speech for the defence, it was suggested that the deceased might have cut his own throat. At that very moment, the figure, with its throat in the dreadful condition referred to (this it had concealed before), stood at the speaker's elbow, motioning across and across its windpipe, now with the right hand, now with the left, vigorously suggesting to the speaker himself the impossibility of such a wound having been self-inflicted by either hand. For another instance: a witness to character, a woman, deposed to the prisoner's being the most amiable of mankind. The figure at that instant stood on the floor before her, looking her full in the face, and pointing out the prisoner's evil countenance with an extended arm and an outstretched finger.

The third change now to be added impressed me strongly as the most marked and striking of all. I do not theorise upon it; I accurately state it, and there leave it. Although the Appearance was not itself perceived by those whom it addressed, its coming close to such persons was invariably attended by some trepidation or disturbance on their part. It seemed to me as if it were prevented, by laws to which I was not amenable, from fully revealing itself to others, and yet as if it could invisibly, dumbly, and darkly overshadow their minds. When the leading counsel for the defence suggested that hypothesis of suicide, and the figure stood at the learned gentleman's elbow, frightfully sawing at its severed throat, it is undeniable that the counsel faltered in his speech, lost for a few seconds the thread of his ingenious discourse, wiped his forehead with his handkerchief, and turned extremely pale. When the witness to character was confronted by the Appearance, her eyes most certainly did follow the direction of its pointed finger, and rest in great hesitation and trouble upon the prisoner's face. Two additional illustrations will suffice. On the eighth day of the trial, after the pause which was every day made early in the afternoon for a few minutes' rest and refreshment, I came back into Court with the rest of the Jury some little time before the return of the Judges. Standing up in the box and looking about me, I thought the figure was not there, until, chancing to raise my eyes to the gallery, I saw it bending forward, and leaning over a very decent woman, as if to assure itself whether the Judges had resumed their seats or not. Immediately afterwards that woman screamed, fainted, and was carried out. So with the venerable, sagacious, and patient Judge who conducted the trial. When the case was over, and he settled himself and his papers to sum up, the murdered man, entering by the Judges' door, advanced to his Lordship's desk, and looked eagerly over his shoulder at the pages of his notes which he was turning. A change came over his Lordship's face; his hand stopped; the peculiar shiver, that I knew so well, passed over him; he faltered, 'Excuse me, gentlemen, for a few moments. I am somewhat oppressed by the vitiated air;' and did not recover until he had drunk a glass of water.

Through all the monotony of six of those interminable ten days—the same Judges and others on the bench, the same Murderer in the dock, the same lawyers at the table, the same tones of question and answer rising to the roof of the court, the same scratching of the Judge's pen, the same ushers going in and out, the same lights kindled at the same hour when there had been any natural light of day, the same foggy curtain outside the great windows when it was foggy, the same rain pattering and dripping when it was rainy, the same footmarks of turnkeys and prisoner day after day on the same sawdust, the same keys locking and unlocking the same heavy doors—through all the wearisome monotony which made me feel as if I had been Foreman of the Jury for a vast cried of time, and Piccadilly had flourished coevally with Babylon, the murdered man never lost one trace of his distinctness in my eyes, nor was he at any moment less distinct than anybody else. I must not omit, as a matter of fact, that I never once saw the Appearance which I call by the name of the murdered man look at the Murderer. Again and again I wondered, 'Why does he not?' But he never did.

Nor did he look at me, after the production of the miniature, until the last closing minutes of the trial arrived. We retired to consider, at seven minutes before ten at night. The idiotic vestryman and his two parochial parasites gave us so much trouble that we twice returned into Court to beg to have certain extracts from the Judge's notes re-read. Nine of us had not the smallest doubt about those passages, neither, I believe, had anyone in the Court; the dunder-headed triumvirate, having no idea but obstruction, disputed them for that very reason. At length we prevailed, and finally the Jury returned into Court at ten minutes past twelve.

The murdered man at that time stood directly opposite the Jury-box, on the other side of the Court. As I took my place, his eyes rested on me with great attention; he seemed satisfied, and slowly shook a great gray veil, which he carried on his arm for the first time, over his head and whole form. As I gave in our verdict, 'Guilty,' the veil collapsed, all was gone, and his place was empty. The Murderer, being asked by the Judge, according to usage, whether he had anything to say before sentence of Death should be passed upon him, indistinctly muttered something which was described in the leading newspapers of the following day as 'a few rambling, incoherent, and half-audible words, in which he was understood to complain that he had not had a fair trial, because the Foreman of the Jury was prepossessed against him.' The remarkable declaration that he really made was this: '*My Lord, I knew I was a doomed man, when the foreman of my jury came into the box. My Lord, I knew he would never let me off, because, before I was taken, he somehow got to my bedside in the night, woke me, and put a rope round my neck.*'

24

AN OCCURRENCE AT OWL CREEK BRIDGE

Ambrose Bierce

...a blinding white light blazes all about him with a sound like the shock of a cannon—then all is darkness and silence!

A man stood upon a railroad bridge in northern Alabama, looking down into the swift water twenty feet below. The man's hands were behind his back, the wrists bound with a cord. A rope closely encircled his neck. It was attached to a stout cross-timber above his head and the slack fell to the level of his knees. Some loose boards laid upon the ties supporting the rails of the railway supplied a footing for him and his executioners—two private soldiers of the Federal army, directed by a sergeant who in civil life may have been a deputy sheriff. At a short remove upon the same temporary platform was an officer in the uniform of his rank, armed. He was a captain. A sentinel at each end of the bridge stood with his rifle in the position known as 'support,' that is to say, vertical in front of the left shoulder, the hammer resting on the forearm thrown straight across the chest—a formal and unnatural position, enforcing an erect carriage of the body. It did not appear to be the duty of these two men to know what was occurring at the center of the bridge; they merely blockaded the two ends of the foot planking that traversed it.

Beyond one of the sentinels nobody was in sight; the railroad ran straight away into a forest for a hundred yards, then, curving, was lost to view. Doubtless there was an outpost farther along. The other bank of the stream was open ground—a gentle slope topped with a stockade of vertical tree trunks, loopholed for rifles, with a single embrasure through which protruded the muzzle of a brass cannon commanding the bridge. Midway up the slope between the bridge and fort were the spectators—a single company of infantry in line, at 'parade rest,' the butts of their rifles on the ground, the barrels inclining slightly backward against the right shoulder, the hands crossed upon the stock. A lieutenant stood at the right of the line, the point of his sword upon the ground, his left hand resting upon his right. Excepting the group of four at the center of the bridge, not a man moved. The company faced the bridge, staring stonily, motionless.

The sentinels, facing the banks of the stream, might have been statues to adorn the bridge. The captain stood with folded arms, silent, observing the work of his subordinates, but making no sign. Death is a dignitary who when he comes announced is to be received with formal manifestations of respect, even by those most familiar with him. In the code of military etiquette silence and fixity are forms of deference.

The man who was engaged in being hanged was apparently about thirty-five years of age. He was a civilian, if one might judge from his habit, which was that of a planter. His features were good—a straight nose, firm mouth, broad forehead, from which his long, dark hair was combed straight back, falling behind his ears to the collar of his well fitting frock coat. He wore a moustache and pointed beard, but no whiskers; his eyes were large and dark gray, and had a kindly expression which one would hardly have expected in one whose neck was in the hemp. Evidently this was no vulgar assassin. The liberal military code makes provision for hanging many kinds of persons, and gentlemen are not excluded.

The preparations being complete, the two private soldiers stepped aside and each drew away the plank upon which he had been standing.

The sergeant turned to the captain, saluted and placed himself immediately behind that officer, who in turn moved apart one pace.

These movements left the condemned man and the sergeant standing on the two ends of the same plank, which spanned three of the cross-ties of the bridge. The end upon which the civilian stood almost, but not quite, reached a fourth. This plank had been held in place by the weight of the captain; it was now held by that of the sergeant. At a signal from the former the latter would step aside, the plank would tilt and the condemned man go down between two ties. The arrangement commended itself to his judgement as simple and effective. His face had not been covered nor his eyes bandaged. He looked a moment at his 'unsteadfast footing,' then let his gaze wander to the swirling water of the stream racing madly beneath his feet. A piece of dancing driftwood caught his attention and his eyes followed it down the current. How slowly it appeared to move! What a sluggish stream!

He closed his eyes in order to fix his last thoughts upon his wife and children. The water, touched to gold by the early sun, the brooding mists under the banks at some distance down the stream, the fort, the soldiers, the piece of drift—all had distracted him. And now he became conscious of a new disturbance. Striking through the thought of his dear ones was a sound which he could neither ignore nor understand, a sharp, distinct, metallic percussion like the stroke of a blacksmith's hammer upon the anvil; it had the same ringing quality.

He wondered what it was, and whether immeasurably distant or nearby—it seemed both. Its recurrence was regular, but as slow as the tolling of a death knell. He awaited each new stroke with impatience and—he knew not why—apprehension. The intervals of silence grew progressively longer; the delays became maddening. With their greater infrequency the sounds increased in strength and sharpness. They hurt his ear like the thrust of a knife; he feared he would shriek. What he heard was the ticking of his watch.

He unclosed his eyes and saw again the water below him. 'If I could free my hands,' he thought, 'I might throw off the noose and spring into the stream. By diving I could evade the bullets and, swimming vigorously, reach the bank, take to the woods and get away home. My home, thank God, is as yet outside their lines; my wife and little ones are still beyond the invader's farthest advance.'

As these thoughts, which have here to be set down in words, were flashed into the doomed man's brain rather than evolved from it the captain nodded to the sergeant. The sergeant stepped aside.

II

Peyton Farquhar was a well to do planter, of an old and highly respected Alabama family. Being a slave owner and like other slave owners a politician, he was naturally an original secessionist and ardently devoted to the Southern cause. Circumstances of an imperious nature, which it is unnecessary to relate here, had prevented him from taking service with that gallant army which had fought the disastrous campaigns ending with the fall of Corinth, and he chafed under the inglorious restraint, longing for the release of his energies, the larger life of the soldier, the opportunity for distinction. That opportunity, he felt, would come, as it comes to all in wartime.

Meanwhile he did what he could. No service was too humble for him to perform in the aid of the South, no adventure too perilous for him to undertake if consistent with the character of a civilian who was at heart a soldier, and who in good faith and without too much qualification assented to at least a part of the frankly villainous dictum that all is fair in love and war.

One evening while Farquhar and his wife were sitting on a rustic bench near the entrance to his grounds, a gray-clad soldier rode up to the gate and asked for a drink of water. Mrs Farquhar was only too happy to serve him with her own white hands. While she was fetching the water her husband approached the dusty horseman and inquired eagerly for news from the front.

'The Yanks are repairing the railroads,' said the man, 'and are getting ready for another advance. They have reached the Owl Creek bridge, put it in order and built a stockade on the north bank. The commandant has issued an order, which is posted everywhere, declaring that any civilian caught interfering with the railroad, its bridges, tunnels, or trains will be summarily hanged. I saw the order.'

'How far is it to the Owl Creek bridge?' Farquhar asked.

'About thirty miles.'

'Is there no force on this side of the creek?'

'Only a picket post half a mile out, on the railroad, and a single sentinel at this end of the bridge.'

'Suppose a man—a civilian and student of hanging—should elude the picket post and perhaps get the better of the sentinel,' said Farquhar, smiling, 'what could he accomplish?'

The soldier reflected. 'I was there a month ago,' he replied. 'I observed that the flood of last winter had lodged a great quantity of driftwood against the wooden pier at this end of the bridge. It is now dry and would burn like tinder.'

The lady had now brought the water, which the soldier drank. He thanked her ceremoniously, bowed to her husband and rode away. An hour later, after nightfall, he repassed the plantation, going northward in the direction from which he had come. He was a Federal scout.

III

As Peyton Farquhar fell straight downward through the bridge he lost consciousness and was as one already dead. From this state he was awakened—ages later, it seemed to him—by the pain of a sharp pressure upon his throat, followed by a sense of suffocation. Keen, poignant agonies seemed to shoot from his neck downward through every fiber of his body and limbs. These pains appeared to flash along well-defined lines of ramification and to beat with an inconceivably rapid periodicity. They seemed like streams of pulsating fire heating him to an intolerable temperature. As to his head, he was conscious of nothing but a feeling of fullness—of congestion. These sensations were unaccompanied by thought. The intellectual part of his nature was already effaced; he had power only to feel, and feeling was torment. He was conscious of motion. Encompassed in a luminous cloud, of which he was now merely the fiery heart, without material substance, he swung through unthinkable arcs of oscillation, like a vast pendulum. Then all at once, with terrible suddenness, the light about him shot upward with the noise of a loud splash; a frightful roaring was in his ears, and all was cold and dark. The power of thought was restored; he knew that the rope had broken and he had fallen into the stream. There was no additional strangulation; the noose about his neck was already suffocating him and kept the water from his lungs. To die of hanging at the bottom of a river!—the idea seemed to him ludicrous. He opened his eyes in the darkness and saw above him a gleam of light, but how distant, how inaccessible! He was still sinking, for the light became fainter and fainter until it was a mere glimmer. Then it began to grow and brighten, and he knew that he was rising toward the surface—knew it with reluctance, for he was now very comfortable. 'To be hanged and drowned,' he thought, 'that is not so bad; but I do not wish to be shot. No; I will not be shot; that is not fair.'

He was not conscious of an effort, but a sharp pain in his wrist apprised him that he was trying to free his hands. He gave the struggle his attention, as an idler might observe the feat of a juggler, without interest in the outcome. What splendid effort!—what magnificent, what superhuman strength! Ah, that was a fine endeavor!

Bravo! The cord fell away; his arms parted and floated upward, the hands dimly seen on each side in the growing light. He watched them with a new interest as first one and then the other pounced upon the noose at his neck. They tore it away and thrust it fiercely aside, its undulations resembling those of a water snake. 'Put it back, put it back !' He thought he shouted these words to his hands, for the undoing of the noose had been succeeded by the direst pang that he had yet experienced. His neck ached horribly; his brain was on fire, his heart, which had been fluttering faintly, gave a great leap, trying to force itself out at his mouth. His whole body was racked and wrenched with an insupportable anguish! But his disobedient hands gave no heed to the command. They beat the water vigorously with quick, downward strokes, forcing him to the surface. He felt his head emerge; his eyes were blinded by the sunlight; his chest expanded convulsively, and with a supreme and crowning agony his lungs engulfed a great draught of air, which instantly he expelled in a shriek!

He was now in full possession of his physical senses. They were, indeed, preternaturally keen and alert. Something in the awful disturbance of his organic system had so exalted and refined them that they made record of things never before perceived. He felt the ripples upon his face and heard their separate sounds as they struck.

He looked at the forest on the bank of the stream, saw the individual trees, the leaves and the veining of each leaf—he saw the very insects upon them: the locusts, the brilliant bodied flies, the gray spiders stretching their webs from twig to twig. He noted the prismatic colours in all the dewdrops upon a million blades of grass.

The humming of the gnats that danced above the eddies of the stream, the beating of the dragon flies' wings, the strokes of the water spiders' legs, like oars which had lifted their boat—all these made audible music. A fish slid along beneath his eyes and he heard the rush of its body parting the water.

He had come to the surface facing down the stream; in a moment the visible world seemed to wheel slowly round, himself the pivotal point, and he saw the bridge, the fort, the soldiers upon the bridge, the captain, the sergeant, the two privates, his executioners. They were in silhouette against the blue sky. They shouted and gesticulated, pointing at him. The captain had drawn his pistol, but did not fire; the others were unarmed. Their movements were grotesque and horrible, their forms gigantic.

Suddenly he heard a sharp report and something struck the water smartly within a few inches of his head, spattering his face with spray. He heard a second report, and saw one of the sentinels with his rifle at his shoulder, a light cloud of blue smoke rising from the muzzle. The man in the water saw the eye of the man on the bridge gazing into his own through the sights of the rifle. He observed that it was a gray eye and remembered having read that gray eyes were keenest, and that all famous marksmen had them. Nevertheless, this one had missed.

A counter-swirl had caught Farquhar and turned him half round; he was again looking at the forest on the bank opposite the fort. The sound of a clear, high voice in a monotonous singsong now rang out behind him and came across the water with a distinctness that pierced and subdued all other sounds, even the beating of the ripples in his ears.

Although no soldier, he had frequented camps enough to know the dread significance of that deliberate, drawling, aspirated chant; the lieutenant on shore was taking a part in the morning's work. How coldly and pitilessly—with what an even, calm intonation, presaging, and enforcing tranquility in the men—with what accurately measured interval fell those cruel words:

'Company!...Attention!...Shoulder arms!...Ready!...Aim!... Fire!'

Farquhar dived—dived as deeply as he could. The water roared in his ears like the voice of Niagara, yet he heard the dull thunder of the volley and, rising again toward the surface, met shining bits of metal, singularly flattened, oscillating slowly downward. Some of them touched him on the face and hands, then fell away, continuing their descent. One lodged between his collar and neck; it was uncomfortably warm and he snatched it out.

As he rose to the surface, gasping for breath, he saw that he had been a long time under water; he was perceptibly farther downstream—nearer to safety. The soldiers had almost finished reloading; the metal ramrods flashed all at once in the sunshine as they were drawn from the barrels, turned in the air, and thrust into their sockets. The two sentinels fired again, independently and ineffectually.

The hunted man saw all this over his shoulder; he was now swimming vigorously with the current. His brain was as energetic as his arms and legs; he thought with the rapidity of lightning:

'The officer,' he reasoned, 'will not make that martinet's error a second time. It is as easy to dodge a volley as a single shot. He has probably already given the command to fire at will. God help me, I cannot dodge them all!'

An appalling splash within two yards of him was followed by a loud, rushing sound, diminuendo, which seemed to travel back through the air to the fort and died in an explosion which stirred the very river to its deeps! A rising sheet of water curved over him, fell down upon him, blinded him, strangled him! The cannon had taken a hand in the game. As he shook his head free from the commotion of the smitten water he heard the deflected shot humming through the air ahead, and in an instant it was cracking and smashing the branches in the forest beyond.

'They will not do that again,' he thought; 'the next time they will use a charge of grape. I must keep my eye upon the gun; the smoke will apprise me—the report arrives too late; it lags behind the missile. That is a good gun.'

Suddenly he felt himself whirled round and round—spinning like a top. The water, the banks, the forests, the now distant bridge, fort and men, all were commingled and blurred. Objects were represented by their colours only; circular horizontal streaks of colour—that was all he saw. He had been caught in a vortex and was being whirled on with a velocity of advance and gyration that made him giddy and sick. In a few moments he was flung upon the gravel at the foot of the left bank of the stream—the southern bank—and behind a projecting point which concealed him from his enemies. The sudden arrest of his motion, the abrasion of one of his hands on the gravel, restored him, and he wept with delight. He dug his fingers into the sand, threw it over himself in handfuls and audibly blessed it. It looked like diamonds, rubies, emeralds; he could think of nothing beautiful which it did not resemble. The trees upon the bank were giant garden plants; he noted a definite order in their arrangement, inhaled the fragrance of their blooms. A strange roseate light shone through the spaces among their trunks and the wind made in their branches the music of Aeolian harps. He had no wish to perfect his escape—he was content to remain in that enchanting spot until retaken.

A whiz and a rattle of grapeshot among the branches high above his head roused him from his dream. The baffled cannoneer had fired him a random farewell. He sprang to his feet, rushed up the sloping bank, and plunged into the forest.

All that day he traveled, laying his course by the rounding sun. The forest seemed interminable; nowhere did he discover a break in it, not even a woodman's road. He had not known that he lived in so wild a region. There was something uncanny in the revelation.

By nightfall he was fatigued, footsore, famished. The thought of his wife and children urged him on. At last he found a road which led him in what he knew to be the right direction. It was as wide and straight as a city street, yet it seemed untraveled. No fields bordered it, no dwelling anywhere. Not so much as the barking of a dog suggested human habitation. The black bodies of the trees formed a straight wall on both sides, terminating on the horizon in a point, like a diagram in a lesson in perspective. Overhead, as he looked up through this rift in the wood, shone great golden stars looking unfamiliar and grouped in strange constellations. He was sure they were arranged in some order which had a secret and malign significance. The wood on either side was full of singular noises, among which—once, twice, and again—he distinctly heard whispers in an unknown tongue.

His neck was in pain and lifting his hand to it he found it

horribly swollen. He knew that it had a circle of black where the rope had bruised it. His eyes felt congested; he could no longer close them. His tongue was swollen with thirst; he relieved its fever by thrusting it forward from between his teeth into the cold air. How softly the turf had carpeted the untraveled avenue—he could no longer feel the roadway beneath his feet!

Doubtless, despite his suffering, he had fallen asleep while walking, for now he sees another scene—perhaps he has merely recovered from a delirium. He stands at the gate of his own home. All is as he left it, and all bright and beautiful in the morning sunshine. He must have traveled the entire night. As he pushes open the gate and passes up the wide white walk, he sees a flutter of female garments; his wife, looking fresh and cool and sweet, steps down from the veranda to meet him. At the bottom of the steps she stands waiting, with a smile of ineffable joy, an attitude of matchless grace and dignity. Ah, how beautiful she is! He springs forwards with extended arms. As he is about to clasp her he feels a stunning blow upon the back of the neck; a blinding white light blazes all about him with a sound like the shock of a cannon—then all is darkness and silence!

Peyton Farquhar was dead; his body, with a broken neck, swung gently from side to side beneath the timbers of the Owl Creek bridge.

25

THURNLEY ABBEY

Perceval Landon

...it was the rarest thing for a light to be seen at the Abbey after dark...

Three years ago I was on my way out to the East, and as an extra day in London was of some importance, I took the Friday evening mail-train to Brindisi instead of the usual Thursday morning Marseilles express.

Many people shrink from the long forty-eight-hour train journey through Europe, and the subsequent rush across the Mediterranean on the nineteen-knot *Isis* or *Osiris*; but there is really very little discomfort on either the train or the mail-boat, and unless there is actually nothing for me to do, I always like to save the extra day and a half in London before I say goodbye to her for one of my longer tramps. This time—it was early, I remember, in the shipping season, probably about the beginning of September—there were few passengers, and I had a compartment in the P. & O. Indian express to myself all the way from Calais. All Sunday I watched the blue waves dimpling the Adriatic, and the pale rosemary along the cuttings; the plain white towns, with their flat roofs and their bold 'duomos', and the grey-green gnarled olive orchards of Apulia. The journey was just like any other. We ate in the dining-car as often and as long as we decently could. We slept after luncheon; we dawdled the afternoon away with yellow-backed novels; sometimes we exchanged platitudes in the smoking-room, and it was there that I met Alastair Colvin.

Colvin was a man of middle height, with a resolute, well-cut jaw; his hair was turning grey; his moustache was sun-whitened, otherwise he was clean-shaven—obviously a gentleman, and obviously also a preoccupied man. He had no great wit. When spoken to, he made the usual remarks in the right way, and I dare say he refrained from banalities only because he spoke less than the rest of us; most of the time he buried himself in the Wagon-lit Company's time-table, but seemed unable to concentrate his attention on anyone page of it. He found that I had been over the Siberian railway, and for a quarter of an hour he discussed it with me. Then he lost interest in it, and rose to go to his compartment. But he came back again very soon, and seemed glad to pick up the conversation again.

Of course this did not seem to me to be of any importance. Most travellers by train become a trifle infirm of purpose after thirty-six hours' rattling. But Colvin's restless way I noticed in somewhat marked contrast with the man's personal importance and dignity; especially ill suited was it to his finely made large hand with strong, broad, regular nails and its few lines. As I looked at his hand I noticed a long, deep, and recent scar of ragged shape. However, it is absurd to pretend that I thought anything was unusual. I went off at five o'clock on Sunday afternoon to sleep away the hour or two that had still to be got through before we arrived at Brindisi.

Once there, we few passengers transhipped our hand baggage, verified our berths—there were only a score of us in all—and then, after an aimless ramble of half an hour in Brindisi, we returned to dinner at the Hotel International, not wholly surprised that the town had been the death of Virgil. If I remember rightly, there is a gaily painted hall at the International—I do not wish to advertise anything, but there is no other place in Brindisi at which to await the coming of the mails—and after dinner I was looking with awe at a trellis overgrown with blue vines, when Colvin moved across the room to my table. He picked up *Il Secolo*, but almost immediately gave up the pretence of reading it. He turned squarely to me and said:

'Would you do me a favour?'

One doesn't do favours to stray acquaintances on Continental expresses without knowing something more of them than I knew of Colvin. But I smiled in a noncommittal way, and asked him what he wanted. I wasn't wrong in part of my estimate of him; he said bluntly:

'Will you let me sleep in your cabin on the *Osiris*?' And he coloured a little as he said it.

Now, there is nothing more tiresome than having to put up with a stable-companion at sea, and I asked him rather pointedly:

'Surely there is room for all of us?' I thought that perhaps he had been partnered off with some mangy Levantine, and wanted to escape from him at all hazards.

Colvin, still somewhat confused, said: 'Yes; I am in a cabin by myself. But you would do me the greatest favour if you would allow me to share yours.'

This was all very well, but, besides the fact that I always sleep better when alone, there had been some recent thefts on board English liners, and I hesitated, frank and honest and self-conscious as Colvin was. Just then the mail-train came in with a clatter and a rush of escaping steam, and I asked him to see me again about it on the boat when we started. He answered me curtly—I suppose he saw the mistrust in my manner—'I am a member of White's.' I smiled to myself as he said it, but I remembered in a moment that the man—if he were really what he claimed to be, and I make no doubt that he was—must have been sorely put to it before he urged the fact as a guarantee of his respectability to a total stranger at a Brindisi hotel.

That evening, as we cleared the red and green harbour-lights of Brindisi, Colvin explained. This is his story in his own words.

'When I was travelling in India some years ago, I made the acquaintance of a youngish man in the Woods and Forests. We camped out together for a week, and I found him a pleasant companion. John Broughton was a light-hearted soul when off duty, but a steady and capable man in any of the small emergencies that continually arise in that department. He was liked and trusted by the natives, and though a trifle over-pleased with himself when he escaped to civilization at Simla or Calcutta, Broughton's future was well assured in Government service, when a fair-sized estate was unexpectedly left to him, and he joyfully shook the dust of the Indian plains from his feet and returned to England. For five years he drifted about London. I saw him now and then. We dined together about every eighteen months, and I could trace pretty exactly the gradual sickening of Broughton with a merely idle life. He then set out on a couple of long voyages, returned as restless as before, and at last told me that he had decided to marry and settle down at his place, Thurnley Abbey, which had long been empty. He spoke about looking after the property and standing for his constituency in the usual way. Vivien Wilde, his fiancée, had, I suppose, begun to take him in hand. She was a pretty girl with a deal of fair hair and rather an exclusive manner; deeply religious in a narrow school, she was still kindly and high-spirited, and I thought that Broughton was in luck. He was quite happy and full of information about his future.

'Among other things, I asked him about Thurnley Abbey. He confessed that he hardly knew the place. The last tenant, a man called Clarke, had lived in one wing for fifteen years and seen no one. He had been a miser and a hermit. It was the rarest thing for a light to be seen at the Abbey after dark. Only the barest necessities of life were ordered, and the tenant himself received them at the side-door. His one half-caste manservant, after a month's stay in the house, had abruptly left without warning, and had returned to the Southern States. One thing Broughton complained bitterly about: Clarke had wilfully spread the rumour among the villagers that the Abbey was haunted, and had even condescended to play childish tricks with spirit-lamps and salt in order to scare trespassers away at night. He had been detected in the act of this tomfoolery, but the story spread, and no one, said Broughton, would venture near the house except in broad daylight. The hauntedness of Thurnley Abbey was now, he said with a grin, part of the gospel of the countryside, but he and his young wife were going to change all that. Would I propose myself any time I liked? I, of course, said I would, and equally, of course, intended to do nothing of the sort without a definite invitation.

'The house was put in thorough repair, though not a stick of the old furniture and tapestry were removed. Floors and ceilings were relaid: the roof was made watertight again, and the dust of half a century was scoured out. He showed me some photographs of the place. It was called an Abbey, though as a matter of fact it had been only the infirmary of the long-vanished Abbey of Clouster some five miles away. The larger part of this building remained as it had been in pre-Reformation days, but a wing had been added in Jacobean times, and that part of the house had been kept in something like repair by Mr Clarke. He had in both the ground and first floors set a heavy timber door, strongly barred with iron, in the passage between the earlier and the Jacobean parts of the house, and had entirely neglected the former. So there had been a good deal of work to be done.

'Broughton, whom I saw in London two or three times about this period, made a deal of fun over the positive refusal of the workmen to remain after sundown. Even after the electric light had been put into every room, nothing would induce them to remain, though, as Broughton observed, electric light was death on ghosts. The legend of the Abbey's ghosts had gone far and wide, and the men would take no risks. They went home in batches of five and six, and even during the daylight hours there was an inordinate amount of talking between one and another, if either happened to be out of sight of his companion. On the whole, though nothing of any sort or kind had been conjured up even by their heated imaginations during their five months' work upon the Abbey, the belief in the ghosts was rather strengthened than otherwise in Thurnley because of the men's confessed nervousness, and local tradition declared itself in favour of the ghost of an immured nun.

'"Good old nun!" said Broughton.

'I asked him whether in general he believed in the possibility of ghosts, and, rather to my surprise, he said that he couldn't say he entirely disbelieved in them. A man in India had told him one morning in camp that he believed that his mother was dead in England, as her vision had come to his tent the night before. He had not been alarmed, but had said nothing, and the figure vanished again. As a matter of fact, the next possible dak-walla brought on a telegram announcing the mother's death. "There the thing was," said Broughton. But at Thurnley he was practical enough. He roundly cursed the idiotic selfishness of Clarke, whose silly antics had caused all the inconvenience. At the same time, he couldn't refuse to sympathize to some extent with the ignorant workmen. "My own idea," said he, "is that if a ghost ever does come in one's way, one ought to speak to it."

'I agreed. Little as I knew of the ghost world and its conventions, I had always remembered that a spook was in honour bound to wait to be spoken to. It didn't seem much to do, and I felt that the sound of one's own voice would at any rate reassure oneself as to one's wakefulness. But there are few ghosts outside Europe—few, that is, that a white man can see—and I had never been troubled with any. However, as I have said, I told Broughton that I agreed.

'So the wedding took place, and I went to it in a tall hat which I bought for the occasion, and the new Mrs Broughton smiled very nicely at me afterwards. As it had to happen, I took the Orient Express that evening and was not in England again for nearly six months. Just before I came back I got a letter from Broughton. He asked if I could see him in London or come to Thurnley, as he thought I should be better able to help him than anyone else he knew. His wife sent a nice message to me at the end, so I was reassured about at least one thing. I wrote from Budapest that I would come and see him at Thurnley two days after my arrival in London, and as I sauntered out of the Pannonia into the Kerepesi Utcza to post my letters, I wondered of what earthly service I could be to Broughton. I had been out with him after tiger on foot, and I could imagine few men better able at a pinch to manage their own business. However, I had nothing to do, so after dealing with some small accumulations of business during my absence, I packed a kit-bag and departed to Euston.

'I was met by Broughton's great limousine at Thurnley Road station, and after a drive of nearly seven miles we echoed through the sleepy streets of Thurnley village, into which the main gates of the park thrust themselves, splendid with pillars and spreadeagles and tom-cats rampant atop of them. I never was a herald, but I know that the Broughtons have the right to supporters—Heaven knows why! From the gates a quadruple avenue of beech-trees led inwards for a quarter of a mile. Beneath them a neat strip of fine turf edged the road and ran back until the poison of the dead beech-leaves killed it under the trees. There were many wheel-tracks on the road, and a comfortable little pony trap jogged past me laden with a country parson and his wife and daughter. Evidently there was some garden party going on at the Abbey. The road dropped away to the right at the end of the avenue, and I could see the Abbey across a wide pasturage and a broad lawn thickly dotted with guests.

'The end of the building was plain. It must have been almost mercilessly austere when it was first built, but time had crumbled the edges and toned the stone down to an orange-lichened grey wherever it showed behind its curtain of magnolia, jasmine, and ivy. Further on was the three-storied Jacobean house, tall and handsome. There had not been the slightest attempt to adapt the one to the other, but the kindly ivy had glossed over the touching-point. There was a tall flèche in the middle of the building, surmounting a small bell tower. Behind the house there rose the mountainous verdure of Spanish chestnuts all the way up the hill.

'Broughton had seen me coming from afar, and walked across from his other guests to welcome me before turning me over to the butler's care. This man was sandy-haired and rather inclined to be talkative. He could, however, answer hardly any questions about the house; he had, he said, only been there three weeks. Mindful of what Broughton had told me, I made no enquiries about ghosts, though the room into which I was shown might have justified anything. It was a very large low room with oak beams projecting from the white ceiling. Every inch of the walls, including the doors, was covered with tapestry, and a remarkably fine Italian fourpost bedstead, heavily draped, added to the darkness and dignity of the place. All the furniture was old, well made and dark. Underfoot there was a plain green pile carpet, the only new thing about the room except the electric light fittings and the jugs and basins. Even the looking-glass on the dressing-table was an old pyramidal Venetian glass set in heavy repoussé frame of tarnished silver.

'After a few minutes' cleaning up, I went downstairs and out upon the lawn, where I greeted my hostess. The people gathered there were of the usual country type, all anxious to be pleased and roundly curious as to the new master of the Abbey. Rather to my surprise, and quite to my pleasure, I rediscovered Glenham, whom I had known well in old days in Barotseland: he lived quite close, as he remarked with a grin. I ought to have known. "But," he added, "I don't live in a place like this." He swept his hand to the long, low lines of the Abbey in obvious admiration, and then, to my intense interest, muttered beneath his breath, "Thank God!" He saw that I had overheard him, and turning to me said decidedly, "Yes, 'thank God' I said, and I meant it. I wouldn't live at the Abbey for all Broughton's money."

'"But surely," I demurred, "you know that old Clarke was discovered in the very act of setting light to his bug-a-boos?"

'Glenham shrugged his shoulders. "Yes, I know about that. But there is something wrong with the place still. All I can say is that Broughton is a different man since he has lived here. I don't believe that he will remain much longer. But—you're staying here?—well, you'll hear all about it tonight. There's a big dinner, I understand." The conversation turned off to old reminiscences, and Glenham soon after had to go.

'Before I went to dress that evening I had twenty minutes'

talk with Broughton in his library. There was no doubt that the man was altered, gravely altered. He was nervous and fidgety, and I found him looking at me only when my eye was off him. I naturally asked him what he wanted of me. I told him I would do anything I could, but that I couldn't conceive what he lacked that I could provide. He said with a lustreless smile that there was, however, something, and that he would tell me the following morning. It struck me that he was somehow ashamed of himself and perhaps ashamed of the part he was asking me to play. However, I dismissed the subject from my mind and went up to dress in my palatial room. As I shut the door a draught blew out the Queen of Sheba from the wall, and I noticed that the tapestries were not fastened to the wall at the bottom. I have always held very practical views about spooks, and it has often seemed to me that the slow waving in firelight of loose tapestry upon a wall would account for 99 per cent of the stories one hears. Certainly the dignified undulation of this lady with her attendants and huntsmen—one of whom was untidily cutting the throat of a fallow deer upon the very steps on which King Solomon, a grey-faced Flemish nobleman with the order of the Golden Fleece, awaited his fair visitor—gave colour to my hypothesis.

'Nothing much happened at dinner. The people were very much like those of the garden party. A young woman next to me seemed anxious to know what was being read in London. As she was far more familiar than I with the most recent magazines and literary supplements, I found salvation in being myself instructed in the tendencies of modern fiction. All true art, she said, was shot through and through with melancholy. How vulgar were the attempts at wit that marked so many modern books! From the beginning of literature it had always been tragedy that embodied the highest attainment of every age. To call such works morbid merely begged the question. No thoughtful man—she looked sternly at me through the steel rim of her glasses—could fail to agree with me. Of course, as one would, I immediately and properly said that I slept with

Pett Ridge and Jacobs under my pillow at night, and that if *Jorrocks* weren't quite so large and cornery, I would add him to the company. She hadn't read any of them, so I was saved—for a time. But I remember grimly that she said that the dearest wish of her life was to be in some awful and soul-freezing situation of horror, and I remember that she dealt hardly with the hero of Nat Paynter's vampire story, between nibbles at her brown-bread ice. She was a cheerless soul, and I couldn't help thinking that if there were many such in the neighbourhood, it was not surprising that old Glenham had been stuffed with some nonsense or other about the Abbey. Yet nothing could well have been less creepy than the glitter of silver and glass, and the subdued lights and cackle of conversation all round the dinner-table.

'After the ladies had gone I found myself talking to the rural dean. He was a thin, earnest man, who at once turned the conversation to old Clarke's buffooneries. But, he said, Mr Broughton had introduced such a new and cheerful spirit, not only into the Abbey, but, he might say, into the whole neighbourhood, that he had great hopes that the ignorant superstitions of the past were from henceforth destined to oblivion. Thereupon his other neighbour, a portly gentleman of independent means and position, audibly remarked "Amen", which damped the rural dean, and we talked of partridges past, partridges present, and pheasants to come. At the other end of the table Broughton sat with a couple of his friends, red-faced hunting men. Once I noticed that they were discussing me, but I paid no attention to it at the time. I remembered it a few hours later.

'By eleven all the guests were gone, and Broughton, his wife, and I were alone together under the fine plaster ceiling of the Jacobean drawing-room. Mrs Broughton talked about one or two of the neighbours, and then, with a smile, said that she knew I would excuse her, shook hands with me, and went off to bed. I am not very good at analysing things, but I felt that she talked a little uncomfortably and with a suspicion of effort, smiled rather conventionally, and was obviously glad to go. These things seem trifling enough to repeat, but I had throughout the faint feeling that everything was not square. Under the circumstances, this was enough to set me wondering what on earth the service could be that I was to render—wondering also whether the whole business were not some ill-advised jest in order to make me come down from London for a mere shooting-party.

'Broughton said little after she had gone. But he was evidently labouring to bring the conversation round to the so-called haunting of the Abbey. As soon as I saw this, of course I asked him directly about it. He then seemed at once to lose interest in the matter. There was no doubt about it: Broughton was somehow a changed man, and to my mind he had changed in no way for the better. Mrs Broughton seemed no sufficient cause. He was clearly very fond of her, and she of him. I reminded him that he was going to tell me what I could do for him in the morning, pleaded my journey, lighted a candle, and went upstairs with him. At the end of the passage leading into the old house he grinned weakly and said, "Mind, if you see a ghost, do talk to it; you said you would." He stood irresolutely a moment and then turned away. At the door of his dressing-room he paused once more: "I'm here," he called out, "if you should want anything. Good night," and he shut his door.

'I went along the passage to my room, undressed, switched on a lamp beside my bed, read a few pages of *The Jungle Book*, and then, more than ready for sleep, turned the light off and went fast asleep.

'Three hours later I woke up. There was not a breath of wind outside. There was not even a flicker of light from the fireplace. As I lay there, an ash tinkled slightly as it cooled, but there was hardly a gleam of the dullest red in the grate. An owl cried among the silent Spanish chestnuts on the slope outside. I idly reviewed the events of the day, hoping that I should fall off to sleep again before I reached dinner. But at the end I seemed as wakeful as ever. There was no help for it.

I must read my *Jungle Book* again till I felt ready to go off, so I fumbled for the pear at the end of the cord that hung down inside the bed, and I switched on the bedside lamp. The sudden glory dazzled me for a moment. I felt under my pillow for my hook with half-shut eyes. Then, growing used to the light, I happened to look down to the foot of my bed.

'I can never tell you really what happened then. Nothing I could ever confess in the most abject words could even faintly picture to you what I felt. I know that my heart stopped dead, and my throat shut automatically. In one instinctive movement I crouched back up against the head-boards of the bed, staring at the horror. The movement set my heart going again, and the sweat dripped from every pore. I am not a particularly religious man, but I had always believed that God would never allow any supernatural appearance to present itself to man in such a guise and in such circumstances that harm, either bodily or mental, could result to him. I can only tell you that at that moment both my life and my reason rocked unsteadily on their seats.'

The other *Osiris* passengers had gone to bed. Only he and I remained leaning over the starboard railing, which rattled uneasily now and then under the fierce vibration of the over-engined mail-boat. Far over, there were the lights of a few fishing-smacks riding out the night, and a great rush of white combing and seething water fell out and away from us overside.

At last Colvin went on:

'Leaning over the foot of my bed, looking at me, was a figure swathed in a rotten and tattered veiling. This shroud passed over the head, but left both eyes and the right side of the face bare. It then followed the line of the arm down to where the hand grasped the bed-end. The face was not entirely that of a skull, though the eyes and the flesh of the face were totally gone. There was a thin, dry skin drawn tightly over the features, and there was some skin left on the hand. One wisp of hair crossed the forehead. It was perfectly still. I looked at it, and it looked at me, and my brains turned dry and hot in my head. I had still got the pear of the electric lamp in my hand,

and I played idly with it; only I dared not turn the light out again. I shut my eyes, only to open them in a hideous terror the same second. The thing had not moved. My heart was thumping, and the sweat cooled me as it evaporated. Another cinder tinkled in the grate, and a panel creaked in the wall.

'My reason failed me. For twenty minutes, or twenty seconds, I was able to think of nothing else but this awful figure, till there came, hurtling through the empty channels of my senses, the remembrance that Broughton and his friends had discussed me furtively at dinner. The dim possibility of its being a hoax stole gratefully into my unhappy mind, and once there, one's pluck came creeping back along a thousand tiny veins. My first sensation was one of blind unreasoning thankfulness that my brain was going to stand the trial. I am not a timid man, but the best of us needs some human handle to steady him in time of extremity, and in this faint but growing hope that after all it might be only a brutal hoax, I found the fulcrum that I needed. At last I moved.

'How I managed to do it I cannot tell you, but with one spring towards the foot of the bed I got within arm's-length and struck out one fearful blow with my fist at the thing. It crumbled under it, and my hand was cut to the bone. With a sickening revulsion after my terror, I dropped half-fainting across the end of the bed. So it was merely a foul trick after all. No doubt the trick had been played many a time before: no doubt Broughton and his friends had had some large bet among themselves as to what I should do when I discovered the gruesome thing. From my state of abject terror I found myself transported into an insensate anger. I shouted curses upon Broughton. I dived rather than climbed over the bed-end on to the sofa. I tore at the robed skeleton—how well the whole thing had been carried out, I thought—I broke the skull against the floor, and stamped upon its dry bones. I flung the head away under the bed, and rent the brittle bones of the trunk in pieces. I snapped the thin thigh-bones across my knee, and flung them in different directions. The shin-bones

I set up against a stool and broke with my heel. I raged like a Berserker against the loathly thing, and stripped the ribs from the backbone and slung the breastbone against the cupboard. My fury increased as the work of destruction went on. I tore the frail rotten veil into twenty pieces, and the dust went up over everything, over the clean blotting-paper and the silver inkstand. At last my work was done. There was but a raffle of broken bones and strips of parchment and crumbling wool. Then, picking up a piece of the skull—it was the cheek and temple bone of the right side, I remember—I opened the door and went down the passage to Broughton's dressing-room. I remember still how my sweat-dripping pyjamas clung to me as I walked. At the door I kicked and entered.

'Broughton was in bed. He had already turned the light on and seemed shrunken and horrified. For a moment he could hardly pull himself together. Then I spoke. I don't know what I said. Only I know that from a heart full and over-full with hatred and contempt, spurred on by shame of my own recent cowardice, I let my tongue run on. He answered nothing. I was amazed at my own fluency. My hair still clung lankily to my wet temples, my hand was bleeding profusely, and I must have looked a strange sight. Broughton huddled himself up at the head of the bed just as I had. Still he made no answer, no defence. He seemed preoccupied with something besides my reproaches, and once or twice moistened his lips with his tongue. But he could say nothing though he moved his hands now and then, just as a baby who cannot speak moves its hands.

'At last the door into Mrs Broughton's room opened and she came in, white and terrified. "What is it? What is it? Oh, in God's name! What is it?" she cried again and again, and then she went up to her husband and sat on the bed in her night-dress, and the two faced me. I told her what the matter was. I spared her husband not a word for her presence there. Yet he seemed hardly to understand. I told the pair that I had spoiled their cowardly joke for them. Broughton looked up.

'"I have smashed the foul thing into a hundred pieces," I

said. Broughton licked his lips again and his mouth worked. "By God!" I shouted, "it would serve you right if I thrashed you within an inch of your life. I will take care that not a decent man or woman of my acquaintance ever speaks to you again. And there," I added, throwing the broken piece of the skull upon the floor beside his bed, "there is a souvenir for you, of your damned work tonight!"

'Broughton saw the bone, and in a moment it was his turn to frighten me. He squealed like a hare caught in a trap. He screamed and screamed till Mrs Broughton, almost as bewildered as myself, held on to him and coaxed him like a child to be quiet. But Broughton—and as he moved I thought that ten minutes ago I perhaps looked as terribly ill as he did—thrust her from him, and scrambled out of the bed on to the floor, and still screaming put out his hand to the bone. It had blood on it from my hand. He paid no attention to me whatever. In truth I said nothing. This was a new turn indeed to the horrors of the evening. He rose from the floor with the bone in his hand and stood silent. He seemed to be listening. "Time, time, perhaps," he muttered, and almost at the same moment fell at full length on the carpet, cutting his head against the fender. The bone flew from his hand and came to rest near the door. I picked Broughton up, haggard and broken, with blood over his face. He whispered hoarsely and quickly, "Listen. listen!" We listened.

'After ten seconds' utter quiet, I seemed to hear something. I could not be sure, but at last there was no doubt. There was a quiet sound as of one moving along the passage. Little regular steps came towards us over the hard oak flooring. Broughton moved to where his wife sat, white and speechless, on the bed, and pressed her face into his shoulder.

'Then, the last thing that I could see as he turned the light out, he fell forward with his own head pressed into the pillow of the bed. Something in their company, something in their cowardice, helped me, and I faced the open doorway of the room, which was outlined fairly clearly against the dimly lighted passage. I put out one hand and touched Mrs Broughton's shoulder in the darkness. But at the last moment I too failed. I sank on my knees and put my face in the bed. Only we all heard. The footsteps came to the door, and there they stopped. The piece of bone was lying a yard inside the door. There was a rustle of moving stuff, and the thing was in the room. Mrs Broughton was silent: I could hear Broughton's voice praying, muffled in the pillow: I was cursing my own cowardice. Then the steps moved out again on the oak boards of the passage, and I heard the sounds dying away. In a flash of remorse I went to the door and looked out. At the end of the corridor I thought I saw something that moved away. A moment later the passage was empty. I stood with my forehead agaanst the jamb of the door almost physically sick.

'"You can turn the light on," I said, and there was an answering flare. There was no bone at my feet. Mrs Broughton had fainted. Broughton was almost useless, and it took me ten minutes to bring her to. Broughton only said one thing worth remembering. For the most part he went on muttering prayers. But I was glad afterwards to recollect that he had said that thing. He said in a colourless voice, half as a question, half as a reproach, "You didn't speak to her."

'We spent the remainder of the night together. Mrs Broughton actually fell off into a kind of sleep before dawn, but she suffered so horribly in her dreams that I shook her into consciousness again. Never was dawn so long in coming. Three or four times Broughton spoke to himself. Mrs Broughton would then just tighten her hold on his arm, but she could say nothing. As for me, I can honestly say that I grew worse as the hours passed and the light strengthened. The two violent reactions had battered down my steadiness of view, and I felt that the foundations of my life had been built upon the sand. I said nothing, and after binding up my hand with a towel, I did not move. It was better so. They helped me and I helped them, and we all three knew that our reason had gone very near to ruin that night. At last, when the light came in pretty strongly, and the birds outside were chattering and singing, we felt that we must do something. Yet we never moved. You might have thought that we should particularly dislike being found as we were by the servants: yet nothing of that kind mattered a straw, and an overpowering listlessness bound us as we sat, until Chapman, Broughton's man, actually knocked and opened the door. None of us moved. Broughton, speaking hardly and stiffly, said, "Chapman you can come back in five minutes." Chapman was a discreet man, but it would have made no difference to us if he had carried his news to the "room" at once.

'We looked at each other and I said I must go back. I meant to wait outside till Chapman returned. I simply dared not re-enter my bedroom alone. Broughton roused himself and said that he would come with me. Mrs Broughton agreed to remain in her own room for five minutes if the blinds were drawn up and all the doors left open.

'So Broughton and I, leaning stiffly one against the other, went down to my room. By the morning light that filtered past the blinds we could see our way, and I released the blinds. There was nothing wrong in the room from end to end, except smears of my own blood on the end of the bed, on the sofa, and on the carpet where I had torn the thing to pieces.'

Colvin had finished his story. There was nothing to say. Seven bells stuttered out from the fo'c'sle, and the answering cry wailed through the darkness. I took him downstairs.

'Of course I am much better now, but it is a kindness of you to let me sleep in your cabin.'

26

DEATH AND THE WOMAN

Gertrude Atherton

The latter deadened the rattle of the streets...

Her husband was dying, and she was alone with him. Nothing could exceed the desolation of her surroundings. She and the man who was going from her were in the third-floor-back of a New York boarding-house. It was summer, and the other boarders were in the country; all the servants except the cook had been dismissed, and she, when not working, slept profoundly on the fifth floor. The landlady also was out of town on a brief holiday.

The window was open to admit the thick unstirring air; no sound rose from the row of long narrow yards, nor from the tall deep houses annexed. The latter deadened the rattle of the streets. At intervals the distant *Elevated* lumbered protestingly along, its grunts and screams muffled by the hot suspended ocean.

She sat there plunged in the profoundest grief that can come to the human soul, for in all other agony hope flickers, however forlornly. She gazed dully at the unconscious breathing form of the man who had been friend, and companion, and lover, during five years of youth too vigorous and hopeful to be warped by uneven fortune. It was wasted by disease; the face was shrunken; the night-garment hung loosely about a body which had never been disfigured by flesh, but had been muscular with exercise and full-blooded with health. She was glad that the body was changed; glad that its beauty, too, had gone some other-where than into the coffin. She had loved his hands as apart from himself; loved their strong warm magnetism. They lay limp and yellow on the quilt: she knew that they were already cold, and that moisture was gathering on them. For a moment something convulsed within her. They had gone too. She repeated the words twice, and, after them, 'forever.' All the while the sweetness of their pressure came back to her.

She leaned suddenly over him. He was in there still, somewhere. Where? If he had not ceased to breathe, the Ego, the Soul, the Personality was still in the sodden clay which had shaped to give it speech. Why could it not manifest itself to her? Was it still conscious in there, unable to project itself through the disintegrating matter which was the only medium its Creator had vouchsafed it? Did it struggle there, seeing her agony, sharing it, longing for the complete disintegration which should put an end to its torment? She called his name, she even shook him slightly, mad to tear the body apart and find her mate, yet even in that tortured moment realizing that violence would hasten his going.

The dying man took no notice of her, and she opened his gown and put her cheek to his heart, calling him again. There had never been more perfect union; how could the bond still be so strong if he were not at the other end of it? He was there, her other part; until dead he must be living. There was no intermediate state. Why should he be as entombed and unresponding as if the screws were in the lid? But the faintly beating heart did not quicken beneath her lips. She extended her arms suddenly, describing eccentric lines, above, about him, rapidly opening and closing her hands as if to clutch some escaping object; then sprang to her feet, and went to the window. She feared insanity. She had asked to be left alone with her dying husband, and she did not wish to lose her reason and shriek, with a crowd of people about her.

The green plots in the yards were not apparent, she noticed. Something heavy, like a pall, rested upon them. Then she understood that the day was over and that night was coming.

She returned swiftly to the bedside, wondering if she had

remained away hours or seconds, and if he were dead. His face was still discernible, and Death had not relaxed it. She laid her own against it, then withdrew it with shuddering flesh, her teeth smiting each other as if an icy wind had passed.

She let herself fall back in the chair, clasping her hands against her heart, watching with expanding eyes the white sculptured face which, in the glittering dark, was becoming less defined of outline. If she lit the gas it would draw mosquitoes, and she could not shut from him the little air he must be mechanically grateful for. And she did not want to see the opening eye—the falling jaw.

Her vision became so fixed that at length she saw nothing, and closed her eyes and waited for the moisture to rise and relieve the strain. When she opened them his face had disappeared; the humid waves above the house-tops put out even the light of the stars, and night was come.

Fearfully, she approached her ear to his lips; he still breathed. She made a motion to kiss him, then threw herself back in a quiver of agony—they were not the lips she had known, and she would have nothing less.

His breathing was so faint that in her half-reclining position she could not hear it, could not be aware of the moment of his death. She extended her arm resolutely and laid her hand on his heart. Not only must she feel his going, but, so strong had been the comradeship between them, it was a matter of loving honour to stand by him to the last.

She sat there in the hot heavy night, pressing her hand hard against the ebbing heart of the unseen, and awaited Death. Suddenly an odd fancy possessed her. Where was Death? Why was he tarrying? Who was detaining him? From what quarter would he come? He was taking his leisure, drawing near with footsteps as measured as those of men keeping time to a funeral march. By a wayward deflection she thought of the slow music that was always turned on in the theatre when the heroine was about to appear, or something eventful to happen. She had always thought that sort of thing ridiculous and inartistic. So had he.

She drew her brows together angrily, wondering at her levity, and pressed her relaxed palm against the heart it kept guard over. For a moment the sweat stood on her face; then the pent-up breath burst from her lungs. He still lived.

Once more the fancy wantoned above the stunned heart. Death—where was he? What a curious experience: to be sitting alone in a big house—she knew that the cook had stolen out—waiting for Death to come and snatch her husband from her. No; he would not snatch, he would steal upon his prey as noiselessly as the approach of Sin to Innocence—an invisible, unfair, sneaking enemy, with whom no man's strength could grapple. If he would only come like a man, and take his chances like a man! Women had been known to reach the hearts of giants with the dagger's point. But he would creep upon her.

She gave an exclamation of horror. Something was creeping over the window-sill. Her limbs palsied, but she struggled to her feet and looked back, her eyes dragged about against her own volition. Two small green stars glared menacingly at her just above the sill; then the cat possessing them leaped downward, and the stars disappeared.

She realized that she was horribly frightened. 'Is it possible?' she thought. 'Am I afraid of Death, and of Death that has not yet come? I have always been rather a brave woman; he used to call me heroic; but then with him it was impossible to fear anything. And I begged them to leave me alone with him as the last of earthly boons. Oh, shame!'

But she was still quaking as she resumed her seat, and laid her hand again on his heart. She wished that she had asked Mary to sit outside the door; there was no bell in the room. To call would be worse than desecrating the house of God, and she would not leave him for one moment. To return and find him dead—gone alone!

Her knees smote each other. It was idle to deny it; she was in a state of unreasoning terror. Her eyes rolled apprehensively about; she wondered if she should see It when It came; wondered how far off It was now. Not very far; the heart was barely pulsing. She had heard of the power of the corpse to drive brave men to frenzy, and had wondered, having no morbid horror of the dead. But this! To wait—and wait—and wait—perhaps for hours—past the midnight—on to the small hours—while that awful, determined, leisurely Something stole nearer and nearer.

She bent to him who had been her protector with a spasm of anger. Where was the indomitable spirit that had held her all these years with such strong and loving clasp? How could he leave her? How could he desert her? Her head fell back and moved restlessly against the cushion; moaning with the agony of loss, she recalled him as he had been. Then fear once more took possession of her, and she sat erect, rigid, breathless, awaiting the approach of Death.

Suddenly, far down in the house, on the first floor, her strained hearing took note of a sound—a wary, muffled sound, as if someone were creeping up the stair, fearful of being heard. Slowly! It seemed to count a hundred between the laying down of each foot. She gave a hysterical gasp. Where was the slow music?

Her face, her body, were wet—as if a wave of death-sweat had broken over them. There was a stiff feeling at the roots of her hair; she wondered if it were really standing erect. But she could not raise her hand to ascertain. Possibly it was only the colouring matter freezing and bleaching. Her muscles were flabby, her nerves twitched helplessly.

She knew that it was Death who was coming to her through the silent deserted house; knew that it was the sensitive ear of her intelligence that heard him, not the dull, coarse-grained ear of the body.

He toiled up the stair painfully, as if he were old and tired with much work. But how could he afford to loiter, with all the work he had to do? Every minute, every second, he must be in demand to hook his cold, hard finger about a soul struggling to escape from its putrefying tenement. But probably he had his emissaries, his minions: for only those worthy of the honour did he come in person.

He reached the first landing and crept like a cat down the hall to the next stair, then crawled slowly up as before. Light as the footfalls were, they were squarely planted, unfaltering; slow, they never halted.

Mechanically she pressed her jerking hand closer against the heart; its beats were almost done. They would finish, she calculated, just as those footfalls paused beside the bed.

She was no longer a human being; she was an Intelligence and an Ear. Not a sound came from without, even the *Elevated* appeared to be temporarily off duty; but inside the big quiet house that footfall was waxing louder, louder, until iron feet crashed on iron stairs and echo thundered.

She had counted the steps—one—two—three—irritated beyond endurance at the long deliberate pauses between. As they climbed and clanged with slow precision she continued to count, audibly and with equal precision, noting their hollow reverberation. How many steps had the stair? She wished she knew. No need! The colossal trampling announced the lessening distance in an increasing volume of sound not to be misunderstood. It turned the curve; it reached the landing; it advanced—slowly—down the hall; it paused before her door. Then knuckles of iron shook the frail panels. Her nerveless tongue gave no invitation. The knocking became more imperious; the very walls vibrated. The handle turned, swiftly and firmly. With a wild instinctive movement she flung herself into the arms of her husband.

When Mary opened the door and entered the room she found a dead woman lying across a dead man.

27

THE DANCING PARTNER

Jerome K. Jerome

The affair was becoming horrible...

'This story,' commenced MacShaugnassy, 'comes from Furtwangen, a small town in the Black Forest. There lived there a very wonderful old fellow named Nicholaus Geibel. His business was the making of mechanical toys, at which work he had acquired an almost European reputation. He made rabbits that would emerge from the heart of a cabbage, flop their ears, smooth their whiskers, and disappear again; cats that would wash their faces, and mew so naturally that dogs would mistake them for real cats and fly at them; dolls with phonographs concealed within them, that would raise their hats and say, "Good morning; how do you do?" and some that would even sing a song.

'But, he was something more than a mere mechanic; he was an artist. His work was with him a hobby, almost a passion. His shop was filled with all manner of strange things that never would, or could, be sold—things he had made for the pure love of making them. He had contrived a mechanical donkey that would trot for two hours by means of stored electricity, and trot, too, much faster than the live article, and with less need for exertion on the part of the driver, a bird that would shoot up into the air, fly round and round in a circle, and drop to earth at the exact spot from where it started; a skeleton that, supported by an upright iron bar, would dance a hornpipe, a life-size lady doll that could play the fiddle, and a gentleman with a hollow inside who could smoke a pipe and drink more lager beer than any three average German students put together, which is saying much.

'Indeed, it was the belief of the town that old Geibel could make a man capable of doing everything that a respectable man need want to do. One day he made a man who did too much, and it came about in this way:

'Young Doctor Follen had a baby, and the baby had a birthday. Its first birthday put Doctor Follen's household into somewhat of a flurry, but on the occasion of its second birthday, Mrs Doctor Follen gave a ball in honour of the event. Old Geibel and his daughter Olga were among the guests.

'During the afternoon of the next day some three or four of Olga's bosom friends, who had also been present at the ball, dropped in to have a chat about it. They naturally fell to discussing the men, and to criticizing their dancing. Old Geibel was in the room, but he appeared to be absorbed in his newspaper, and the girls took no notice of him.

'"There seem to be fewer men who can dance at every ball you go to," said one of the girls.

'"Yes, and don't the ones who can give themselves airs?" said another; "they make quite a favour of asking you."

'"And how stupidly they talk," added a third. "They always say exactly the same things: 'How charming you are looking tonight.' 'Do you often go to Vienna? Oh, you should, it's delightful.' 'What a charming dress you have on.' 'What a warm day it has been.' 'Do you like Wagner?' I do wish they'd think of something new."

'"Oh, I never mind how they talk," said a fourth. "If a man dances well he may be a fool for all I care."

'"He generally is," slipped in a thin girl, rather spitefully.

'"I go to a ball to dance," continued the previous speaker, not noticing the interruption. "All I ask is that he shall hold me firmly, take me round steadily, and not get tired before I do."

'"A clockwork figure would be the thing for you," said the girl who had interrupted.

'"Bravo!" cried one of the others, clapping her hands, "what a capital idea!"

'"What's a capital idea?" they asked.

'"Why, a clockwork dancer, or, better still, one that would go by electricity and never run down."

'The girls took up the idea with enthusiasm.

'"Oh, what a lovely partner he would make," said one; "he would never kick you, or tread on your toes."

'"Or tear your dress," said another.

'"Or get out of step."

'"Or get giddy and lean on you."

'"And he would never want to mop his face with his handkerchief. I do hate to see a man do that after every dance."

'"And wouldn't want to spend the whole evening in the supper-room."

'"Why, with a phonograph inside him to grind out all the stock remarks, you would not be able to tell him from a real man," said the girl who had first suggested the idea. "Oh yes, you would," said the thin girl, "he would be so much nicer."

'Old Geibel had laid down his paper, and was listening with both his ears. On one of the girls glancing in his direction, however, he hurriedly hid himself again behind it.

'After the girls were gone, he went into his workshop, where Olga heard him walking up and down, and every now and then chuckling to himself; and that night he talked to her a good deal about dancing and dancing men—asked what dances were most popular—what steps were gone through, with many other questions bearing on the subject.

'Then for a couple of weeks he kept much to his factory, and was very thoughtful and busy, though prone at unexpected moments to break into a quiet low laugh, as if enjoying a joke that nobody else knew of.

'A month later another ball took place in Furtwangen. On this occasion it was given by old Wenzel, the wealthy timber merchant, to celebrate his niece's betrothal, and Geibel and his daughter were again among the invited.

'When the hour arrived to set out, Olga sought her father.

Not finding him in the house, she tapped at the door of his workshop. He appeared in his shirt-sleeves, looking hot but radiant.

'"Don't wait for me," he said, "you go on, I'll follow you. I've got something to finish."

'As she turned to obey he called after her, "Tell them I'm going to bring a young man with me—such a nice young man, and an excellent dancer. All the girls will like him." Then he laughed and closed the door.

'Her father generally kept his doings secret from everybody, but she had a pretty shrewd suspicion of what he had been planning, and so, to a certain extent, was able to prepare the guests for what was coming. Anticipation ran high, and the arrival of the famous mechanist was eagerly awaited.

'At length the sound of wheels was heard outside, followed by a great commotion in the passage, and old Wenzel himself, his jolly face red with excitement and suppressed laughter, burst into the room and announced in stentorian tones:

'"Herr Geibel—and a friend."

'Herr Geibel and his "friend" entered, greeted with shouts of laughter and applause, and advanced to the centre of the room.

'"Allow me, ladies and gentlemen," said Herr Geibel, "to introduce you to my friend, Lieutenant Fritz. Fritz, my dear fellow, bow to the ladies and gentlemen."

'Geibel placed his hand encouragingly on Fritz's shoulder, and the Lieutenant bowed low, accompanying the action with a harsh clicking noise in his throat, unpleasantly suggestive of a death-rattle. But that was only a detail.

'"He walks a little stiffly" (old Geibel took his arm and walked him forward a few steps. He certainly did walk stiffly), "but then, walking is not his forte. He is essentially a dancing man. I have only been able to teach him the waltz as yet, but at that he is faultless. Come, which of you ladies may I introduce him to as a partner? He keeps perfect time; he never gets tired; he won't kick you or tread on your dress; he will hold you as firmly as you like, and go as quickly or as slowly as you please;

he never gets giddy; and he is full of conversation. Come, speak up for yourself, my boy."

'The old gentleman twisted one of the bottons at the back of his coat, and immediately Fritz opened his mouth, and in thin tones that appeared to proceed from the back of his head, remarked suddenly, "May I have the pleasure?" and then shut his mouth again with a snap.

'That Lieutenant Fritz had made a strong impression on the company was undoubted, yet none of the girls seemed inclined to dance with him. They looked askance at his waxen face, with his staring eyes and fixed smile, and shuddered. At last old Geibel came to the girl who had conceived the idea.

'"It is your own suggestion, carried out to the letter," said Geibel, "an electric dancer. You owe it to the gentleman to give him a trial."

'She was a bright, saucy little girl, fond of a frolic. Her host added his entreaties, and she consented.

'Herr Geibel fixed the figure to her. Its right arm was screwed round her waist, and held her firmly; its delicately-jointed left hand was made to fasten itself upon her right. The old toymaker showed her how to regulate its speed, and how to stop it, and release herself.

'"It will take you round in a complete circle," he explained; "be careful that no one knocks against you, and alters its course."

'The music struck up. Old Geibel put the current in motion, and Annette and her strange partner began to dance.

'For a while everyone stood watching them. The figure performed its purpose admirably. Keeping perfect time and step, and holding its little partner tight clasped in an unyielding embrace, it revolved steadily, pouring forth at the same time a constant flow of squeaky conversation, broken by brief intervals of grinding silence.

'"How charming you are looking tonight," it remarked in its thin, far-away voice. "What a lovely day it has been. Do you like dancing? How well our steps agree. You will give me another, won't you? Oh, don't be so cruel. What a charming gown you have on. Isn't waltzing delightful? I could go on dancing for ever—with you. Have you had supper?"

'As she grew more familiar with the uncanny creature, the girl's nervousness wore off, and she entered into the fun of the thing.

'"Oh, he's just lovely," she cried, laughing. "I could go on dancing with him all my life."

'Couple after couple now joined them, and soon all the dancers in the room were whirling round behind them. Nicholaus Geibel stood looking on, beaming with childish delight at his success.

'Old Wenzel approached him, and whispered something in his ear. Geibel laughed and nodded, and the two worked their way quietly towards the door.

'"This is the young people's house tonight," said Wenzel, so soon as they were outside; "you and I will have a quiet pipe and a glass of hock, over in the countinghouse."

'Meanwhile the dancing grew more fast and furious. Little Annette loosened the screw regulating her partner's rate of progress, and the figure flew round with her swifter and swifter. Couple after couple dropped out exhausted, but they only went the faster, till at length they remained dancing alone.

'Madder and madder became the waltz. The music lagged behind: the musicians, unable to keep pace, ceased, and sat staring. The younger guests applauded, but the older faces began to grow anxious.

'"Hadn't you better stop, dear," said one of the women, "you'll make yourself so tired."

'But Annette did not answer.

'"I believe she's fainted," cried out a girl who had caught sight of her face as it was swept by.

'One of the men sprang forward and clutched at the figure, but its impetus threw him down on to the floor, where its steel-cased feet laid bare his cheek. The thing evidently did not intend to part with its prize so easily.

'Had anyone retained a cool head, the figure, one cannot

help thinking, might easily have been stopped. Two or three men acting in concert might have lifted it bodily off the floor, or have jammed it into a corner. But few human heads are capable of remaining cool under excitement. Those who are not present think how stupid must have been those who were; those who are reflect afterwards how simple it would have been to do this, that, or the other, if only they had thought of it at the time.

'The women grew hysterical. The men shouted contradictory directions to one another. Two of them made a bungling rush at the figure, which had the end result of forcing it out of its orbit at the centre of the room, and sending it crashing against the walls and furniture. A stream of blood showed itself down the girl's white frock, and followed her along the floor. The affair was becoming horrible. The women rushed screaming from the room. The men followed them.

'One sensible suggestion was made: "Find Geibel—fetch Geibel."

'No one had noticed him leave the room, no one knew where he was. A party went in search of him. The others, too unnerved to go back into the ballroom, crowded outside the door and listened. They could hear the steady whir of the wheels upon the polished floor as the thing spun round and round; the dull thud as every now and again it dashed itself and its burden against some opposing object and ricocheted off in a new direction.

'And everlastingly it talked in that thin ghostly voice, repeating over and over the same formula: "How charming you look tonight. What a lovely day it has been. Oh, don't be so cruel. I could go on dancing for ever—with you. Have you had supper?"

'Of course they sought Geibel everywhere but where he was. They looked in every room in the house, then they rushed off in a body to his own place, and spent precious minutes waking up his deaf old housekeeper. At last it occurred to one of the party that Wenzel was missing also, and then the idea of the counting-house across the yard presented itself to them, and there they found him.

'He rose up, very pale, and followed them; and he and old Wenzel forced their way through the crowd of guests gathered outside, and entered the room, and locked the door behind them.

'From within there came the muffled sound of low voices and quick steps, followed by a confused scuffling noise, then silence, then the low voices again.

'After a time the door opened, and those near it pressed forward to enter, but old Wenzel's broad head and shoulders barred the way.

'"I want you—and you, Bekler," he said, addressing a couple of the elder men. His voice was calm, but his face was deadly white. "The rest of you, please go—get the women away as quickly as you can."

'From that day old Nicholaus Geibel confined himself to the making of mechanical rabbits, and cats that mewed and washed their faces.'

28

THE OPEN WINDOW

Saki

Framton shivered slightly and turned towards...

'My aunt will be down presently, Mr Nuttel,' said a very self-possessed young lady of fifteen; 'in the meantime you must try and put up with me.'

Framton Nuttel endeavoured to say the correct something which should duly flatter the niece of the moment without unduly discounting the aunt that was to come. Privately he doubted more than ever whether these formal visits on a succession of total strangers would do much towards helping the nerve cure which he was supposed to be undergoing.

'I know how it will be,' his sister had said when he was preparing to migrate to this rural retreat; 'you will bury yourself down there and not speak to a living soul, and your nerves will be worse than ever from moping. I shall just give you letters of introduction to all the people I know there. Some of them, as far as I can remember, were quite nice.'

Framton wondered whether Mrs Sappleton, the lady to whom he was presenting one of the letters of introduction, came into the nice division.

'Do you know many of the people round here?' asked the niece, when she judged that they had had sufficient silent communion.

'Hardly a soul,' said Framton. 'My sister was staying here, at the rectory, you know, some four years ago, and she gave me letters of introduction to some of the people here.'

He made the last statement in a tone of distinct regret.

'Then you know practically nothing about my aunt?' pursued the self-possessed young lady.

'Only her name and address,' admitted the caller. He was wondering whether Mrs Sappleton was in the married or widowed state. An undefinable something about the room seemed to suggest masculine habitation.

'Her great tragedy happened just three years ago,' said the child; 'that would be since your sister's time.'

'Her tragedy?' asked Framton; somehow in this restful country spot tragedies seemed out of place.

'You may wonder why we keep that window wide open on an October afternoon,' said the niece, indicating a large French window that opened on to a lawn.

'It is quite warm for the time of the year,' said Framton; 'but has that window got anything to do with the tragedy?'

'Out through that window, three years ago to a day, her husband and her two young brothers went off for their day's shooting. They never came back. In crossing the moor to their favourite snipe-shooting ground they were all three engulfed in a treacherous piece of bog. It had been that dreadful wet summer, you know, and places that were safe in other years gave way suddenly without warning. Their bodies were never recovered. That was the dreadful part of it.' Here the child's voice lost its self-possessed note and became falteringly human. 'Poor aunt always thinks that they will come back someday, they and the little brown spaniel that was lost with them, and walk in at that window just as they used to do. That is why the window is kept open every evening till it is quite dusk. Poor dear aunt, she has often told me how they went out, her husband with his white waterproof coat over his arm, and Ronnie, her youngest brother, singing "Bertie, why do you bound?" as he always did to tease her, because she said it got on her nerves. Do you know, sometimes on still, quiet evenings like this, I almost get a creepy feeling that they will all walk in through that window—'

She broke off with a little shudder. It was a relief to Framton when the aunt bustled into the room with a whirl of apologies for being late in making her appearance.

'I hope Vera has been amusing you?' she said.

'She has been very interesting,' said Framton.

'I hope you don't mind the open window,' said Mrs Sappleton briskly; 'my husband and brothers will be home directly from shooting, and they always come in this way. They've been out for snipe in the marshes today, so they'll make a fine mess over my poor carpets. So like you menfolk, isn't it?'

She rattled on cheerfully about the shooting and the scarcity of birds, and the prospects for duck in the winter. To Framton it was all purely horrible. He made a desperate but only partially successful effort to turn the talk on to a less ghastly topic; he was conscious that his hostess was giving him only a fragment of her attention, and her eyes were constantly straying past him to the open window and the lawn beyond. It was certainly an unfortunate coincidence that he should have paid his visit on this tragic anniversary.

'The doctors agree in ordering me complete rest, an absence of mental excitement and avoidance of anything in the nature of violent physical exercise,' announced Framton, who laboured under the tolerably widespread delusion that total strangers and chance acquaintances are hungry for the least detail of one's ailments and infirmities, their cause and cure. 'On the matter of diet they are not so much in agreement,' he continued.

'No?' said Mrs Sappleton, in a voice which only replaced a yawn at the last moment. Then she suddenly brightened into alert attention—but not to what Framton was saying.

'Here they are at last!' she cried. 'Just in time for tea, and don't they look as if they were muddy up to the eyes!'

Framton shivered slightly and turned towards the niece with a look intended to convey sympathetic comprehension. The child was staring out through the open window with a dazed horror in her eyes. In a chill shock of nameless fear Framton swung round in his seat and looked in the same direction.

In the deepening twilight three figures were walking across

the lawn towards the window, they all carried guns under their arms, and one of them was additionally burdened with a white coat hung over his shoulders. A tired brown spaniel kept close at their heels. Noiselessly they neared the house, and then a hoarse young voice chanted out of the dusk: 'I said, Bertie, why do you bound?'

Framton grabbed wildly at his stick and hat; the hall door, the gravel drive and the front gate were dimly noted stages in his headlong retreat. A cyclist coming along the road had to run into the hedge to avoid imminent collision.

'Here we are, my dear,' said the bearer of the white mackintosh, coming in through the window, 'fairly muddy, but most of it's dry. Who was that who bolted out as we came up?'

'A most extraordinary man, a Mr Nuttel,' said Mrs Sappleton; 'could only talk about his illnesses, and dashed off without a word of goodbye or apology when you arrived. One would think he had seen a ghost.'

'I expect it was the spaniel,' said the niece calmly; 'he told me he had a horror of dogs. He was once hunted into a cemetery somewhere on the banks of the Ganges by a pack of pariah dogs and had to spend the night in a newly dug grave with the creatures snarling and grinning and foaming just above him. Enough to make anyone lose their nerve.'

Romance at short notice was her speciality.

29

LOST HEARTS

M.R. James

...Who was the old man whose picture hung on the staircase, sitting at a table, with a skull under his hand?

It was, as far as I can ascertain, in September of the year 1811 that a post-chaise drew up before the door of Aswarby Hall, in the heart of Lincolnshire. The little boy who was the only passenger in the chaise, and who jumped out as soon as it had stopped, looked about him with the keenest curiosity during the short interval that elapsed between the ringing of the bell and the opening of the hall door. He saw a tall, square, red-brick house, built in the reign of Anne; a stone-pillared porch had been added in the purer classical style of 1790; the windows of the house were many, tall and narrow, with small panes and thick white woodwork. A pediment, pierced with a round window, crowned the front. There were wings to right and left, connected by curious glazed galleries, supported by colonnades, with the central block. These wings plainly contained the stables and offices of the house. Each was surmounted by an ornamental cupola with a gilded vane.

An evening light shone on the building, making the window-panes glow like so many fires. Away from the Hall in front stretched a flat park studded with oaks and fringed with firs, which stood out against the sky. The clock in the church-tower, buried in trees on the edge of the park, only its golden weather-cock catching the light, was striking six, and the sound came gently beating down the wind. It was altogether a pleasant impression, though tinged with the sort of melancholy appropriate to an evening in early autumn, that was conveyed to the mind of the boy who was standing in the porch waiting for the door to open to him.

The post-chaise had brought him from Warwickshire, where, some six months before, he had been left an orphan. Now, owing to the generous offer of his elderly cousin, Mr Abney, he had come to live at Aswarby. The offer was unexpected, because all who knew anything of Mr Abney looked upon him as a somewhat austere recluse, into whose steady-going household the advent of a small boy would import a new and, it seemed, incongruous element. The truth is that very little was known of Mr Abney's pursuits or temper. The Professor of Greek at Cambridge had been heard to say that no one knew more of the religious beliefs of the later pagans than did the owner of Aswarby. Certainly his library contained all the then available books bearing on the Mysteries, the Orphic poems, the worship of Mithras, and the Neo–Platonists. In the marble-paved hall stood a fine group of Mithras slaying a bull, which had been imported from the Levant at great expense by the owner. He had contributed a description of it to the Gentleman's Magazine, and he had written a remarkable series of articles in the Critical Museum on the superstitions of the Romans of the Lower Empire. He was looked upon, in fine, as a man wrapped up in his books, and it was a matter of great surprise among his neighbours that he should ever have heard of his orphan cousin, Stephen Elliott, much more that he should have volunteered to make him an inmate of Aswarby Hall.

Whatever may have been expected by his neighbours, it is certain that Mr Abney—the tall, the thin, the austere—seemed inclined to give his young cousin a kindly reception. The moment the front-door was opened he darted out of his study, rubbing his hands with delight.

'How are you, my boy?—how are you? How old are you?' said he—'that is, you are not too much tired, I hope, by your journey to eat your supper?'

'No, thank you, sir,' said Master Elliott; 'I am pretty well.'

'That's a good lad,' said Mr Abney. 'And how old are you, my boy?'

It seemed a little odd that he should have asked the question twice in the first two minutes of their acquaintance.

'I'm twelve years old next birthday, sir,' said Stephen.

'And when is your birthday, my dear boy? Eleventh of September, eh? That's well—that's very well. Nearly a year hence, isn't it? I like—ha, ha!—I like to get these things down in my book. Sure it's twelve? Certain?'

'Yes, quite sure, sir.'

'Well, well! Take him to Mrs Bunch's room, Parkes, and let him have his tea—supper—whatever it is.'

'Yes, sir,' answered the staid Mr Parkes; and conducted Stephen to the lower regions.

Mrs Bunch was the most comfortable and human person whom Stephen had as yet met at Aswarby. She made him completely at home; they were great friends in a quarter of an hour: and great friends they remained. Mrs Bunch had been born in the neighbourhood some fifty-five years before the date of Stephen's arrival, and her residence at the Hall was of twenty years' standing. Consequently, if anyone knew the ins and outs of the house and the district, Mrs Bunch knew them; and she was by no means disinclined to communicate her information.

Certainly there were plenty of things about the Hall and the Hall gardens which Stephen, who was of an adventurous and inquiring turn, was anxious to have explained to him. 'Who built the temple at the end of the laurel walk? Who was the old man whose picture hung on the staircase, sitting at a table, with a skull under his hand?' These and many similar points were cleared up by the resources of Mrs Bunch's powerful intellect. There were others, however, of which the explanations furnished were less satisfactory.

One November evening Stephen was sitting by the fire in the housekeeper's room reflecting on his surroundings.

'Is Mr Abney a good man, and will he go to heaven?' he suddenly asked, with the peculiar confidence which children possess in the ability of their elders to settle these questions, the decision of which is believed to be reserved for other tribunals.

'Good?—bless the child!' said Mrs Bunch. 'Master's as kind a soul as ever I see! Didn't I never tell you of the little boy as he took in out of the street, as you may say, this seven years back? And the little girl, two years after I first come here?'

'No. Do tell me all about them, Mrs Bunch—now, this minute!'

'Well,' said Mrs Bunch, 'the little girl I don't seem to recollect so much about. I know master brought her back with him from his walk one day, and give orders to Mrs Ellis, as was housekeeper then, as she should be took every care with. And the pore child hadn't no one belonging to her—she telled me so her own self—and here she lived with us a matter of three weeks it might be; and then, whether she were somethink of a gipsy in her blood or what not, but one morning she out of her bed afore any of us had opened a eye, and neither track nor yet trace of her have I set eyes on since. Master was wonderful put about, and had all the ponds dragged; but it's my belief she was had away by them gipsies, for there was singing round the house for as much as an hour the night she went, and Parkes, he declare as he heard them a-calling in the woods all that afternoon. Dear, dear! A hodd child she was, so silent in her ways and all, but I was wonderful taken up with her, so domesticated she was—surprising.'

'And what about the little boy?' said Stephen.

'Ah, that pore boy!' sighed Mrs Bunch. 'He were a foreigner—Jevanny he called hisself—and he come a-tweaking his 'urdy-gurdy round and about the drive one winter day, and master 'ad him in that minute, and ast all about where he came from, and how old he was, and how he made his way, and where was his relatives, and all as kind as heart could wish. But it went the same way with him. They're a hunruly lot, them foreign nations, I do suppose, and he was off one fine morning just the same as the girl. Why he went and what he done was our question for as much as a year after; for he never took his 'urdy-gurdy, and there it lays on the shelf.'

The remainder of the evening was spent by Stephen in miscellaneous cross-examination of Mrs Bunch and in efforts to extract a tune from the hurdy-gurdy.

That night he had a curious dream. At the end of the passage at the top of the house, in which his bedroom was situated, there was an old disused bathroom. It was kept locked, but the upper half of the door was glazed, and, since the muslin curtains which used to hang there had long been gone, you could look in and see the lead-lined bath affixed to the wall on the right hand, with its head towards the window.

On the night of which I am speaking, Stephen Elliott found himself, as he thought, looking through the glazed door. The moon was shining through the window, and he was gazing at a figure which lay in the bath.

His description of what he saw reminds me of what I once beheld myself in the famous vaults of St Michan's Church in Dublin, which possesses the horrid property of preserving corpses from decay for centuries. A figure inexpressibly thin and pathetic, of a dusty leaden colour, enveloped in a shroud-like garment, the thin lips crooked into a faint and dreadful smile, the hands pressed tightly over the region of the heart.

As he looked upon it, a distant, almost inaudible moan seemed to issue from its lips, and the arms began to stir. The terror of the sight forced Stephen backwards and he awoke to the fact that he was indeed standing on the cold boarded floor of the passage in the full light of the moon. With a courage which I do not think can be common among boys of his age, he went to the door of the bathroom to ascertain if the figure of his dreams were really there. It was not, and he went back to bed.

Mrs Bunch was much impressed next morning by his story, and went so far as to replace the muslin curtain over the glazed door of the bathroom. Mr Abney, moreover, to whom he confided his experiences at breakfast, was greatly interested and made notes of the matter in what he called 'his book'.

The spring equinox was approaching, as Mr Abney frequently

reminded his cousin, adding that this had been always considered by the ancients to be a critical time for the young: that Stephen would do well to take care of himself, and to shut his bedroom window at night; and that Censorinus had some valuable remarks on the subject. Two incidents that occurred about this time made an impression upon Stephen's mind.

The first was after an unusually uneasy and oppressed night that he had passed—though he could not recall any particular dream that he had had.

The following evening Mrs Bunch was occupying herself in mending his nightgown.

'Gracious me, Master Stephen!' she broke forth rather irritably, 'how do you manage to tear your nightdress all to flinders this way? Look here, sir, what trouble you do give to poor servants that have to darn and mend after you!'

There was indeed a most destructive and apparently wanton series of slits or scorings in the garment, which would undoubtedly require a skilful needle to make good. They were confined to the left side of the chest—long, parallel slits about six inches in length, some of them not quite piercing the texture of the linen. Stephen could only express his entire ignorance of their origin: he was sure they were not there the night before.

'But,' he said, 'Mrs Bunch, they are just the same as the scratches on the outside of my bedroom door: and I'm sure I never had anything to do with making them.'

Mrs Bunch gazed at him open-mouthed, then snatched up a candle, departed hastily from the room, and was heard making her way upstairs. In a few minutes she came down.

'Well,' she said, 'Master Stephen, it's a funny thing to me how them marks and scratches can 'a' come there—too high up for any cat or dog to 'ave made 'em, much less a rat: for all the world like a Chinaman's finger-nails, as my uncle in the tea-trade used to tell us of when we was girls together. I wouldn't say nothing to master, not if I was you, Master Stephen, my dear; and just turn the key of the door when you go to your bed.'

'I always do, Mrs Bunch, as soon as I've said my prayers.'

'Ah, that's a good child: always say your prayers, and then no one can't hurt you.'

Herewith Mrs Bunch addressed herself to mending the injured nightgown, with intervals of meditation, until bed-time. This was on a Friday night in March, 1812.

On the following evening the usual duet of Stephen and Mrs Bunch was augmented by the sudden arrival of Mr Parkes, the butler, who as a rule kept himself rather to himself in his own pantry. He did not see that Stephen was there: he was, moreover, flustered and less slow of speech than was his wont.

'Master may get up his own wine, if he likes, of an evening,' was his first remark. 'Either I do it in the daytime or not at all, Mrs Bunch. I don't know what it may be: very like it's the rats, or the wind got into the cellars; but I'm not so young as I was, and I can't go through with it as I have done.'

'Well, Mr Parkes, you know it is a surprising place for the rats, is the Hall.'

'I'm not denying that, Mrs Bunch; and, to be sure, many a time I've heard the tale from the men in the shipyards about the rat that could speak. I never laid no confidence in that before; but tonight, if I'd demeaned myself to lay my ear to the door of the further bin, I could pretty much have heard what they was saying.'

'Oh, there, Mr Parkes, I've no patience with your fancies! Rats talking in the wine-cellar indeed!'

'Well, Mrs Bunch, I've no wish to argue with you: all I say is, if you choose to go to the far bin, and lay your ear to the door, you may prove my words this minute.'

'What nonsense you do talk, Mr Parkes—not fit for children to listen to! Why, you'll be frightening Master Stephen there out of his wits.'

'What! Master Stephen?' said Parkes, awaking to the consciousness of the boy's presence. 'Master Stephen knows well enough when I'm a-playing a joke with you, Mrs Bunch.'

In fact, Master Stephen knew much too well to suppose that Mr Parkes had in the first instance intended a joke. He was interested, not altogether pleasantly, in the situation; but all his questions were unsuccessful in inducing the butler to give any more detailed account of his experiences in the wine-cellar.

◆

We have now arrived at March 24, 1812. It was a day of curious experiences for Stephen: a windy, noisy day, which filled the house and the gardens with a restless impression. As Stephen stood by the fence of the grounds, and looked out into the park, he felt as if an endless procession of unseen people were sweeping past him on the wind, borne on resistlessly and aimlessly, vainly striving to stop themselves, to catch at something that might arrest their flight and bring them once again into contact with the living world of which they had formed a part. After luncheon that day Mr Abney said:

'Stephen, my boy, do you think you could manage to come to me tonight as late as eleven o'clock in my study? I shall be busy until that time, and I wish to show you something connected with your future life which it is most important that you should know. You are not to mention this matter to Mrs Bunch nor to anyone else in the house; and you had better go to your room at the usual time.'

Here was a new excitement added to life: Stephen eagerly grasped at the opportunity of sitting up till eleven o'clock. He looked in at the library door on his way upstairs that evening, and saw a brazier, which he had often noticed in the corner of the room, moved out before the fire; an old silver-gilt cup stood on the table, filled with red wine, and some written sheets of paper lay near it. Mr Abney was sprinkling some incense on the brazier from a round silver box as Stephen passed, but did not seem to notice his step.

The wind had fallen, and there was a still night and a full moon. At about ten o'clock Stephen was standing at the open window of his bedroom, looking out over the country. Still as the night was, the mysterious population of the distant moonlit woods was not yet lulled to rest. From time to time strange cries as of lost and despairing wanderers sounded from across the mere. They might be the notes of owls or water-birds, yet they did not quite resemble either sound. Were not they coming nearer? Now they sounded from the nearer side of the water, and in a few moments they seemed to be floating about among the shrubberies. Then they ceased; but just as Stephen was thinking of shutting the window and resuming his reading of *Robinson Crusoe*, he caught sight of two figures standing on the gravelled terrace that ran along the garden side of the Hall—the figures of a boy and girl, as it seemed; they stood side by side, looking up at the windows. Something in the form of the girl recalled irresistibly his dream of the figure in the bath. The boy inspired him with more acute fear.

Whilst the girl stood still, half smiling, with her hands clasped over her heart, the boy, a thin shape, with black hair and ragged clothing, raised his arms in the air with an appearance of menace and of unappeasable hunger and longing. The moon shone upon his almost transparent hands, and Stephen saw that the nails were fearfully long and that the light shone through them. As he stood with his arms thus raised, he disclosed a terrifying spectacle. On the left side of his chest there opened a black and gaping rent; and there fell upon Stephen's brain, rather than upon his ear, the impression of one of those hungry and desolate cries that he had heard resounding over the woods of Aswarby all that evening. In another moment this dreadful pair had moved swiftly and noiselessly over the dry gravel, and he saw them no more.

Inexpressibly frightened as he was, he determined to take his candle and go down to Mr Abney's study, for the hour appointed for their meeting was near at hand. The study or library opened out of the front-hall on one side, and Stephen, urged on by his terrors, did not take long in getting there. To effect an entrance was not so easy. It was not locked, he felt sure, for the key was on the outside of the door as usual. His repeated knocks produced no answer. Mr Abney was engaged: he was speaking. What! Why did he try to cry out? And why was the cry choked in his throat? Had he, too, seen the mysterious children? But now everything was quiet, and the door yielded to Stephen's terrified and frantic pushing.

◆

On the table in Mr Abney's study certain papers were found which explained the situation to Stephen Elliott when he was of an age to understand them. The most important sentences were as follows:

'It was a belief very strongly and generally held by the ancients—of whose wisdom in these matters I have had such experience as induces me to place confidence in their assertions—that by enacting certain processes, which to us moderns have something of a barbaric complexion, a very remarkable enlightenment of the spiritual faculties in man may be attained: that, for example, by absorbing the personalities of a certain number of his fellow-creatures, an individual may gain a complete ascendancy over those orders of spiritual beings which control the elemental forces of our universe.

'It is recorded of Simon Magus that he was able to fly in the air, to become invisible, or to assume any form he pleased, by the agency of the soul of a boy whom, to use the libellous phrase employed by the author of the *Clementine Recognitions*, he had "murdered". I find it set down, moreover, with considerable detail in the writings of Hermes Trismegistus, that similar happy results may be produced by the absorption of the hearts of not less than three human beings below the age of twenty-one years. To the testing of the truth of this receipt I have devoted the greater part of the last twenty years, selecting as the corpora vilia of my experiment such persons as could conveniently be removed without occasioning a sensible gap in society. The first step I effected by the removal of one Phoebe Stanley, a girl of gipsy extraction, on March 24, 1792. The second, by the removal of a wandering Italian lad, named Giovanni Paoli, on the night of March 23, 1805. The final "victim"—to employ a word repugnant in the highest degree to my feelings—must be my cousin, Stephen Elliott. His day must be this March 24, 1812.

'The best means of effecting the required absorption is to remove the heart from the living subject, to reduce it to ashes, and to mingle them with about a pint of some red wine, preferably port. The remains of the first two subjects, at least, it will be well to conceal: a disused bathroom or wine-cellar will be found convenient for such a purpose. Some annoyance may be experienced from the psychic portion of the subjects, which popular language dignifies with the name of ghosts. But the man of philosophic temperament—to whom alone the experiment is appropriate—will be little prone to attach importance to the feeble efforts of these beings to wreak their vengeance on him. I contemplate with the liveliest satisfaction the enlarged and emancipated existence which the experiment, if successful, will confer on me; not only placing me beyond the reach of human justice (so-called), but eliminating to a great extent the prospect of death itself.'

Mr Abney was found in his chair, his head thrown back, his face stamped with an expression of rage, fright, and mortal pain. In his left side was a terrible lacerated wound, exposing the heart. There was no blood on his hands, and a long knife that lay on the table was perfectly clean. A savage wild-cat might have inflicted the injuries. The window of the study was open, and it was the opinion of the coroner that Mr Abney had met his death by the agency of some wild creature. But Stephen Elliott's study of the papers I have quoted led him to a very different conclusion.

30

A DEAD WOMAN'S SECRET

Guy de Maupassant

The nun was wildly-kissing the dead woman's hand, an ivory hand as white as the large crucifix lying across the bed...

The woman had died without pain, quietly, as a woman should whose life had been blameless. Now she was resting in her bed, lying on her back, her eyes closed, her features calm, her long white hair carefully arranged as though she had done it up ten minutes before dying. The whole pale countenance of the dead woman was so collected, so calm, so resigned that one could feel what a sweet soul had lived in that body, what a quiet existence this old soul had led, how easy and pure the death of this parent had been.

Kneeling beside the bed, her son, a magistrate with inflexible principles, and her daughter, Marguerite, known as Sister Eulalie, were weeping as though their hearts would break. She had, from childhood up, armed them with a strict moral code, teaching them religion, without weakness, and duty, without compromise. He, the man, had become a judge and handled the law as a weapon with which he smote the weak ones without pity. She, the girl, influenced by the virtue which had bathed her in this austere family, had become the bride of the Church through her loathing for man.

They had hardly known their father, knowing only that he had made their mother most unhappy, without being told any other details.

The nun was wildly-kissing the dead woman's hand, an ivory hand as white as the large crucifix lying across the bed.

On the other side of the long body the other hand seemed still to be holding the sheet in the death grasp; and the sheet had preserved the little creases as a memory of those last movements which precede eternal immobility.

A few light taps on the door caused the two sobbing heads to look up, and the priest, who had just come from dinner, returned. He was red and out of breath from his interrupted digestion, for he had made himself a strong mixture of coffee and brandy in order to combat the fatigue of the last few nights and of the wake which was beginning.

He looked sad, with that assumed sadness of the priest for whom death is a bread winner. He crossed himself and approached with his professional gesture: 'Well, my poor children! I have come to help you pass these last sad hours.' But Sister Eulalie suddenly arose. 'Thank you, father, but my brother and I prefer to remain alone with her. This is our last chance to see her, and we wish to be together, all three of us, as we—we—used to be when we were small and our poor mo—mother—'

Grief and tears stopped her; she could not continue.

Once more serene, the priest bowed, thinking of his bed. 'As you wish, my children.' He kneeled, crossed himself, prayed, arose and went out quietly, murmuring: 'She was a saint!'

They remained alone; the dead woman and her children. The ticking of the clock, hidden in the shadow, could be heard distinctly, and through the open window drifted in the sweet smell of hay and of woods, together with the soft moonlight. No other noise could be heard over the land except the occasional croaking of the frog or the chirping of some belated insect. An infinite peace, a divine melancholy, a silent serenity surrounded this dead woman, seemed to be breathed out from her and to appease nature itself.

Then the judge, still kneeling, his head buried in the bed clothes, cried in a voice altered by grief and deadened by the sheets and blankets: 'Mamma, mamma, mamma!' And his sister, frantically striking her forehead against the woodwork, convulsed, twitching and trembling as in an epileptic fit, moaned: 'Jesus, Jesus, mamma, Jesus!' And both of them, shaken by a storm of grief, gasped and choked.

The crisis slowly calmed down and they began to weep quietly, just as on the sea when a calm follows a squall.

A rather long time passed and they arose and looked at their dead. And the memories, those distant memories, yesterday so dear, today so torturing, came to their minds with all the little forgotten details, those little intimate familiar details which bring back to life the one who has left. They recalled to each other circumstances, words, smiles, intonations of the mother who was no longer to speak to them. They saw her again happy and calm. They remembered things which she had said, and a little motion of the hand, like beating time, which she often used when emphasizing something important.

And they loved her as they never had loved her before. They measured the depth of their grief, and thus they discovered how lonely they would find themselves.

It was their prop, their guide, their whole youth, all the best part of their lives which was disappearing. It was their bond with life, their mother, their mamma, the connecting link with their forefathers which they would thenceforth miss. They now became solitary, lonely beings; they could no longer look back.

The nun said to her brother: 'You remember how mamma used always to read her old letters; they are all there in that drawer. Let us, in turn, read them; let us live her whole life through tonight beside her! It would be like a road to the cross, like making the acquaintance of her mother, of our grandparents, whom we never knew, but whose letters are there and of whom she so often spoke, do you remember?'

Out of the drawer they took about ten little packages of yellow paper, tied with care and arranged one beside the other. They threw these relics on the bed and chose one of them on which the word 'Father' was written. They opened and read it.

It was one of those old-fashioned letters which one finds in old family desk drawers, those epistles which smell of another century. The first one started: 'My dear,' another one: 'My beautiful little girl,' others: 'My dear child,' or: 'My dear daughter.' And suddenly the nun began to read aloud, to read over to the dead woman her whole history, all her tender memories. The judge, resting his elbow on the bed, was listening with his eyes fastened on his mother. The motionless body seemed happy.

Sister Eulalie, interrupting herself, said suddenly:

'These ought to be put in the grave with her; they ought to be used as a shroud and she ought to be buried in it.' She took another package, on which no name was written. She began to read in a firm voice: 'My adored one, I love you wildly. Since yesterday I have been suffering the tortures of the damned, haunted by our memory. I feel your lips against mine, your eyes in mine, your breast against mine. I love you, I love you! You have driven me mad. My arms open, I gasp, moved by a wild desire to hold you again. My whole soul and body cries out for you, wants you. I have kept in my mouth the taste of your kisses—'

The judge had straightened himself up. The nun stopped reading. He snatched the letter from her and looked for the signature. There was none, but only under the words, 'The man who adores you,' the name 'Henry.' Their father's name was Rene. Therefore this was not from him. The son then quickly rummaged through the package of letters, took one out and read: 'I can no longer live without your caresses.' Standing erect, severe as when sitting on the bench, he looked unmoved at the dead woman. The nun, straight as a statue, tears trembling in the corners of her eyes, was watching her brother, waiting. Then he crossed the room slowly, went to the window and stood there, gazing out into the dark night.

When he turned around again Sister Eulalie, her eyes dry now, was still standing near the bed, her head bent down.

He stepped forward, quickly picked up the letters and threw them pell-mell back into the drawer. Then he closed the curtains of the bed.

When daylight made the candles on the table turn pale

the son slowly left his armchair, and without looking again at the mother upon whom he had passed sentence, severing the tie that united her to son and daughter, he said slowly: 'Let us now retire, sister.'

31

THE MASQUE OF THE RED DEATH

Edgar Allan Poe

Blood was its Avatar and its seal
—the redness and the horror of blood...

The 'Red Death' had long devastated the country. No pestilence had ever been so fatal, or so hideous. Blood was its Avatar and its seal—the redness and the horror of blood. There were sharp pains, and sudden dizziness, and then profuse bleeding at the pores, with dissolution. The scarlet stains upon the body and especially upon the face of the victim, were the pest ban which shut him out from the aid and from the sympathy of his fellow-men. And the whole seizure, progress and termination of the disease, were the incidents of half an hour.

But the Prince Prospero was happy and dauntless and sagacious. When his dominions were half depopulated, he summoned to his presence a thousand hale and light-hearted friends from among the knights and dames of his court, and with these retired to the deep seclusion of one of his castellated abbeys. This was an extensive and magnificent structure, the creation of the prince's own eccentric yet august taste. A strong and lofty wall girdled it in. This wall had gates of iron. The courtiers, having entered, brought furnaces and massy hammers and welded the bolts. They resolved to leave means neither of ingress nor egress to the sudden impulses of despair or of frenzy from within. The abbey was amply provisioned. With such precautions the courtiers might bid defiance to contagion. The external world could take care of itself. In the meantime it was folly to grieve, or to think. The prince had provided all the appliances of pleasure. There were buffoons, there were improvisatori, there were ballet-dancers, there were musicians, there was Beauty, there was wine. All these and security were within. Without was the 'Red Death'.

It was towards the close of the fifth or sixth month of his seclusion, and while the pestilence raged most furiously abroad, that the Prince Prospero entertained his thousand friends at a masked ball of the most unusual magnificence.

It was a voluptuous scene, that masquerade. But first let me tell of the rooms in which it was held. These were seven—an imperial suite.

In many palaces, however, such suites form a long and straight vista, while the folding doors slide back nearly to the walls on either hand, so that the view of the whole extent is scarcely impeded. Here the case was very different, as might have been expected from the duke's love of the *bizarre*. The apartments were so irregularly disposed that the vision embraced but little more than one at a time. There was a sharp turn at every twenty or thirty yards, and at each turn a novel effect. To the right and left, in the middle of each wall, a tall and narrow Gothic window looked out upon a closed corridor which pursued the windings of the suite. These windows were of stained glass whose colour varied in accordance with the prevailing hue of the decorations of the chamber into which it opened. That at the eastern extremity was hung, for example in blue—and vividly blue were its windows. The second chamber was purple in its ornaments and tapestries, and here the panes were purple. The third was green throughout, and so were the casements. The fourth was furnished and lighted with orange—the fifth with white—the sixth with violet. The seventh apartment was closely shrouded in black velvet tapestries that hung all over the ceiling and down the walls, falling in heavy folds upon a carpet of the same material and hue. But in this chamber only, the colour of the windows failed to correspond with the decorations. The panes here were scarlet—a deep blood colour. Now in no one of the seven apartments was there any lamp or candelabrum, amid the profusion of golden ornaments that lay scattered to and fro or depended from the roof.

There was no light of any kind emanating from lamp or candle within the suite of chambers. But in the corridors that followed the suite, there stood, opposite to each window, a heavy tripod, bearing a brazier of fire, that projected its rays through the tinted glass and so glaringly illumined the room. And thus were produced a multitude of gaudy and fantastic appearances. But in the western or black chamber the effect of the fire-light that streamed upon the dark hangings through the blood-tinted panes, was ghastly in the extreme, and produced so wild a look upon the countenances of those who entered, that there were few of the company bold enough to set foot within its precincts at all.

It was in this apartment, also, that there stood against the western wall, a gigantic clock of ebony. Its pendulum swung to and fro with a dull, heavy, monotonous clang; and when the minute-hand made the circuit of the face, and the hour was to be stricken, there came from the brazen lungs of the clock a sound which was clear and loud and deep and exceedingly musical, but of so peculiar a note and emphasis that, at each lapse of an hour, the musicians of the orchestra were constrained to pause, momentarily, in their performance, to harken to the sound; and thus the waltzers perforce ceased their evolutions; and there was a brief disconcert of the whole gay company; and, while the chimes of the clock yet rang, it was observed that the giddiest grew pale, and the more aged and sedate passed their hands over their brows as if in confused revery or meditation. But when the echoes had fully ceased, a light laughter at once pervaded the assembly; the musicians looked at each other and smiled as if at their own nervousness and folly, and made whispering vows, each to the other, that the next chiming of the clock should produce in them no similar emotion; and then, after the lapse of sixty minutes, (which embrace three thousand and six hundred seconds of the Time that flies,) there came yet another chiming of the clock, and then were the same disconcert and tremulousness and meditation as before.

But, in spite of these things, it was a gay and magnificent revel. The tastes of the duke were peculiar. He had a fine eye for colours and effects. He disregarded the *decora* of mere fashion. His plans were bold and fiery, and his conceptions glowed with barbaric lustre. There are some who would have thought him mad. His followers felt that he was not. It was necessary to hear and see and touch him to be sure that he was not.

He had directed, in great part, the movable embellishments of the seven chambers, upon occasion of this great *fete*; and it was his own guiding taste which had given character to the masqueraders. Be sure they were grotesque. There were much glare and glitter and piquancy and phantasm—much of what has been since seen in 'Hernani '. There were arabesque figures with unsuited limbs and appointments. There were delirious fancies such as the madman fashions. There were much of the beautiful, much of the wanton, much of the *bizarre*, something of the terrible, and not a little of that which might have excited disgust.

To and fro in the seven chambers there stalked, in fact, a multitude of dreams. And these—the dreams—writhed in and about, taking hue from the rooms, and causing the wild music of the orchestra to seem as the echo of their steps. And, anon, there strikes the ebony clock which stands in the hall of the velvet. And then, for a moment, all is still, and all is silent save the voice of the clock. The dreams are stiff-frozen as they stand. But the echoes of the chime die away—they have endured but an instant—and a light, half-subdued laughter floats after them as they depart. And now again the music swells, and the dreams live, and writhe to and fro more merrily than ever, taking hue from the many tinted windows through which stream the rays from the tripods. But to the chamber which lies most westwardly of the seven, there are now none of the maskers who venture; for the night is waning away; and there flows a ruddier light through the blood-coloured panes; and the blackness of the sable drapery appals; and to him whose foot falls upon the sable carpet, there comes from the near clock of ebony a muffled peal more solemnly emphatic than any which reaches *their* ears who indulged in the more remote gaieties of the other apartments.

But these other apartments were densely crowded, and in them beat feverishly the heart of life. And the revel went whirlingly on, until at length there commenced the sounding of midnight upon the clock. And then the music ceased, as I have told; and the evolutions of the waltzers were quieted; and there was an uneasy cessation of all things as before. But now there were twelve strokes to be sounded by the bell of the clock; and thus it happened, perhaps, that more of thought crept, with more of time, into the meditations of the thoughtful among those who revelled. And thus too, it happened, perhaps, that before the last echoes of the last chime had utterly sunk into silence, there were many individuals in the crowd who had found leisure to become aware of the presence of a masked figure which had arrested the attention of no single individual before. And the rumour of this new presence having spread itself whisperingly around, there arose at length from the whole company a buzz, or murmur, expressive of disapprobation and surprise—then, finally, of terror, of horror, and of disgust.

In an assembly of phantasms such as I have painted, it may well be supposed that no ordinary appearance could have excited such sensation. In truth the masquerade licence of the night was nearly unlimited; but the figure in question had out-Heroded Herod, and gone beyond the bounds of even the prince's indefinite decorum. There are chords in the hearts of the most reckless which cannot be touched without emotion. Even with the utterly lost, to whom life and death are equally jests, there are matters of which no jest can be made. The whole company, indeed, seemed now deeply to feel that in the costume and bearing of the stranger neither wit nor propriety existed. The figure was tall and gaunt, and shrouded from head to foot in the habiliments of the grave. The mask which concealed the visage was made so nearly to resemble the countenance of a stiffened corpse that the closest scrutiny must have had difficulty in detecting the cheat. And yet all this might have been endured, if not approved, by the mad revellers around. But the mummer had gone so far as to assume the type of the Red Death. His vesture was dabbled in blood—and his broad brow, with all the features of the face, was besprinkled with the scarlet horror.

When the eyes of the Prince Prospero fell upon this spectral image (which, with a slow and solemn movement, as if more fully to sustain its role, stalked to and fro among the waltzers) he was seen to be convulsed, in the first moment with a strong shudder either of terror or distaste; but, in the next, his brow reddened with rage.

'Who dares,'—he demanded hoarsely of the courtiers who stood near him—'who dares insult us with this blasphemous mockery? Seize him and unmask him—that we may know whom we have to hang, at sunrise, from the battlements!'

It was in the eastern or blue chamber in which stood the Prince Prospero as he uttered these words. They rang throughout the seven rooms loudly and clearly, for the prince was a bold and robust man, and the music had become hushed at the waving of his hand.

It was in the blue room where stood the prince, with a group of pale courtiers by his side. At first, as he spoke, there was a slight rushing movement of this group in the direction of the intruder, who at the moment was also near at hand, and now, with deliberate and stately step, made closer approach to the speaker. But from a certain nameless awe with which the mad assumptions of the mummer had inspired the whole party, there were found none who put forth hand to seize him; so that, unimpeded, he passed within a yard of the prince's person; and, while the vast assembly, as if with one impulse, shrank from the centres of the rooms to the walls, he made his way uninterruptedly, but with the same solemn and measured step which had distinguished him from the first, through the blue chamber to the purple—through the purple to the green—through the green to the orange—through this again to the white—and even thence to the violet, ere a decided movement had been made to arrest him. It was then, however, that the Prince Prospero, maddening with rage and the shame of his own momentary cowardice, rushed hurriedly through the six chambers, while none followed him on account of a deadly terror that had seized upon all. He bore aloft a drawn dagger, and had approached, in rapid impetuosity, to within three or four feet of the retreating figure, when the latter, having attained the extremity of the velvet apartment, turned suddenly and confronted his pursuer. There was a sharp cry—and the dagger dropped gleaming upon the sable carpet, upon which, instantly afterwards, fell prostrate in death the Prince Prospero. Then, summoning the wild courage of despair, a throng of the revellers at once threw themselves into the black apartment, and, seizing the mummer, whose tall figure stood erect and motionless within the shadow of the ebony clock, gasped in unutterable horror at finding the grave cerements and corpse-like mask, which they handled with so violent a rudeness, untenanted by any tangible form.

And now was acknowledged the presence of the Red Death. He had come like a thief in the night. And one by one dropped the revellers in the blood-bedewed halls of their revel, and died each in the despairing posture of his fall. And the life of the ebony clock went out with that of the last of the gay. And the flames of the tripods expired.

And Darkness and Decay and the Red Death held illimitable dominion over all.

32

JOHN CHARRINGTON'S WEDDING

Edith Nesbit

Mr Charrington was thrown from the dogcart on his way to the station at half past one. Killed on the spot!

No one ever thought that May Forster would marry John Charrington; but he thought differently, and things which John Charrington intended had a queer way of coming to pass. He asked her to marry him before he went up to Oxford. She laughed and refused him. He asked her again next time he came home. Again she laughed, tossed her dainty blonde head and again refused. A third time he asked her; she said it was becoming a confirmed bad habit, and laughed at him more than ever.

John was not the only man who wanted to marry her: she was the belle of our village coterie, and we were all in love with her more or less; it was a sort of fashion, like masher collars or Inverness capes. Therefore we were as much annoyed as surprised when John Charrington walked into our little local Club—we held it in a loft over the saddler's, I remember—and invited us all to his wedding.

'Your wedding?'

'You don't mean it?'

'Who's the happy pair? When's it to be?'

John Charrington filled his pipe and lighted it before he replied. Then he said: 'I'm sorry to deprive you fellows of your only joke—but Miss Forster and I are to be married in September.'

'You don't mean it?'

'He's got the mitten again, and it's turned his head.'

'No,' I said, rising, 'I see it's true. Lend me a pistol, someone—or a first-class fare to the other end of Nowhere. Charrington has bewitched the only pretty girl in our twenty-mile radius. Was it mesmerism, or a love-potion, Jack?'

'Neither, sir, but a gift you'll never have—perseverance—and the best luck a man ever had in this world.'

There was something in his voice that silenced me, and all chaff of the other fellows failed to draw him further.

The queer thing about it was that when we congratulated Miss Forster, she blushed and smiled and dimpled, for all the world as though she were in love with him, and had been in love with him all the time. Upon my word, I think she had. Women are strange creatures.

We were all asked to the wedding. In Brixham everyone who was anybody knew everybody else who was anyone. My sisters were, I truly believe, more interested in the trousseau than the bride herself, and I was to be best man. The coming marriage was much canvassed at afternoon tea-tables, and at our little Club over the saddler's, and the question was always asked, 'Does she care for him?'

I used to ask that question myself in the early days of their engagement, but after a certain evening in August I never asked it again. I was coming home from the Club through the churchyard. Our church is on a thyme-grown hill, and the turf about it is so thick and soft that one's footsteps are noiseless.

I made no sound as I vaulted the low lichened wall, and threaded my way between the tombstones. It was at the same instant that I heard John Charrington's voice, and saw her. May was sitting on a low flat gravestone, her face turned towards the full splendour of the western sun. Its expression ended, at once and for ever, any question of love for him; it was transfigured to a beauty I should not have believed possible, even to that beautiful little face.

John lay at her feet, and it was his voice that broke the stillness of the golden August evening.

'My dear, my dear, I believe I should come back from the dead if you wanted me!'

I coughed at once to indicate my presence, and passed on into the shadow fully enlightened.

The wedding was to be early in September. Two days before I had to run up to town on business. The train was late, of course, for we are on the South-Eastern, and as I stood grumbling with my watch in my hand, whom should I see but John Charrington and May Forster. They were walking up and down the unfrequented end of the platform, arm in arm, looking into each other's eyes, careless of the sympathetic interest of the porters.

Of course I knew better than to hesitate a moment before burying myself in the booking-office, and it was not till the train drew up at the platform, that I obtrusively passed the pair with my Gladstone, and took the corner in a first-class smoking-carriage. I did this with as good an air of not seeing them as I could assume. I pride myself on my discretion, but if John were travelling alone I wanted his company. I had it.

'Hullo, old man,' came his cheery voice as he swung his bag into my carriage; 'here's luck; I was expecting a dull journey!'

'Where are you off to?' I asked, discretion still bidding me turn my eyes away, though I saw, without looking, that hers were red-rimmed.

'To old Branbridge's,' he answered, shutting the door and leaning out for a last word with his sweetheart.

'Oh, I wish you wouldn't go, John,' she was saying in a low, earnest voice. 'I feel certain something will happen.'

'Do you think I should let anything happen to keep me, and the day after tomorrow our wedding day?'

'Don't go,' she answered, with a pleading intensity which would have sent my Gladstone onto the platform and me after it. But she wasn't speaking to me. John Charrington was made differently: he rarely changed his opinions, never his resolutions.

He only stroked the little ungloved hands that lay on the carriage door.

'I must, May. The old boy's been awfully good to me, and now he's dying I must go and see him, but I shall come home in time for—' the rest of the parting was lost in a whisper and in the rattling lurch of the starting train.

'You're sure to come?' she spoke as the train moved.

'Nothing shall keep me,' he answered; and we steamed out. After he had seen the last of the little figure on the platform he leaned back in his corner and kept silence for a minute.

When he spoke it was to explain to me that his godfather, whose heir he was, lay dying at Peasmarsh Place, some fifty miles away, and had sent for John, and John had felt bound to go.

'I shall be surely back tomorrow,' he said, 'or, if not, the day after, in heaps of time. Thank heaven; one hasn't to get up in the middle of the night to get married nowadays!'

'And suppose Mr Branbridge dies?'

'Alive or dead I mean to be married on Thursday!' John answered, lighting a cigar and unfolding The Times.

At Peasmarsh station we said 'goodbye', and he got out, and I saw him ride off; I went on to London, where I stayed the night.

When I got home the next afternoon—a very wet one, by the way—my sister greeted me with:

'Where's Mr Charrington?'

'Goodness knows,' I answered testily. Every man, since Cain, has resented that kind of question.

'I thought you might have heard from him,' she went on, 'as you're to give him away tomorrow.'

'Isn't he back?' I asked, for I had confidently expected to find him at home.

'No, Geoffrey,' my sister Fanny always had a way of jumping to conclusions, especially such conclusions as were least favourable to her fellow-creatures—'he has not returned, and, what is more, you may depend upon it he won't. You mark my words, there'll be no wedding tomorrow.'

My sister Fanny has a power of annoying me which no other human being possesses.

'You mark my words,' I retorted with asperity, 'you had better give up making such a thundering idiot of yourself. There'll be more wedding tomorrow than ever you'll take the first part in.' A prophecy which, by the way, came true.

But though I could snarl confidently to my sister, I did not feel so comfortable when late that night, I, standing on the doorstep of John's house, heard that he had not returned. I went home gloomily through the rain. Next morning brought a brilliant blue sky, gold sun, and all such softness of air and beauty of cloud as go to make up a perfect day. I woke with a vague feeling of having gone to bed anxious, and of being rather averse to facing that anxiety in the light of full wakefulness.

But with my shaving-water came a note from John which relieved my mind and sent me up to the Forsters with a light heart.

May was in the garden. I saw her blue gown through the hollyhocks as the lodge gates swung to behind me. So I did not go up to the house, but turned aside down the turfed path.

'He's written to you too,' she said, without preliminary greeting, when I reached her side.

'Yes, I'm to meet him at the station at three, and come straight on to the church.'

Her face looked pale, but there was a brightness in her eyes, and a tender quiver about the mouth that spoke of renewed happiness.

'Mr Branbridge begged him so to stay another night that he had not the heart to refuse,' she went on. 'He is so kind, but I wish he hadn't stayed.'

I was at the station at half past two. I felt rather annoyed with John. It seemed a sort of slight to the beautiful girl who loved him, that he should come as it were out of breath, and with the dust of travel upon him, to take her hand, which some of us would have given the best years of our lives to take.

But when the three o'clock train glided in, and glided out again having brought no passengers to our little station, I was more than annoyed. There was no other train for thirty-five minutes; I calculated that, with much hurry, we might just get to the church in time for the ceremony; but, oh, what a fool to miss that first train! What other man could have done it?

That thirty-five minutes seemed a year, as I wandered round the station reading the advertisements and the timetables, and the company's bye-laws, and getting more and more angry with John Charrington. This confidence in his own power of getting everything he wanted the minute he wanted it was leading him too far. I hate waiting. Everyone does, but I believe I hate it more than anyone else. The three thirty-five was late, of course.

I ground my pipe between my teeth and stamped with impatience as I watched the signals. Click. The signal went down. Five minutes later I flung myself into the carriage that I had brought for John.

'Drive to the church!' I said, as someone shut the door. 'Mr Charrington hasn't come by this train.'

Anxiety now replaced anger. What had become of the man? Could he have been taken suddenly ill? I had never known him have a day's illness in his life. And even so he might have telegraphed. Some awful accident must have happened to him. The thought that he had played her false never—no, not for a moment—entered my head. Yes, something terrible had happened to him, and on me lay the task of telling his bride. I almost wished the carriage would upset and break my head so that someone else might tell her, not I, who—but that's nothing to do with this story.

It was five minutes to four as we drew up at the churchyard gate. A double row of eager onlookers lined the path from lychgate to porch. I sprang from the carriage and passed up between them. Our gardener had a good front place near the door. I stopped.

'Are they waiting still, Byles?' I asked, simply to gain time, for of course I knew they were by the waiting crowd's attentive attitude.

'Waiting, sir? No, no, sir; why, it must be over by now.'

'Over! Then Mr Charrington's come?'

'To the minute, sir; must have missed you somehow, and I say, sir,' lowering his voice, 'I never see Mr John the least bit so afore, but my opinion is he's been drinking pretty free. His clothes was all dusty and his face like a sheet. I tell you I didn't like the looks of him at all, and the folks inside are saying all sorts of things. You'll see, something's gone very wrong with Mr John, and he's tried liquor. He looked like a ghost, and in he went with his eyes straight before him, with never a look or a word for none of us: him that was always such a gentleman!'

I had never heard Byles make so long a speech. The crowd in the churchyard were talking in whispers and getting ready rice and slippers to throw at the bride and bridegroom. The ringers were ready with their hands on the ropes to ring out the merry peal as the bride and bridegroom should come out.

A murmur from the church announced them; out they came. Byles was right. John Charrington did not look himself. There was dust on his coat, his hair was disarranged. He seemed to have been in some row, for there was a black mark above his eyebrow. He was deathly pale. But his pallor was not greater than that of the bride, who might have been carved in ivory—dress, veil, orange blossoms, face and all.

As they passed out the ringers stooped—there were six of them—and then, on the ears expecting the gay wedding peal, came the slow tolling of the passing bell.

A thrill of horror at so foolish a jest from the ringers passed through us all. But the ringers themselves dropped the ropes and fled like rabbits out into the sunlight. The bride shuddered, and grey shadows came about her mouth, but the bridegroom led her on down the path where the people stood with the handfuls of rice; but the handfuls were never thrown, and the wedding bells never rang. In vain the ringers were urged to remedy their mistake: they protested with many whispered expletives that they would see themselves further first.

In a hush like the hush in the chamber of death the bridal pair passed into their carriage and its door slammed behind them.

Then the tongues were loosed. A babel of anger, wonder,

conjecture from the guests and the spectators.

'If I'd seen his condition, sir,' said old Forster to me as we drove off, 'I would have stretched him on the floor of the church, sir, by heaven I would, before I'd have let him marry my daughter!'

Then he put his head out of the window.

'Drive like hell,' he cried to the coachman; 'don't spare the horses.'

He was obeyed. We passed the bride's carriage. I forbore to look at it, and old Forster turned his head away and swore. We reached home before it.

We stood in the doorway, in the blazing afternoon sun, and in about half a minute we heard wheels crunching the gravel. When the carriage stopped in front of the steps old Forster and I ran down.

'Great heaven, the carriage is empty! And yet—'

I had the door open in a minute, and this is what I saw . . .

No sign of John Charrington; and of May, his wife, only a huddled heap of white satin lying half on the floor of the carriage and half on the seat.

'I drove straight here, sir,' said the coachman, as the bride's father lifted her out; 'and I'll swear no one got out of the carriage.'

We carried her into the house in her bridal dress and drew back her veil. I saw her face. Shall I ever forget it? White, white and drawn with agony and horror, bearing such a look of terror as I have never seen since except in dreams. And her hair, her radiant blonde hair, I tell you it was white like snow.

As we stood, her father and I, half mad with the horror and mystery of it, a boy came up the avenue—a telegraph boy. They brought the orange envelope to me. I tore it open.

Mr Charrington was thrown from the dogcart on his way to the station at half past one. Killed on the spot!

And he was married to May Forster in our parish church at half past three, in presence of half the parish.

'I shall be married, dead, or alive!'

What had passed in that carriage on the homeward drive? No one knows—no one will ever know. Oh, May! Oh, my dear!

Before a week was over they laid her beside her husband in our little churchyard on the thyme-covered hill—the churchyard where they had kept their love-trysts.

Thus was accomplished John Charrington's wedding.

33
EX OBLIVIONE
H.P. Lovecraft

...ugly trifles of existence began to drive me to madness like the small drops of water that torturers let fall ceaselessly upon one spot of their victims body.

When the last days were upon me, and the ugly trifles of existence began to drive me to madness like the small drops of water that torturers let fall ceaselessly upon one spot of their victims body, I loved the irradiate refuge of sleep. In my dreams I found a little of the beauty I had vainly sought in life, and wandered through old gardens and enchanted woods.

Once when the wind was soft and scented I heard the south calling, and sailed endlessly and languorously under strange stars.

Once when the gentle rain fell I glided in a barge down a sunless stream under the earth till I reached another world of purple twilight, iridescent arbours, and undying roses.

And once I walked through a golden valley that led to shadowy groves and ruins, and ended in a mighty wall green with antique vines, and pierced by a little gate of bronze.

Many times I walked through that valley, and longer and longer would I pause in the spectral half-light where the giant trees squirmed and twisted grotesquely, and the grey ground stretched damply from trunk to trunk, some times disclosing the mould-stained stones of buried temples. And always the goal of my fancies was the mighty vine-grown wall with the little gate of bronze therein.

After a while, as the days of waking became less and less

bearable from their greyness and sameness, I would often drift in opiate peace through the valley and the shadowy groves, and wonder how I might seize them for my eternal dwelling-place, so that I need no more crawl back to a dull world stript of interest and new colours. And as I looked upon the little gate in the mighty wall, I felt that beyond it lay a dream-country from which, once it was entered, there would be no return.

So each night in sleep I strove to find the hidden latch of the gate in the ivied antique wall, though it was exceedingly well hidden. And I would tell myself that the realm beyond the wall was not more lasting merely, but more lovely and radiant as well.

Then one night in the dream-city of Zakarion I found a yellowed papyrus filled with the thoughts of dream-sages who dwelt of old in that city, and who were too wise ever to be born in the waking world. Therein were written many things concerning the world of dream, and among them was lore of a golden valley and a sacred grove with temples, and a high wall pierced by a little bronze gate. When I saw this lore, I knew that it touched on the scenes I had haunted, and I therefore read long in the yellowed papyrus.

Some of the dream-sages wrote gorgeously of the wonders beyond the irrepassable gate, but others told of horror and disappointment. I knew not which to believe, yet longed more and more to cross for ever into the unknown land; for doubt and secrecy are the lure of lures, and no new horror can be more terrible than the daily torture of the commonplace. So when I learned of the drug which would unlock the gate and drive me through, I resolved to take it when next I awaked.

Last night I swallowed the drug and floated dreamily into the golden valley and the shadowy groves; and when I came this time to the antique wall, I saw that the small gate of bronze was ajar. From beyond came a glow that weirdly lit the giant twisted trees and the tops of the buried temples, and I drifted on songfully, expectant of the glories of the land from whence I should never return.

But as the gate swung wider and the sorcery of the drug and the dream pushed me through, I knew that all sights and glories were at an end; for in that new realm was neither land nor sea, but only the white void of unpeopled and illimitable space. So, happier than I had ever dared hope to be, I dissolved again into that native infinity of crystal oblivion from which the daemon Life had called me for one brief and desolate hour.

34
THE PICTURE IN THE HOUSE

H.P. Lovecraft

Most horrible of all sights are the little unpainted wooden houses remote from travelled ways...

Searchers after horror haunt strange, far places. For them are the catacombs of Ptolemais, and the carven mausolea of the nightmare countries. They climb to the moonlit towers of ruined Rhine castles, and falter down black cobwebbed steps beneath the scattered stones of forgotten cities in Asia. The haunted wood and the desolate mountain are their shrines, and they linger around the sinister monoliths on uninhabited islands. But the true epicure in the terrible, to whom a new thrill of unutterable ghastliness is the chief end and justification of existence, esteems most of all the ancient, lonely farmhouses of backwoods New England; for there the dark elements of strength, solitude, grotesqueness and ignorance combine to form the perfection of the hideous.

Most horrible of all sights are the little unpainted wooden houses remote from travelled ways, usually squatted upon some damp grassy slope or leaning against some gigantic outcropping of rock. Two hundred years and more they have leaned or squatted there, while the vines have crawled and the trees have swelled and spread. They are almost hidden now in lawless luxuriances of green and guardian shrouds of shadow; but the small-paned windows still stare shockingly, as if blinking through a lethal stupor which wards off madness by dulling the memory of unutterable things.

In such houses have dwelt generations of strange people,

whose like the world has never seen. Seized with a gloomy and fanatical belief which exiled them from their kind, their ancestors sought the wilderness for freedom. There the scions of a conquering race indeed flourished free from the restrictions of their fellows, but cowered in an appalling slavery to the dismal phantasms of their own minds. Divorced from the enlightenment of civilization, the strength of these Puritans turned into singular channels; and in their isolation, morbid self-repression, and struggle for life with relentless Nature, there came to them dark furtive traits from the prehistoric depths of their cold Northern heritage. By necessity practical and by philosophy stern, these folks were not beautiful in their sins. Erring as all mortals must, they were forced by their rigid code to seek concealment above all else; so that they came to use less and less taste in what they concealed. Only the silent, sleepy, staring houses in the backwoods can tell all that has lain hidden since the early days, and they are not communicative, being loath to shake off the drowsiness which helps them forget. Sometimes one feels that it would be merciful to tear down these houses, for they must often dream.

It was to a time-battered edifice of this description that I was driven one afternoon in November, 1896, by a rain of such chilling copiousness that any shelter was preferable to exposure. I had been travelling for some time amongst the people of the Miskatonic Valley in quest of certain genealogical data; and from the remote, devious, and problematical nature of my course, had deemed it convenient to employ a bicycle despite the lateness of the season. Now I found myself upon an apparently abandoned road which I had chosen as the shortest cut to Arkham, overtaken by the storm at a point far from any town, and confronted with no refuge save the antique and repellent wooden building which blinked with bleared windows from between two huge leafless elms near the foot of a rocky hill. Distant though it is from the remnant of a road, this house none the less impressed me unfavorably the very moment I espied it. Honest, wholesome structures do not stare at travellers so slyly and hauntingly, and in my genealogical researches I had encountered legends of a century before which biased me against places of this kind. Yet the force of the elements was such as to overcome my scruples, and I did not hesitate to wheel my machine up the weedy rise to the closed door which seemed at once so suggestive and secretive.

I had somehow taken it for granted that the house was abandoned, yet as I approached it I was not so sure, for though the walks were indeed overgrown with weeds, they seemed to retain their nature a little too well to argue complete desertion. Therefore instead of trying the door I knocked, feeling as I did so a trepidation I could scarcely explain. As I waited on the rough, mossy rock which served as a door-step, I glanced at the neighbouring windows and the panes of the transom above me, and noticed that although old, rattling, and almost opaque with dirt, they were not broken. The building, then, must still be inhabited, despite its isolation and general neglect. However, my rapping evoked no response, so after repeating the summons I tried the rusty latch and found the door unfastened. Inside was a little vestibule with walls from which the plaster was falling, and through the doorway came a faint but peculiarly hateful odor. I entered, carrying my bicycle, and closed the door behind me. Ahead rose a narrow staircase, flanked by a small door probably leading to the cellar, while to the left and right were closed doors leading to rooms on the ground floor.

Leaning my cycle against the wall I opened the door at the left, and crossed into a small low-ceiled chamber but dimly lighted by its two dusty windows and furnished in the barest and most primitive possible way. It appeared to be a kind of sitting-room, for it had a table and several chairs, and an immense fireplace above which ticked an antique clock on a mantel. Books and papers were very few, and in the prevailing gloom I could not readily discern the titles. What interested me was the uniform air of archaism as displayed in every visible detail. Most of the houses in this region I had found rich in relics of the past, but here the antiquity was curiously complete; for in all the room I could not discover a single article of definitely post-revolutionary date. Had the furnishings been less humble, the place would have been a collector's paradise.

As I surveyed this quaint apartment, I felt an increase in that aversion first excited by the bleak exterior of the house. Just what it was that I feared or loathed, I could by no means define; but something in the whole atmosphere seemed redolent of unhallowed age, of unpleasant crudeness, and of secrets which should be forgotten. I felt disinclined to sit down, and wandered about examining the various articles which I had noticed. The first object of my curiosity was a book of medium size lying upon the table and presenting such an antediluvian aspect that I marvelled at beholding it outside a museum or library. It was bound in leather with metal fittings, and was in an excellent state of preservation; being altogether an unusual sort of volume to encounter in an abode so lowly. When I opened it to the title page my wonder grew even greater, for it proved to be nothing less rare than Pigafetta's account of the Congo region, written in Latin from the notes of the sailor Lopex and printed at Frankfurt in 1598. I had often heard of this work, with its curious illustrations by the brothers De Bry, hence for a moment forgot my uneasiness in my desire to turn the pages before me. The engravings were indeed interesting, drawn wholly from imagination and careless descriptions, and represented negroes with white skins and Caucasian features; nor would I soon have closed the book had not an exceedingly trivial circumstance upset my tired nerves and revived my sensation of disquiet. What annoyed me was merely the persistent way in which the volume tended to fall open of itself at Plate XII, which represented in gruesome detail a butcher's shop of the cannibal Anziques. I experienced some shame at my susceptibility to so slight a thing, but the drawing nevertheless disturbed me, especially in connection with some adjacent passages descriptive of Anzique gastronomy.

I had turned to a neighbouring shelf and was examining its meagre literary contents—an eighteenth century Bible, a *Pilgrim's*

Progress of like period, illustrated with grotesque woodcuts and printed by the almanack-maker Isaiah Thomas, the rotting bulk of Cotton Mather's *Magnalia Christi Americana*, and a few other books of evidently equal age—when my attention was aroused by the unmistakable sound of walking in the room overhead. At first astonished and startled, considering the lack of response to my recent knocking at the door, I immediately afterward concluded that the walker had just awakened from a sound sleep, and listened with less surprise as the footsteps sounded on the creaking stairs. The tread was heavy, yet seemed to contain a curious quality of cautiousness; a quality which I disliked the more because the tread was heavy. When I had entered the room I had shut the door behind me. Now, after a moment of silence during which the walker may have been inspecting my bicycle in the hall, I heard a fumbling at the latch and saw the paneled portal swing open again.

In the doorway stood a person of such singular appearance that I should have exclaimed aloud but for the restraints of good breeding. Old, white-bearded, and ragged, my host possessed a countenance and physique which inspired equal wonder and respect. His height could not have been less than six feet, and despite a general air of age and poverty he was stout and powerful in proportion. His face, almost hidden by a long beard which grew high on the cheeks, seemed abnormally ruddy and less wrinkled than one might expect; while over a high forehead fell a shock of white hair little thinned by the years. His blue eyes, though a trifle bloodshot, seemed inexplicably keen and burning. But for his horrible unkemptness the man would have been as distinguished-looking as he was impressive. This unkemptness, however, made him offensive despite his face and figure. Of what his clothing consisted I could hardly tell, for it seemed to me no more than a mass of tatters surmounting a pair of high, heavy boots; and his lack of cleanliness surpassed description.

The appearance of this man, and the instinctive fear he inspired, prepared me for something like enmity; so that I almost shuddered through surprise and a sense of uncanny incongruity when he motioned me to a chair and addressed me in a thin, weak voice full of fawning respect and ingratiating hospitality. His speech was very curious, an extreme form of Yankee dialect I had thought long extinct; and I studied it closely as he sat down opposite me for conversation.

'Ketched in the rain, be ye?' he greeted. 'Glad ye was nigh the haouse en' hed the sense ta come right in. I calc'late I was alseep, else I'd a heerd ye—I ain't as young as I uster be, an' I need a paowerful sight o' naps naowadays. Trav'lin fur? I hain't seed many folks 'long this rud sence they tuk off the Arkham stage.'

I replied that I was going to Arkham, and apologized for my rude entry into his domicile, whereupon he continued.

'Glad ta see ye, young Sir—new faces is scurce arount here, an' I hain't got much ta cheer me up these days. Guess yew hail from Bosting, don't ye? I never ben thar, but I kin tell a taown man when I see 'im—we hed one fer deestrick schoolmaster in 'eighty-four, but he quit suddent an' no one never heerd on 'im sence—' here the old man lapsed into a kind of chuckle, and made no explanation when I questioned him. He seemed to be in an aboundingly good humor, yet to possess those eccentricities which one might guess from his grooming. For some time he rambled on with an almost feverish geniality, when it struck me to ask him how he came by so rare a book as Pigafetta's *Regnum Congo*. The effect of this volume had not left me, and I felt a certain hesitancy in speaking of it, but curiosity overmastered all the vague fears which had steadily accumulated since my first glimpse of the house. To my relief, the question did not seem an awkward one, for the old man answered freely and volubly.

'Oh, that Afriky book? Cap'n Ebenezer Holt traded me thet in 'sixty-eight—him as was kilt in the war.' Something about the name of Ebenezer Holt caused me to look up sharply. I had encountered it in my genealogical work, but not in any record since the Revolution. I wondered if my host could help me in the task at which I was labouring, and resolved to ask him about it later on. He continued.

'Ebenezer was on a Salem merchantman for years, an' picked up a sight o' queer stuff in every port. He got this in London, I guess—he uster like ter buy things at the shops. I was up ta his haouse onct, on the hill, tradin' hosses, when I see this book. I relished the picters, so he give it in on a swap. 'Tis a queer book—here, leave me git on my spectacles—' The old man fumbled among his rags, producing a pair of dirty and amazingly antique glasses with small octagonal lenses and steel bows. Donning these, he reached for the volume on the table and turned the pages lovingly.

'Ebenezer cud read a leetle o' this—'tis Latin—but I can't. I had two er three schoolmasters read me a bit, and Passon Clark, him they say got draownded in the pond—kin yew make anything outen it?' I told him that I could, and translated for his benefit a paragraph near the beginning. If I erred, he was not scholar enough to correct me; for he seemed childishly pleased at my English version. His proximity was becoming rather obnoxious, yet I saw no way to escape without offending him. I was amused at the childish fondness of this ignorant old man for the pictures in a book he could not read, and wondered how much better he could read the few books in English which adorned the room. This revelation of simplicity removed much of the ill-defined apprehension I had felt, and I smiled as my host rambled on:

'Queer haow picters kin set a body thinkin'. Take this un here near the front. Hey yew ever seed trees like thet, with big leaves a floppin' over an' daown? And them men—them can't be niggers—they dew beat all. Kinder like Injuns, I guess, even ef they be in Afriky. Some o' these here critters looks like monkeys, or half monkeys an' half men, but I never heerd o' nothin' like this un.' Here he pointed to a fabulous creature of the artist, which one might describe as a sort of dragon with the head of an alligator.

'But naow I'll show ye the best un—over here nigh the middle—' The old man's speech grew a trifle thicker and his eyes assumed a brighter glow; but his fumbling hands, though seemingly clumsier than before, were entirely adequate to their mission. The book fell open, almost of its own accord and as if from frequent consultation at this place, to the repellent twelfth plate showing a butcher's shop amongst the Anzique cannibals. My sense of restlessness returned, though I did not exhibit it. The especially bizarre thing was that the artist had made his Africans look like white men—the limbs and quarters hanging about the walls of the shop were ghastly, while the butcher with his axe was hideously incongruous. But my host seemed to relish the view as much as I disliked it.

'What d'ye think o' this—ain't never see the like hereabouts, eh? When I see this I telled Eb Holt, "That's suthin' ta stir ye up an' make yer blood tickle." When I read in Scripter about slayin'—like them Midianites was slew—I kinder think things, but I ain't got no picter of it. Here a body kin see all they is to it—I s'pose 'tis sinful, but ain't we all born an' livin' in sin?—Thet feller bein' chopped up gives me a tickle every time I look at 'im—I hey ta keep lookin' at 'im—see whar the butcher cut off his feet? Thar's his head on thet bench, with one arm side of it, an' t'other arm's on the other side o' the meat block.'

As the man mumbled on in his shocking ecstasy the expression on his hairy, spectacled face became indescribable, but his voice sank rather than mounted. My own sensations can scarcely be recorded. All the terror I had dimly felt before rushed upon me actively and vividly, and I knew that I loathed the ancient and abhorrent creature so near me with an infinite intensity. His madness, or at least his partial perversion, seemed beyond dispute. He was almost whispering now, with a huskiness more terrible than a scream, and I trembled as I listened.

'As I says, 'tis queer haow picters sets ye thinkin'. D'ye know, young Sir, I'm right sot on this un here. Arter I got the book off Eb I uster look at it a lot, especial when I'd heerd Passon Clark rant o' Sundays in his big wig. Onct I tried suthin' funny—here, young Sir, don't git skeert—all I done was ter look at the picter afore I kilt the sheep for market—killin' sheep was kinder more fun arter lookin' at it—' The tone of the old man now sank very low, sometimes becoming so faint that his words were hardly audible. I listened to the rain, and to the rattling of the bleared, small-paned windows, and marked a rumbling of approaching thunder quite unusual for the season. Once a terrific flash and peal shook the frail house to its foundations, but the whisperer seemed not to notice it.

'Killin' sheep was kinder more fun—but d'ye know, 'twan't quite satisfyin'. Queer haow a cravin' gits a holt on ye—As ye love the Almighty, young man, don't tell nobody, but I swar ter Gawd thet picter begun to make me hungry fer victuals I couldn't raise nor buy—here, set still, what's ailin' ye?—I didn't do nothin', only I wondered haow 'twud be ef I did—They say meat makes blood an' flesh, an' gives ye new life, so I wondered ef 'twudn't make a man live longer an' longer ef 'twas more the same—' But the whisperer never continued. The interruption was not produced by my fright, nor by the rapidly increasing storm amidst whose fury I was presently to open my eyes on a smoky solitude of blackened ruins. It was produced by a very simple though somewhat unusual happening.

The open book lay flat between us, with the picture staring repulsively upward. As the old man whispered the words 'more the same' a tiny splattering impact was heard, and something showed on the yellowed paper of the upturned volume. I thought of the rain and of a leaky roof, but rain is not red. On the butcher's shop of the Anzique cannibals a small red spattering glistened picturesquely, lending vividness to the horror of the engraving. The old man saw it, and stopped whispering even before my expression of horror made it necessary; saw it and glanced quickly toward the floor of the room he had left an hour before. I followed his glance, and beheld just above us on the loose plaster of the ancient ceiling a large irregular spot of wet crimson which seemed to spread even as I viewed it. I did not shriek or move, but merely shut my eyes. A moment later came the titanic thunderbolt of thunderbolts; blasting that accursed house of unutterable secrets and bringing the oblivion which alone saved my mind.

35

THE CATS OF ULTHAR

H.P. Lovecraft

... the cat is cryptic, and close to strange things which men cannot see.

It is said that in Ulthar, which lies beyond the river Skai, no man may kill a cat; and this I can verily believe as I gaze upon him who sitteth purring before the fire. For the cat is cryptic, and close to strange things which men cannot see. He is the soul of antique Aegyptus, and bearer of tales from forgotten cities in Meroe and Ophir. He is the kin of the jungle's lords, and heir to the secrets of hoary and sinister Africa. The Sphinx is his cousin and he speaks her language; but he is more ancient than the Sphinx and remembers that which she hath forgotten.

In Ulthar, before ever the burgesses forbade the killing of cats, there dwelt an old cotter and his wife who delighted to trap and slay the cats of their neighbours. Why they did this I know not; save that many hate the voice of the cat in the night, and take it ill that cats should run stealthily about yards and gardens at twilight. But whatever the reason, this old man and woman took pleasure in trapping and slaying every cat which came near to their hovel; and from some of the sounds heard after dark, many villagers fancied that the manner of slaying was exceedingly peculiar. But the villagers did not discuss such things with the old man and his wife; because of the habitual expression on the withered faces of the two, and because their cottage was so small and so darkly hidden under spreading oaks at the back of a neglected yard. In truth, much as the owners of cats hated these odd folk, they feared them more; and instead of berating them as brutal assassins, merely took care that no cherished pet or mouser should stray toward the remote hovel under the dark trees. When through some unavoidable oversight a cat was missed and sounds heard after dark, the loser would lament impotently; or console himself by thanking Fate that it was not one of his children who had thus vanished. For the people of Ulthar were simple and knew not whence it is all cats first came.

One day a caravan of strange wanderers from the South entered the narrow cobbled streets of Ulthar. Dark wanderers they were, and unlike the other roving folk who passed through the village twice every year. In the market-place they told fortunes for silver and bought gay beads from the merchants. What was the land of these wanderers none could tell; but it was seen that they were given to strange prayers, and that they had painted on the sides of their wagons strange figures with human bodies and the heads of cats, hawks, rams and lions. And the leader of the caravan wore a headdress with two horns and a curious disk betwixt the horns.

There was in this singular caravan a little boy with no father or mother, but only a tiny black kitten to cherish. The plague had not been kind to him, yet had left him this small furry thing to mitigate his sorrow; and when one is very young, one can find great relief in the lively antics of a black kitten. So the boy, whom the dark people called Menes, smiled more often than he wept as he sat playing with his graceful kitten on the steps of an oddly painted wagon.

On the third morning of the wanderers' stay in Ulthar, Menes could not find his kitten; and as he sobbed aloud in the market-place certain villagers told him of the old man and his wife, and of sounds heard in the night. And when he heard these things his sobbing gave place to meditation, and finally to prayer. He stretched out his arms toward the sun and prayed in a tongue no villager could understand; though indeed the villagers did not try very hard to understand, since their attention was mostly taken up by the sky and the odd shapes the clouds were assuming. It was very peculiar, but as the little boy uttered his petition there seemed to form overhead the shadowy, nebulous figures of exotic things; of hybrid creatures crowned with horn-flanked disks. Nature is full of such illusions to impress the imaginative.

That night the wanderers left Ulthar and were never seen again. And the householders were troubled when they noticed that in all the village there was not a cat to be found. From each hearth the familiar cat had vanished; cats large and small, black, grey, striped, yellow and white. Old Kranon, the burgomaster, swore that the dark folk had taken the cats away in revenge for the killing of Menes's kitten; and cursed the caravan and the little boy. But Nith, the lean notary, declared that the old cotter and his wife were more likely persons to suspect; for their hatred of cats was notorious and increasingly bold. Still, no one durst complain to the sinister couple; even when little Atal, the innkeepers' son, vowed that he had at twilight seen all the cats of Ulthar in that accursed yard under the trees, pacing very slowly and solemnly in a circle around the cottage, two abreast, as if in performance of some unheard-of rite of beasts. The villagers did not know how much to believe from so small a boy; and though they feared that the evil pair had charmed the cats to their death, they preferred not to chide the old cotter till they met him outside his dark and repellent yard.

So Ulthar went to sleep in vain anger; and when the people awakened at dawn, behold! Every cat was back at his accustomed hearth! Large and small, black, grey, striped, yellow and white, none was missing. Very sleek and fat did the cats appear, and sonorous with purring content. The citizens talked with one another of the affair, and marveled not a little. Old Kranon again insisted that it was the dark folk who had taken them, since cats did not return alive from the cottage of the ancient man and his wife. But all agreed on one thing: that the refusal of all the cats to eat their portions of meat or drink their saucers of milk was exceedingly curious. And for two whole days the sleek, lazy cats of Ulthar would touch no food, but only doze by the fire or in the sun.

It was fully a week before the villagers noticed that no lights were appearing at dusk in the windows of the cottage under the trees. Then the lean Nith remarked that no one had seen the old man or his wife since the night the cats were away. In another week the burgomaster decided to overcome his fears and call at the strangely silent dwelling as a matter of duty, though in so doing he was careful to take with him Shang the blacksmith and Thul the cutter of stone as witnesses. And when they had broken down the frail door they found only this: two cleanly picked human skeletons on the earthen floor, and a number of singular beetles crawling in the shadowy corners.

There was subsequently much talk among the burgesses of Ulthar. Zath, the coroner, disputed at length with Nith, the lean notary; and Kranon and Shang and Thul were overwhelmed with questions. Even little Atal, the innkeepers' son, was closely questioned and given a sweetmeat as reward. They talked of the old cotter and his wife, of the caravan of dark wanderers, of small Menes and his black kitten, of the prayer of Menes and of the sky during that prayer, of the doings of the cats on the night the caravan left, and of what was later found in the cottage under the dark trees in the repellent yard.

And in the end the burgesses passed that remarkable law which is told of by traders in Hatheg and discussed by travelers in Nir; namely, that in Ulthar no man may kill a cat.

36

THE BLACK CAT

Edgar Allan Poe

But tomorrow I die, and today
I would unburthen my soul...

For the most wild, yet most homely narrative which I am about to pen, I neither expect nor solicit belief. Mad indeed would I be to expect it, in a case where my very senses reject their own evidence. Yet, mad am I not—and very surely do I not dream. But tomorrow I die, and today I would unburthen my soul. My immediate purpose is to place before the world, plainly, succinctly, and without comment, a series of mere household events. In their consequences, these events have terrified—have tortured—have destroyed me. Yet I will not attempt to expound them. To me, they have presented little but Horror—to many they will seem less terrible than barroques. Hereafter, perhaps, some intellect may be found which will reduce my phantasm to the common-place—some intellect more calm, more logical, and far less excitable than my own, which will perceive, in the circumstances I detail with awe, nothing more than an ordinary succession of very natural causes and effects.

From my infancy I was noted for the docility and humanity of my disposition. My tenderness of heart was even so conspicuous as to make me the jest of my companions. I was especially fond of animals, and was indulged by my parents with a great variety of pets. With these I spent most of my time, and never was so happy as when feeding and caressing them. This peculiarity of character grew with my growth, and in my manhood, I derived from it one of my principal sources of pleasure. To those who have cherished an affection for a faithful and sagacious dog, I need hardly be at the trouble of explaining the nature or the intensity of the gratification thus derivable. There is something in the unselfish and self-sacrificing love of a brute, which goes directly to the heart of him who has had frequent occasion to test the paltry friendship and gossamer fidelity of mere Man.

I married early, and was happy to find in my wife a disposition not uncongenial with my own. Observing my partiality for domestic pets, she lost no opportunity of procuring those of the most agreeable kind. We had birds, goldfish, a fine dog, rabbits, a small monkey, and a cat.

This latter was a remarkably large and beautiful animal, entirely black, and sagacious to an astonishing degree. In speaking of his intelligence, my wife, who at heart was not a little tinctured with superstition, made frequent allusion to the ancient popular notion, which regarded all black cats as witches in disguise. Not that she was ever serious upon this point—and I mention the matter at all for no better reason than that it happens, just now, to be remembered.

Pluto—this was the cat's name—was my favorite pet and playmate. I alone fed him, and he attended me wherever I went about the house. It was even with difficulty that I could prevent him from following me through the streets.

Our friendship lasted, in this manner, for several years, during which my general temperament and character—through the instrumentality of the Fiend Intemperance—had (I blush to confess it) experienced a radical alteration for the worse. I grew, day by day, more moody, more irritable, more regardless of the feelings of others. I suffered myself to use intemperate language to my wife. At length, I even offered her personal violence. My pets, of course, were made to feel the change in my disposition. I not only neglected, but ill-used them. For Pluto, however, I still retained sufficient regard to restrain me from maltreating him, as I made no scruple of maltreating the rabbits, the monkey, or even the dog, when by accident, or through affection, they came in my way. But my disease grew upon me—for what disease is like Alcohol!—and at length even Pluto, who was now becoming old, and consequently somewhat peevish—even Pluto began to experience the effects of my ill temper.

One night, returning home, much intoxicated, from one of my haunts about town, I fancied that the cat avoided my presence. I seized him; when, in his fright at my violence, he inflicted a slight wound upon my hand with his teeth. The fury of a demon instantly possessed me. I knew myself no longer. My original soul seemed, at once, to take its flight from my body and a more than fiendish malevolence, gin-nurtured, thrilled every fibre of my frame. I took from my waistcoat-pocket a pen knife, opened it, grasped the poor beast by the throat, and deliberately cut one of its eyes from the socket! I blush, I burn, I shudder, while I pen the damnable atrocity.

When reason returned with the morning—when I had slept off the fumes of the night's debauch—I experienced a sentiment half of horror, half of remorse, for the crime of which I had been guilty; but it was, at best, a feeble and equivocal feeling, and the soul remained untouched. I again plunged into excess, and soon drowned in wine all memory of the deed.

In the meantime the cat slowly recovered. The socket of the lost eye presented, it is true, a frightful appearance, but he no longer appeared to suffer any pain. He went about the house as usual, but, as might be expected, fled in extreme terror at my approach. I had so much of my old heart left, as to be at first grieved by this evident dislike on the part of a creature which had once so loved me. But this feeling soon gave place to irritation. And then came, as if to my final and irrevocable overthrow, the spirit of *perverseness*. Of this spirit philosophy takes no account. Yet I am not more sure that my soul lives, than I am that perverseness is one of the primitive impulses of the human heart—one of the indivisible primary faculties, or sentiments, which give direction to the character of Man. Who has not, a hundred times, found himself committing a vile or a silly action, for no other reason than because he knows he should not? Have we not a perpetual inclination, in the teeth of our best judgment, to violate that which is Law, merely because we understand it to be such? This spirit of perverseness, I say, came to my final overthrow. It was this unfathomable longing of the soul to vex itself—to offer violence to its own nature—to do wrong for the wrong's sake only—that urged me to continue and finally to consummate the injury I had inflicted upon the unoffending brute. One morning, in cool blood, I slipped a noose about its neck and hung it to the limb of a tree;—hung it with the tears streaming from my eyes, and with the bitterest remorse at my heart;—hung it because I knew that it had loved me, and because I felt it had given me no reason of offence;—hung it because I knew that in so doing I was committing a sin—a deadly sin that would so jeopardize my immortal soul as to place it—if such a thing were possible—even beyond the reach of the infinite mercy of the Most Merciful and Most Terrible God.

On the night of the day on which this cruel deed was done, I was aroused from sleep by the cry of fire. The curtains of my bed were in flames. The whole house was blazing. It was with great difficulty that my wife, a servant, and myself, made our escape from the conflagration. The destruction was complete. My entire worldly wealth was swallowed up, and I resigned myself thenceforward to despair.

I am above the weakness of seeking to establish a sequence of cause and effect, between the disaster and the atrocity. But I am detailing a chain of facts—and wish not to leave even a possible link imperfect. On the day succeeding the fire, I visited the ruins. The walls, with one exception, had fallen in. This exception was found in a compartment wall, not very thick, which stood about the middle of the house, and against which had rested the head of my bed. The plastering had here, in great measure, resisted the action of the fire—a fact which I attributed to its having been recently spread. About this wall a dense crowd were collected, and many persons seemed to be examining a particular portion of it with very minute and eager attention. The words 'strange!' 'singular!' and other similar expressions, excited my curiosity. I approached and saw, as if graven in bas relief upon the white surface, the figure of a gigantic cat. The impression was given with an accuracy truly marvellous. There was a rope about the animal's neck.

When I first beheld this apparition—for I could scarcely regard it as less—my wonder and my terror were extreme. But at length reflection came to my aid. The cat, I remembered, had been hung in a garden adjacent to the house. Upon the alarm of fire, this garden had been immediately filled by the crowd—by someone of whom the animal must have been cut from the tree and thrown, through an open window, into my chamber. This had probably been done with the view of arousing me from sleep. The falling of other walls had compressed the victim of my cruelty into the substance of the freshly-spread plaster; the lime of which, with the flames, and the ammonia from the carcass, had then accomplished the portraiture as I saw it.

Although I thus readily accounted to my reason, if not altogether to my conscience, for the startling fact just detailed, it did not the less fail to make a deep impression upon my fancy. For months I could not rid myself of the phantasm of the cat; and, during this period, there came back into my spirit a half-sentiment that seemed, but was not, remorse. I went so far as to regret the loss of the animal, and to look about me, among the vile haunts which I now habitually frequented, for another pet of the same species, and of somewhat similar appearance, with which to supply its place.

One night as I sat, half stupified, in a den of more than infamy, my attention was suddenly drawn to some black object, reposing upon the head of one of the immense hogsheads of Gin, or of Rum, which constituted the chief furniture of the apartment. I had been looking steadily at the top of this hogshead for some minutes, and what now caused me surprise was the fact that I had not sooner perceived the object thereupon. I approached it, and touched it with my hand. It was a black cat—a very large one—fully as large as Pluto, and closely resembling him in every respect but one. Pluto had not a white hair upon any portion of his body; but this cat had a large, although indefinite splotch of white, covering nearly the whole region of the breast. Upon my touching him, he immediately arose, purred loudly, rubbed against my hand, and appeared delighted with my notice. This, then, was the very creature of which I was in search. I at once offered to purchase it of the landlord; but this person made no claim to it—knew nothing of it—had never seen it before.

I continued my caresses, and, when I prepared to go home, the animal evinced a disposition to accompany me. I permitted it to do so; occasionally stooping and patting it as I proceeded. When it reached the house it domesticated itself at once, and became immediately a great favorite with my wife.

For my own part, I soon found a dislike to it arising within me. This was just the reverse of what I had anticipated; but—I know not how or why it was—its evident fondness for myself rather disgusted and annoyed. By slow degrees, these feelings of disgust and annoyance rose into the bitterness of hatred. I avoided the creature; a certain sense of shame, and the remembrance of my former deed of cruelty, preventing me from physically abusing it. I did not, for some weeks, strike, or otherwise violently ill use it; but gradually—very gradually—I came to look upon it with unutterable loathing, and to flee silently from its odious presence, as from the breath of a pestilence.

What added, no doubt, to my hatred of the beast, was the discovery, on the morning after I brought it home, that, like Pluto, it also had been deprived of one of its eyes. This circumstance, however, only endeared it to my wife, who, as I have already said, possessed, in a high degree, that humanity of feeling which had once been my distinguishing trait, and the source of many of my simplest and purest pleasures.

With my aversion to this cat, however, its partiality for myself seemed to increase. It followed my footsteps with a pertinacity which it would be difficult to make the reader comprehend. Whenever I sat, it would crouch beneath my chair, or spring upon my knees, covering me with its loathsome caresses. If I arose to walk it would get between my feet and thus nearly throw me down, or, fastening its long and sharp claws in my dress, clamber, in this manner, to my breast. At such times, although I longed to destroy it with a blow, I was yet withheld from so doing, partly by a memory of my former crime, but chiefly—let me confess it at once—by absolute dread of the beast.

This dread was not exactly a dread of physical evil—and yet I should be at a loss how otherwise to define it. I am almost ashamed to own—yes, even in this felon's cell, I am almost ashamed to own—that the terror and horror with which the animal inspired me, had been heightened by one of the merest chimaeras it would be possible to conceive. My wife had called my attention, more than once, to the character of the mark of white hair, of which I have spoken, and which constituted the sole visible difference between the strange beast and the one I had destroyed. The reader will remember that this mark, although large, had been originally very indefinite; but, by slow degrees—degrees nearly imperceptible, and which for a long time my Reason struggled to reject as fanciful—it had, at length, assumed a rigorous distinctness of outline. It was now the representation of an object that I shudder to name—and for this, above all, I loathed, and dreaded, and would have rid myself of the monster had I dared—it was now, I say, the image of a hideous—of a ghastly thing—of the *gallows*!—Oh, mournful and terrible engine of Horror and of Crime—of Agony and of Death !

And now was I indeed wretched beyond the wretchedness of mere Humanity. And a brute beast—whose fellow I had contemptuously destroyed—a brute beast to work out for me—for me a man, fashioned in the image of the High God—so much of insufferable wo! Alas! Neither by day nor by night knew I the blessing of Rest any more! During the former the creature left me no moment alone; and, in the latter, I started, hourly, from dreams of unutterable fear, to find the hot breath of the thing upon my face, and its vast weight—an incarnate Night-Mare that I had no power to shake off—incumbent eternally upon my heart!

Beneath the pressure of torments such as these, the feeble remnant of the good within me succumbed. Evil thoughts became my sole intimates—the darkest and most evil of thoughts. The moodiness of my usual temper increased to hatred of all things and of all mankind; while, from the sudden, frequent, and ungovernable outbursts of a fury to which I now blindly abandoned myself, my uncomplaining wife—alas!—was the most usual and the most patient of sufferers.

One day she accompanied me, upon some household errand, into the cellar of the old building which our poverty compelled us to inhabit. The cat followed me down the steep stairs, and, nearly throwing me headlong, exasperated me to madness. Uplifting an axe, and forgetting, in my wrath, the childish dread which had hitherto stayed my hand, I aimed a blow at the animal which, of course, would have proved instantly fatal had it descended as I wished. But this blow was arrested by the hand of my wife. Goaded, by the interference, into a rage more than demoniacal, I withdrew my arm from her grasp and buried the axe in her brain. She fell dead upon the spot, without a groan.

This hideous murder accomplished, I set myself forthwith, and with entire deliberation, to the task of concealing the body. I knew that I could not remove it from the house, either by day or by night, without the risk of being observed by the neighbours. Many projects entered my mind. At one period I thought of cutting the corpse into minute fragments, and destroying them by fire. At another, I resolved to dig a grave for it in the floor of the cellar. Again, I deliberated about casting it in the well in the yard—about packing it in a box, as if merchandize, with the usual arrangements, and so getting a porter to take it from the house. Finally I hit upon what I considered a far better expedient than either of these. I determined to wall it up in the cellar—as the monks of the middle ages are recorded to have walled up their victims.

For a purpose such as this the cellar was well adapted. Its walls were loosely constructed, and had lately been plastered throughout with a rough plaster, which the dampness of the atmosphere had prevented from hardening. Moreover, in one of the walls was a projection, caused by a false chimney, or fireplace, that had been filled up, and made to resemble the red of the cellar. I made no doubt that I could readily displace the bricks at this point, insert the corpse, and wall the whole up as before, so that no eye could detect anything suspicious. And in this calculation I was not deceived. By means of a crowbar I easily dislodged the bricks, and, having carefully deposited the body against the inner wall, I propped it in that position, while, with little trouble, I relaid the whole structure as it originally stood. Having procured mortar, sand, and hair, with every possible precaution, I prepared a plaster which could not be distinguished from the old, and with this I very carefully went over the new brickwork. When I had finished, I felt satisfied that all was right. The wall did not present the slightest appearance of having been disturbed. The rubbish on the floor was picked up with the minutest care. I looked around triumphantly, and said to myself—'Here at least, then, my labour has not been in vain.'

My next step was to look for the beast which had been the cause of so much wretchedness; for I had, at length, firmly resolved to put it to death. Had I been able to meet with it, at the moment, there could have been no doubt of its fate; but it appeared that the crafty animal had been alarmed at the violence of my previous anger, and forebore to present itself in my present mood. It is impossible to describe, or to imagine, the deep, the blissful sense of relief which the absence of the detested creature occasioned in my bosom. It did not make its appearance during the night—and thus for one night at least, since its introduction into the house, I soundly and tranquilly slept; aye, slept even with the burden of murder upon my soul!

The second and the third day passed, and still my tormentor

came not. Once again I breathed as a freeman. The monster, in terror, had fled the premises forever! I should behold it no more! My happiness was supreme! The guilt of my dark deed disturbed me but little. Some few inquiries had been made, but these had been readily answered. Even a search had been instituted—but of course nothing was to be discovered. I looked upon my future felicity as secured.

Upon the fourth day of the assassination, a party of the police came, very unexpectedly, into the house, and proceeded again to make rigorous investigation of the premises. Secure, however, in the inscrutability of my place of concealment, I felt no embarrassment whatever. The officers bade me accompany them in their search. They left no nook or corner unexplored. At length, for the third or fourth time, they descended into the cellar. I quivered not in a muscle. My heart beat calmly as that of one who slumbers in innocence. I walked the cellar from end to end. I folded my arms upon my bosom, and roamed easily to and fro. The police were thoroughly satisfied and prepared to depart. The glee at my heart was too strong to be restrained. I burned to say if but one word, by way of triumph, and to render doubly sure their assurance of my guiltlessness.

'Gentlemen,' I said at last, as the party ascended the steps, 'I delight to have allayed your suspicions. I wish you all health, and a little more courtesy. By the bye, gentlemen, this—this is a very well constructed house.' (In the rabid desire to say something easily, I scarcely knew what I uttered at all.) 'I may say an excellently well constructed house. These walls—are you going, gentlemen?—these walls are solidly put together;' and here, through the mere frenzy of bravado, I rapped heavily, with a cane which I held in my hand, upon that very portion of the brick-work behind which stood the corpse of the wife of my bosom.

But may God shield and deliver me from the fangs of the Arch-Fiend ! No sooner had the reverberation of my blows sunk into silence, than I was answered by a voice from within the tomb!—By a cry, at first muffled and broken, like the sobbing of a child, and then quickly swelling into one long, loud, and continuous scream, utterly anomalous and inhuman—a howl—a wailing shriek, half of horror and half of triumph, such as might have arisen only out of hell, conjointly from the throats of the dammed in their agony and of the demons that exult in the damnation.

Of my own thoughts it is folly to speak. Swooning, I staggered to the opposite wall. For one instant the party upon the stairs remained motionless, through extremity of terror and of awe. In the next, a dozen stout arms were toiling at the wall. It fell bodily. The corpse, already greatly decayed and clotted with gore, stood erect before the eyes of the spectators. Upon its head, with red extended mouth and solitary eye of fire, sat the hideous beast whose craft had seduced me into murder, and whose informing voice had consigned me to the hangman. I had walled the monster up within the tomb!

37

THE MONKEY'S PAW

W.W. Jacobs

...it's just an ordinary little paw, dried to a mummy...

Without, the night was cold and wet, but in the small parlour of Laburnam Villa the blinds were drawn and the fire burned brightly. Father and son were at chess, the former, who possessed ideas about the game involving radical changes, putting his king into such sharp and unnecessary perils that it even provoked comment from the white-haired old lady knitting placidly by the fire.

'Hark at the wind,' said Mr White, who, having seen a fatal mistake after it was too late, was amiably desirous of preventing his son from seeing it.

'I'm listening,' said the latter, grimly surveying the board as he stretched out his hand. 'Check.'

'I should hardly think that he'd come tonight,' said his father, with his hand poised over the board.

'Mate,' replied the son.

'That's the worst of living so far out,' bawled Mr White, with sudden and unlooked-for violence; 'of all the beastly, slushy, out-of-the-way places to live in, this is the worst. Pathway's a bog, and the road's a torrent. I don't know what people are thinking about. I suppose because only two houses in the road are let, they think it doesn't matter.'

'Never mind, dear,' said his wife, soothingly; 'perhaps you'll win the next one.'

Mr White looked up sharply, just in time to intercept a knowing glance between mother and son. The words died away on his lips, and he hid a guilty grin in his thin grey beard.

'There he is,' said Herbert White, as the gate banged to loudly and heavy footsteps came toward the door.

The old man rose with hospitable haste, and opening the door, was heard condoling with the new arrival. The new arrival also condoled with himself, so that Mrs White said, 'Tut, tut!' and coughed gently as her husband entered the room, followed by a tall, burly man, beady of eye and rubicund of visage.

'Sergeant-Major Morris,' he said, introducing him.

The Sergeant-Major shook hands, and taking the proffered seat by the fire, watched contentedly while his host got out whiskey and tumblers and stood a small copper kettle on the fire.

At the third glass his eyes got brighter, and he began to talk, the little family circle regarding with eager interest this visitor from distant parts, as he squared his broad shoulders in the chair and spoke of wild scenes and doughty deeds; of wars and plagues and strange peoples.

'Twenty-one years of it,' said Mr White, nodding at his wife and son. 'When he went away he was a slip of a youth in the warehouse. Now look at him.'

'He don't look to have taken much harm,' said Mrs White, politely.

'I'd like to go to India myself,' said the old man, 'just to look round a bit, you know.'

'Better where you are,' said the Sergeant-Major, shaking his head. He put down the empty glass, and sighing softly, shook it again.

'I should like to see those old temples and fakirs and jugglers,' said the old man. 'What was that you started telling me the other day about a monkey's paw or something, Morris?'

'Nothing,' said the soldier, hastily. 'Leastways nothing worth hearing.'

'Monkey's paw?' said Mrs White, curiously.

'Well, it's just a bit of what you might call magic, perhaps,' said the Sergeant-Major, offhandedly.

His three listeners leaned forward eagerly. The visitor

absent-mindedly put his empty glass to his lips and then set it down again. His host filled it for him.

'To look at,' said the Sergeant-Major, fumbling in his pocket, 'it's just an ordinary little paw, dried to a mummy.'

He took something out of his pocket and proffered it. Mrs White drew back with a grimace, but her son, taking it, examined it curiously.

'And what is there special about it?' inquired Mr White as he took it from his son, and having examined it, placed it upon the table.

'It had a spell put on it by an old fakir,' said the sergeant-major, 'a very holy man. He wanted to show that fate ruled people's lives, and that those who interfered with it did so to their sorrow. He put a spell on it so that three separate men could each have three wishes from it.'

His manner was so impressive that his hearers were conscious that their light laughter jarred somewhat.

'Well, why don't you have three, sir?' said Herbert White, cleverly.

The soldier regarded him in the way that middle age is wont to regard presumptuous youth. 'I have,' he said, quietly, and his blotchy face whitened.

'And did you really have the three wishes granted?' asked Mrs White.

'I did,' said the Sergeant-Major, and his glass tapped against his strong teeth.

'And has anybody else wished?' persisted the old lady.

'The first man had his three wishes. Yes,' was the reply; 'I don't know what the first two were, but the third was for death. That's how I got the paw.'

His tones were so grave that a hush fell upon the group.

'If you've had your three wishes, it's no good to you now, then, Morris,' said the old man at last. 'What do you keep it for?'

The soldier shook his head. 'Fancy, I suppose,' he said, slowly. 'I did have some idea of selling it, but I don't think I will. It has caused enough mischief already. Besides, people won't buy. They think it's a fairy tale; some of them, and those who do think anything of it want to try it first and pay me afterward.'

'If you could have another three wishes,' said the old man, eyeing him keenly, 'would you have them?'

'I don't know,' said the other. 'I don't know.'

He took the paw, and dangling it between his forefinger and thumb, suddenly threw it upon the fire. White, with a slight cry, stooped down and snatched it off.

'Better let it burn,' said the soldier, solemnly.

'If you don't want it, Morris,' said the other, 'give it to me.'

'I won't,' said his friend, doggedly. 'I threw it on the fire. If you keep it, don't blame me for what happens. Pitch it on the fire again like a sensible man.'

The other shook his head and examined his new possession closely. 'How do you do it?' he inquired.

'Hold it up in your right hand and wish aloud,' said the sergeant-major, 'but I warn you of the consequences.'

'Sounds like the Arabian Nights,' said Mrs White, as she rose and began to set the supper. 'Don't you think you might wish for four pairs of hands for me?'

Her husband drew the talisman from pocket, and then all three burst into laughter as the Sergeant-Major, with a look of alarm on his face, caught him by the arm.

'If you must wish,' he said, gruffly, 'wish for something sensible.'

Mr White dropped it back in his pocket, and placing chairs, motioned his friend to the table. In the business of supper the talisman was partly forgotten, and afterward the three sat listening in an enthralled fashion to a second instalment of the soldier's adventures in India.

'If the tale about the monkey's paw is not more truthful than those he has been telling us,' said Herbert, as the door closed behind their guest, just in time for him to catch the last train, 'we sha'nt make much out of it.'

'Did you give him anything for it, father?' inquired Mrs

White, regarding her husband closely.

'A trifle,' said he, colouring slightly. 'He didn't want it, but I made him take it. And he pressed me again to throw it away.'

'Likely,' said Herbert, with pretended horror. 'Why, we're going to be rich, and famous and happy. Wish to be an emperor, father, to begin with; then you can't be henpecked.'

He darted round the table, pursued by the maligned Mrs White armed with an antimacassar.

Mr White took the paw from his pocket and eyed it dubiously. 'I don't know what to wish for, and that's a fact,' he said, slowly. 'It seems to me I've got all I want.'

'If you only cleared the house, you'd be quite happy, wouldn't you?' said Herbert, with his hand on his shoulder. 'Well, wish for two hundred pounds, then; that'll just do it.'

His father, smiling shamefacedly at his own credulity, held up the talisman, as his son, with a solemn face, somewhat marred by a wink at his mother, sat down at the piano and struck a few impressive chords.

'I wish for two hundred pounds,' said the old man distinctly.

A fine crash from the piano greeted the words, interrupted by a shuddering cry from the old man. His wife and son ran toward him.

'It moved,' he cried, with a glance of disgust at the object as it lay on the floor.

'As I wished, it twisted in my hand like a snake.'

'Well, I don't see the money,' said his son as he picked it up and placed it on the table, 'and I bet I never shall.'

'It must have been your fancy, father,' said his wife, regarding him anxiously.

He shook his head. 'Never mind, though; there's no harm done, but it gave me a shock all the same.'

They sat down by the fire again while the two men finished their pipes. Outside, the wind was higher than ever, and the old man started nervously at the sound of a door banging upstairs. A silence unusual and depressing settled upon all three, which lasted until the old couple rose to retire for the night.

'I expect you'll find the cash tied up in a big bag in the middle of your bed,' said Herbert, as he bade them good-night, 'and something horrible squatting up on top of the wardrobe watching you as you pocket your ill-gotten gains.'

He sat alone in the darkness, gazing at the dying fire, and seeing faces in it. The last face was so horrible and so simian that he gazed at it in amazement. It got so vivid that, with a little uneasy laugh, he felt on the table for a glass containing a little water to throw over it. His hand grasped the monkey's paw, and with a little shiver he wiped his hand on his coat and went up to bed.

In the brightness of the wintry sun next morning as it streamed over the breakfast table he laughed at his fears. There was an air of prosaic wholesomeness about the room which it had lacked on the previous night, and the dirty, shrivelled little paw was pitched on the sideboard with a carelessness which betokened no great belief in its virtues.

'I suppose all old soldiers are the same,' said Mrs White. 'The idea of our listening to such nonsense! How could wishes be granted in these days? And if they could, how could two hundred pounds hurt you, father?'

'Might drop on his head from the sky,' said the frivolous Herbert.

'Morris said the things happened so naturally,' said his father, 'that you might if you so wished attribute it to coincidence.'

'Well, don't break into the money before I come back,' said Herbert as he rose from the table. 'I'm afraid it'll turn you into a mean, avaricious man, and we shall have to disown you.'

His mother laughed, and following him to the door, watched him down the road; and returning to the breakfast table, was very happy at the expense of her husband's credulity. All of which did not prevent her from scurrying to the door at the postman's knock, nor prevent her from referring somewhat shortly to retired sergeant-majors of bibulous habits when she found that the post brought a tailor's bill.

'Herbert will have some more of his funny remarks, I

expect, when he comes home,' she said, as they sat at dinner.

'I dare say,' said Mr White, pouring himself out some beer; 'but for all that, the thing moved in my hand; that I'll swear to.'

'You thought it did,' said the old lady soothingly.

'I say it did,' replied the other. 'There was no thought about it; I had just—What's the matter?'

His wife made no reply. She was watching the mysterious movements of a man outside, who, peering in an undecided fashion at the house, appeared to be trying to make up his mind to enter. In mental connection with the two hundred pounds, she noticed that the stranger was well dressed, and wore a silk hat of glossy newness. Three times he paused at the gate, and then walked on again. The fourth time he stood with his hand upon it, and then with sudden resolution flung it open and walked up the path. Mrs White at the same moment placed her hands behind her, and hurriedly unfastening the strings of her apron, put that useful article of apparel beneath the cushion of her chair.

She brought the stranger, who seemed ill at ease, into the room. He gazed at her furtively, and listened in a preoccupied fashion as the old lady apologized for the appearance of the room, and her husband's coat, a garment which he usually reserved for the garden. She then waited as patiently as her sex would permit, for him to broach his business, but he was at first strangely silent.

'I—was asked to call,' he said at last, and stooped and picked a piece of cotton from his trousers. 'I come from "Maw and Meggins."'

The old lady started. 'Is anything the matter?' she asked, breathlessly. 'Has anything happened to Herbert? What is it? What is it?'

Her husband interposed. 'There, there, mother,' he said, hastily. 'Sit down, and don't jump to conclusions. You've not brought bad news, I'm sure, sir;' and he eyed the other wistfully.

'I'm sorry—' began the visitor.

'Is he hurt?' demanded the mother, wildly.

The visitor bowed in assent. 'Badly hurt,' he said, quietly, 'but he is not in any pain.'

'Oh, thank God!' said the old woman, clasping her hands. 'Thank God for that! Thank——'

She broke off suddenly as the sinister meaning of the assurance dawned upon her and she saw the awful confirmation of her fears in the other's averted face. She caught her breath, and turning to her slower-witted husband, laid her trembling old hand upon his. There was a long silence.

'He was caught in the machinery,' said the visitor at length in a low voice.

'Caught in the machinery,' repeated Mr White, in a dazed fashion, 'yes.'

He sat staring blankly out at the window, and taking his wife's hand between his own, pressed it as he had been wont to do in their old courting-days nearly forty years before.

'He was the only one left to us,' he said, turning gently to the visitor. 'It is hard.'

The other coughed, and rising, walked slowly to the window. 'The firm wished me to convey their sincere sympathy with you in your great loss,' he said, without looking round. 'I beg that you will understand I am only their servant and merely obeying orders.'

There was no reply; the old woman's face was white, her eyes staring, and her breath inaudible; on the husband's face was a look such as his friend the sergeant might have carried into his first action.

'I was to say that Maw and Meggins disclaim all responsibility,' continued the other. 'They admit no liability at all, but in consideration of your son's services, they wish to present you with a certain sum as compensation.'

Mr White dropped his wife's hand, and rising to his feet, gazed with a look of horror at his visitor. His dry lips shaped the words, 'How much?'

'Two hundred pounds,' was the answer.

Unconscious of his wife's shriek, the old man smiled faintly, put out his hands like a sightless man, and dropped, a senseless heap, to the floor.

◆

In the huge new cemetery, some two miles distant, the old people buried their dead, and came back to a house steeped in shadow and silence. It was all over so quickly that at first they could hardly realize it, and remained in a state of expectation as though of something else to happen—something else which was to lighten this load, too heavy for old hearts to bear.

But the days passed, and expectation gave place to resignation—the hopeless resignation of the old, sometimes miscalled, apathy. Sometimes they hardly exchanged a word, for now they had nothing to talk about, and their days were long to weariness.

It was about a week after that the old man, waking suddenly in the night, stretched out his hand and found himself alone. The room was in darkness, and the sound of subdued weeping came from the window. He raised himself in bed and listened.

'Come back,' he said, tenderly. 'You will be cold.'

'It is colder for my son,' said the old woman, and wept afresh.

The sound of her sobs died away on his ears. The bed was warm, and his eyes heavy with sleep. He dozed fitfully, and then slept until a sudden wild cry from his wife awoke him with a start.

'The paw!' she cried wildly. 'The monkey's paw!'

He started up in alarm. 'Where? Where is it? What's the matter?'

She came stumbling across the room toward him. 'I want it,' she said, quietly. 'You've not destroyed it?'

'It's in the parlour, on the bracket,' he replied, marvelling. 'Why?'

She cried and laughed together, and bending over, kissed his cheek.

'I only just thought of it,' she said, hysterically. 'Why didn't

I think of it before? Why didn't you think of it?'

'Think of what?' he questioned.

'The other two wishes,' she replied, rapidly. 'We've only had one.'

'Was not that enough?' he demanded, fiercely.

'No,' she cried, triumphantly; 'we'll have one more. Go down and get it quickly, and wish our boy alive again.'

The man sat up in bed and flung the bedclothes from his quaking limbs. 'Good God, you are mad!' he cried, aghast.

'Get it,' she panted; 'get it quickly, and wish—Oh, my boy, my boy!'

Her husband struck a match and lit the candle. 'Get back to bed,' he said, unsteadily. 'You don't know what you are saying.'

'We had the first wish granted,' said the old woman, feverishly; 'why not the second?'

'A coincidence,' stammered the old man.

'Go and get it and wish,' cried his wife, quivering with excitement.

The old man turned and regarded her, and his voice shook. 'He has been dead ten days, and besides he—I would not tell you else, but—I could only recognize him by his clothing. If he was too terrible for you to see then, how now?'

'Bring him back,' cried the old woman, and dragged him toward the door. 'Do you think I fear the child I have nursed?'

He went down in the darkness, and felt his way to the parlour, and then to the mantelpiece. The talisman was in its place, and a horrible fear that the unspoken wish might bring his mutilated son before him ere he could escape from the room seized upon him, and he caught his breath as he found that he had lost the direction of the door. His brow cold with sweat, he felt his way round the table, and groped along the wall until he found himself in the small passage with the unwholesome thing in his hand.

Even his wife's face seemed changed as he entered the room. It was white and expectant, and to his fears seemed to have an unnatural look upon it. He was afraid of her.

'Wish!' she cried, in a strong voice.

'It is foolish and wicked,' he faltered.

'Wish!' repeated his wife.

He raised his hand. 'I wish my son alive again.'

The talisman fell to the floor, and he regarded it fearfully. Then he sank trembling into a chair as the old woman, with burning eyes, walked to the window and raised the blind.

He sat until he was chilled with the cold, glancing occasionally at the figure of the old woman peering through the window. The candle-end, which had burned below the rim of the china candlestick, was throwing pulsating shadows on the ceiling and walls, until, with a flicker larger than the rest, it expired. The old man, with an unspeakable sense of relief at the failure of the talisman, crept back to his bed, and a minute or two afterward the old woman came silently and apathetically beside him.

Neither spoke, but lay silently listening to the ticking of the clock. A stair creaked, and a squeaky mouse scurried noisily through the wall. The darkness was oppressive, and after lying for some time screwing up his courage, he took the box of matches, and striking one, went downstairs for a candle.

At the foot of the stairs the match went out, and he paused to strike another; and at the same moment a knock, so quiet and stealthy as to be scarcely audible, sounded on the front door.

The matches fell from his hand and spilled in the passage. He stood motionless, his breath suspended until the knock was repeated. Then he turned and fled swiftly back to his room, and closed the door behind him. A third knock sounded through the house.

'What's that?' cried the old woman, starting up.

'A rat,' said the old man in shaking tones—'a rat. It passed me on the stairs.'

His wife sat up in bed listening. A loud knock resounded through the house.

'It's Herbert!' she screamed. 'It's Herbert!'

She ran to the door, but her husband was before her, and catching her by the arm, held her tightly.

'What are you going to do?' he whispered hoarsely.

'It's my boy; it's Herbert!' she cried, struggling mechanically. 'I forgot it was two miles away. What are you holding me for? Let go. I must open the door.'

'For God's sake don't let it in,' cried the old man, trembling.

'You're afraid of your own son,' she cried, struggling. 'Let me go. I'm coming, Herbert; I'm coming.'

There was another knock, and another. The old woman with a sudden wrench broke free and ran from the room. Her husband followed to the landing, and called after her appealingly as she hurried downstairs. He heard the chain rattle back and the bottom bolt drawn slowly and stiffly from the socket. Then the old woman's voice, strained and panting.

'The bolt,' she cried, loudly. 'Come down. I can't reach it.'

But her husband was on his hands and knees groping wildly on the floor in search of the paw. If he could only find it before the thing outside got in. A perfect fusillade of knocks reverberated through the house, and he heard the scraping of a chair as his wife put it down in the passage against the door. He heard the creaking of the bolt as it came slowly back, and at the same moment he found the monkey's paw, and frantically breathed his third and last wish.

The knocking ceased suddenly, although the echoes of it were still in the house. He heard the chair drawn back, and the door opened. A cold wind rushed up the staircase, and a long loud wail of disappointment and misery from his wife gave him courage to run down to her side, and then to the gate beyond. The street lamp flickering opposite shone on a quiet and deserted road.

38

THE TELL-TALE HEART

Edgar Allan Poe

...It is the beating of his hideous heart!

True!—Nervous—very, very dreadfully nervous I had been and am; but why will you say that I am mad? The disease had sharpened my senses—not destroyed—not dulled them. Above all was the sense of hearing acute. I heard all things in the heaven and in the earth. I heard many things in hell. How, then, am I mad? Hearken! and observe how healthily—how calmly I can tell you the whole story.

It is impossible to say how first the idea entered my brain; but once conceived, it haunted me day and night. Object there was none. Passion there was none. I loved the old man. He had never wronged me. He had never given me insult. For his gold I had no desire. I think it was his eye! Yes, it was this! He had the eye of a vulture—a pale blue eye, with a film over it. Whenever it fell upon me, my blood ran cold; and so by degrees—very gradually—I made up my mind to take the life of the old man, and thus rid myself of the eye forever.

Now this is the point. You fancy me mad. Madmen know nothing. But you should have seen me. You should have seen how wisely I proceeded—with what caution—with what foresight—with what dissimulation I went to work! I was never kinder to the old man than during the whole week before I killed him. And every night, about midnight, I turned the latch of his door and opened it—oh so gently! And then, when I had made an opening sufficient for my head, I put in a dark lantern, all closed, closed, that no light shone out, and then I thrust in my head. Oh, you would have laughed to see how cunningly I thrust it in! I moved it slowly—very, very slowly, so that I might not disturb the old man's sleep. It took me an hour to place my whole head within the opening so far that I could see him as he lay upon his bed. Ha! Would a madman have been so wise as this? And then, when my head was well in the room, I undid the lantern cautiously—oh, so cautiously—cautiously (for the hinges creaked)—I undid it just so much that a single thin ray fell upon the vulture eye. And this I did for seven long nights—every night just at midnight—but I found the eye always closed; and so it was impossible to do the work; for it was not the old man who vexed me, but his Evil Eye. And every morning, when the day broke, I went boldly into the chamber, and spoke courageously to him, calling him by name in a hearty tone, and inquiring how he has passed the night. So you see he would have been a very profound old man, indeed, to suspect that every night, just at twelve, I looked in upon him while he slept.

Upon the eighth night I was more than usually cautious in opening the door. A watch's minute hand moves more quickly than did mine. Never before that night had I felt the extent of my own powers—of my sagacity. I could scarcely contain my feelings of triumph. To think that there I was, opening the door, little by little, and he not even to dream of my secret deeds or thoughts. I fairly chuckled at the idea; and perhaps he heard me; for he moved on the bed suddenly, as if startled. Now you may think that I drew back—but no. His room was as black as pitch with the thick darkness, (for the shutters were close fastened, through fear of robbers,) and so I knew that he could not see the opening of the door, and I kept pushing it on steadily, steadily. I had my head in, and was about to open the lantern, when my thumb slipped upon the tin fastening, and the old man sprang up in bed, crying out—'Who's there?' I kept quite still and said nothing. For a whole hour I did not move a muscle, and in the meantime I did not hear him lie down. He was still sitting up in the bed listening;—just as I have done, night after night, hearkening to the death watches in the wall.

Presently I heard a slight groan, and I knew it was the groan of mortal terror. It was not a groan of pain or of grief—oh, no!—it was the low stifled sound that arises from the bottom of the soul when overcharged with awe. I knew the sound well. Many a night, just at midnight, when all the world slept, it has welled up from my own bosom, deepening, with its dreadful echo, the terrors that distracted me. I say I knew it well. I knew what the old man felt, and pitied him, although I chuckled at heart. I knew that he had been lying awake ever since the first slight noise, when he had turned in the bed. His fears had been ever since growing upon him. He had been trying to fancy them causeless, but could not. He had been saying to himself—'It is nothing but the wind in the chimney—it is only a mouse crossing the floor,' or 'It is merely a cricket which has made a single chirp.' Yes, he had been trying to comfort himself with these suppositions: but he had found all in vain. All in vain; because Death, in approaching him had stalked with his black shadow before him, and enveloped the victim. And it was the mournful influence of the unperceived shadow that caused him to feel—although he neither saw nor heard—to feel the presence of my head within the room.

When I had waited a long time, very patiently, without hearing him lie down, I resolved to open a little—a very, very little crevice in the lantern. So I opened it—you cannot imagine how stealthily, stealthily—until, at length a simple dim ray, like the thread of the spider, shot from out the crevice and fell full upon the vulture eye. It was open—wide, wide open—and I grew furious as I gazed upon it. I saw it with perfect distinctness—all a dull blue, with a hideous veil over it that chilled the very marrow in my bones; but I could see nothing else of the old man's face or person: for I had directed the ray as if by instinct, precisely upon the damned spot. And have I not told you that what you mistake for madness is but over-acuteness of the sense?—Now, I say, there came to my ears a low, dull, quick sound, such as a watch makes when enveloped in cotton. I knew that sound well, too. It was the beating of the old man's heart. It increased my fury, as the beating of a drum stimulates the soldier into courage.

But even yet I refrained and kept still. I scarcely breathed. I held the lantern motionless. I tried how steadily I could maintain the ray upon the eye. Meantime the hellish tattoo of the heart increased. It grew quicker and quicker, and louder and louder every instant. The old man's terror must have been extreme! It grew louder, I say, louder every moment!—Do you mark me well? I have told you that I am nervous: so I am. And now at the dead hour of the night, amid the dreadful silence of that old house, so strange a noise as this excited me to uncontrollable terror. Yet, for some minutes longer I refrained and stood still. But the beating grew louder, louder! I thought the heart must burst. And now a new anxiety seized me—the sound would be heard by a neighbour! The old man's hour had come! With a loud yell, I threw open the lantern and leaped into the room. He shrieked once—once only. In an instant I dragged him to the floor, and pulled the heavy bed over him. I then smiled gaily, to find the deed so far done. But, for many minutes, the heart beat on with a muffled sound. This, however, did not vex me; it would not be heard through the wall. At length it ceased. The old man was dead. I removed the bed and examined the corpse. Yes, he was stone, stone dead. I placed my hand upon the heart and held it there many minutes. There was no pulsation. He was stone dead. His eye would trouble me no more.

If still you think me mad, you will think so no longer when I describe the wise precautions I took for the concealment of the body. The night waned, and I worked hastily, but in silence. First of all I dismembered the corpse. I cut off the head and the arms and the legs. I then took up three planks from the flooring of the chamber, and deposited all between the scantlings. I then replaced the boards so cleverly, so cunningly, that no human eye—not even his—could have detected any thing wrong. There was nothing to wash out—no stain of any kind—no blood-spot whatever. I had been too wary for that. A tub had caught all—ha! ha! When I had made an end of these labours, it was four o'clock—still dark as midnight. As the bell sounded the hour, there came a knocking at the street door. I went down to open it with a light heart,—for what had I now to fear? There entered three men, who introduced themselves, with perfect suavity, as officers of the police. A shriek had been heard by a neighbour during the night; suspicion of foul play had been aroused; information had been lodged at the police office, and they (the officers) had been deputed to search the premises. I smiled—for what had I to fear? I bade the gentlemen welcome. The shriek, I said, was my own in a dream. The old man, I mentioned, was absent in the country. I took my visitors all over the house. I bade them search—search well. I led them, at length, to his chamber. I showed them his treasures, secure, undisturbed. In the enthusiasm of my confidence, I brought chairs into the room, and desired them here to rest from their fatigues, while I myself, in the wild audacity of my perfect triumph, placed my own seat upon the very spot beneath which reposed the corpse of the victim.

The officers were satisfied. My manner had convinced them. I was singularly at ease. They sat, and while I answered cheerily, they chatted of familiar things. But, ere long, I felt myself getting pale and wished them gone. My head ached, and I fancied a ringing in my ears: but still they sat and still chatted. The ringing became more distinct—it continued and became more distinct: I talked more freely to get rid of the feeling: but it continued and gained definiteness—until, at length, I found that the noise was not within my ears. No doubt I now grew very pale—but I talked more fluently, and with a heightened voice. Yet the sound increased—and what could I do? It was a low, dull, quick sound—much such a sound as a watch makes when enveloped in cotton. I gasped for breath—and yet the officers heard it not. I talked more quickly—more vehemently; but the noise steadily increased. I arose and argued about trifles, in a high key and with violent gesticulations; but the noise steadily increased. Why would they not be gone? I paced the floor to and fro with heavy strides, as if excited to fury by the observations of the men—but the noise steadily increased. Oh God! What could I do? I foamed—I raved—I swore! I swung the chair upon which I had been sitting, and grated it upon the boards, but the noise arose over all and continually increased. It grew louder—louder—louder! And still the men chatted pleasantly, and smiled. Was it possible they heard not? Almighty God!—No, no! They heard!—They suspected!—They knew!—They were making a mockery of my horror!—This I thought, and this I think. But anything was better than this agony! Anything was more tolerable than this derision! I could bear those hypocritical smiles no longer! I felt that I must scream or die! And now—again!—hark! Louder! Louder! Louder! Louder!

'Villains' I shrieked, 'dissemble no more! I admit the deed!—Tear up the planks! Here, here!—It is the beating of his hideous heart!'

39

THE CALL OF CTHULHU

H.P. Lovecraft

Excerpted from 'The Call of Cthulhu' (1928)

*...some obscure lesion of the heart,
induced by the brisk ascent of so steep a hill
by so elderly a man, was responsible for the end...*

The most merciful thing in the world, I think, is the inability of the human mind to correlate all its contents. We live on a placid island of ignorance in the midst of black seas of infinity, and it was not meant that we should voyage far. The sciences, each straining in its own direction, have hitherto harmed us little; but some day the piecing together of dissociated knowledge will open up such terrifying vistas of reality, and of our frightful position therein, that we shall either go mad from the revelation or flee from the light into the peace and safety of a new dark age.

Theosophists have guessed at the awesome grandeur of the cosmic cycle wherein our world and human race form transient incidents. They have hinted at strange survivals in terms which would freeze the blood if not masked by a bland optimism. But it is not from them that there came the single glimpse of forbidden eons which chills me when I think of it and maddens me when I dream of it. That glimpse, like all dread glimpses of truth, flashed out from an accidental piecing together of separated things—in this case an old newspaper item and the notes of a dead professor. I hope that no one else will accomplish this piecing out; certainly, if I live, I shall never knowingly supply a link in so hideous a chain. I think that the professor, too, intented to keep silent regarding the part he knew, and that he would have destroyed his notes had not sudden death seized him.

My knowledge of the thing began in the winter of 1926-27 with the death of my great-uncle, George Gammell Angell, Professor Emeritus of Semitic Languages in Brown University, Providence, Rhode Island. Professor Angell was widely known as an authority on ancient inscriptions, and had frequently been resorted to by the heads of prominent museums; so that his passing at the age of ninety-two may be recalled by many. Locally, interest was intensified by the obscurity of the cause of death. The professor had been stricken whilst returning from the Newport boat; falling suddenly; as witnesses said, after having been jostled by a nautical-looking negro who had come from one of the queer dark courts on the precipitous hillside which formed a short cut from the waterfront to the deceased's home in Williams Street. Physicians were unable to find any visible disorder, but concluded after perplexed debate that some obscure lesion of the heart, induced by the brisk ascent of so steep a hill by so elderly a man, was responsible for the end. At the time I saw no reason to dissent from this dictum, but latterly I am inclined to wonder—and more than wonder.

As my great-uncle's heir and executor, for he died a childless widower, I was expected to go over his papers with some thoroughness; and for that purpose moved his entire set of files and boxes to my quarters in Boston.

Much of the material which I correlated will be later published by the American Archaeological Society, but there was one box which I found exceedingly puzzling, and which I felt much averse from showing to other eyes. It had been locked and I did not find the key till it occurred to me to examine the personal ring which the professor carried in his pocket. Then, indeed, I succeeded in opening it, but when I did so seemed only to be confronted by a greater and more closely locked barrier. For what could be the meaning of the queer clay bas-relief and the disjointed jottings, ramblings, and cuttings which

I found? Had my uncle, in his latter years become credulous of the most superficial impostures? I resolved to search out the eccentric sculptor responsible for this apparent disturbance of an old man's peace of mind.

The bas-relief was a rough rectangle less than an inch thick and about five by six inches in area; obviously of modern origin. Its designs, however, were far from modern in atmosphere and suggestion; for, although the vagaries of cubism and futurism are many and wild, they do not often reproduce that cryptic regularity which lurks in prehistoric writing. And writing of some kind the bulk of these designs seemed certainly to be; though my memory, despite much familiarity with the papers and collections of my uncle, failed in any way to identify this particular species, or even hint at its remotest affiliations.

Above these apparent hieroglyphics was a figure of evident pictorial intent, though its impressionistic execution forbade a very clear idea of its nature.

It seemed to be a sort of monster, or symbol representing a monster, of a form which only a diseased fancy could conceive. If I say that my somewhat extravagant imagination yielded simultaneous pictures of an octopus, a dragon, and a human caricature, I shall not be unfaithful to the spirit of the thing. A pulpy, tentacled head surmounted a grotesque and scaly body with rudimentary wings; but it was the general outline of the whole which made it most shockingly frightful. Behind the figure was a vague suggestions of a Cyclopean architectural background.

The writing accompanying this oddity was, aside from a stack of press cuttings, in Professor Angell's most recent hand; and made no pretense to literary style. What seemed to be the main document was headed 'CTHULHU CULT' in characters painstakingly printed to avoid the erroneous reading of a word so unheard-of. This manuscript was divided into two sections, the first of which was headed '1925—Dream and Dream Work of H.A. Wilcox, 7 Thomas St., Providence, R. I.', and the second, 'Narrative of Inspector John R. Legrasse, 121

Bienville St., New Orleans, La., at 1908 A. A. S. Mtg.—Notes on Same, & Prof. Webb's Acct.' The other manuscript papers were brief notes, some of them accounts of the queer dreams of different persons, some of them citations from theosophical books and magazines (notably W. Scott-Elliot's *Atlantis and the Lost Lemuria*), and the rest comments on long -surviving secret societies and hidden cults, with references to passages in such mythological and anthropological source-books as Frazer's *Golden Bough* and Miss Murray's *Witch-Cult in Western Europe*. The cuttings largely alluded to outre mental illness and outbreaks of group folly or mania in the spring of 1925.

The first half of the principal manuscript told a very particular tale. It appears that on March 1st, 1925, a thin, dark young man of neurotic and excited aspect had called upon Professor Angell bearing the singular clay bas-relief, which was then exceedingly damp and fresh. His card bore the name of Henry Anthony Wilcox, and my uncle had recognized him as the youngest son of an excellent family slightly known to him, who had latterly been studying sculpture at the Rhode Island School of Design and living alone at the Fleur-de-Lys Building near that institution. Wilcox was a precocious youth of known genius but great eccentricity, and had from chidhood excited attention through the strange stories and odd dreams he was in the habit of relating. He called himself 'psychically hypersensitive', but the staid folk of the ancient commercial city dismissed him as merely 'queer.' Never mingling much with his kind, he had dropped gradually from social visibility, and was now known only to a small group of esthetes from other towns. Even the Providence Art Club, anxious to preserve its conservatism, had found him quite hopeless.

On the ocassion of the visit, ran the professor's manuscript, the sculptor abruptly asked for the benefit of his host's archeological knowledge in identifying the hieroglyphics of the bas-relief. He spoke in a dreamy, stilted manner which suggested pose and alienated sympathy; and my uncle showed some sharpness in replying, for the conspicuous freshness of the tablet implied kinship with anything but archeology. Young Wilcox's rejoinder, which impressed my uncle enough to make him recall and record it verbatim, was of a fantastically poetic cast which must have typified his whole conversation, and which I have since found highly characteristic of him. He said, 'It is new, indeed, for I made it last night in a dream of strange cities; and dreams are older than brooding Tyre, or the contemplative Sphinx, or garden-girdled Babylon.'

It was then that he began that rambling tale which suddenly played upon a sleeping memory and won the fevered interest of my uncle. There had been a slight earthquake tremor the night before, the most considerable felt in New England for some years; and Wilcox's imagination had been keenly affected. Upon retiring, he had had an unprecedented dream of great Cyclopean cities of Titan blocks and sky-flung monoliths, all dripping with green ooze and sinister with latent horror. Hieroglyphics had covered the walls and pillars, and from some undetermined point below had come a voice that was not a voice; a chaotic sensation which only fancy could transmute into sound, but which he attempted to render by the almost unpronounceable jumble of letters: 'Cthulhu fhtagn.'

This verbal jumble was the key to the recollection which excited and disturbed Professor Angell. He questioned the sculptor with scientific minuteness; and studied with frantic intensity the bas-relief on which the youth had found himself working, chilled and clad only in his night clothes, when waking had stolen bewilderingly over him. My uncle blamed his old age, Wilcox afterwards said, for his slowness in recognizing both hieroglyphics and pictorial design. Many of his questions seemed highly out of place to his visitor, especially those which tried to connect the latter with strange cults or societies; and Wilcox could not understand the repeated promises of silence which he was offered in exchange for an admission of membership in some widespread mystical or paganly religious body. When Professor Angell became convinced that the sculptor was indeed ignorant of any cult or system of cryptic lore, he besieged his visitor with demands for future reports of dreams. This bore regular fruit, for after the first interview the manuscript records daily calls of the young man, during which he related startling fragments of nocturnal imagery whose burden was always some terrible Cyclopean vista of dark and dripping stone, with a subterrene voice or intelligence shouting monotonously in enigmatical sense-impacts uninscribable save as gibberish. The two sounds frequently repeated are those rendered by the letters 'Cthulhu' and 'R'lyeh.'

On March 23, the manuscript continued, Wilcox failed to appear; and inquiries at his quarters revealed that he had been stricken with an obscure sort of fever and taken to the home of his family in Waterman Street. He had cried out in the night, arousing several other artists in the building, and had manifested since then only alternations of unconsciousness and delirium. My uncle at once telephoned the family, and from that time forward kept close watch of the case; calling often at the Thayer Street office of Dr Tobey, whom he learned to be in charge. The youth's febrile mind, apparently, was dwelling on strange things; and the doctor shuddered now and then as he spoke of them. They included not only a repetition of what he had formerly dreamed, but touched wildly on a gigantic thing 'miles high' which walked or lumbered about.

He at no time fully described this object but occasional frantic words, as repeated by Dr Tobey, convinced the professor that it must be identical with the nameless monstrosity he had sought to depict in his dream-sculpture. Reference to this object, the doctor added, was invariably a prelude to the young man's subsidence into lethargy. His temperature, oddly enough, was not greatly above normal; but the whole condition was otherwise such as to suggest true fever rather than mental disorder.

On April 2 at about 3 p.m. every trace of Wilcox's malady suddenly ceased. He sat upright in bed, astonished to find himself at home and completely ignorant of what had happened in dream or reality since the night of March 22. Pronounced well by his physician, he returned to his quarters in three days;

but to Professor Angell he was of no further assistance. All traces of strange dreaming had vanished with his recovery, and my uncle kept no record of his night-thoughts after a week of pointless and irrelevant accounts of thoroughly usual visions.

Here the first part of the manuscript ended, but references to certain of the scattered notes gave me much material for thought—so much, in fact, that only the ingrained skepticism then forming my philosophy can account for my continued distrust of the artist. The notes in question were those descriptive of the dreams of various persons covering the same period as that in which young Wilcox had had his strange visitations. My uncle, it seems, had quickly instituted a prodigiously far-flung body of inquires amongst nearly all the friends whom he could question without impertinence, asking for nightly reports of their dreams, and the dates of any notable visions for some time past. The reception of his request seems to have varied; but he must, at the very least, have received more responses than any ordinary man could have handled without a secretary. This original correspondence was not preserved, but his notes formed a thorough and really significant digest. Average people in society and business—New England's traditional 'salt of the earth'—gave an almost completely negative result, though scattered cases of uneasy but formless nocturnal impressions appear here and there, always between March 23 and and April 2—the period of young Wilcox's delirium. Scientific men were little more affected, though four cases of vague description suggest fugitive glimpses of strange landscapes, and in one case there is mentioned a dread of something abnormal.

It was from the artists and poets that the pertinent answers came, and I know that panic would have broken loose had they been able to compare notes. As it was, lacking their original letters, I half suspected the compiler of having asked leading questions, or of having edited the correspondence in corroboration of what he had latently resolved to see. That is why I continued to feel that Wilcox, somehow cognizant of the old data which my uncle had possessed, had been imposing on the veteran scientist. These responses from esthetes told a disturbing tale. From February 28 to April 2 a large proportion of them had dreamed very bizarre things, the intensity of the dreams being immeasurably the stronger during the period of the sculptor's delirium. Over a fourth of those who reported anything, reported scenes and half-sounds not unlike those which Wilcox had described; and some of the dreamers confessed acute fear of the gigantic nameless thing visible toward the last. One case, which the note describes with emphasis, was very sad. The subject, a widely known architect with leanings toward theosophy and occultism, went violently insane on the date of young Wilcox's seizure, and expired several months later after incessant screamings to be saved from some escaped denizen of hell. Had my uncle referred to these cases by name instead of merely by number, I should have attempted some corroboration and personal investigation; but as it was, I succeeded in tracing down only a few. All of these, however, bore out the notes in full. I have often wondered if all the the objects of the professor's questioning felt as puzzled as did this fraction. It is well that no explanation shall ever reach them.

The press cuttings, as I have intimated, touched on cases of panic, mania, and eccentricity during the given period. Professor Angell must have employed a cutting bureau, for the number of extracts was tremendous, and the sources scattered throughout the globe. Here was a nocturnal suicide in London, where a lone sleeper had leaped from a window after a shocking cry. Here likewise a rambling letter to the editor of a paper in South America, where a fanatic deduces a dire future from visions he has seen. A dispatch from California describes a theosophist colony as donning white robes en masse for some "glorious fulfiment" which never arrives, whilst items from India speak guardedly of serious native unrest toward the end of March 22-23.

The west of Ireland, too, is full of wild rumour and legendry, and a fantastic painter named Ardois-Bonnot hangs a blasphemous Dream Landscape in the Paris spring salon of

1926. And so numerous are the recorded troubles in insane asylums that only a miracle can have stopped the medical fraternity from noting strange parallelisms and drawing mystified conclusions. A weird bunch of cuttings, all told; and I can at this date scarcely envisage the callous rationalism with which I set them aside. But I was then convinced that young Wilcox had known of the older matters mentioned by the professor.

40

A VENDETTA

Guy de Maupassant

... three windows looked out over this wild and desolate scene.

Paolo Saverini's widow lived alone with her son in a poor little house on the ramparts of Bonifacio. The town, built on a spur of the mountains, in places actually overhanging the sea, looks across a channel bristling with reefs, to the lower shores of Sardinia. At its foot, on the other side and almost completely surrounding it, is the channel that serves as its harbour, cut in the cliff like a gigantic corridor. Through a long circuit between steep walls, the channel brings to the very foot of the first houses the little Italian or Sardinian fishing-boats, and, every fortnight, the old steamboat that runs to and from Ajaccio.

Upon the white mountain the group of houses form a whiter patch still. They look like the nests of wild birds, perched so upon the rock, dominating that terrible channel through which hardly ever a ship risks a passage. The unresting wind harasses the sea and eats away the bare shore, clad with a sparse covering of grass; it rushes into the ravine and ravages its two sides. The trailing wisps of white foam round the black points of countless rocks that everywhere pierce the waves, look like rags of canvas floating and heaving on the surface of the water.

The widow Saverini's house held for dear life to the very edge of the cliff; its three windows looked out over this wild and desolate scene.

She lived there alone with her son Antoine and their bitch Semillante, a large, thin animal with long, shaggy hair, of the sheep-dog breed. The young man used her for hunting.

One evening, after a quarrel, Antoine Saverini was treacherously slain by a knife-thrust from Nicolas Ravolati, who got away to Sardinia the same night.

When his old mother received his body, carried home by bystanders, she did not weep, but for a long time stayed motionless, looking at it; then, stretching out her wrinkled hand over the body, she swore vendetta against him. She would have no one stay with her, and shut herself up with the body, together with the howling dog. The animal howled continuously, standing at the foot of the bed, her head thrust towards her master, her tail held tightly between her legs. She did not stir, nor did the mother, who crouched over the body with her eyes fixed steadily upon it, and wept great silent tears.

The young man, lying on his back, clad in his thick serge coat with a hole torn across the front, looked as though he slept; but everywhere there was blood; on the shirt, torn off for the first hasty dressing; on his waistcoat, on his breeches, on his face, on his hands. Clots of blood had congealed in his beard and in his hair.

The old mother began to speak to him. At the sound of her voice the dog was silent.

'There, there, you shall be avenged, my little one, my boy, my poor child. Sleep, sleep, you shall be avenged, do you hear! Your mother swears it! And your mother always keeps her word; you know she does.'

Slowly she bent over him, pressing her cold lips on the dead lips.

Then Semillante began to howl once more. She uttered long cries, monotonous, heart-rending, horrible cries.

They remained there, the pair of them, the woman and the dog, till morning.

Antoine Saverini was buried next day, and before long there was no more talk of him in Bonifacio.

He had left neither brothers nor close cousins. No man was there to carry on the vendetta. Only his mother, an old woman, brooded over it.

On the other side of the channel she watched from morning till night a white speck on the coast. It was a little Sardinian village, Longosardo, where Corsican bandits fled for refuge when too hard pressed. They formed almost the entire population of this hamlet, facing the shores of their own country, and there they awaited a suitable moment to come home, to return to the maquis of Corsica. She knew that Nicolas Ravolati had taken refuge in this very village.

All alone, all day long, sitting by the window, she looked over there and pondered revenge. How could she do it without another's help, so feeble as she was, so near to death? But she had promised, she had sworn upon the body. She could not forget, she could not wait. What was she to do? She could no longer sleep at night, she had no more sleep nor peace; obstinately she searched for a way. The dog slumbered at her feet and sometimes, raising her head, howled into the empty spaces. Since her master had gone, she often howled thus, as though she were calling him, as though her animal soul, inconsolable, had retained an ineffaceable memory of him.

One night, as Semillante was beginning to moan again, the mother had a sudden idea, an idea quite natural to a vindictive and ferocious savage. She meditated on it till morning, then, rising at the approach of day, she went to church. She prayed, kneeling on the stones, prostrate before God, begging Him to aid her, to sustain her, to grant her poor worn-out body the strength necessary to avenge her son.

Then she returned home. There stood in the yard an old barrel with its sides stove in, which held the rain-water; she overturned it, emptied it, and fixed it to the ground with stakes and stones; then she chained up Semillante in this kennel, and went into the house.

Next she began to walk up and down her room, taking no rest, her eyes still turned to the coast of Sardinia. He was there, the murderer.

All day long and all night long the dog howled. In the

morning the old woman took her some water in a bowl, but nothing else; no soup, no bread.

Another day went by. Semillante, exhausted, was asleep. Next day her eyes were shining, her hair on end, and she tugged desperately at the chain.

Again the old woman gave her nothing to eat. The animal, mad with hunger, barked hoarsely. Another night went by.

When day broke, Mother Saverini went to her neighbour to ask him to give her two trusses of straw. She took the old clothes her husband had worn and stuffed them with the straw into the likeness of a human figure.

Having planted a post in the ground opposite Semillante's kennel, she tied the dummy figure to it, which looked now as though it were standing. Then she fashioned a head with a roll of old linen.

The dog, surprised, looked at this straw man, and was silent, although devoured with hunger.

Then the woman went to the pork-butcher and bought a long piece of black pudding. She returned home, lit a wood fire in her yard, close to the kennel, and grilled the black pudding. Semillante, maddened, leapt about and foamed at the mouth, her eyes fixed on the food, the flavour of which penetrated to her very stomach.

Then with the smoking sausage the mother made a collar for the straw man. She spent a long time lashing it round his neck, as though to stuff it right in. When it was done, she unchained the dog.

With a tremendous bound the animal leapt upon the dummy's throat and with her paws on his shoulders began to rend it. She fell back with a piece of the prey in her mouth, then dashed at it again, sank her teeth into the cords, tore away a few fragments of food, fell back again, and leapt once more, ravenous.

With great bites she rent away the face, and tore the whole neck to shreds.

The old woman watched, motionless and silent, a gleam

in her eyes. Then she chained up her dog again, made her go without food for two more days, and repeated the strange performance.

For three months she trained the dog to this struggle, the conquest of a meal by fangs. She no longer chained her up, but launched her upon the dummy with a sign.

She had taught the dog to rend and devour it without hiding food in its throat. Afterwards she would reward the dog with the gift of the black pudding she had cooked for her.

As soon as she saw the man, Semillante would tremble, then turn her eyes towards her mistress, who would cry 'Off!' in a whistling tone, raising her finger.

When she judged that the time was come, Mother Saverini went to confession and took communion one Sunday morning with an ecstatic fervour; then, putting on a man's clothes, like an old ragged beggar, she bargained with a Sardinian fisherman, who took her, accompanied by the dog, to the other side of the straits.

In a canvas bag she had a large piece of black pudding. Semillante had had nothing to eat for two days. Every minute the old woman made her smell the savoury food, stimulating her hunger with it.

They came to Longosardo. The Corsican woman was limping slightly. She went to the baker's and inquired for Nicolas Ravolati's house. He had resumed his old occupation, that of a joiner. He was working alone at the back of his shop.

The old woman pushed open the door and called him:

'Hey! Nicolas!'

He turned round; then, letting go of her dog, she cried:

'Off, off, bite him, bite him!'

The maddened beast dashed forward and seized his throat.

The man put out his arms, clasped the dog, and rolled upon the ground. For a few minutes he writhed, beating the ground with his feet; then he remained motionless while Semillante nuzzled at his throat and tore it out in ribbons.

Two neighbours, sitting at their doors, plainly recollected

having seen a poor old man come out with a lean black dog which ate, as it walked, something brown that its master was giving to it.

In the evening the old woman returned home. That night she slept well.

41
THE TERROR

Guy de Maupassant

...my state of mind is so wretched
that you will pity me and despise me...

You say you cannot possibly understand it, and I believe you. You think I am losing my mind? Perhaps I am, but for other reasons than those you imagine, my dear friend.

Yes, I am going to be married, and will tell you what has led me to take that step.

I may add that I know very little of the girl who is going to become my wife tomorrow; I have only seen her four or five times. I know that there is nothing unpleasing about her, and that is enough for my purpose. She is small, fair, and stout; so, of course, the day after tomorrow I shall ardently wish for a tall, dark, thin woman.

She is not rich, and belongs to the middle classes. She is a girl such as you may find by the gross, well adapted for matrimony, without any apparent faults, and with no particularly striking qualities. People say of her:

'Mlle. Lajolle is a very nice girl,' and tomorrow they will say: 'What a very nice woman Madame Raymon is.' She belongs, in a word, to that immense number of girls whom one is glad to have for one's wife, till the moment comes when one discovers that one happens to prefer all other women to that particular woman whom one has married.

'Well,' you will say to me, 'what on earth did you get married for?'

I hardly like to tell you the strange and seemingly

improbable reason that urged me on to this senseless act; the fact, however, is that I am afraid of being alone.

I don't know how to tell you or to make you understand me, but I do not want to be alone any longer at night. I want to feel that there is someone close to me, touching me, a being who can speak and say something, no matter what it be.

I wish to be able to awaken somebody by my side, so that I may be able to ask some sudden question, a stupid question even, if I feel inclined, so that I may hear a human voice, and feel that there is some waking soul close to me, someone whose reason is at work; so that when I hastily light the candle I may see some human face by my side—because—because—I am ashamed to confess it—because I am afraid of being alone.

Oh, you don't understand me yet.

I am not afraid of any danger; if a man were to come into the room, I should kill him without trembling. I am not afraid of ghosts, nor do I believe in the supernatural. I am not afraid of dead people, for I believe in the total annihilation of every being that disappears from the face of this earth.

Well—yes, well, it must be told: I am afraid of myself, afraid of that horrible sensation of incomprehensible fear.

You may laugh, if you like. It is terrible, and I cannot get over it. I am afraid of the walls, of the furniture, of the familiar objects; which are animated, as far as I am concerned, by a kind of animal life. Above all, I am afraid of my own dreadful thoughts, of my reason, which seems as if it were about to leave me, driven away by a mysterious and invisible agony.

At first I feel a vague uneasiness in my mind, which causes a cold shiver to run all over me. I look round, and of course nothing is to be seen, and I wish that there were something there, no matter what, as long as it were something tangible. I am frightened merely because I cannot understand my own terror.

If I speak, I am afraid of my own voice. If I walk, I am afraid of I know not what, behind the door, behind the curtains, in the cupboard, or under my bed, and yet all the time I know there is nothing anywhere, and I turn round suddenly because I am afraid of what is behind me, although there is nothing there, and I know it.

I become agitated. I feel that my fear increases, and so I shut myself up in my own room, get into bed, and hide under the clothes; and there, cowering down, rolled into a ball, I close my eyes in despair, and remain thus for an indefinite time, remembering that my candle is alight on the table by my bedside, and that I ought to put it out, and yet—I dare not do it.

It is very terrible, is it not, to be like that?

Formerly I felt nothing of all that. I came home quite calm, and went up and down my apartment without anything disturbing my peace of mind. Had anyone told me that I should be attacked by a malady—for I can call it nothing else—of most improbable fear, such a stupid and terrible malady as it is, I should have laughed outright. I was certainly never afraid of opening the door in the dark. I went to bed slowly, without locking it, and never got up in the middle of the night to make sure that everything was firmly closed.

It began last year in a very strange manner on a damp autumn evening. When my servant had left the room, after I had dined, I asked myself what I was going to do. I walked up and down my room for some time, feeling tired without any reason for it, unable to work, and even without energy to read. A fine rain was falling, and I felt unhappy, a prey to one of those fits of despondency, without any apparent cause, which make us feel inclined to cry, or to talk, no matter to whom, so as to shake off our depressing thoughts.

I felt that I was alone, and my rooms seemed to me to be more empty than they had ever been before. I was in the midst of infinite and overwhelming solitude. What was I to do? I sat down, but a kind of nervous impatience seemed to affect my legs, so I got up and began to walk about again. I was, perhaps, rather feverish, for my hands, which I had clasped behind me, as one often does when walking slowly, almost seemed to burn one another. Then suddenly a cold shiver ran down my back, and I thought the damp air might have penetrated into my rooms, so I lit the fire for the first time that year, and sat down again and looked at the flames. But soon I felt that I could not possibly remain quiet, and so I got up again and determined to go out, to pull myself together, and to find a friend to bear me company.

I could not find anyone, so I walked to the boulevard to try and meet some acquaintance or other there.

It was wretched everywhere, and the wet pavement glistened in the gaslight, while the oppressive warmth of the almost impalpable rain lay heavily over the streets and seemed to obscure the light of the lamps.

I went on slowly, saying to myself: 'I shall not find a soul to talk to.'

I glanced into several cafes, from the Madeleine as far as the Faubourg Poissoniere, and saw many unhappy-looking individuals sitting at the tables who did not seem even to have enough energy left to finish the refreshments they had ordered.

For a long time I wandered aimlessly up and down, and about midnight I started for home. I was very calm and very tired. My janitor opened the door at once, which was quite unusual for him, and I thought that another lodger had probably just come in.

When I go out I always double-lock the door of my room, and I found it merely closed, which surprised me; but I supposed that some letters had been brought up for me in the course of the evening.

I went in, and found my fire still burning so that it lighted up the room a little, and, while in the act of taking up a candle, I noticed somebody sitting in my armchair by the fire, warming his feet, with his back toward me.

I was not in the slightest degree frightened. I thought, very naturally, that some friend or other had come to see me. No doubt the porter, to whom I had said I was going out, had lent him his own key. In a moment I remembered all the circumstances of my return, how the street door had been opened immediately, and that my own door was only latched and not locked.

I could see nothing of my friend but his head, and he had evidently gone to sleep while waiting for me, so I went up to him to rouse him. I saw him quite distinctly; his right arm was hanging down and his legs were crossed; the position of his head, which was somewhat inclined to the left of the armchair, seemed to indicate that he was asleep. 'Who can it be?' I asked myself. I could not see clearly, as the room was rather dark, so I put out my hand to touch him on the shoulder, and it came in contact with the back of the chair. There was nobody there; the seat was empty.

I fairly jumped with fright. For a moment I drew back as if confronted by some terrible danger; then I turned round again, impelled by an imperious standing upright, panting with fear, so upset that I could not collect my thoughts, and ready to faint.

But I am a cool man, and soon recovered myself. I thought: 'It is a mere hallucination, that is all,' and I immediately began to reflect on this phenomenon. Thoughts fly quickly at such moments.

I had been suffering from an hallucination, that was an incontestable fact. My mind had been perfectly lucid and had acted regularly and logically, so there was nothing the matter with the brain. It was only my eyes that had been deceived; they had had a vision, one of those visions which lead simple folk to believe in miracles. It was a nervous seizure of the optical apparatus, nothing more; the eyes were rather congested, perhaps.

I lit my candle, and when I stooped down to the fire in doing so I noticed that I was trembling, and I raised myself up with a jump, as if somebody had touched me from behind.

I was certainly not by any means calm.

I walked up and down a little, and hummed a tune or two. Then I double-locked the door and felt rather reassured;

now, at any rate, nobody could come in.

I sat down again and thought over my adventure for a long time; then I went to bed and blew out my light.

For some minutes all went well; I lay quietly on my back, but presently an irresistible desire seized me to look round the room, and I turned over on my side.

My fire was nearly out, and the few glowing embers threw a faint light on the floor by the chair, where I fancied I saw the man sitting again.

I quickly struck a match, but I had been mistaken; there was nothing there. I got up, however, and hid the chair behind my bed, and tried to get to sleep, as the room was now dark; but I had not forgotten myself for more than five minutes, when in my dream I saw all the scene which I had previously witnessed as clearly as if it were reality. I woke up with a start, and having lit the candle, sat up in bed, without venturing even to try to go to sleep again.

Twice, however, sleep overcame me for a few moments in spite of myself, and twice I saw the same thing again, till I fancied I was going mad. When day broke, however, I thought that I was cured, and slept peacefully till noon.

It was all past and over. I had been feverish, had had the nightmare. I know not what. I had been ill, in fact, but yet thought I was a great fool.

I enjoyed myself thoroughly that evening. I dined at a restaurant and afterward went to the theatre, and then started for home. But as I got near the house I was once more seized by a strange feeling of uneasiness. I was afraid of seeing him again. I was not afraid of him, not afraid of his presence, in which I did not believe; but I was afraid of being deceived again. I was afraid of some fresh hallucination, afraid lest fear should take possession of me.

For more than an hour I wandered up and down the pavement; then, feeling that I was really too foolish, I returned home. I breathed so hard that I could hardly get upstairs, and remained standing outside my door for more than ten minutes; then suddenly I had a courageous impulse and my will asserted itself. I inserted my key into the lock, and went into the apartment with a candle in my hand. I kicked open my bedroom door, which was partly open, and cast a frightened glance toward the fireplace. There was nothing there. A-h! What a relief and what a delight! What a deliverance! I walked up and down briskly and boldly, but I was not altogether reassured, and kept turning round with a jump; the very shadows in the corners disquieted me.

I slept badly, and was constantly disturbed by imaginary noises, but did not see him; no, that was all over.

Since that time I have been afraid of being alone at night. I feel that the spectre is there, close to me, around me; but it has not appeared to me again.

And supposing it did, what would it matter, since I do not believe in it, and know that it is nothing?

However, it still worries me, because I am constantly thinking of it. His right arm hanging down and his head inclined to the left like a man who was asleep—I don't want to think about it!

Why, however, am I so persistently possessed with this idea? His feet were close to the fire!

He haunts me; it is very stupid, but who and what is he? I know that he does not exist except in my cowardly imagination, in my fears, and in my agony. There—enough of that!

Yes, it is all very well for me to reason with myself, to stiffen my backbone, so to say; but I cannot remain at home because I know he is there. I know I shall not see him again; he will not show himself again; that is all over. But he is there, all the same, in my thoughts. He remains invisible, but that does not prevent his being there. He is behind the doors, in the closed cupboard, in the wardrobe, under the bed, in every dark corner. If I open the door or the cupboard, if I take the candle to look under the bed and throw a light on the dark places he is there no longer, but I feel that he is behind me. I turn round, certain that I shall not see him, that I shall never see him again; but for all that, he is behind me.

It is very stupid, it is dreadful; but what am I to do? I cannot help it.

But if there were two of us in the place I feel certain that he would not be there any longer, for he is there just because I am alone, simply and solely because I am alone!

42

GHOSTS

Guy de Maupassant

... I fear, be the ruin of Austria, receive a staggering blow...

Just at the time when the *concordat* was in its most flourishing condition, a young man belonging to a wealthy and highly respected middle class family went to the office of the Head of the Police at P— and begged for his help and advice, which was immediately promised him.

'My father threatens to disinherit me,' the young man then began, 'although I have never offended against the laws of the State, of morality or of his paternal authority, merely because I do not share his blind reverence for the Catholic Church and her Ministers. On that account he looks upon me, not merely as Latitudinarian, but as a perfect Atheist, and a faithful old manservant of ours, who is much attached to me, and who accidentally saw my father's will, told me in confidence that he had left all his property to the Jesuits. I think this is highly suspicious, and I fear that the priests have been maligning me to my father. Until less than a year ago, we used to live very quietly and happily together, but ever since he has had so much to do with the clergy, our domestic peace and happiness are at an end.'

'What you have told me,' the official replied, 'is as likely as it is regrettable, but I fail to see how I can interfere in the matter. Your father is in the full possession of all his mental faculties, and can dispose of all his property exactly as he pleases. I also think that your protest is premature; you must wait until his will can legally take effect, and then you can invoke the aid of justice; I am sorry to say that I can do nothing for you.'

'I think you will be able to,' the young man replied; 'for I believe that a very clever piece of deceit is being carried on here.'

'How? Please explain yourself more clearly.'

'When I remonstrated with him, yesterday evening, he referred to my dead mother, and at last assured me, in a voice of the deepest conviction, that she had frequently appeared to him, and had threatened him with all the torments of the damned, if he did not disinherit his son, who had fallen away from God, and leave all his property to the Church. Now I do not believe in ghosts.'

'Neither do I,' the police director replied; 'but I cannot well do anything on this dangerous ground, if I had nothing but superstitions to go upon. You know how the Church rules all our affairs since the *concordat* with Rome, and if I investigate this matter, and obtain no results, I am risking my post. It would be very different if you could adduce any proofs for your suspicions. I do not deny that I should like to see the clerical party, which will, I fear, be the ruin of Austria, receive a staggering blow; try, therefore, to get to the bottom of this business, and then we will talk it over again.'

About a month passed, without the young Latitudinarian being heard of; but then he suddenly came one evening, evidently in a great state of excitement, and told him that he was in a position to expose the priestly deceit which he had mentioned, if the authorities would assist him. The police director asked for further information.

'I have obtained a number of important clues,' the young man said. 'In the first place, my father confessed to me, that my mother did not appear to him in our house, but in the churchyard where she is buried. My mother was consumptive for many years, and a few weeks before her death she went to the village of S— where she died and was buried. In addition to this, I found out from our footman, that my father has already left the house twice, late at night, in company of X— the Jesuit priest, and that on both occasions he did not return till morning.

Each time he was remarkably uneasy and low-spirited after his return, and had three masses said for my dead mother. He also told me just now, that he has to leave home this evening on business, but immediately he told me that, our footman saw the Jesuit go out of the house. We may, therefore, assume that he intends this evening to consult the spirit of my dead mother again, and this would be an excellent opportunity for getting on the track of the matter, if you do not object to opposing the most powerful force in the Empire, for the sake of such an insignificant individual as myself.'

'Every citizen has an equal right to the protection of the State,' the police director replied; 'and I think that I have shown often enough, that I am not wanting in courage to perform my duty, no matter how serious the consequences may be; but only very young men act without any prospects of success, as they are carried away by their feelings. When you came to me the first time, I was obliged to refuse your request for assistance, but today your shares have risen in value. It is now eight o'clock, and I shall expect you in two hours' time, here in my office. At present, all you have to do is to hold your tongue; everything else is my affair.'

As soon as it was dark, four men got into a closed carriage in the yard of the police office, and were driven in the direction of the village of S—; their carriage, however, did not enter the village, but stopped at the edge of a small wood in the immediate neighbourhood. Here they all four alighted; they were the police director, accompanied by the young Latitudinarian, a police sergeant and an ordinary policeman, who was, however, dressed in plain clothes.

'The first thing for us to do is to examine the locality carefully,' the police director said; 'it is eleven o'clock and the exorcisers of ghosts will not arrive before midnight, so we have time to look round us, and to take our measure.'

The four men went to the churchyard, which lay at the end of the village, near the little wood. Everything was as still as death, and not a soul was to be seen. The sexton was evidently sitting in the public house, for they found the door of his cottage locked, as well as the door of the little chapel that stood in the middle of the churchyard.

'Where is your mother's grave?' the police director asked; as there were only a few stars visible, it was not easy to find it, but at last they managed it, and the police director looked about in the neighbourhood of it.

'The position is not a very favorable one for us,' he said at last; 'there is nothing here, not even a shrub, behind which we could hide.'

But just then the policeman said that he had tried to get into the sexton's hut through the door or the window, and that at last he had succeeded in doing so by breaking open a square in a window, which had been mended with paper, and that he had opened it and obtained possession of the key, which he brought to the police director.

His plans were very quickly settled. He had the chapel opened and went in with the young Latitudinarian; then he told the police sergeant to lock the door behind him and to put the key back where he had found it, and to shut the window of the sexton's cottage carefully. Lastly, he made arrangements as to what they were to do, in case anything unforeseen should occur, whereupon the sergeant and the constable left the churchyard, and lay down in a ditch at some distance from the gate, but opposite to it.

Almost as soon as the clock struck half-past eleven, they heard steps near the chapel, whereupon the police director and the young Latitudinarian went to the window, in order to watch the beginning of the exorcism, and as the chapel was in total darkness, they thought that they should be able to see, without being seen; but matters turned out differently from what they expected.

Suddenly, the key turned in the lock, and they barely had time to conceal themselves behind the altar, before two men came in, one of whom was carrying a dark lantern. One was the young man's father, an elderly man of the middle class, who seemed very unhappy and depressed, the other the Jesuit father K— a tall, thin, big-boned man, with a thin, bilious face, in which two large gray eyes shone restlessly under their bushy, black eyebrows. He lit the tapers, which were standing on the altar, and then began to say a Requiem Mass; while the old man knelt on the altar steps and served him.

When it was over, the Jesuit took the book of the Gospels and the holy water sprinkler, and went slowly out of the chapel, while the old man followed him, with the holy water basin in one hand and a taper in the other. Then the police director left his hiding place, and stooping down, so as not to be seen, he crept to the chapel window, where he cowered down carefully, and the young man followed his example. They were now looking straight on his mother's grave.

The Jesuit, followed by the superstitious old man, walked three times round the grave; then he remained standing before it, and by the light of the taper, he read a few passages from the Gospel; then he dipped the holy water sprinkler three times into the holy water basin, and sprinkled the grave three times; then both returned to the chapel, knelt down outside it with their faces towards the grave, and began to pray aloud, until at last the Jesuit sprang up, in a species of wild ecstasy, and cried out three times in a shrill voice:

'Exsurge! Exsurge! Exsurge!'

Scarcely had the last word of the exorcism died away, when thick, blue smoke rose out of the grave, which rapidly grew into a cloud, and began to assume the outlines of a human body, until at last a tall, white figure stood behind the grave, and beckoned with its hand.

'Who art thou?' the Jesuit asked solemnly, while the old man began to cry.

'When I was alive, I was called Anna Maria B—' the ghost replied in a hollow voice.

'Will you answer all my questions?' the priest continued.

'As far as I can.'

'Have you not yet been delivered from purgatory by our

prayers, and all the masses for your soul, which we have said for you?'

'Not yet, but soon, soon I shall be.'

'When?'

'As soon as that blasphemer, my son, has been punished.'

'Has that not already happened? Has not your husband disinherited his lost son, and made the Church his heir, in his place?'

'That is not enough.'

'What must he do besides?'

'He must deposit his will with the Judicial Authorities, as his last will and testament, and drive the reprobate out of his house.'

'Consider well what you are saying. Must this really be?'

'It must, or otherwise I shall have to languish in purgatory much longer,' the sepulchral voice replied with a deep sigh; but the next moment it yelled out in terror:

'Oh! Good Lord!' and the ghost began to run away as fast as it could. A shrill whistle was heard, and then another, and the police director laid his hand on the shoulder of the exorcisor, accompanied with the remark:

'You are in custody.'

Meanwhile, the police sergeant and the policeman, who had come into the churchyard, had caught the ghost, and dragged it forward. It was the sexton, who had put on a flowing, white dress, and who wore a wax mask, which bore striking resemblance to his mother, as the son declared.

When the case was heard, it was proved that the mask had been very skillfully made from a portrait of the deceased woman. The Government gave orders that the matter should be investigated as secretly as possible, and left the punishment of Father K—to the spiritual authorities, which was a matter of course, at a time when priests were outside the jurisdiction of the Civil Authorities; and it is needless to say that he was very comfortable during his imprisonment, in a monastery in a part of the country which abounded with game and trout.

The only valuable result of the amusing ghost story was, that it brought about a reconciliation between father and son, and the former, as a matter of fact, felt such deep respect for priests and their ghosts in consequence of the apparition, that a short time after his wife had left purgatory for the last time, in order to talk with him, he turned *Protestant*.

43

THE HAND

Guy de Maupassant

I simply believe that the legitimate owner of the hand was not dead, that he came to get it with his remaining one...

All were crowding around M. Bermutier, the judge, who was giving his opinion about the Saint-Cloud mystery. For a month this inexplicable crime had been the talk of Paris. Nobody could make head or tail of it.

M. Bermutier, standing with his back to the fireplace, was talking, citing the evidence, discussing the various theories, but arriving at no conclusion.

Some women had risen, in order to get nearer to him, and were standing with their eyes fastened on the clean-shaven face of the judge, who was saying such weighty things. They were shaking and trembling, moved by fear and curiosity, and by the eager and insatiable desire for the horrible, which haunts the soul of every woman. One of them, paler than the others, said during a pause:

'It's terrible. It verges on the supernatural. The truth will never be known.'

The judge turned to her: 'True, madame, it is likely that the actual facts will never be discovered. As for the word "supernatural" which you have just used, it has nothing to do with the matter. We are in the presence of a very cleverly conceived and executed crime, so well enshrouded in mystery that we cannot disentangle it from the involved circumstances which surround it. But once I had to take charge of an affair in which the uncanny seemed to play a part. In fact, the case became so confused that it had to be given up.'

Several women exclaimed at once: 'Oh! Tell us about it!'

M. Bermutier smiled in a dignified manner, as a judge should, and went on: 'Do not think, however, that I, for one minute, ascribed anything in the case to supernatural influences. I believe only in normal causes. But if, instead of using the word "supernatural" to express what we do not understand, we were simply to make use of the word "inexplicable", it would be much better. At any rate, in the affair of which I am about to tell you, it is especially the surrounding, preliminary circumstances which impressed me. Here are the facts:

'I was, at that time, a judge at Ajaccio, a little white city on the edge of a bay which is surrounded by high mountains.

'The majority of the cases which came up before me concerned vendettas. There are some that are superb, dramatic, ferocious, heroic. We find there the most beautiful causes for revenge of which one could dream, enmities hundreds of years old, quieted for a time but never extinguished; abominable stratagems, murders becoming massacres and almost deeds of glory. For two years I heard of nothing but the price of blood, of this terrible Corsican prejudice which compels revenge for insults meted out to the offending person and all his descendants and relatives. I had seen old men, children, cousins murdered; my head was full of these stories.

'One day I learned that an Englishman had just hired a little villa at the end of the bay for several years. He had brought with him a French servant, whom he had engaged on the way at Marseilles.

'Soon this peculiar person, living alone, only going out to hunt and fish, aroused a widespread interest. He never spoke to anyone, never went to the town, and every morning he would practise for an hour or so with his revolver and rifle.

'Legends were built up around him. It was said that he was some high personage, fleeing from his fatherland for political reasons; then it was affirmed that he was in hiding after having committed some abominable crime. Some particularly horrible circumstances were even mentioned.

'In my judicial position I thought it necessary to get some information about this man, but it was impossible to learn anything. He called himself Sir John Rowell.

'I therefore had to be satisfied with watching him as closely as I could, but I could see nothing suspicious about his actions.

'However, as rumours about him were growing and becoming more widespread, I decided to try to see this stranger myself, and I began to hunt regularly in the neighbourhood of his grounds.

'For a long time I watched without finding an opportunity. At last it came to me in the shape of a partridge which I shot and killed right in front of the Englishman. My dog fetched it for me, but, taking the bird, I went at once to Sir John Rowell and, begging his pardon, asked him to accept it.

'He was a big man, with red hair and beard, very tall, very broad, a kind of calm and polite Hercules. He had nothing of the so-called British stiffness, and in a broad English accent he thanked me warmly for my attention. At the end of a month we had had five or six conversations.

'One night, at last, as I was passing before his door, I saw him in the garden, seated astride a chair, smoking his pipe. I bowed and he invited me to come in and have a glass of beer. I needed no urging.

'He received me with the most punctilious English courtesy, sang the praises of France and of Corsica, and declared that he was quite in love with this country.

'Then, with great caution and under the guise of a vivid interest, I asked him a few questions about his life and his plans. He answered without embarrassment, telling me that he had travelled a great deal in Africa, in the Indies, in America. He added, laughing: "I have had many adventures."

'Then I turned the conversation on hunting, and he gave me the most curious details on hunting the hippopotamus, the tiger, the elephant and even the gorilla.

'I said: "Are all these animals dangerous?"

'He smiled: "Oh, no! Man is the worst."

'And he laughed a good broad laugh, the wholesome laugh of a contented Englishman.

'"I have also frequently been man-hunting."

'Then he began to talk about weapons, and he invited me to come in and see different makes of guns.

'His parlour was draped in black, black silk embroidered in gold. Big yellow flowers, as brilliant as fire, were worked on the dark material.

'He said: "It is a Japanese material."

'But in the middle of the widest panel a strange thing attracted my attention. A black object stood out against a square of red velvet. I went up to it; it was a hand, a human hand. Not the clean white hand of a skeleton, but a dried black hand, with yellow nails, the muscles exposed and traces of old blood on the bones, which were cut off as clean as though it had been chopped off with an axe, near the middle of the forearm.

'Around the wrist, an enormous iron chain, riveted and soldered to this unclean member, fastened it to the wall by a ring, strong enough to hold an elephant in leash.

'I asked: "What is that?"

'The Englishman answered quietly: "That is my best enemy. It comes from America, too. The bones were severed by a sword and the skin cut off with a sharp stone and dried in the sun for a week."

'I touched these human remains, which must have belonged to a giant. The uncommonly long fingers were attached by enormous tendons which still had pieces of skin hanging to them in places. This hand was terrible to see; it made one think of some savage vengeance.

'I said: "This man must have been very strong."

'The Englishman answered quietly: "Yes, but I was stronger than he. I put on this chain to hold him."

'I thought that he was joking. I said: "This chain is useless now, the hand won't run away."

'Sir John Rowell answered seriously: "It always wants to go away. This chain is needed."

'I glanced at him quickly, questioning his face, and I asked myself: "Is he an insane man or a practical joker?"

'But his face remained inscrutable, calm and friendly. I turned to other subjects, and admired his rifles.

'However, I noticed that he kept three loaded revolvers in the room, as though constantly in fear of some attack.

'I paid him several calls. Then I did not go any more. People had become used to his presence; everybody had lost interest in him.

'A whole year rolled by. One morning, toward the end of November, my servant awoke me and announced that Sir John Rowell had been murdered during the night.

'Half an hour later I entered the Englishman's house, together with the police commissioner and the captain of the gendarmes. The servant, bewildered and in despair, was crying before the door. At first I suspected this man, but he was innocent.

'The guilty party could never be found.

'On entering Sir John's parlour, I noticed the body, stretched out on its back, in the middle of the room.

'His vest was torn, the sleeve of his jacket had been pulled off, everything pointed to a violent struggle.

'The Englishman had been strangled! His face was black, swollen and frightful, and seemed to express a terrible fear. He held something between his teeth, and his neck, pierced by five or six holes which looked as though they had been made by some iron instrument, was covered with blood.

'A physician joined us. He examined the finger marks on the neck for a long time and then made this strange announcement:

'"It looks as though he had been strangled by a skeleton."

'A cold chill seemed to run down my back, and I looked over to where I had formerly seen the terrible hand. It was no longer there. The chain was hanging down, broken.

'I bent over the dead man and, in his contracted mouth, I found one of the fingers of this vanished hand, cut—or rather sawed off by the teeth down to the second knuckle.

'Then the investigation began. Nothing could be discovered.

No door, window or piece of furniture had been forced. The two watch dogs had not been aroused from their sleep.

'Here, in a few words, is the testimony of the servant: For a month his master had seemed excited. He had received many letters, which he would immediately burn.

'Often, in a fit of passion which approached madness, he had taken a switch and struck wildly at this dried hand riveted to the wall, and which had disappeared, no one knows how, at the very hour of the crime.

'He would go to bed very late and carefully lock himself in. He always kept weapons within reach. Often at night he would talk loudly, as though he were quarrelling with someone.

'That night, somehow, he had made no noise, and it was only on going to open the windows that the servant had found Sir John murdered. He suspected no one.

'I communicated what I knew of the dead man to the judges and public officials. Throughout the whole island a minute investigation was carried on. Nothing could be found out.

'One night, about three months after the crime, I had a terrible nightmare. I seemed to see the horrible hand running over my curtains and walls like an immense scorpion or spider. Three times I awoke, three times I went to sleep again; three times I saw the hideous object galloping round my room and moving its fingers like legs.

'The following day the hand was brought me, found in the cemetery, on the grave of Sir John Rowell, who had been buried there because we had been unable to find his family. The first finger was missing.

'Ladies, there is my story. I know nothing more.'

The women, deeply stirred, were pale and trembling. One of them exclaimed: 'But that is neither a climax nor an explanation! We will be unable to sleep unless you give us your opinion of what had occurred.'

The judge smiled severely: 'Oh! Ladies, I shall certainly spoil your terrible dreams. I simply believe that the legitimate owner of the hand was not dead, that he came to get it with his remaining one. But I don't know how. It was a kind of vendetta.'

One of the women murmured: 'No, it can't be that.'

And the judge, still smiling, said: 'Didn't I tell you that my explanation would not satisfy you?'

44
THE OUTSIDER
H.P. Lovecraft

Ghastly and terrible was that dead, stairless cylinder of rock; black, ruined, and deserted, and sinister with startled bats whose wings made no noise...

That night the Baron dreamt of many a woe;
And all his warrior-guests, with shade and form
Of witch, and demon, and large coffin-worm,
Were long be-nightmared.
—Keats.

Unhappy is he to whom the memories of childhood bring only fear and sadness. Wretched is he who looks back upon lone hours in vast and dismal chambers with brown hangings and maddening rows of antique books, or upon awed watches in twilight groves of grotesque, gigantic, and vine-encumbered trees that silently wave twisted branches far aloft. Such a lot the gods gave to me—to me, the dazed, the disappointed; the barren, the broken. And yet I am strangely content, and cling desperately to those sere memories, when my mind momentarily threatens to reach beyond to the other.

I know not where I was born, save that the castle was infinitely old and infinitely horrible; full of dark passages and having high ceilings where the eye could find only cobwebs and shadows. The stones in the crumbling corridors seemed always hideously damp, and there was an accursed smell everywhere, as of the piled-up corpses of dead generations. It was never light, so that I used sometimes to light candles and gaze steadily at them for relief; nor was there any sun outdoors, since the terrible trees grew high above the topmost accessible tower. There was one black tower which reached above the trees into the unknown outer sky, but that was partly ruined and could not be ascended save by a well-nigh impossible climb up the sheer wall, stone by stone.

I must have lived years in this place, but I cannot measure the time. Beings must have cared for my needs, yet I cannot recall any person except myself; or anything alive but the noiseless rats and bats and spiders. I think that whoever nursed me must have been shockingly aged, since my first conception of a living person was that of something mockingly like myself, yet distorted, shrivelled, and decaying like the castle. To me there was nothing grotesque in the bones and skeletons that strowed some of the stone crypts deep down among the foundations. I fantastically associated these things with every-day events, and thought them more natural than the coloured pictures of living beings which I found in many of the mouldy books. From such books I learned all that I know. No teacher urged or guided me, and I do not recall hearing any human voice in all those years—not even my own; for although I had read of speech, I had never thought to try to speak aloud. My aspect was a matter equally unthought of, for there were no mirrors in the castle, and I merely regarded myself by instinct as akin to the youthful figures I saw drawn and painted in the books. I felt conscious of youth because I remembered so little.

Outside, across the putrid moat and under the dark mute trees, I would often lie and dream for hours about what I read in the books; and would longingly picture myself amidst gay crowds in the sunny world beyond the endless forest. Once I tried to escape from the forest, but as I went farther from the castle the shade grew denser and the air more filled with brooding fear; so that I ran frantically back lest I lose my way in a labyrinth of nighted silence.

So through endless twilights I dreamed and waited, though

I knew not what I waited for. Then in the shadowy solitude my longing for light grew so frantic that I could rest no more, and I lifted entreating hands to the single black ruined tower that reached above the forest into the unknown outer sky. And at last I resolved to scale that tower, fall though I might; since it were better to glimpse the sky and perish, than to live without ever beholding day.

In the dank twilight I climbed the worn and aged stone stairs till I reached the level where they ceased, and thereafter clung perilously to small footholds leading upward. Ghastly and terrible was that dead, stairless cylinder of rock; black, ruined, and deserted, and sinister with startled bats whose wings made no noise. But more ghastly and terrible still was the slowness of my progress; for climb as I might, the darkness overhead grew no thinner, and a new chill as of haunted and venerable mould assailed me. I shivered as I wondered why I did not reach the light, and would have looked down had I dared. I fancied that night had come suddenly upon me, and vainly groped with one free hand for a window embrasure, that I might peer out and above, and try to judge the height I had attained.

All at once, after an infinity of awesome, sightless crawling up that concave and desperate precipice, I felt my head touch a solid thing, and I knew I must have gained the roof, or at least some kind of floor. In the darkness I raised my free hand and tested the barrier, finding it stone and immovable. Then came a deadly circuit of the tower, clinging to whatever holds the slimy wall could give; till finally my testing hand found the barrier yielding, and I turned upward again, pushing the slab or door with my head as I used both hands in my fearful ascent. There was no light revealed above, and as my hands went higher I knew that my climb was for the nonce ended; since the slab was the trap-door of an aperture leading to a level stone surface of greater circumference than the lower tower, no doubt the floor of some lofty and capacious observation chamber. I crawled through carefully, and tried to prevent the heavy slab from falling back into place; but failed in the latter attempt. As I lay exhausted on the stone floor I heard the eerie echoes of its fall, but hoped when necessary to pry it open again.

Believing I was now at a prodigious height, far above the accursed branches of the wood, I dragged myself up from the floor and fumbled about for windows, that I might look for the first time upon the sky, and the moon and stars of which I had read. But on every hand I was disappointed; since all that I found were vast shelves of marble, bearing odious oblong boxes of disturbing size. More and more I reflected, and wondered what hoary secrets might abide in this high apartment so many aeons cut off from the castle below. Then unexpectedly my hands came upon a doorway, where hung a portal of stone, rough with strange chiselling. Trying it, I found it locked; but with a supreme burst of strength I overcame all obstacles and dragged it open inward. As I did so there came to me the purest ecstasy I have ever known; for shining tranquilly through an ornate grating of iron, and down a short stone passageway of steps that ascended from the newly found doorway, was the radiant full moon, which I had never before seen save in dreams and in vague visions I dared not call memories.

Fancying now that I had attained the very pinnacle of the castle, I commenced to rush up the few steps beyond the door; but the sudden veiling of the moon by a cloud caused me to stumble, and I felt my way more slowly in the dark. It was still very dark when I reached the grating—which I tried carefully and found unlocked, but which I did not open for fear of falling from the amazing height to which I had climbed. Then the moon came out.

Most daemoniacal of all shocks is that of the abysmally unexpected and grotesquely unbelievable. Nothing I had before undergone could compare in terror with what I now saw; with the bizarre marvels that sight implied. The sight itself was as simple as it was stupefying, for it was merely this: instead of a dizzying prospect of treetops seen from a lofty eminence, there stretched around me on a level through the grating nothing less than *the solid ground,* decked and diversified by marble slabs and columns, and overshadowed by an ancient stone church, whose ruined spire gleamed spectrally in the moonlight.

Half unconscious, I opened the grating and staggered out upon the white gravel path that stretched away in two directions. My mind, stunned and chaotic as it was, still held the frantic craving for light; and not even the fantastic wonder which had happened could stay my course. I neither knew nor cared whether my experience was insanity, dreaming, or magic; but was determined to gaze on brilliance and gaiety at any cost. I knew not who I was or what I was, or what my surroundings might be; though as I continued to stumble along I became conscious of a kind of fearsome latent memory that made my progress not wholly fortuitous. I passed under an arch out of that region of slabs and columns, and wandered through the open country; sometimes following the visible road, but sometimes leaving it curiously to tread across meadows where only occasional ruins bespoke the ancient presence of a forgotten road. Once I swam across a swift river where crumbling, mossy masonry told of a bridge long vanished.

Over two hours must have passed before I reached what seemed to be my goal, a venerable ivied castle in a thickly wooded park; maddeningly familiar, yet full of perplexing strangeness to me. I saw that the moat was filled in, and that some of the well-known towers were demolished; whilst new wings existed to confuse the beholder. But what I observed with chief interest and delight were the open windows—gorgeously ablaze with light and sending forth sound of the gayest revelry. Advancing to one of these I looked in and saw an oddly dressed company, indeed; making merry, and speaking brightly to one another. I had never, seemingly, heard human speech before; and could guess only vaguely what was said. Some of the faces seemed to hold expressions that brought up incredibly remote recollections; others were utterly alien.

I now stepped through the low window into the brilliantly lighted room, stepping as I did so from my single bright moment of hope to my blackest convulsion of despair and realisation. The nightmare was quick to come; for as I entered, there occurred immediately one of the most terrifying demonstrations I had ever conceived. Scarcely had I crossed the sill when there descended upon the whole company a sudden and unheralded fear of hideous intensity, distorting every face and evoking the most horrible screams from nearly every throat. Flight was universal, and in the clamour and panic several fell in a swoon and were dragged away by their madly fleeing companions. Many covered their eyes with their hands, and plunged blindly and awkwardly in their race to escape; overturning furniture and stumbling against the walls before they managed to reach one of the many doors.

The cries were shocking; and as I stood in the brilliant apartment alone and dazed, listening to their vanishing echoes, I trembled at the thought of what might be lurking near me unseen. At a casual inspection the room seemed deserted, but when I moved toward one of the alcoves I thought I detected a presence there—a hint of motion beyond the golden-arched doorway leading to another and somewhat similar room. As I approached the arch I began to perceive the presence more clearly; and then, with the first and last sound I ever uttered—a ghastly ululation that revolted me almost as poignantly as its noxious cause—I beheld in full, frightful vividness the inconceivable, indescribable, and unmentionable monstrosity which had by its simple appearance changed a merry company to a herd of delirious fugitives.

I cannot even hint what it was like, for it was a compound of all that is unclean, uncanny, unwelcome, abnormal, and detestable. It was the ghoulish shade of decay, antiquity, and desolation; the putrid, dripping eidolon of unwholesome revelation; the awful baring of that which the merciful earth should always hide. God knows it was not of this world—or no longer of this world—yet to my horror I saw in its eaten-away and bone-revealing outlines a leering, abhorrent travesty on the human shape; and in its mouldy, disintegrating apparel an unspeakable quality that chilled me even more.

I was almost paralysed, but not too much so to make a feeble effort toward flight; a backward stumble which failed to break the spell in which the nameless, voiceless monster held me. My eyes, bewitched by the glassy orbs which stared loathsomely into them, refused to close; though they were mercifully blurred, and shewed the terrible object but indistinctly after the first shock. I tried to raise my hand to shut out the sight, yet so stunned were my nerves that my arm could not fully obey my will. The attempt, however, was enough to disturb my balance; so that I had to stagger forward several steps to avoid falling. As I did so I became suddenly and agonisingly aware of the *nearness* of the carrion thing, whose hideous hollow breathing I half fancied I could hear. Nearly mad, I found myself yet able to throw out a hand to ward off the foetid apparition which pressed so close; when in one cataclysmic second of cosmic nightmarishness and hellish accident *my fingers touched the rotting outstretched paw of the monster beneath the golden arch.*

I did not shriek, but all the fiendish ghouls that ride the night-wind shrieked for me as in that same second there crashed down upon my mind a single and fleeting avalanche of soul-annihilating memory. I knew in that second all that had been; I remembered beyond the frightful castle and the trees, and recognised the altered edifice in which I now stood; I recognised, most terrible of all, the unholy abomination that stood leering before me as I withdrew my sullied fingers from its own.

But in the cosmos there is balm as well as bitterness, and that balm is nepenthe. In the supreme horror of that second I forgot what had horrified me, and the burst of black memory vanished in a chaos of echoing images. In a dream I fled from that haunted and accursed pile, and ran swiftly and silently in the moonlight. When I returned to the churchyard place of marble and went down the steps I found the stone trap-door immovable; but I was not sorry, for I had hated the antique castle and the trees. Now I ride with the mocking and friendly ghouls on the night-wind, and play by day amongst the catacombs of Nephren-Ka in the sealed and unknown valley of Hadoth by the Nile. I know that light is not for me, save that of the moon over the rock tombs of Neb, nor any gaiety save the unnamed feasts of Nitokris beneath the Great Pyramid; yet in my new wildness and freedom I almost welcome the bitterness of alienage.

For although nepenthe has calmed me, I know always that I am an outsider; a stranger in this century and among those who are still men. This I have known ever since I stretched out my fingers to the abomination within that great gilded frame; stretched out my fingers and touched *a cold and unyielding surface of polished glass.*

45

THE DAMNED THING

Ambrose Bierce

I am not mad; there are colours that we cannot see...

By the light of a tallow candle which had been placed on one end of a rough table a man was reading something written in a book. It was an old account book, greatly worn; and the writing was not, apparently, very legible, for the man sometimes held the page close to the flame of the candle to get a stronger light on it. The shadow of the book would then throw into obscurity a half of the room, darkening a number of faces and figures; for besides the reader, eight other men were present. Seven of them sat against the rough log walls, silent, motionless, and the room being small, not very far from the table. By extending an arm anyone of them could have touched the eighth man, who lay on the table, face upward, partly covered by a sheet, his arms at his sides. He was dead.

The man with the book was not reading aloud, and no one spoke; all seemed to be waiting for something to occur; the dead man only was without expectation. From the blank darkness outside came in, through the aperture that served for a window, all the ever unfamiliar noises of night in the wilderness—the long nameless note of a distant coyote; the stilly pulsing thrill of tireless insects in trees; strange cries of night birds, so different from those of the birds of day; the drone of great blundering beetles, and all that mysterious chorus of small sounds that seem always to have been but half heard when they have suddenly ceased, as if conscious of an indiscretion. But nothing of all this was noted in that company;

its members were not overmuch addicted to idle interest in matters of no practical importance; that was obvious in every line of their rugged faces—obvious even in the dim light of the single candle. They were evidently men of the vicinity—farmers and woodsmen.

The person reading was a trifle different; one would have said of him that he was of the world, worldly, albeit there was that in his attire which attested a certain fellowship with the organisms of his environment. His coat would hardly have passed muster in San Francisco; his foot-gear was not of urban origin, and the hat that lay by him on the floor (he was the only one uncovered) was such that if one had considered it as an article of mere personal adornment he would have missed its meaning. In countenance the man was rather prepossessing, with just a hint of sternness; though that he may have assumed or cultivated, as appropriate to one in authority. For he was a coroner. It was by virtue of his office that he had possession of the book in which he was reading; it had been found among the dead man's effects—in his cabin, where the inquest was now taking place.

When the coroner had finished reading he put the book into his breast pocket. At that moment the door was pushed open and a young man entered. He, clearly, was not of mountain birth and breeding: he was clad as those who dwell in cities. His clothing was dusty, however, as from travel. He had, in fact, been riding hard to attend the inquest.

The coroner nodded; no one else greeted him.

'We have waited for you,' said the coroner. 'It is necessary to have done with this business tonight.'

The young man smiled. 'I am sorry to have kept you,' he said. 'I went away, not to evade your summons, but to post to my newspaper an account of what I suppose I am called back to relate.'

The coroner smiled.

'The account that you posted to your newspaper,' he said, 'differs, probably, from that which you will give here under oath.'

'That,' replied the other, rather hotly and with a visible flush, 'is as you please. I used manifold paper and have a copy of what I sent. It was not written as news, for it is incredible, but as fiction. It may go as a part of my testimony under oath.'

'But you say it is incredible.'

'That is nothing to you, sir, if I also swear that it is true.'

The coroner was silent for a time, his eyes upon the floor. The men about the sides of the cabin talked in whispers, but seldom withdrew their gaze from the face of the corpse. Presently the coroner lifted his eyes and said: 'We will resume the inquest.'

The men removed their hats. The witness was sworn.

'What is your name?' the coroner asked.

'William Harker.'

'Age?'

'Twenty-seven.'

'You knew the deceased, Hugh Morgan?'

'Yes.'

'You were with him when he died?'

'Near him.'

'How did that happen—your presence, I mean ?'

'I was visiting him at this place to shoot and fish. A part of my purpose, however, was to study him and his odd, solitary way of life. He seemed a good model for a character in fiction. I sometimes write stories.'

'I sometimes read them.'

'Thank you.'

'Stories in general—not yours.'

Some of the jurors laughed. Against a sombre background humour shows high lights. Soldiers in the intervals of battle laugh easily, and a jest in the death chamber conquers by surprise.

'Relate the circumstances of this man's death,' said the coroner. 'You may use any notes or memoranda that you please.'

The witness understood. Pulling a manuscript from his breast pocket he held it near the candle and turning the leaves until he found the passage that he wanted began to read.

II: What may Happen in a Field of Wild Oats

'...The sun had hardly risen when we left the house. We were looking for quail, each with a shotgun, but we had only one dog. Morgan said that our best ground was beyond a certain ridge that he pointed out, and we crossed it by a trail through the chaparral. On the other side was comparatively level ground, thickly covered with wild oats. As we emerged from the chaparral Morgan was but a few yards in advance. Suddenly we heard, at a little distance to our right and partly in front, a noise as of some animal thrashing about in the bushes, which we could see were violently agitated.

'"We've started a deer," I said. "I wish we had brought a rifle."

'Morgan, who had stopped and was intently watching the agitated chaparral, said nothing, but had cocked both barrels of his gun and was holding it in readiness to aim. I thought him a trifle excited, which surprised me, for he had a reputation for exceptional coolness, even in moments of sudden and imminent peril.

'"Oh, come," I said. "You are not going to fill up a deer with quail-shot, are you?"

'Still he did not reply; but catching a sight of his face as he turned it slightly toward me I was struck by the intensity of his look. Then I understood that we had serious business in hand, and my first conjecture was that we had "jumped" a grizzly. I advanced to Morgan's side, cocking my piece as I moved.

'The bushes were now quiet and the sounds had ceased, but Morgan was as attentive to the place as before.

'"What is it? What the devil is it?" I asked.

'"That Damned Thing!" he replied, without turning his head. His voice was husky and unnatural. He trembled visibly.

'I was about to speak further, when I observed the wild oats near the place of the disturbance moving in the most inexplicable way. I can hardly describe it. It seemed as if stirred by a streak of wind, which not only bent it, but pressed it down—crushed it so that it did not rise; and this movement was slowly prolonging itself directly toward us.

'Nothing that I had ever seen had affected me so strangely as this unfamiliar and unaccountable phenomenon, yet I am unable to recall any sense of fear. I remember—and tell it here because, singularly enough, I recollected it then—that once in looking carelessly out of an open window I momentarily mistook a small tree close at hand for one of a group of larger trees at a little distance away. It looked the same size as the others, but being more distinctly and sharply defined in mass and detail seemed out of harmony with them. It was a mere falsification of the law of aerial perspective, but it startled, almost terrified me. We so rely upon the orderly operation of familiar natural laws that any seeming suspension of them is noted as a menace to our safety, a warning of unthinkable calamity. So now the apparently causeless movement of the herbage and the slow, undeviating approach of the line of disturbance were distinctly disquieting. My companion appeared actually frightened, and I could hardly credit my senses when I saw him suddenly throw his gun to his shoulder and fire both barrels at the agitated grain! Before the smoke of the discharge had cleared away I heard a loud savage cry—a scream like that of a wild animal—and flinging his gun upon the ground Morgan sprang away and ran swiftly from the spot. At the same instant I was thrown violently to the ground by the impact of something unseen in the smoke—some soft, heavy substance that seemed thrown against me with great force.

'Before I could get upon my feet and recover my gun, which seemed to have been struck from my hands, I heard Morgan crying out as if in mortal agony, and mingling with his cries were such hoarse, savage sounds as one hears from fighting dogs. Inexpressibly terrified, I struggled to my feet and looked in the direction of Morgan's retreat; and may Heaven in mercy spare me from another sight like that! At a distance of less than thirty yards was my friend, down upon one knee, his head thrown back at a frightful angle, hatless, his long hair in disorder and his whole body in violent movement from side to side, backward and forward. His right arm was lifted and seemed to lack the hand—at least, I could see none. The other arm was invisible. At times, as my memory now reports this extraordinary scene, I could discern but a part of his body; it was as if he had been partly blotted out—I cannot otherwise express it—then a shifting of his position would bring it all into view again.

'All this must have occurred within a few seconds, yet in that time Morgan assumed all the postures of a determined wrestler vanquished by superior weight and strength. I saw nothing but him, and him not always distinctly. During the entire incident his shouts and curses were heard, as if through an enveloping uproar of such sounds of rage and fury as I had never heard from the throat of man or brute!

'For a moment only I stood irresolute, then throwing down my gun I ran forward to my friend's assistance. I had a vague belief that he was suffering from a fit, or some form of convulsion. Before I could reach his side he was down and quiet. All sounds had ceased, but with a feeling of such terror as even these awful events had not inspired I now saw again the mysterious movement of the wild oats, prolonging itself from the trampled area about the prostrate man toward the edge of a wood. It was only when it had reached the wood that I was able to withdraw my eyes and look at my companion. He was dead.'

III: A Man Though Naked may be in Rags

The coroner rose from his seat and stood beside the dead man. Lifting an edge of the sheet he pulled it away, exposing the entire body, altogether naked and showing in the candle-light a clay-like yellow. It had, however, broad maculations of bluish black, obviously caused by extravasated blood from contusions. The chest and sides looked as if they had been beaten with a bludgeon. There were dreadful lacerations; the skin was torn in strips and shreds.

The coroner moved round to the end of the table and undid a silk handkerchief which had been passed under the chin and knotted on the top of the head. When the handkerchief was drawn away it exposed what had been the throat. Some of the jurors who had risen to get a better view repented their curiosity and turned away their faces. Witness Harker went to the open window and leaned out across the sill, faint and sick. Dropping the handkerchief upon the dead man's neck the coroner stepped to an angle of the room and from a pile of clothing produced one garment after another, each of which he held up a moment for inspection. All were torn, and stiff with blood. The jurors did not make a closer inspection. They seemed rather uninterested. They had, in truth, seen all this before; the only thing that was new to them being Harker's testimony.

'Gentlemen,' the coroner said, 'we have no more evidence, I think. Your duty has been already explained to you; if there is nothing you wish to ask you may go outside and consider your verdict.'

The foreman rose—a tall, bearded man of sixty, coarsely clad.

'I should like to ask one question, Mr Coroner,' he said. 'What asylum did this yer last witness escape from?'

'Mr Harker,' said the coroner gravely and tranquilly, 'from what asylum did you last escape?' Harker flushed crimson again, but said nothing, and the seven jurors rose and solemnly filed out of the cabin.

'If you have done insulting me, sir,' said Harker, as soon as he and the officer were left alone with the dead man, 'I suppose I am at liberty to go?'

'Yes.'

Harker started to leave, but paused, with his hand on the door latch. The habit of his profession was strong in him—stronger than his sense of personal dignity. He turned about and said:

'The book that you have there—I recognize it as Morgan's diary. You seemed greatly interested in it; you read in it while I was testifying. May I see it? The public would like—'

'The book will cut no figure in this matter,' replied the official, slipping it into his coat pocket; 'all the entries in it were made before the writer's death.'

As Harker passed out of the house the jury reentered and stood about the table, on which the now covered corpse showed under the sheet with sharp definition. The foreman seated himself near the candle, produced from his breast pocket a pencil and scrap of paper and wrote rather laboriously the following verdict, which with various degrees of effort all signed:

'We, the jury, do find that the remains come to their death at the hands of a mountain lion, but some of us thinks, all the same, they had fits.'

IV: An Explanation from the Tomb

In the diary of the late Hugh Morgan are certain interesting entries having, possibly, a scientific value as suggestions. At the inquest upon his body the book was not put in evidence; possibly the coroner thought it not worth while to confuse the jury. The date of the first of the entries mentioned cannot be ascertained; the upper part of the leaf is torn away; the part of the entry remaining follows:

'...would run in a half-circle, keeping his head turned always toward the centre, and again he would stand still, barking furiously. At last he ran away into the brush as fast as he could go. I thought at first that he had gone mad, but on returning to the house found no other alteration in his manner than what was obviously due to fear of punishment.

'Can a dog see with his nose? Do odours impress some cerebral centre with images of the thing that emitted them? . . .

'Sept 2—Looking at the stars last night as they rose above the crest of the ridge east of the house, I observed them successively disappear—from left to right. Each was eclipsed but an instant, and only a few at the same time, but along the entire length of the ridge all that were within a degree or two of the crest were blotted out. It was as if something had passed along between me and them; but I could not see it, and the stars were not thick enough to define its outline. Ugh! don't like this. . .'

Several weeks' entries are missing, three leaves being torn from the book.

'Sept 27—It has been about here again—I find evidences of its presence every day. I watched again all last night in the same cover, gun in hand, double-charged with buckshot. In the morning the fresh footprints were there, as before. Yet I would have sworn that I did not sleep—indeed, I hardly sleep at all. It is terrible, insupportable! If these amazing experiences are real I shall go mad; if they are fanciful I am mad already.

'Oct 3—I shall not go—it shall not drive me away. No, this is my house, my land. God hates a coward...

'Oct 5—I can stand it no longer; I have invited Harker to pass a few weeks with me—he has a level head. I can judge from his manner if he thinks me mad.

'Oct 7—I have the solution of the mystery; it came to me last night—suddenly, as by revelation. How simple—how terribly simple!

'There are sounds that we cannot hear. At either end of the scale are notes that stir no chord of that imperfect instrument, the human ear. They are too high or too grave. I have observed a flock of blackbirds occupying an entire tree-top—the tops of several trees—and all in full song. Suddenly—in a moment—at absolutely the same instant—all spring into the air and fly away. How? They could not all see one another—whole tree-tops intervened. At no point could a leader have been visible to all. There must have been a signal of warning or command, high and shrill above the din, but by me unheard. I have observed, too, the same simultaneous flight when all were silent, among not only blackbirds, but other birds—quail, for example, widely separated by bushes—even on opposite sides of a hill.

'It is known to seamen that a school of whales basking or sporting on the surface of the ocean, miles apart, with the convexity of the earth between, will sometimes dive at the same instant—all gone out of sight in a moment. The signal has been sounded—too grave for the ear of the sailor at the masthead and his comrades on the deck—who nevertheless feel its vibrations in the ship as the stones of a cathedral are stirred by the bass of the organ.

'As with sounds, so with colours. At each end of the solar spectrum the chemist can detect the presence of what are known as "actinic" rays. They represent colours—integral colours in the composition of light—which we are unable to discern. The human eye is an imperfect instrument; its range is but a few octaves of the real "chromatic scale". I am not mad; there are colours that we cannot see.

'And, God help me! the Damned Thing is of such a colour!'

46

THE GHOST IN MASTER B.'S ROOM

Charles Dickens

For six nights, I had been worried thus in Master B.'s room, when I began to perceive that things were going wrong...

When I established myself in the triangular garret which had gained so distinguished a reputation, my thoughts naturally turned to Master B. My speculations about him were uneasy and manifold. Whether his Christian name was Benjamin, Bissextile (from his having been born in Leap Year), Bartholomew, or Bill. Whether the initial letter belonged to his family name, and that was Baxter, Black, Brown, Barker, Buggins, Baker, or Bird. Whether he was a foundling, and had been baptized B. Whether he was a lion-hearted boy, and B. was short for Briton, or for Bull. Whether he could possibly have been kith and kin to an illustrious lady who brightened my own childhood, and had come of the blood of the brilliant Mother Bunch?

With these profitless meditations I tormented myself much. I also carried the mysterious letter into the appearance and pursuits of the deceased; wondering whether he dressed in Blue, wore Boots (he couldn't have been Bald), was a boy of Brains, liked Books, was good at Bowling, had any skill as a Boxer, even in his Buoyant Boyhood Bathed from a Bathing-machine at Bognor, Bangor, Bournemouth, Brighton, or Broadstairs, like a Bounding Billiard Ball?

So, from the first, I was haunted by the letter B.

It was not long before I remarked that I never by any hazard had a dream of Master B., or of anything belonging to him. But, the instant I awoke from sleep, at whatever hour of the night, my thoughts took him up, and roamed away, trying to attach his initial letter to something that would fit it and keep it quiet.

For six nights, I had been worried thus in Master B.'s room, when I began to perceive that things were going wrong.

The first appearance that presented itself was early in the morning when it was but just daylight and no more. I was standing shaving at my glass, when I suddenly discovered, to my consternation and amazement, that I was shaving—not myself—I am fifty—but a boy. Apparently Master B.!

I trembled and looked over my shoulder; nothing there. I looked again in the glass, and distinctly saw the features and expression of a boy, who was shaving, not to get rid of a beard, but to get one. Extremely troubled in my mind, I took a few turns in the room, and went back to the looking-glass, resolved to steady my hand and complete the operation in which I had been disturbed. Opening my eyes, which I had shut while recovering my firmness, I now met in the glass, looking straight at me, the eyes of a young man of four or five and twenty. Terrified by this new ghost, I closed my eyes, and made a strong effort to recover myself. Opening them again, I saw, shaving his cheek in the glass, my father, who has long been dead. Nay, I even saw my grandfather too, whom I never did see in my life.

Although naturally much affected by these remarkable visitations, I determined to keep my secret, until the time agreed upon for the present general disclosure. Agitated by a multitude of curious thoughts, I retired to my room, that night, prepared to encounter some new experience of a spectral character. Nor was my preparation needless, for, waking from an uneasy sleep at exactly two o'clock in the morning, what were my feelings to find that I was sharing my bed with the skeleton of Master B.!

I sprang up, and the skeleton sprang up also. I then heard a plaintive voice saying, 'Where am I? What is become of me?' and, looking hard in that direction, perceived the ghost of Master B.

The young spectre was dressed in an obsolete fashion: or rather, was not so much dressed as put into a case of inferior pepper-and-salt cloth, made horrible by means of shining buttons. I observed that these buttons went, in a double row, over each shoulder of the young ghost, and appeared to descend his back. He wore a frill round his neck. His right hand (which I distinctly noticed to be inky) was laid upon his stomach; connecting this action with some feeble pimples on his countenance, and his general air of nausea, I concluded this ghost to be the ghost of a boy who had habitually taken a great deal too much medicine.

'Where am I?' said the little spectre, in a pathetic voice. 'And why was I born in the Calomel days, and why did I have all that Calomel given me?'

I replied, with sincere earnestness, that upon my soul I couldn't tell him.

'Where is my little sister,' said the ghost, 'and where my angelic little wife, and where is the boy I went to school with?'

I entreated the phantom to be comforted, and above all things to take heart respecting the loss of the boy he went to school with. I represented to him that probably that boy never did, within human experience, come out well, when discovered. I urged that I myself had, in later life, turned up several boys whom I went to school with, and none of them had at all answered. I expressed my humble belief that that boy never did answer. I represented that he was a mythic character, a delusion, and a snare. I recounted how, the last time I found him, I found him at a dinner party behind a wall of white cravat, with an inconclusive opinion on every possible subject, and a power of silent boredom absolutely titanic. I related how, on the strength of our having been together at 'Old Doylance's', he had asked himself to breakfast with me (a social offence of the largest magnitude); how, fanning my weak embers of belief in Doylance's boys, I had let him in; and how, he had proved to be a fearful wanderer about the earth, pursuing the race of Adam with inexplicable notions concerning the currency, and with a proposition that the Bank of England should, on pain of being abolished, instantly strike off and circulate, God knows how many thousand millions of ten-and-sixpenny notes.

The ghost heard me in silence, and with a fixed stare. 'Barber!' it apostrophised me when I had finished.

'Barber?' I repeated—for I am not of that profession.

'Condemned,' said the ghost, 'to shave a constant change of customers—now, me—now, a young man—now, thyself as thou art—now, thy father—now, thy grandfather; condemned, too, to lie down with a skeleton every night, and to rise with it every morning—'

(I shuddered on hearing this dismal announcement.)

'Barber! Pursue me!'

I had felt, even before the words were uttered, that I was under a spell to pursue the phantom. I immediately did so, and was in Master B.'s room no longer.

Most people know what long and fatiguing night journeys had been forced upon the witches who used to confess, and who, no doubt, told the exact truth—particularly as they were always assisted with leading questions, and the Torture was always ready. I asseverate that, during my occupation of Master B.'s room, I was taken by the ghost that haunted it, on expeditions fully as long and wild as any of those. Assuredly, I was presented to no shabby old man with a goat's horns and tail (something between Pan and an old clothesman), holding conventional receptions, as stupid as those of real life and less decent; but, I came upon other things which appeared to me to have more meaning.

Confident that I speak the truth and shall be believed, I declare without hesitation that I followed the ghost, in the first instance on a broom-stick, and afterwards on a rocking-horse. The very smell of the animal's paint—especially when I brought it out, by making him warm—I am ready to swear to. I followed the ghost, afterwards, in a hackney coach; an institution with the peculiar smell of which, the present generation is unacquainted, but to which I am again ready to swear as a combination of stable, dog with the mange, and very old bellows. (In this, I appeal to previous generations to confirm or refute me.) I pursued the phantom, on a headless donkey: at least, upon a donkey who was so interested in the state of his stomach that his head was always down there, investigating it; on ponies, expressly born to kick up behind; on roundabouts and swings, from fairs; in the first cab—another forgotten institution where the fare regularly got into bed, and was tucked up with the driver.

Not to trouble you with a detailed account of all my travels in pursuit of the ghost of Master B., which were longer and more wonderful than those of Sinbad the Sailor, I will confine myself to one experience from which you may judge of many.

I was marvellously changed. I was myself, yet not myself. I was conscious of something within me, which has been the same all through my life, and which I have always recognised under all its phases and varieties as never altering, and yet I was not the I who had gone to bed in Master B.'s room. I had the smoothest of faces and the shortest of legs, and I had taken another creature like myself, also with the smoothest of faces and the shortest of legs, behind a door, and was confiding to him a proposition of the most astounding nature.

This proposition was, that we should have a Seraglio.

The other creature assented warmly. He had no notion of respectability, neither had I. It was the custom of the East, it was the way of the good Caliph Haroun Alraschid (let me have the corrupted name again for once, it is so scented with sweet memories!), the usage was highly laudable, and most worthy of imitation. 'O, yes! Let us,' said the other creature with a jump, 'have a Seraglio.'

It was not because we entertained the faintest doubts of the meritorious character of the Oriental establishment we proposed to import, that we perceived it must be kept a secret from Miss Griffin. It was because we knew Miss Griffin to be bereft of human sympathies, and incapable of appreciating the greatness of the great Haroun. Mystery impenetrably shrouded from Miss Griffin, then, let us entrust it to Miss Bule.

We were ten in Miss Griffin's establishment by Hampstead Ponds; eight ladies and two gentlemen. Miss Bule, whom I judge to have attained the ripe age of eight or nine, took the lead in society. I opened the subject to her in the course of the day, and proposed that she should become the Favourite.

Miss Bule, after struggling with the diffidence so natural to, and charming in, her adorable sex, expressed herself as flattered by the idea, but wished to know how it was proposed to provide for Miss Pipson? Miss Bule—who was understood to have vowed towards that young lady, a friendship, halves, and no secrets, until death, on the Church Service and Lessons complete in two volumes with case and lock—Miss Bule said she could not, as the friend of Pipson, disguise from herself, or me, that Pipson was not one of the common.

Now, Miss Pipson, having curly hair and blue eyes (which was my idea of anything mortal and feminine that was called Fair), I promptly replied that I regarded Miss Pipson in the light of a Fair Circassian.

'And what then?' Miss Bule pensively asked.

I replied that she must be inveigled by a Merchant, brought to me veiled, and purchased as a slave.

(The other creature had already fallen into the second male place in the State, and was set apart for Grand Vizier. He afterwards resisted this disposal of events, but had his hair pulled until he yielded.)

'Shall I not be jealous?' Miss Bule inquired, casting down her eyes.

'Zobeide, no,' I replied; 'you will ever be the favourite Sultana; the first place in my heart, and on my throne, will be ever yours.'

Miss Bule, upon that assurance, consented to propound the idea to her seven beautiful companions. It occurring to me, in the course of the same day, that we knew we could trust a grinning and good-natured soul called Tabby, who was the serving drudge of the house, and had no more figure than one of the beds, and upon whose face there was always more or less black-lead, I slipped into Miss Bule's hand after supper, a little note to that effect; dwelling on the black-lead as being in a manner deposited by the finger of Providence, pointing Tabby out for Mesrour, the celebrated chief of the Blacks of the Hareem.

There were difficulties in the formation of the desired institution, as there are in all combinations. The other creature showed himself of a low character, and, when defeated in aspiring to the throne, pretended to have conscientious scruples about prostrating himself before the Caliph; wouldn't call him Commander of the Faithful; spoke of him slightingly and inconsistently as a mere 'chap;' said he, the other creature, 'wouldn't play'—Play!—and was otherwise coarse and offensive. This meanness of disposition was, however, put down by the general indignation of an united Seraglio, and I became blessed in the smiles of eight of the fairest of the daughters of men.

The smiles could only be bestowed when Miss Griffin was looking another way, and only then in a very wary manner, for there was a legend among the followers of the Prophet that she saw with a little round ornament in the middle of the pattern on the back of her shawl. But every day after dinner, for an hour, we were all together, and then the Favourite and the rest of the Royal Hareem competed who should most beguile the leisure of the Serene Haroun reposing from the cares of State—which were generally, as in most affairs of State, of an arithmetical character, the Commander of the Faithful being a fearful boggler at a sum.

On these occasions, the devoted Mesrour, chief of the Blacks of the Hareem, was always in attendance (Miss Griffin usually ringing for that officer, at the same time, with great vehemence), but never acquitted himself in a manner worthy of his historical reputation. In the first place, his bringing a broom into the Divan of the Caliph, even when Haroun wore on his shoulders the red robe of anger (Miss Pipson's pelisse), though it might be got over for the moment, was never to be quite satisfactorily accounted for. In the second place, his breaking out into grinning exclamations of 'Lork you pretties!' was neither Eastern nor respectful. In the third place, when specially instructed to say 'Bismillah!' he always said 'Hallelujah!' This officer, unlike his class, was too good-humoured altogether, kept his mouth open far too wide, expressed approbation to an incongruous extent, and even once—it was on the occasion of the purchase of the Fair Circassian for five hundred thousand purses of gold, and cheap, too—embraced the Slave, the Favourite, and the Caliph, all round. (Parenthetically let me say God bless Mesrour, and may there have been sons and daughters on that tender bosom, softening many a hard day since!)

Miss Griffin was a model of propriety, and I am at a loss to imagine what the feelings of the virtuous woman would have been, if she had known, when she paraded us down the Hampstead Road two and two, that she was walking with a stately step at the head of Polygamy and Mahomedanism. I believe that a mysterious and terrible joy with which the contemplation of Miss Griffin, in this unconscious state, inspired us, and a grim sense prevalent among us that there was a dreadful power in our knowledge of what Miss Griffin (who knew all things that could be learnt out of book) didn't know, were the main-spring of the preservation of our secret. It was wonderfully kept, but was once upon the verge of self-betrayal. The danger and escape occurred upon a Sunday. We were all ten ranged in a conspicuous part of the gallery at church, with Miss Griffin at our head—as we were every Sunday—advertising the establishment in an unsecular sort of way—when the description of Solomon in his domestic glory happened to be read. The moment that monarch was thus referred to, conscience whispered me, 'Thou, too, Haroun!' The officiating minister had a cast in his eye, and it assisted conscience by giving him the appearance of reading personally at me. A crimson blush, attended by a fearful perspiration, suffused my features. The Grand Vizier became more dead than alive, and the whole Seraglio reddened as if the sunset of Bagdad shone direct upon their lovely faces. At this portentous time the awful Griffin rose, and balefully surveyed the children of Islam. My own impression was, that Church and State had entered into a conspiracy with Miss Griffin to expose us, and that we should all be put into white sheets, and exhibited in the centre aisle. But, so Westerly—if I may be allowed the expression as opposite to Eastern associations—was Miss Griffin's sense of rectitude, that she merely suspected Apples, and we were saved.

I have called the Seraglio, united. Upon the question, solely, whether the Commander of the Faithful durst exercise a right of kissing in that sanctuary of the palace, were its peerless inmates divided. Zobeide asserted a counter-right in the Favourite to scratch, and the Fair Circassian put her face, for refuge, into a green baize bag, originally designed for books. On the other hand, a young antelope of transcendent beauty from the fruitful plains of Camden Town (whence she had been brought, by traders, in the half-yearly caravan that crossed the intermediate desert after the holidays), held more liberal opinions, but stipulated for limiting the benefit of them to that dog, and son of a dog, the Grand Vizier—who had no rights, and was not in question. At length, the difficulty was compromised by the installation of a very youthful slave as Deputy. She, raised upon a stool, officially received upon her cheeks the salutes intended by the gracious Haroun for other Sultanas, and was privately rewarded from the coffers of the Ladies of the Hareem.

And now it was, at the full height of enjoyment of my bliss, that I became heavily troubled. I began to think of my mother, and what she would say to my taking home at Midsummer eight of the most beautiful of the daughters of men, but all unexpected. I thought of the number of beds we made up at our house, of my father's income, and of the baker, and my despondency redoubled. The Seraglio and malicious Vizier, divining the cause of their Lord's unhappiness, did their utmost to augment it. They professed unbounded fidelity, and declared that they would live and die with him. Reduced to the utmost wretchedness by these protestations of attachment, I lay awake, for hours at a time, ruminating on my frightful lot. In my despair, I think I might have taken an early opportunity of falling on my knees before Miss Griffin, avowing my resemblance to Solomon, and praying to be dealt with according to the outraged laws of my country, if an unthought-of means of escape had not opened before me.

One day, we were out walking, two and two—on which occasion the Vizier had his usual instructions to take note of the boy at the turnpike, and if he profanely gazed (which he always did) at the beauties of the Hareem, to have him bowstrung in the course of the night—and it happened that our hearts were veiled in gloom. An unaccountable action on the part of the antelope had plunged the State into disgrace. That charmer, on the representation that the previous day was her birthday, and that vast treasures had been sent in a hamper for its celebration (both baseless assertions), had secretly but most pressingly invited thirty-five neighbouring princes and princesses to a ball and supper: with a special stipulation that they were 'not to be fetched till twelve'. This wandering of the antelope's fancy, led to the surprising arrival at Miss Griffin's door, in divers equipages and under various escorts, of a great company in full dress, who were deposited on the top step in a flush of high expectancy, and who were dismissed in tears. At the beginning of the double knocks attendant on these ceremonies, the antelope had retired to a back attic, and bolted herself in; and at every new arrival, Miss Griffin had gone so much more and more distracted, that at last she had been seen to tear her front. Ultimate capitulation on the part of the offender, had been followed by solitude in the linen-closet, bread and water and a lecture to all, of vindictive length, in which Miss Griffin had used expressions: Firstly, 'I believe you all of you knew of it;' Secondly, 'Every one of you is as wicked as another;' Thirdly, 'A pack of little wretches.'

Under these circumstances, we were walking drearily along;

and I especially, with my Moosulmaun responsibilities heavy on me, was in a very low state of mind; when a strange man accosted Miss Griffin, and, after walking on at her side for a little while and talking with her, looked at me. Supposing him to be a minion of the law, and that my hour was come, I instantly ran away, with the general purpose of making for Egypt.

The whole Seraglio cried out, when they saw me making off as fast as my legs would carry me (I had an impression that the first turning on the left, and round by the public-house, would be the shortest way to the Pyramids), Miss Griffin screamed after me, the faithless Vizier ran after me, and the boy at the turnpike dodged me into a corner, like a sheep, and cut me off. Nobody scolded me when I was taken and brought back; Miss Griffin only said, with a stunning gentleness, this was very curious! Why had I run away when the gentleman looked at me?

If I had had any breath to answer with, I dare say I should have made no answer; having no breath, I certainly made none. Miss Griffin and the strange man took me between them, and walked me back to the palace in a sort of state; but not at all (as I couldn't help feeling, with astonishment) in culprit state.

When we got there, we went into a room by ourselves, and Miss Griffin called in to her assistance, Mesrour, chief of the dusky guards of the Hareem. Mesrour, on being whispered to, began to shed tears. 'Bless you, my precious!' said that officer, turning to me; 'your Pa's took bitter bad!'

I asked, with a fluttered heart, 'Is he very ill?'

'Lord temper the wind to you, my lamb!' said the good Mesrour, kneeling down, that I might have a comforting shoulder for my head to rest on, 'your Pa's dead!'

Haroun Alraschid took to flight at the words; the Seraglio vanished; from that moment, I never again saw one of the eight of the fairest of the daughters of men.

I was taken home, and there was Debt at home as well as Death, and we had a sale there. My own little bed was so superciliously looked upon by a Power unknown to me, hazily called 'The Trade,' that a brass coal-scuttle, a roasting-jack, and a birdcage, were obliged to be put into it to make a lot of it, and then it went for a song. So I heard mentioned, and I wondered what song, and thought what a dismal song it must have been to sing!

Then, I was sent to a great, cold, bare, school of big boys; where everything to eat and wear was thick and clumpy, without being enough; where everybody, large and small, was cruel; where the boys knew all about the sale, before I got there, and asked me what I had fetched, and who had bought me, and hooted at me, 'Going, going, gone!' I never whispered in that wretched place that I had been Haroun, or had had a Seraglio: for, I knew that if I mentioned my reverses, I should be so worried, that I should have to drown myself in the muddy pond near the playground, which looked like the beer.

Ah me, ah me! No other ghost has haunted the boy's room, my friends, since I have occupied it, than the ghost of my own childhood, the ghost of my own innocence, the ghost of my own airy belief. Many a time have I pursued the phantom: never with this man's stride of mine to come up with it, never with these man's hands of mine to touch it, never more to this man's heart of mine to hold it in its purity. And here you see me working out, as cheerfully and thankfully as I may, my doom of shaving in the glass a constant change of customers, and of lying down and rising up with the skeleton allotted to me for my mortal companion.

47

THE STORY OF AN HOUR

Kate Chopin

When the doctors came they said
she had died of heart disease—of the joy that kills.

Knowing that Mrs Mallard was afflicted with a heart trouble, great care was taken to break to her as gently as possible the news of her husband's death.

It was her sister Josephine who told her, in broken sentences; veiled hints that revealed in half concealing. Her husband's friend Richards was there, too, near her. It was he who had been in the newspaper office when intelligence of the railroad disaster was received, with Brently Mallard's name leading the list of 'killed'. He had only taken the time to assure himself of its truth by a second telegram, and had hastened to forestall any less careful, less tender friend in bearing the sad message.

She did not hear the story as many women have heard the same, with a paralyzed inability to accept its significance. She wept at once, with sudden, wild abandonment, in her sister's arms. When the storm of grief had spent itself she went away to her room alone. She would have no one follow her.

There stood, facing the open window, a comfortable, roomy armchair. Into this she sank, pressed down by a physical exhaustion that haunted her body and seemed to reach into her soul.

She could see in the open square before her house the tops of trees that were all aquiver with the new spring life. The delicious breath of rain was in the air. In the street below a peddler was crying his wares. The notes of a distant song which someone was singing reached her faintly, and countless sparrows were twittering in the eaves.

There were patches of blue sky showing here and there through the clouds that had met and piled one above the other in the west facing her window.

She sat with her head thrown back upon the cushion of the chair, quite motionless, except when a sob came up into her throat and shook her, as a child who has cried itself to sleep continues to sob in its dreams.

She was young, with a fair, calm face, whose lines bespoke repression and even a certain strength. But now there was a dull stare in her eyes, whose gaze was fixed away off yonder on one of those patches of blue sky. It was not a glance of reflection, but rather indicated a suspension of intelligent thought.

There was something coming to her and she was waiting for it, fearfully. What was it? She did not know; it was too subtle and elusive to name. But she felt it, creeping out of the sky, reaching toward her through the sounds, the scents, the colour that filled the air.

Now her bosom rose and fell tumultuously. She was beginning to recognize this thing that was approaching to possess her, and she was striving to beat it back with her will—as powerless as her two white slender hands would have been. When she abandoned herself a little whispered word escaped her slightly parted lips. She said it over and over under the breath: 'free, free, free!' The vacant stare and the look of terror that had followed it went from her eyes. They stayed keen and bright. Her pulses beat fast, and the coursing blood warmed and relaxed every inch of her body.

She did not stop to ask if it were or were not a monstrous joy that held her. A clear and exalted perception enabled her to dismiss the suggestion as trivial. She knew that she would weep again when she saw the kind, tender hands folded in death; the face that had never looked save with love upon her, fixed and grey and dead. But she saw beyond that bitter moment a long procession of years to come that would belong to her absolutely. And she opened and spread her arms out to them in welcome.

There would be no one to live for during those coming years; she would live for herself. There would be no powerful will bending hers in that blind persistence with which men and women believe they have a right to impose a private will upon a fellow-creature. A kind intention or a cruel intention made the act seem no less a crime as she looked upon it in that brief moment of illumination.

And yet she had loved him—sometimes. Often she had not. What did it matter! What could love, the unsolved mystery, count for in the face of this possession of self-assertion which she suddenly recognized as the strongest impulse of her being!

'Free! Body and soul free!' she kept whispering.

Josephine was kneeling before the closed door with her lips to the keyhold, imploring for admission. 'Louise, open the door! I beg; open the door—you will make yourself ill. What are you doing, Louise? For heaven's sake open the door.'

'Go away. I am not making myself ill.' No; she was drinking in a very elixir of life through that open window.

Her fancy was running riot along those days ahead of her. Spring days, and summer days, and all sorts of days that would be her own. She breathed a quick prayer that life might be long. It was only yesterday she had thought with a shudder that life might be long.

She arose at length and opened the door to her sister's importunities. There was a feverish triumph in her eyes, and she carried herself unwittingly like a goddess of Victory. She clasped her sister's waist, and together they descended the stairs. Richards stood waiting for them at the bottom.

Someone was opening the front door with a latchkey. It was Brently Mallard who entered, a little travel-stained, composedly carrying his grip-sack and umbrella. He had been far from the scene of the accident, and did not even know there had been one. He stood amazed at Josephine's piercing cry; at Richards' quick motion to screen him from the view of his wife.

When the doctors came they said she had died of heart disease—of the joy that kills.

48
FISHER'S GHOST
John Lang

Suddenly Fisher disappeared...

In the colony of New South Wales, at a place called Penrith, distant from Sydney about thirty-seven miles, lived a farmer named Fisher. He had been, originally, transported, but had become free by servitude. Unceasing toil, and great steadiness of character, had acquired for him a considerable property, for a person in his station of life. His lands and stock were not worth less than four thousand pounds. He was unmarried and was about forty-five years old.

Suddenly Fisher disappeared; and one of his neighbours—a man named Smith—gave out that he had gone to England, but would return in two or three years. Smith produced a document, purporting to be executed by Fisher; and, according to this document, Fisher had appointed Smith to act as his agent during his absence. Fisher was a man of very singular habits and eccentric character and his silence about his departure, instead of creating surprise, was declared to be 'exactly like him'.

About six months after Fisher's disappearance, an old man called Ben Weir, who had a small farm near Penrith and who always drove his own cart to market, was returning from Sydney one night when he beheld, seated on a rail which bounded the road—Fisher. The night was very dark and the distance of the fence from the middle of the road was, at least, twelve yards. Weir, nevertheless, saw Fisher's figure seated on the rail. He pulled his old mare up, and called out, 'Fisher, is that you?' No answer was returned; but there, still on the rail, sat the form of the man with whom he had been on the most intimate terms. Weir—who was not drunk, though he had taken several glasses of strong liquor on the road—jumped off his cart and approached the rail. To his surprise, the form vanished.

'Well,' exclaimed old Weir, 'this is very curious, anyhow;' and, breaking several branches of a sapling so as to mark the exact spot, he remounted his cart, put his old mare into a jog-trot and soon reached his home.

Ben was not likely to keep this vision a secret from his old woman. All that he had seen he faithfully related to her.

'Hold your nonsense, Ben!' was old Betty's reply. 'You know you have been a drinking and disturbing of your imagination. Ain't Fisher agone to England? And if he had a comeback, do you think we shouldn't a heard on it?'

'Ay, Betty!' said old Ben, 'but he'd a cruel gash in his forehead and the blood was all fresh like. Faith, it makes me shudder to think on't. It were his ghost.'

'How can you talk so foolish, Ben?' said the old woman. 'You must be drunk surely to get on about ghosteses.'

'I tell thee I am not drunk,' rejoined old Ben, angrily. 'There's been foul play, Betty; I'm sure on't. There sat Fisher on the rail—not more than a matter of two mile from this. Egad, it were on his own fence that he sat. There he was, in his shirt-sleeves, with his arms a folded; just as he used to sit when he was a waiting for anybody coming up the road. Bless you, Betty, I seed 'im till I was as close as I am to thee; when, all on a sudden, he vanished, like smoke.'

'Nonsense, Ben: don't talk of it,' said old Betty, 'or the neighbours will only laugh at you. Come to bed and you'll forget all about it before tomorrow morning.'

Old Ben went to bed; but he did not next morning forget all about what he had seen on the previous night: on the contrary, he was more positive than before. However, at the earnest and often repeated request of the old woman, he promised not to mention having seen Fisher's ghost, for fear that it might expose him to ridicule.

On the following Thursday night, when old Ben was returning from market—again in his cart—he saw, seated upon the same rail, the identical apparition. He had purposely abstained from drinking that day and was in the full possession of all his senses. On this occasion old Ben was too much alarmed to stop. He urged the old mare on and got home as speedily as possible. As soon as he had unharnessed and fed the mare and taken his purchases out of the cart, he entered his cottage, lighted his pipe, sat over the fire with his better half and gave her an account of how he had disposed of his produce and what he had brought back from Sydney in return. After this he said to her, 'Well, Betty, I'm not drunk tonight, anyhow, am I?'

'No,' said Betty. 'You are quite sober, sensible like, tonight, Ben; and therefore you have come home without any ghost in your head. Ghosts! Don't believe there is such things.'

'Well, you are satisfied I am not drunk; but perfectly sober,' said the old man.

'Yes, Ben,' said Betty.

'Well, then,' said Ben, 'I tell thee what, Betty. I saw Fisher tonight agin!'

'Stuff!' cried old Betty.

'You may say stuff,' said the old farmer; 'but I tell you what—I saw him as plainly as I did last Thursday night. Smith is a bad 'un! Do you think Fisher would ever have left this country without coming to bid you and me goodbye?'

'It's all fancy!' said old Betty. 'Now drink your grog and smoke your pipe and think no more about the ghost. I won't hear on't.'

'I'm as fond of my grog and my pipe as most men,' said old Ben; 'but I'm not going to drink anything tonight. It may be all fancy, as you call it, but I am now going to tell Mr Grafton all I saw, and what I think;' and with these words he got up and left the house.

Mr Grafton was a gentleman who lived about a mile from old Weir's farm. He had been formerly a lieutenant in the navy, but was now on half-pay and was a settler in the new colony;

he was, moreover, in the commission of the peace.

When old Ben arrived at Mr Grafton's house, Mr Grafton was about to retire to bed; but he requested old Ben might be shown in. He desired the farmer to take a seat by the fire and then enquired what was the latest news in Sydney.

'The news in Sydney, sir, is very small,' said old Ben; 'wheat is falling, but maize still keeps its price—seven and sixpence a bushel: but I want to tell you, sir, something that will astonish you.'

'What is it, Ben?' asked Mr Grafton.

'Why, sir,' resumed old Ben, 'you know I am not a weak-minded man, nor a fool, exactly; for I was born and bred in Yorkshire.'

'No, Ben, I don't believe you to be weak-minded, nor do I think you a fool,' said Mr Grafton; 'but what can you have to say that you come at this late hour and that you require such a preface?'

'That I have seen the ghost of Fisher, sir,' said the old man; and he detailed the particulars of which the reader is already in possession.

Mr Grafton was at first disposed to think with old Betty, that Ben had seen Fisher's Ghost through an extra glass or two of rum on the first night; and that on the second night, when perfectly sober, he was unable to divest himself of the idea previously entertained. But after a little consideration the words 'How very singular!' involuntarily escaped him.

'Go home, Ben,' said Mr Grafton, 'and let me see you tomorrow at sunrise. We will go together to the place where you say you saw the ghost.'

Mr Grafton used to encourage the aboriginal natives of New South Wales (that race which has been very aptly described 'the last link in the human chain') to remain about his premises. At the head of a little tribe then encamped on Mr Grafton's estate, was a sharp young man named Johnny Crook. The peculiar faculty of the aboriginal natives of New South Wales, of tracking the human foot not only over grass but over the hardest rock; and of tracking the whereabouts of runaways by signs imperceptible to civilised eyes, is well known; and this man, Johnny Crook, was famous for his skill in this particular art of tracking. He had recently been instrumental in the apprehension of several desperate bushrangers whom he had tracked over twenty-seven miles of rocky country and fields, which they had crossed bare-footed, in the hope of checking the black fellow in the progress of his keen pursuit with the horse police.

When old Ben Weir made his appearance in the morning at Mr Grafton's house, the black chief, Johnny Crook, was summoned to attend. He came and brought with him several of his subjects. The party set out, old Weir showing the way. The leaves on the branches of the saplings which he had broken on the first night of seeing the ghost were withered and sufficiently pointed out the exact rail on which the phantom was represented to have sat. There were stains upon the rail. Johnny Crook, who had then no idea of what he was required for, pronounced these stains to be 'White man's blood;' and, after searching about for some time, he pointed to a spot whereon he said a human body had been laid.

In New South Wales long droughts are not very uncommon; and not a single shower of rain had fallen for seven months previously—not sufficient even to lay the dust upon the roads.

In consequence of the time that had elapsed, Crook had no small difficulty to contend with; but in about two hours he succeeded in tracking the footsteps of one man to the unfrequented side of a pond at some distance. He gave it as his opinion that another man had been dragged thither. The savage walked round and round the pond, eagerly examining its borders and the sedges and weeds springing up around it. At first he seemed baffled. No clue had been washed ashore to show that anything unusual had been sunk in the pond; but, having finished this examination, he laid himself down on his face and looked keenly along the surface of the smooth and stagnant water. Presently he jumped up, uttered a cry peculiar to the natives when gratified by finding some long-sought object, clapped his hands and, pointing to the middle of the pond to where the decomposition of some sunken substance had produced a slimy coating streaked with prismatic colours, he exclaimed, 'White man's fat!' The pond was immediately searched; and, below the spot indicated, the remains of a body were discovered. A large stone and a rotted silk handkerchief were found near the body; these had been used to sink it.

That it was the body of Fisher there could be no question. It might have been identified by the teeth; but on the waistcoat there were some large brass buttons which were immediately recognised, both by Mr Grafton and by old Ben Weir, as Fisher's property. He had worn those buttons on his waistcoat for several years.

Leaving the body by the side of the pond and old Ben and the blacks to guard it, Mr Grafton cantered up to Fisher's house. Smith was not only in possession of all the missing man's property, but had removed to Fisher's house. It was about a mile and a half distant. He enquired for Mr Smith. Mr Smith, who was at breakfast, came out and invited Mr Grafton to alight; Mr Grafton accepted the invitation and after a few desultory observations said, 'Mr Smith, I am anxious to purchase a piece of land on the other side of the road, belonging to this estate, and I would give a fair price for it. Have you the power to sell?'

'Oh yes, sir,' replied Smith. 'The power which I hold from Fisher is a general power;' and he forthwith produced a document purporting to be signed by Fisher, but which was not witnessed.

'If you are not very busy, I should like to show you the piece of land I allude to,' said Mr Grafton.

'Oh certainly, sir. I am quite at your service,' said Smith; and he then ordered his horse to be saddled.

It was necessary to pass the pond where the remains of Fisher's body were then exposed. When they came near to the spot, Mr Grafton, looking Smith full in the face, said, 'Mr Smith, I wish to show you something. Look here!' He pointed to the decomposed body and narrowly watching Mr Smith's countenance, remarked: 'These are the remains of Fisher. How do you account for their being found in this pond?'

Smith, with the greatest coolness, got off his horse, minutely examined the remains and then admitted that there was no doubt they were Fisher's. He confessed himself at a loss to account for their discovery, unless it could be (he said) that somebody had waylaid him on the road when he left his home for Sydney; had murdered him for the gold and banknotes which he had about his person and had then thrown him into the pond. 'My hands, thank heaven!' he concluded, 'are clean. If my old friend could come to life again, he would tell you that I had no hand in his horrible murder.'

Mr Grafton knew not what to think. He was not a believer in ghosts. Could it be possible, he began to ask himself, that old Weir had committed this crime and—finding it weigh heavily on his conscience and fearing that he might be detected—had trumped up the story about the ghost—had pretended that he was led to the spot by supernatural agency—and thus by bringing the murder voluntarily to light, hoped to stifle all suspicion? But then, he considered Weir's excellent character, his kind disposition and good-nature. These at once put to flight his suspicion of Weir; but still he was by no means satisfied of Smith's guilt, much as appearances were against him.

Fisher's servants were examined and stated that their master had often talked of going to England on a visit to his friends and of leaving Mr Smith to manage his farm; and that though they were surprised when Mr Smith came and said he had 'gone at last', they did not think it at all unlikely that he had done so. An inquest was held and a verdict of wilful murder found against Thomas Smith. He was thereupon transmitted to Sydney for trial, at the ensuing sessions, in the Supreme Court. The case naturally excited great interest in the colony; and public opinion respecting Smith's guilt was evenly balanced.

The day of trial came; and the court was crowded almost to suffocation. The Attorney-General very truly remarked that there were circumstances connected with the case which were without any precedent in the annals of jurisprudence. The only witnesses were old Weir and Mr Grafton. Smith, who defended himself with great composure and ability, cross-examined them at considerable length and with consummate skill. The prosecution having closed, Smith addressed the jury (which consisted of military officers) in his defence. He admitted that the circumstances were strong against him; but he most ingeniously proceeded to explain them. The power of attorney, which he produced, he contended had been regularly granted by Fisher and he called several witnesses who swore that they believed the signature to be that of the deceased. He, further, produced a will, which had been drawn up by Fisher's attorney, and by that will Fisher had appointed Smith his sole executor, in the event of his death. He declined, he said, to throw any suspicion on Weir; but he would appeal to the common sense of the jury whether the ghost story was entitled to any credit; and, if it were not, to ask themselves why it had been invented? He alluded to the fact—which in cross-examination Mr Grafton swore to—that when the remains were first shown to him, he did not conduct himself as a guilty man would have been likely to do, although he was horror-stricken on beholding the hideous spectacle. He concluded by invoking the Almighty to bear witness that he was innocent of the diabolical crime for which he had been arraigned. The judge (the late Sir Francis Forbes) recapitulated the evidence. It was not an easy matter to deal with that part of it which had reference to the apparition: and if the charge of the judge had any leaning one way or the other, it was decidedly in favour of an acquittal. The jury retired; but, after deliberating for seven hours, they returned to the court, with a verdict of guilty.

The judge then sentenced the prisoner to be hanged on the following Monday. It was on a Thursday night that he was convicted. On the Sunday, Smith expressed a wish to see a clergyman. His wish was instantly attended to, when he confessed that he, and he alone, committed the murder; and that it was upon the very rail where Weir swore that he had seen Fisher's ghost sitting, that he had knocked out Fisher's brains with a tomahawk. The power of attorney he likewise confessed was a forgery, but declared that the will was genuine.

This is very extraordinary, but is, nevertheless, true in substance, if not in every particular. Most persons who have visited Sydney for any length of time will no doubt have had it narrated to them.

49

THE HORRIBLE

Guy de Maupassant

They had been talking about a frightful accident which had occurred the night before...

The shadows of a balmy night were slowly falling. The women remained in the drawing-room of the villa. The men, seated, or astride of garden chairs, were smoking outside the door of the house, around a table laden with cups and liqueur glasses.

Their lighted cigars shone like eyes in the darkness, which was gradually becoming more dense. They had been talking about a frightful accident which had occurred the night before—two men and three women drowned in the river before the eyes of the guests.

General de G— remarked: 'Yes, these things are affecting, but they are not horrible.

'Horrible, that well-known word, means much more than terrible. A frightful accident like this affects, upsets, terrifies; it does not horrify. In order that we should experience horror, something more is needed than emotion, something more than the spectacle of a dreadful death; there must be a shuddering sense of mystery, or a sensation of abnormal terror, more than natural. A man who dies, even under the most tragic circumstances, does not excite horror; a field of battle is not horrible; blood is not horrible; the vilest crimes are rarely horrible.

'Here are two personal examples which have shown me what is the meaning of horror.

'It was during the war of 1870. We were retreating toward Pont-Audemer, after having passed through Rouen. The army, consisting of about twenty thousand men, twenty thousand routed men, disbanded, demoralized, exhausted, were going to disband at Havre.

'The earth was covered with snow. The night was falling. They had not eaten anything since the day before. They were fleeing rapidly, the Prussians not being far off.

'All the Norman country, sombre, dotted with the shadows of the trees surrounding the farms, stretched out beneath a black, heavy, threatening sky.

'Nothing else could be heard in the wan twilight but the confused sound, undefined though rapid, of a marching throng, an endless tramping, mingled with the vague clink of tin bowls or swords. The men, bent, round-shouldered, dirty, in many cases even in rags, dragged themselves along, hurried through the snow, with a long, broken-backed stride.

'The skin of their hands froze to the butt ends of their muskets, for it was freezing hard that night. I frequently saw a little soldier take off his shoes in order to walk barefoot, as his shoes hurt his weary feet; and at every step he left a track of blood. Then, after some time, he would sit down in a field for a few minutes' rest, and he never got up again. Every man who sat down was a dead man.

'Should we have left behind us those poor, exhausted soldiers, who fondly counted on being able to start afresh as soon as they had somewhat refreshed their stiffened legs? But scarcely had they ceased to move, and to make their almost frozen blood circulate in their veins, than an unconquerable torpor congealed them, nailed them to the ground, closed their eyes, and paralyzed in one second this overworked human mechanism. And they gradually sank down, their foreheads on their knees, without, however, falling over, for their loins and their limbs became as hard and immovable as wood, impossible to bend or to stand upright.

'And the rest of us, more robust, kept straggling on, chilled to the marrow, advancing by a kind of inertia through the night, through the snow, through that cold and deadly country, crushed by pain, by defeat, by despair, above all overcome by the abominable sensation of abandonment, of the end, of death, of nothingness.

'I saw two gendarmes holding by the arm a curious-looking little man, old, beardless, of truly surprising aspect.

'They were looking for an officer, believing that they had caught a spy. The word "spy" at once spread through the midst of the stragglers, and they gathered in a group round the prisoner. A voice exclaimed: "He must be shot!" And all these soldiers who were falling from utter prostration, only holding themselves on their feet by leaning on their guns, felt all of a sudden that thrill of furious and bestial anger which urges on a mob to massacre.

'I wanted to speak. I was at that time in command of a battalion; but they no longer recognized the authority of their commanding officers; they would even have shot me.

'One of the gendarmes said: "He has been following us for the three last days. He has been asking information from everyone about the artillery."

'I took it on myself to question this person.

'"What are you doing? What do you want? Why are you accompanying the army?"

'He stammered out some words in some unintelligible dialect. He was, indeed, a strange being, with narrow shoulders, a sly look, and such an agitated air in my presence that I really no longer doubted that he was a spy. He seemed very aged and feeble. He kept looking at me from under his eyes with a humble, stupid, crafty air.

'The men all round us exclaimed.

'"To the wall! To the wall!"

'I said to the gendarmes: "Will you be responsible for the prisoner?"

'I had not ceased speaking when a terrible shove threw me on my back, and in a second I saw the man seized by the furious soldiers, thrown down, struck, dragged along the side of the road, and flung against a tree. He fell in the snow, nearly dead already.

'And immediately they shot him. The soldiers fired at him, reloaded their guns, fired again with the desperate energy of brutes. They fought with each other to have a shot at him, filed off in front of the corpse, and kept on firing at him, as people at a funeral keep sprinkling holy water in front of a coffin.

'But suddenly a cry arose of "The Prussians! the Prussians!"

'And all along the horizon I heard the great noise of this panic-stricken army in full flight.

'A panic, the result of these shots fired at this vagabond, had filled his very executioners with terror; and, without realizing that they were themselves the originators of the scare, they fled and disappeared in the darkness.

'I remained alone with the corpse, except for the two gendarmes whose duty compelled them to stay with me.

'They lifted up the riddled mass of bruised and bleeding flesh.

'"He must be searched," I said. And I handed them a box of taper matches which I had in my pocket. One of the soldiers had another box. I was standing between the two.

'The gendarme who was examining the body announced: "Clothed in a blue blouse, a white shirt, trousers, and a pair of shoes."

'The first match went out; we lighted a second. The man continued, as he turned out his pockets: "A horn-handled pocketknife, check handkerchief, a snuffbox, a bit of pack thread, a piece of bread."

'The second match went out; we lighted a third. The gendarme, after having felt the corpse for a long time, said: "That is all."

'I said: "Strip him. We shall perhaps find something next his skin."

'And in order that the two soldiers might help each other in this task, I stood between them to hold the lighted match. By the rapid and speedily extinguished flame of the match, I saw them take off the garments one by one, and expose to view that bleeding bundle of flesh, still warm, though lifeless.

'And suddenly one of them exclaimed: "Good God, general, it is a woman!"

'I cannot describe to you the strange and poignant sensation of pain that moved my heart. I could not believe it, and I knelt down in the snow before this shapeless pulp of flesh to see for myself: it was a woman.

'The two gendarmes, speechless and stunned, waited for me to give my opinion on the matter. But I did not know what to think, what theory to adopt.

'Then the brigadier slowly drawled out: "Perhaps she came to look for a son of hers in the artillery, whom she had not heard from."

'And the other chimed in: "Perhaps, indeed, that is so."

'And I, who had seen some very terrible things in my time, began to cry. And I felt, in the presence of this corpse, on that icy cold night, in the midst of that gloomy plain; at the sight of this mystery, at the sight of this murdered stranger, the meaning of that word "horror".

'I had the same sensation last year, while interrogating one of the survivors of the Flatters Mission, an Algerian sharpshooter.

'You know the details of that atrocious drama. It is possible, however, that you are unacquainted with one of them.

'The colonel travelled through the desert into the Soudan, and passed through the immense territory of the Touaregs, who, in that great ocean of sand which stretches from the Atlantic to Egypt and from the Soudan to Algeria, are a kind of pirates, resembling those who ravaged the seas in former days.

'The guides who accompanied the column belonged to the tribe of the Chambaa, of Ouargla.

'Now, one day we encamped in the middle of the desert, and the Arabs declared that, as the spring was still some distance away, they would go with all their camels to look for water.

'One man alone warned the colonel that he had been betrayed. Flatters did not believe this, and accompanied the convoy with the engineers, the doctors, and nearly all his officers.

'They were massacred round the spring, and all the camels

were captured.

'The captain of the Arab Intelligence Department at Ouargla, who had remained in the camp, took command of the survivors, spahis and sharpshooters, and they began to retreat, leaving behind them the baggage and provisions, for want of camels to carry them.

'Then they started on their journey through this solitude without shade and boundless, beneath the devouring sun, which burned them from morning till night.

'One tribe came to tender its submission and brought dates as a tribute. The dates were poisoned. Nearly all the Frenchmen died, and, among them, the last officer.

'There now only remained a few spahis with their quartermaster, Pobeguin, and some native sharpshooters of the Chambaa tribe. They had still two camels left. They disappeared one night, along with two Arabs.

'Then the survivors understood that they would be obliged to eat each other, and as soon as they discovered the flight of the two men with the two camels, those who remained separated, and proceeded to march, one by one, through the soft sand, under the glare of a scorching sun, at a distance of more than a gunshot from each other.

'So they went on all day, and when they reached a spring each of them came to drink at it in turn, as soon as each solitary marcher had moved forward the number of yards arranged upon. And thus they continued marching the whole day, raising everywhere they passed, in that level, burnt up expanse, those little columns of dust which, from a distance, indicate those who are trudging through the desert.

'But one morning one of the travellers suddenly turned round and approached the man behind him. And they all stopped to look.

'The man toward whom the famished soldier drew near did not flee, but lay flat on the ground, and took aim at the one who was coming toward him. When he believed he was within gunshot, he fired. The other was not hit, and he continued then to advance, and levelling his gun, in turn, he killed his comrade.

'Then from all directions the others rushed to seek their share. And he who had killed the fallen man, cutting the corpse into pieces, distributed it.

'And they once more placed themselves at fixed distances, these irreconcilable allies, preparing for the next murder which would bring them together.

'For two days they lived on this human flesh which they divided between them. Then, becoming famished again, he who had killed the first man began killing afresh. And again, like a butcher, he cut up the corpse and offered it to his comrades, keeping only his own portion of it.

'And so this retreat of cannibals continued.

'The last Frenchman, Pobeguin, was massacred at the side of a well, the very night before the supplies arrived.

'Do you understand now what I mean by the horrible?'

This was the story told us a few nights ago by General de G—.

50

MY OWN TRUE GHOST STORY

Rudyard Kipling

But he will insist upon treating his ghosts...

As I came through the Desert thus it was—
As I came through the Desert.
The City of Dreadful Night

Somewhere in the Other World, where there are books and pictures and plays and shop windows to look at, and thousands of men who spend their lives in building up all four, lives a gentleman who writes real stories about the real insides of people; and his name is Mr Walter Besant. But he will insist upon treating his ghosts—he has published half a workshopful of them—with levity. He makes his ghost-seers talk familiarly, and, in some cases, flirt outrageously, with the phantoms.

You may treat anything, from a Viceroy to a Vernacular Paper, with levity; but you must behave reverently toward a ghost, and particularly an Indian one.

There are, in this land, ghosts who take the form of fat, cold, pobby corpses, and hide in trees near the roadside till a traveler passes. Then they drop upon his neck and remain. There are also terrible ghosts of women who have died in child-bed. These wander along the pathways at dusk, or hide in the crops near a village, and call seductively. But to answer their call is death in this world and the next. Their feet are turned backward that all sober men may recognize them. There are ghosts of little children who have been thrown into wells.

These haunt well curbs and the fringes of jungles, and wail under the stars, or catch women by the wrist and beg to be taken up and carried. These and the corpse ghosts, however, are only vernacular articles and do not attack Sahibs. No native ghost has yet been authentically reported to have frightened an Englishman; but many English ghosts have scared the life out of both white and black.

Nearly every other Station owns a ghost. There are said to be two at Simla, not counting the woman who blows the bellows at Syree dâk-bungalow on the Old Road; Mussoorie has a house haunted of a very lively Thing; a White Lady is supposed to do night-watchman round a house in Lahore; Dalhousie says that one of her houses 'repeats' on autumn evenings all the incidents of a horrible horse-and-precipice accident; Murree has a merry ghost, and, now that she has been swept by cholera, will have room for a sorrowful one; there are Officers' Quarters in Mian Mir whose doors open without reason, and whose furniture is guaranteed to creak, not with the heat of June but with the weight of Invisibles who come to lounge in the chairs; Peshawur possesses houses that none will willingly rent; and there is something—not fever—wrong with a big bungalow in Allahabad. The older Provinces simply bristle with haunted houses, and march phantom armies along their main thoroughfares.

Some of the dâk-bungalows on the Grand Trunk Road have handy little cemeteries in their compound—witnesses to the 'changes and chances of this mortal life' in the days when men drove from Calcutta to the Northwest. These bungalows are objectionable places to put up in. They are generally very old, always dirty, while the khansamah is as ancient as the bungalow. He either chatters senilely, or falls into the long trances of age. In both moods he is useless. If you get angry with him, he refers to some Sahib dead and buried these thirty years, and says that when he was in that Sahib's service not a khansamah in the Province could touch him. Then he jabbers and mows and trembles and fidgets among the dishes, and you repent of your irritation.

In these dâk-bungalows, ghosts are most likely to be found, and when found, they should be made a note of. Not long ago it was my business to live in dâk-bungalows. I never inhabited the same house for three nights running, and grew to be learned in the breed. I lived in Government-built ones with red brick walls and rail ceilings, an inventory of the furniture posted in every room, and an excited snake at the threshold to give welcome. I lived in 'converted' ones—old houses officiating as dâk-bungalows—where nothing was in its proper place and there wasn't even a fowl for dinner. I lived in second-hand palaces where the wind blew through open-work marble tracery just as uncomfortably as through a broken pane. I lived in dâk-bungalows where the last entry in the visitors' book was fifteen months old, and where they slashed off the curry-kid's head with a sword. It was my good luck to meet all sorts of men, from sober traveling missionaries and deserters flying from British Regiments, to drunken loafers who threw whisky bottles at all who passed; and my still greater good fortune just to escape a maternity case. Seeing that a fair proportion of the tragedy of our lives out here acted itself in dâk-bungalows, I wondered that I had met no ghosts. A ghost that would voluntarily hang about a dâk-bungalow would be mad of course; but so many men have died mad in dâk-bungalows that there must be a fair percentage of lunatic ghosts.

In due time I found my ghost, or ghosts rather, for there were two of them. Up till that hour I had sympathized with Mr Besant's method of handling them, as shown in *The Strange Case of Mr Lucraft and Other Stories*. I am now in the Opposition.

We will call the bungalow Katmal dâk-bungalow. But *that* was the smallest part of the horror. A man with a sensitive hide has no right to sleep in dâk-bungalows. He should marry. Katmal dâk-bungalow was old and rotten and unrepaired. The floor was of worn brick, the walls were filthy, and the windows were nearly black with grime. It stood on a bypath largely used by native Sub-Deputy Assistants of all kinds, from Finance to

Forests; but real Sahibs were rare. The khansamah, who was nearly bent double with old age, said so.

When I arrived, there was a fitful, undecided rain on the face of the land, accompanied by a restless wind, and every gust made a noise like the rattling of dry bones in the stiff toddy palms outside. The khansamah completely lost his head on my arrival. He had served a Sahib once. Did I know that Sahib? He gave me the name of a well-known man who has been buried for more than a quarter of a century, and showed me an ancient daguerreotype of that man in his prehistoric youth. I had seen a steel engraving of him at the head of a double volume of Memoirs a month before, and I felt ancient beyond telling.

The day shut in and the khansamah went to get me food. He did not go through the pretense of calling it 'khana'—man's victuals. He said 'ratub', and that means, among other things, 'grub'—dog's rations. There was no insult in his choice of the term. He had forgotten the other word, I suppose.

While he was cutting up the dead bodies of animals, I settled myself down, after exploring the dâk-bungalow. There were three rooms, beside my own, which was a corner kennel, each giving into the other through dingy white doors fastened with long iron bars. The bungalow was a very solid one, but the partition walls of the rooms were almost jerry-built in their flimsiness. Every step or bang of a trunk echoed from my room down the other three, and every footfall came back tremulously from the far walls. For this reason I shut the door. There were no lamps—only candles in long glass shades. An oil wick was set in the bathroom.

For bleak, unadulterated misery that dâk-bungalow was the worst of the many that I had ever set foot in. There was no fireplace, and the windows would not open; so a brazier of charcoal would have been useless. The rain and the wind splashed and gurgled and moaned round the house, and the toddy palms rattled and roared. Half a dozen jackals went through the compound singing, and a hyena stood afar off and mocked them. A hyena would convince a Sadducee of the Resurrection of the Dead—the worst sort of Dead. Then came the ratub—a curious meal, half native and half English in composition—with the old khansamah babbling behind my chair about dead and gone English people, and the wind-blown candles playing shadow-bo-peep with the bed and the mosquito-curtains. It was just the sort of dinner and evening to make a man think of every single one of his past sins, and of all the others that he intended to commit if he lived.

Sleep, for several hundred reasons, was not easy. The lamp in the bath-room threw the most absurd shadows into the room, and the wind was beginning to talk nonsense.

Just when the reasons were drowsy with blood-sucking I heard the regular—'Let-us-take-and-heave-him-over' grunt of doolie-bearers in the compound. First one doolie came in, then a second, and then a third. I heard the doolies dumped on the ground, and the shutter in front of my door shook. 'That's someone trying to come in,' I said. But no one spoke, and I persuaded myself that it was the gusty wind. The shutter of the room next to mine was attacked, flung back, and the inner door opened. 'That's some Sub-Deputy Assistant,' I said, 'and he has brought his friends with him. Now they'll talk and spit and smoke for an hour.'

But there were no voices and no footsteps. No one was putting his luggage into the next room. The door shut, and I thanked Providence that I was to be left in peace. But I was curious to know where the doolies had gone. I got out of bed and looked into the darkness. There was never a sign of a doolie. Just as I was getting into bed again, I heard, in the next room, the sound that no man in his senses can possibly mistake—the whir of a billiard ball down the length of the slates when the striker is stringing for break. No other sound is like it. A minute afterwards there was another whir, and I got into bed. I was not frightened—indeed I was not. I was very curious to know what had become of the doolies. I jumped into bed for that reason.

Next minute I heard the double click of a cannon and my hair sat up. It is a mistake to say that hair stands up. The skin of the head tightens and you can feel a faint, prickly, bristling all over the scalp. That is the hair sitting up.

There was a whir and a click, and both sounds could only have been made by one thing—a billiard ball. I argued the matter out at great length with myself; and the more I argued the less probable it seemed that one bed, one table, and two chairs—all the furniture of the room next to mine—could so exactly duplicate the sounds of a game of billiards.

After another cannon, a three-cushion one to judge by the whir, I argued no more. I had found my ghost and would have given worlds to have escaped from that dâk-bungalow. I listened, and with each listen the game grew clearer. There was whir on whir and click on click. Sometimes there was a double click and a whir and another click. Beyond any sort of doubt, people were playing billiards in the next room. And the next room was not big enough to hold a billiard table!

Between the pauses of the wind I heard the game go forward—stroke after stroke. I tried to believe that I could not hear voices; but that attempt was a failure.

Do you know what fear is? Not ordinary fear of insult, injury or death, but abject, quivering dread of something that you cannot see—fear that dries the inside of the mouth and half of the throat—fear that makes you sweat on the palms of the hands, and gulp in order to keep the uvula at work? This is a fine Fear—a great cowardice, and must be felt to be appreciated. The very improbability of billiards in a dâk-bungalow proved the reality of the thing. No man—drunk or sober—could imagine a game at billiards, or invent the spitting crack of a 'screw-cannon'.

A severe course of dâk-bungalows has this disadvantage—it breeds infinite credulity. If a man said to a confirmed dâk-bungalow-haunter:—'There is a corpse in the next room, and there's a mad girl in the next but one, and the woman and man on that camel have just eloped from a place sixty miles away,' the hearer would not disbelieve because he would know that nothing is too wild, grotesque, or horrible to happen in a dâk-bungalow.

This credulity, unfortunately, extends to ghosts. A rational person fresh from his own house would have turned on his side and slept. I did not. So surely as I was given up as a bad carcass by the scores of things in the bed because the bulk of my blood was in my heart, so surely did I hear every stroke of a long game at billiards played in the echoing room behind the iron-barred door. My dominant fear was that the players might want a marker. It was an absurd fear; because creatures who could play in the dark would be above such superfluities. I only know that that was my terror; and it was real.

After a long, long while the game stopped, and the door banged. I slept because I was dead tired. Otherwise I should have preferred to have kept awake. Not for everything in Asia would I have dropped the door-bar and peered into the dark of the next room.

When the morning came, I considered that I had done well and wisely, and inquired for the means of departure.

'By the way, khansamah,' I said, 'what were those three doolies doing in my compound in the night?'

'There were no doolies,' said the khansamah.

I went into the next room and the daylight streamed through the open door. I was immensely brave. I would, at that hour, have played Black Pool with the owner of the big Black Pool down below.

'Has this place always been a dâk-bungalow?' I asked.

'No,' said the khansamah. 'Ten or twenty years ago, I have forgotten how long, it was a billiard room.'

'A how much?'

'A billiard room for the Sahibs who built the Railway. I was khansamah then in the big house where all the Railway-Sahibs lived, and I used to come across with brandy-shrab. These three rooms were all one, and they held a big table on which the Sahibs played every evening. But the Sahibs are all dead now, and the Railway runs, you say, nearly to Kabul.'

'Do you remember anything about the Sahibs?'

'It is long ago, but I remember that one Sahib, a fat man and always angry, was playing here one night, and he said to me:—"Mangal Khan, *brandy-pani do*," and I filled the glass, and he bent over the table to strike, and his head fell lower and lower till it hit the table, and his spectacles came off, and when we—the Sahibs and I myself—ran to lift him. He was dead. I helped to carry him out. Aha, he was a strong Sahib! But he is dead and I, old Mangal Khan, am still living, by your favor.'

That was more than enough! I had my ghost—a firsthand, authenticated article. I would write to the Society for Psychical Research—I would paralyze the Empire with the news! But I would, first of all, put eighty miles of assessed crop land between myself and that dâk-bungalow before nightfall. The Society might send their regular agent to investigate later on.

I went into my own room and prepared to pack after noting down the facts of the case. As I smoked I heard the game begin again,—with a miss in balk this time, for the whir was a short one.

The door was open and I could see into the room. *Click—click*! That was a cannon. I entered the room without fear, for there was sunlight within and a fresh breeze without. The unseen game was going on at a tremendous rate. And well it might, when a restless little rat was running to and fro inside the dingy ceiling-cloth, and a piece of loose window-sash was making fifty breaks off the window-bolt as it shook in the breeze!

Impossible to mistake the sound of billiard balls! Impossible to mistake the whir of a ball over the slate! But I was to be excused. Even when I shut my enlightened eyes the sound was marvelously like that of a fast game.

Entered angrily the faithful partner of my sorrows, Kadir Baksh.

'This bungalow is very bad and low-caste! No wonder the Presence was disturbed and is speckled. Three sets of doolie-bearers came to the bungalow late last night when I was sleeping outside, and said that it was their custom to rest in the rooms set apart for the English people! What honour has the khansamah? They tried to enter, but I told them to go. No wonder, if these Oorias have been here, that the Presence is sorely spotted. It is shame, and the work of a dirty man!'

Kadir Baksh did not say that he had taken from each gang two annas for rent in advance, and then, beyond my earshot, had beaten them with the big green umbrella whose use I could never before divine. But Kadir Baksh has no notions of morality.

There was an interview with the khansamah, but as he promptly lost his head, wrath gave place to pity, and pity led to a long conversation, in the course of which he put the fat Engineer-Sahib's tragic death in three separate stations—two of them fifty miles away. The third shift was to Calcutta, and there the Sahib died while driving a dogcart.

If I had encouraged him the khansamah would have wandered all through Bengal with his corpse.

I did not go away as soon as I intended. I stayed for the night, while the wind and the rat and the sash and the window-bolt played a ding-dong 'hundred and fifty up.' Then the wind ran out and the billiards stopped, and I felt that I had ruined my one genuine, hallmarked ghost story.

Had I only stopped at the proper time, I could have made *anything* out of it.

That was the bitterest thought of all!

ABOUT TERRY O'BRIEN

Terry O'Brien is an academic with three decades of experience in teaching language and communication skills in India and abroad. He also headed a college under the auspices of the University of Delhi.

A prolific writer with several books to his credit, Terry O'Brien is a reputed professional, motivation speaker and a quizmaster.